ORDOWAHL

NINTH PRINCE OF NORDWEG

MATE

ORDOWAHL

NINTH PRINCE OF NORDWEG

MATE

ISBN: 978-0-9970326-8-0

Published October 2019
Revised November 2021
        Words With a Mission (wordswithamission.com)

Other work, also via Words With a Mission:
        Christ – Cosmology   November 2021
        Ordowahl : Manhood   August 2019
                                               Revised November 2021
        An Adult's Garden of Verses   May 2017

BLOG

                                oh-and-another-thing.blog

Dedication

Ruth Marguerite Hinrichs, 1923–2006
Joel Henry Hinrichs, Sr. 1919–2008

Beloved parents, you gave me more than I ever knew, and while I tried to thank you, there is always more to say. I loved you, I miss you, and, in time, may we be reunited at Jesus' feet.

Also to my astonishing late-career trophy wife Jody, a.k.a. JoAnn Glittenberg, RN, MA (Psych), MA PhD (Anthropology), a co-pioneer in the field of cross-cultural nursing, and an anthropologist with many publications.

Special Thanks

Many thanks to the Aspen Grove writers group meeting Wednesday's at the Tattered Cover, Mark Lehnertz, buchmeister. And special thanks to Kevin Chambless who spoke truth with diplomacy.

My greatest thanks go to Lynnette Horner (Letter Perfect Writing and Editing Services,) without whose help this book would be a pale imitation of what you see before you.

Introduction

Look back at an age of old languages and simple truths, a period of tension, danger and war, of death by sword and subtler means, a time of mysterious powers, of mages white and black.

Prince Ordowahl, ninth and last son of Stegnwahl, King of Nordweg, towers over his brothers in body, mind and spirit. They refuse to let him disrupt their "orderly" contest to earn their father's choice as his successor to the Nordwesh throne. The prince is a devout, faithful Christian. This lends him a thoughtful nature. He strives for purity in thought and act. Ordowahl meets his violent age head on yet is gentle toward the weak, and (most of the time) meets wrath with temperance.

Ordowahl has fief Klarenz, a commoner with a knack for mastering any craft or trade, yet who finds himself driven from town to town because his abilities include fascinating women, but not the wit to govern his skill. Ordowahl has left home and made his way against a world inhabited by black magery. Watch him here encounter a very different sort. See him encounter a fitting partner, someone whose own gifts and characteristics stack as high as his own—and whose hidden traits differ from his but provide another great asset.

Embrace the Eleventh Century, the old, the formal, the cruel and harsh, the noble. A sonnet accompanies each chapter; find its meaning trying to bridge from what has taken place to what next shoe may drop. Come with me to a scene "long ago and far, far away"—but here in this galaxy, and grounded in earth and iron.

-Joel

PS: Throughout you'll see names that resemble modern Dutch. A thousand years ago Old English, Old German and Old Dutch were dialects of a broad spectrum that included Old Danish and Old Norse. Since the setting is in today's Nederland, I've tried to stay close to their spellings.

CONTENTS

Ordowahl learned to pronounce these vowels, plus letters j, v, w. They are based on modern Dutch pronunciation, a personal favorite; I have tried to avoid the letter g, because if you're not Dutch, you'd think the speaker was gathering the contents of his or her throat for an aggressive act.

Emluyn	EM looin	(Emmi)	
Ferbliet	fehr BLEAT		
Gendowert	KHEN doe vairt		
Hangendro	hahn **KH**EN droe		
Herrobur	HEH-roe boor	(Heri)	
Jakop	YAH kawp		
Janalei	YAHN a lye	(Jani)	
Joop	YOPE	(Joopi)	
Klarenz	KLAR enz		
Ordowahl	OR doe vall	(Ordi)	
Ornje	ORN yeh		
Rutelyn	ROOT eh lin		
Torwulf	TOR voolf		
Vendink	FEN deenk		
Wilfbur	VEELF boor	(Wils	VEELSS)

Prince Ordowahl of Nordweg, ninth in line,

was deemed "of age" when he turned seventeen.

When two years past, this giant made benign

the dread Black Knight—bedulled his pois'nous sheen.

    And comes the Vice-Count Utrecht. She has been

    a giant of another kind. That face,

    when not of "hear me!" mien, unmans all men.

    Her wit, her poise, her smile, are iron lace.

She's not the sort to trifle with. She'll stay

a single woman 'til she dies. Her life,

revealed while still a child—swept away:

a giant rogue would seize her as his wife!

    They've never met but Utrecht knows. Her hate

    grows from the day they meet—he's not her mate.

Utrecht

ANNO DOMINI MLXX (1070), END OF AUGUST

"Liege," said bondman Klarenz. He broke a long mid-morning silence.

"What is it?"

"Last night we slept at an inn. Thank you."

Ordowahl gave him an indulgent smile. "Tonight we will find lodging in the city of Utrecht in County Vendink. Do you think yourself ready to ignore a woman's passing glance?"

"More to the point, Liege, can you?"

"What an impertinent question. Why do you ask?"

Klarenz ducked the question. "See ahead, Liege, someone not large enough to provide shade comes our way."

Ordowahl looked forward; perhaps two hundred yards distant he spied a horse. *Lovely animal, and with glistening tack. Its rider appears smallish, but even from this distance I can see that he is very self-assured. And there is something odd about his footman, as though he is a doting attendant.* "What do you think, Klarenz? Who comes?"

"Liege, I have heard of the count who sits in Utrecht. He has one heir, a daughter. She is the equal of any man you care to mention. Not you! Liege, not you. But she is formidable. Furthermore she is said to receive court from nobles far and wide, yet rejects each of them."

"Her position as heir or heiress would guarantee a flock of ganders.

"Yes, Liege. She is also said to have a face that plunges Eros's arrow into the best-guarded of men."

Within less than a minute the riders faced each other. Ordowahl saw that the rider was female, as Klarenz had said. She wore a charcoal-gray leather tunic and glossy, sky blue leather pantaloons with matching boots. Her hair fell in a long red-to-orange-to-blonde braid. When she swung her head its end fell past the middle of her back; someone had tied it with a bit of purple ribbon.

She spoke. "Aren't you the man who slit another man's throat while he was down?" She waited for Ordowahl to respond.

"That much is true. Do I see a woman dressed against Scripture, in a man's garments? Do both of us carry shame?"

Her nose twitched, below unsmiling eyes. "In other words, you propose a fact as an insult. I have not made it known that I am Vice-Count Utrecht, Regent of Vendink. Be sure to know your place hereafter." Her nose didn't twitch a second time.

"And I am Ordowahl, Prince of Nordweg, ninth son of King Stegnwahl. I also endured a fact spoken as an insult. I know my place and have told you what it is." He could not put a scowl on his face when looking at her.

"I will judge my own words, Prince—if indeed what you say is true. I've never heard of Nordweg and don't look forward to any sort of acquaintance. I am regent of this county. Whatever business you have here is my concern. State it."

"As you will, Vice-Count. For being youngest son, my place in God's world is undefined. I expect to wait many years for that to change. I wish to take instruction among Utrecht's community of religious scholars. Reading the Vulgate of Jerome during my childhood left a great deal of it living within my head. It itches for scholars to help me search its depths."

"Do you seek the priesthood?"

That idea brings her odd calm. "No, Vice-Count, I have my father's word that I must return to Nordweg and add to the royal family there. I make no plan. In fact, God in heaven seems to have

2

used me in several places already. No doubt He led me here. Each time the reason hides from me. I am here, and I plan to study. Past that, or what I will have for morning meal tomorrow, are blank."

She scoffed, "You believe God in heaven needed you to slit a defenseless throat." She coughed up phlegm and spat at his horse's feet. "Please keep your presence from staining mine." She spurred her horse and brushed past him. Her twenty-years-older footman gave them a nervous smile and hurried to catch up.

Klarenz did his best to stifle a guffaw. He again scanned the skyline for any sight of tower or cook-fire smoke. In an arch tone he said, "Liege, just beyond that horizon to the west, ahead of us, lives a noblewoman whose smile is said to steal men's affections the way a child plucks daisies beside the road, and with the same casual enjoyment."

"So a man's mind is like a little flower. I cannot say she aroused that sort of feeling in me. Did you mean, she should have?"

"We, each of us, have known the company of a woman, and find it as much beyond delightful as sunshine compared to firelight. I am well accustomed by now to doing without. I have sworn an oath to remain celibate until such time as I find a woman whom I may marry. Haven't I heard you making the same pledge at prayer time, nightly since we left Ermsleben?"

"Indeed so, Klarenz. Are you concerned for my chastity too?"

"I should be silent, Liege." Klarenz made yet another scan of the horizon. "But I have heard tales of Count Vendink as well as his daughter. He is so old that he remains housebound except for rare trips out of the city."

"Surely he has a nephew to take his place when he passes from this life?"

"That is the nub of it, Liege. He has settled on his daughter with as much vigor as she rejects the parade of men reaching out for her. In fact her father's intent in the matter is even stronger."

"Though he has an army of her suitors to select from, none of them will become Count on his death?"

"It is that simple. The stories say she is headstrong to a fault. Her smile can turn winter into spring while her frowns freeze and shatter men's hearts. She also performs each of her father's duties that could require him to go beyond the castle walls, with success like his before he made her Regent."

"Klarenz, I've never heard of the like. But, please unfold your mystery. Why is my vow at risk?"

"Liege, we must wait and see. And from what I hear, she will do everything she can to help you remain chaste." Klarenz risked a smirk but turned his head aside so his liege wouldn't see it.

"How else would you expect her to behave? I will be relieved not to have another Gnade Grace to deal with. Another man's child in her belly, you know how well she swived with me in open day and well after dark."

Klarenz ignored his liege's remark. "I see the spire of Saint Martin's Cathedral, which fronts on the city's market square. Yet there is more. I've heard whispers that she fears an interloper. The fated rogue will rip her away from here. It explains part of the mystery."

"And, Klarenz, what is the other part?"

"She accepts suitors, takes them with the grace of a hawk in flight, Liege. Each gets a brief time of awe and sweet kisses."

"Yes, we've gone over that point. What then?"

"And then she sends them away. Always."

"In other words she would be the last to threaten any man's vow of chastity. Are you telling me a fool's tale?"

Klarenz lapsed into silence.

They entered the city square. Prince Ordowahl the Huge, slayer of the Black Knight, from somewhere across an ocean and far to the north, startled everyone. A gigantic man on an enormous stallion—it could be no one else. Two years a vagabond, two years past boyhood, and everywhere receiving stares from all in sight. It would have been a surprise if no one looked up, or made no remark to his neighbor.

He sat on battle stallion Hammerfoot, eighteen hands at the shoulder, yellow-tan coat shining in the morning sun. At his side, bondman Klarenz rode a nondescript gray gelding. Two pack mules followed them.

Utrecht

All whose eyes fell on the giant knew him as slayer of the despised Saxon Black Knight. Immense, with a tall brow, face that looked carved from a tree stump, regal bearing—these and the stallion silenced doubt. Many gaped and pointed as they recalled his harrowing tale and miracle recovery from a deadly wound.

If the prince had cared to observe the women in the square, he'd have see them hold their breath or clutch something to themselves. He lifted his eyes above any gaze. Many men sent him direct stares, some with smiles of surprised admiration. Others held eyes clenched, mouth a thin line, arms crossed, head thrown back—one rooster sizing up another.

Vice-Count Utrecht had circled back behind the prince to observe his entry into her city and reined in her mount at the far edge of the square. Shoulders back, head erect, face composed and chin forward, it was customary for any stranger to notice her rich garb, striking athletic figure, confidence, poise, heart-stopping face.

Ordowahl's attention went to a screaming knight erupting through the crowd as though propelled by insult. Red-faced and flailing his arms, he seemed to have been waiting for the prince to arrive. He leapt in front of Hammerfoot and posed, feet spread and arms waving, voice already ragged.

Prince Ordowahl patted Hammerfoot's neck and tugged on the reins. The stallion had been about to rise up and smash the noisy knight with a front hoof. The fellow stood there, immobile as though he owned the square.

"I say there, you! Criminal," the knight yelled. He gesticulated at both Ordowahl and Klarenz. He appeared to defy both giants, stallion and rider. "Tell me," he demanded, "why did you run your lance through a jouster's charging stallion? Such wantonness against a helpless animal," he said, sneering at the prince. He paused as if to hear an answer then continued. "Not only that, *Prince*, I know you stood over the defenseless, downed knight and slit his throat. I despise you."

It's always a burden to be the center of a hundred staring eyes. Thank you, Father God in heaven, that this angry fellow is pulling them away from me. Out loud Ordowahl said, "You realize that the

5

Black Knight was a sorcerer."

Those watching had heard the tale a dozen times, full of lurid references to the Black Knight's horrific nature. The prince's victory sounded astonishing. A different part of the story had a seamy side, that the giant used a grandmother as concubine. That part supported the knight's disgust.

"Fie!" the knight spat back. "Sorcery and magic are wives' tales, and all Christendom knows this. You confess yourself not only murderer of horses and downed men, but pagan as well?"

The crush of people in the square grew into a crowd, but the giant paid attention only to his accuser. "If you are a Christian then tell this to your priest," and recited something that had to be Church Latin.

The knight waited for him to finish the stream of odd syllables. "Sirrah, this babble you speak, what is that?"

"It is from the Holy Book," said Ordowahl, ignoring the slur. Having a sketchy grasp of the local dialect, he used Saxon speech, knowing most would understand him. "'For now we see as through a glass, darkly, but then face to face: now I know in part, but then shall I know even as also I am known.' The cathedral making one side of this square has priests who must know this passage."

The growing crowd's buzz became hostile.

"Nonsense!" said the knight, shoulders back and chest puffed out. "What is this talk of looking glasses and darkness?" He waved one hand as though dismissing a troublesome insect.

Ordowahl's focus stayed on his accuser while he laid out the meaning. "In Saint Paul's first letter to the believers in Corinth he is saying that he, Paul, knew much of God's action in this world, yet only in part."

The knight showed no twitch of understanding.

"But when his time came to enter into the Heavenly Kingdom, he would know in completeness."

The knight pursed his lips, tilting his head to think about what he'd heard.

Ordowahl continued. "Surely you confess to a priest. If Saint Paul professes incomplete knowledge, then how can your priest know so much about something he has never dealt with?"

Still nothing broke through to the knight.

"In fact, ask him to come out and drive away a demon. Doesn't a demon trace itself back to the same source as a black mage?"

The knight screwed his face into a scowl. He stood mute, hands on hips and elbows out to the side, unmoved.

Ordowahl said, "Be gone, now, my friend, and do not create trouble beyond your stature."

At last self-conscious, the knight scanned himself: feet, legs, torso, arms. Formidable among the people of Utrecht, he could not compare himself to the prince.

"I met and defeated the so-called Black Knight three months ago. Think of him as allied with a demon. He blinded me in the charge, making the horse's murder his act alone."

The knight turned his face aside.

Ordowahl continued. "Even gored through the shoulder, I by the power of Christ found strength to sever the mage from this life. Do you wish to avenge the Black Knight's horse, or perhaps the man himself?"

The knight, still silent, held his ground.

"Knight, I will agree to make combat with you, and with your choice of weapons. Either that or you can buy me ale. We can sit down together, drink in peace and quiet, then instruct one another."

The knight's face did a slow fade. He swallowed and blinked several times, wavered and shifted from foot to foot. He looked up at Ordowahl. "Drink it shall be, good noble," and he led the way to a low building just off the market square.

Out of the corner of his eye Ordowahl recognized the vice-count at the edge of the square. He glimpsed again the lavish clothes and the red-orange braid dangling behind, her flame-red hair. An act of will kept him from giving her an open stare. *No poet can justly laud this beauty.*

Vice-Count Utrecht followed the men into the alehouse. Outside, Klarenz and the vice-count's manservant Joop handled the collection of horses and mules to await their nobles' presence.

The alehouse had four blank walls, with a door left well ajar to admit some daylight. The dirt floor, long seasoned with ale, wine, and vomit, gave the room a musty, sour odor. Someone must have used a sharp axe to carve out the lone table. A half-dozen stools were no better.

Vice-Count Utrecht took her usual seat in a dim corner, unseen by the two men. The alewife, a pleasant widow of early grandmother age, stood behind a rough-hewn counter. A stained apron covered her simple dress. Smoothing the apron, she gave the prince a surprised but ready smile. She looked toward the knight, already a frequent customer.

The knight settled in to drink. Between quaffs of an often refilled mug he made small talk about the weather and horses and jousting but volunteered nothing substantial. Ordowahl watched him unwind.

The knight kept on drinking until he slurred, "Y'know, I really have a much larger bone to pick with you, Sirrah!"

"And what might that be, Knight?" Ordowahl again ignored the slur, other than to pause. *Easy does it. No need to ignite this fellow—he already smolders.* Still in courteous voice he asked, "Does this involve another of my sins? And give me your name, if you will."

"I be Sir Torwulf of Haus Tannhaueffig. The bondman outside tending your livestock is Klarenz of Hammaborg," and he jerked his thumb at the doorway. "Sixteen years ago he swived my second-cousin-aunt. He got her with child while she was in troth to Euwart IV, prince-to-be of Hammaborg." He paused, waiting for some response, then remembered to continue. He stiffened. He sat up straight to unload his anger: "That wretch wrought ripe ruin on a ranking member of my family, Sirrah, and I require restitution."

Hear him out; let him make a demand., even if it's the only way to get him to stop talking.

"You own him. Thus you own his debts, one of which is the very, very, very large dowry that went with her, my second-cousin aunt, the one whose sanctity was sundered by your sly servant's surly swiving!" Torwulf smirked at his witty alliteration.

"So," said Ordowahl, "you allege first claim to recover a princess's dowry?"

Utrecht

Torwulf gazed at Ordowahl with stony eyes, hands on the table, his gaze direct. "In a word, yes! I'll have my family's honor avenged, and I caution you, be glad I don't demand the fool's tool into the bargain."

"Please tell me more, Sir Torwulf of Tannhaueffig. Just how much of the tale do you possess? I want facts before I judge your claim."

Torwulf drew back open-mouthed and shouted his answer. "I buy you ale and you chase me for gossip? The facts, Sirrah, are these: Your bondman Klarenz stuck a child into the belly of a princess-to-be, costing Haus Tannhaueffig a huge dowry. Only one answer will stand."

"And," asked Ordowahl, with calm gravity, "when that answer was asked of the Haus she was to marry into, what did they say?"

Torwulf's eyes bulged. His face grew even redder, if possible. His voice rose to a screech. "Say?" he sputtered. "Say? They demanded another princess and a second dowry!"

"Or, in other words, Haus Tannhaueffig accepted the loss of that first dowry as somehow just. Is that your complaint?"

"My complaint?" He turned his contorted face toward the alewife as though she could supply an answer.

Ordowahl pressed the point. "Or, for that matter, your next-younger second-cousin-aunt, Princess Rigomonde—I heard her forgive Klarenz. Did you receive news that she gave him her forgiveness?"

Torwulf balled his fists. He stood, his whole body rigid. His lips pulled back to bare every possible tooth. His voice quavered. He said, "She spoke only for herself and perhaps her slack-living husband." He stopped to breathe. "No, Prince, that stain on Haus Tannhaueffig lays at the feet, hangs on the tool of your wretched bondman, and is yours to repay—or else," and he stomped out. Curses still slipped from between clenched jaws and fluttering lips.

Vice-Count Utrecht spoke from the shadowy corner. "A word, Prince."

He recognized the rich contralto and turned around to see her in the dimness. Beyond doubt the vice-count. She had witnessed the entire conversation.

"Do you address me?" he asked.

"Indeed, Prince."

The silky contralto voice captivated Ordowahl. As she moved across the doorway and appeared in silhouette, the male clothing didn't hide her woman's frame any better than it had on horseback, outside the city.

He rose. "It is my pleasure, Vice-Count. Please join me." Two manlike strides brought the vice-count to the table. As she turned and her face came into the light he stared at her like any other awed male. She took the stool Torwulf had just vacated and warned Ordowahl, "Look out for that one. He holds a grudge the way a hungry infant holds the teat, sucking at it even after it's empty. You'll meet him again—just be sure you see him coming. You may address me as Utrecht."

Her calm face made a most engaging puzzle. It spoke nothing yet promised much, a mystery he felt compelled to resolve. Ordowahl remembered his manners and gave her a nod as though he understood the fellow just as she described him.

"But, Prince, I confess that I have heard stories, not the true tale." She asked, "If I keep your mug filled, will you share it? I've had no one to set the right line of it. Please tell it in full and all."

He gave her a quiet look, as if trying to make up his mind. She gave it back but included a pro-forma smile. He found it much more than disarming and had to remember to breathe.

At the end of his story the alewife brought over a pitcher and refilled the prince's mug. "Prince—begging the vice-count's pardon for speaking—three wealthy girls, two known and one from another place, each anxious to be bedded by a *seventeen-year-old who ran a hostler's kitchen?*"

Ordowahl smiled. "That describes Klarenz."

"I can see the Hammaborgian prince's need to blame the young swain for the sin of his betrothed." She chuckled. "And condemned to wander ever after? All for trysting three titled trollops? 'Tis tragic." Her smirk matched Sir Torwulf's.

"Indeed, mistress, indeed," said Ordowahl. He gave her a polite nod. *It must be a custom here?*

"Prince," said Utrecht, "part of your story nags at me. How did you divine which manner of person the Black Knight was, and how did you persuade his disciples to shun his memory? I heard that his hold over them was very effective. So when you defeated him, why did they not act against you?"

She sat with elbows on the table, her fingertips steepled. Light from the doorway illuminated her face. The cream-cultured voice and easy smile, as one powerful noble speaking to another, astonished Ordowahl.

His "helpless awed male" face betrayed him, and he saw her relax. *What could have made her so tense to start?* "The first joust, in which the Black Knight fell, should have led them to challenge me, one after another, until I might fall. But a raven's peck restored him to immediate health."

"Yes. That explains the first time you defeated him. Somehow a magical bird's peck, or a magical peck from a bird, revived him." She did nothing to hide her sarcasm.

Ordowahl took a calming breath. "His quick return to vigor calmed their hearts, and his pretense of open friendship restored their good will. But the raven's peck showed that Sir Blackness had allied himself to something not just powerful, but also a proven enemy of God."

"You spoke of a second joust with a very different ending."

He winced but smiled.

"First seeing your lance pierce their liege's horse, then watching you stand over him to slice him at the neck—why didn't they draw swords and run you through where you stood?"

It almost seems she wished they had! "In life he cast a subtle cloud over their minds, like a perfume from a deadly flower. It dissipated when the flies blew out of his corpse and his ravens chased them."

"I can see how that could work. It made you a hero. So why did you leave?"

Yes, and why did I come to Utrecht? You challenge me. "Even the humblest helot or serf is beloved of God and has opportunities each day to show kindness or mercy to those around him," he said, looking Utrecht in the eye, "or her."

She appeared to ignore the gender reference.

"Forgive me if this sounds arrogant, Utrecht, but I believe both that God makes each of us to a purpose, and that mine lies far ahead of me. How far, I do not know."

She made an impatient motion for him to continue.

He hastened to add, "The day I came of age, Father sent me away from the kingdom. But God seems to have used me since then to right a few wrongs, some large, some small. My own behavior hasn't been innocent, for that matter."

A flicker of scorn crossed her face, but he didn't react. "As I said when we met on the road, this city's religious scholars draw me here."

He got back, "I hope your visit is fruitful," with a banal Welcome To The City smile.

"I also have learned that truth depends on who tells it. No one can succeed in telling anything the way God might. Everyone must seek truth, but who can know it? Yet I pursue it as though it were life itself."

"Well, well, Prince, and welcome. I hope your visit will aid your understanding."

She rose from the table without reminding him to stay out of trouble, or to pursue his studies to their conclusion then continue his travels. She didn't say it in so many words, but her abrupt exit said it as if she held up a sign.

She thinks he's tamable, a simpleton.

He thinks she's out of reach, and doesn't care.

The Vice-Count, just as Klarenz said, is spun

of counterpoised details, a swain's despair.

 The prince has no reaction to her save

 the standard gawking stare. She's used to that

 at least. Her sense of pow'r assuaged, the brave

 young prince gets just a welcome-smile-so-flat.

But still, she hears his tale with careful ears

and tries to keep the peace, by warning that

Sir Torwulf is a sorry sport whose beers

will quash his manly wisdom sadly flat.

 With Utrecht gone away and drinking done,

 the prince enjoys the taste of cinnamon.

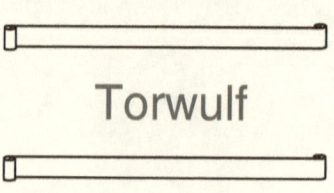

Torwulf

The vice-count blew out the sour, oppressive alehouse air to breathe in the more familiar scents of nearby livestock, cooking oil wafting from food vendors in the marketplace, an undertone of heaped onions waiting for buyers. These made the sunlit outside air a blessing. Sir Torwulf stood waiting, an unhappy surprise. Anger radiated from him with the intensity of stirred coals.

She stepped away from the doorway and eyed him, to be sure he hadn't been waiting for her. She edged Joop to the side. Without invitation, Klarenz joined them. Joop, her nanny of sorts since too early to recall, wore footman's livery as might a doting uncle in costume for her benefit.

Utrecht bit her lip, waiting to see what sort of trouble Sir Torwulf would make. Count Jakop, were he well, would have intervened between two angry men without a thought. The vice-count's own force being more moral than physical, she left the drunken Torwulf to his own fate. She took two deep, calming breaths.

The prince meanwhile had paused to thank the alewife. Utrecht watched him emerge into bright sun and shield his eyes for a moment.

Torwulf yelled, "Die here, thieves!" and drew his sword. A leap should have put his sword tip at Ordowahl's chest. But after too much ale, its point wavered, and his leap was sloppy.

14

Torwulf

Instead of stepping back to draw his sword and skewer errant Sir Torwulf of Haus Tannhaueffig, the prince grasped at his chest and collapsed forward. He tumbled to the ground, drawing his knees and legs to his body. Passing under Torwulf's sword, he uncoiled and sprang to his feet just behind the knight. His sword's point kissed Sir Torwulf's neck. The giant prince asked, "Sir Torwulf, do you yield, or do you forfeit life?"

Torwulf, defender of Haus Tannhaueffig, had turned and tried to make his sword follow the giant's strange move. Now he froze. A shiny, knife-sharp sword rested its deadly point at his neck. He felt it, not yet cut but knew its sharpness. If it were to slice him he'd feel nothing until air hit opened flesh. For a moment he closed his eyes, as if in prayer. His face paled. The hair on his arms and the back of his neck bristled in terror.

"Knight," said Ordowahl, "I credit the honor of Haus Tannhaueffig. You gave warning with your attack, and at risk to your life. Decide now."

Torwulf stood stock-still.

"Continue your attack and end your life, with honor both as knight and as defender of a noble Haus, or convert that honor. Swear allegiance to me and to Nordweg. Pledge fealty to me as my sworn defender."

They spent a full, tense minute staring at each other, not blinking. Torwulf dared not turn his head so he peered out of the corner of one eye.

Some people in the square had heard Torwulf's shout and seen Ordowahl's unorthodox movement. They turned to gawk, but saw neither blood nor body. Vice-Count Utrecht's bored-looking face, plus a flick of her eyes and head, sent the onlookers back to their errands.

Torwulf spoke. "From what I've heard, Prince, despite the way the Black Knight died, it is not in your nature to take a life on a moment's lapse."

"Intemperate behavior shows itself in many such lapses." Ordowahl held his impassive stare.

Torwulf stood, posture still frozen. At length he spoke. "So now

I choose." With Ordowahl holding his sword point motionless, one twitch shy of opening Torwulf's neck, the knight said, "I yield to you, Prince Ordowahl. I tender my life and honor to you and thus to Nordweg. I swear to learn temperate behavior."

Ordowahl nodded. A formal rite would pass Torwulf from honored corpse to honorable defender.

Torwulf began the protocol: "Your cause is my honor, and your wrongs are mine to avenge. I accept you as liege lord. I invite you to command me as a knight sworn to your life and to defend your honor in all things."

Klarenz and Joop had watched the drama alongside Vice-Count Utrecht. Torwulf flicked his eyes toward Klarenz to avoid confusion about his status. "And to your bondman, Prince Nordweg. I forswear any claim against him and invite him to wait upon me in safety and to whatever degree you may grant. Klarenz, I offer you my peace." The knight dropped his sword and knelt in front of Ordowahl.

The prince looked down, stern acceptance on his face. "You have my peace, Sir Torwulf. I touch your head with my sword to accept your pledge of loyalty to me and to Nordweg. Now let us try to perceive God's Will, not our own, and do it."

Torwulf stood and reached out his hand to Klarenz. "Let us be united in service to Nordweg and in holy service to Almighty God."

Klarenz knelt for a moment in front of Torwulf then stood and clasped the man's hand. "You have my peace, too, Sir Torwulf. I'll serve you as best I can." He stooped to retrieve the dropped sword from the dun-colored dust outside the alehouse, wiped it against his leg, and handed it to the knight.

"So now we are three," said Ordowahl. "Sir Torwulf, while we were in there I heard your descriptions of this city. You have the makings of a canny observer and will serve me best as adviser on local custom and politic."

Torwulf cocked his head as if to learn more.

Ordowahl asked him, "What do you know of such things hereabout? How much time have you spent in this place, and what can you tell me about the nobility who dwell here? And," he added, "I remind you that your oath binds you against any attack on me or

16

Klarenz. If by a regrettable impulse you unbind yourself from me, it will not turn out well. You have my grace until you prove me wrong."

Torwulf wiped sweat from his brow and his face inched toward a frown. He stiffened; his honor had just endured a fresh slap. But he realized that the prince was cementing him into a subservient role. His admiration for this prince, and the prince's wisdom, began there. He relaxed, saying, "I thank God, Prince, and ask Him to aid me in service to you."

Vice-Count Utrecht said, aside to Joop, "This one has not just reformed a hothead, but also put him to a good use covering an important lack." Nanny-footman Joop managed a smile.

Ordowahl wasn't done. "One more thing, Sir Torwulf."

"Yes, Prince?"

"Here is a proverb of Solomon. Your priest may find it: 'A hot-tempered man must pay the penalty. If you rescue him, you will have to do it again.'"

Torwulf squeezed his eyes shut and bowed his head.

"This means, Knight, that I have not rescued you, but moved you into a useful role on this earth, in service to Nordweg and to me."

Torwulf opened his eyes but stared at his feet. Much as he wanted to kick at the dust of the street, he held still.

Ordowahl continued. "I show no false fondness but expect good from you, now and forever after."

He looked up. After a moment he said, "Yes, Prince. I affirm that from my heart."

"So now—if the need arises for me to rescue you, dwell on the wisdom of Solomon."

"Yes, Prince. I take your point."

Seeing that Torwulf had passed into the prince's service, Vice-Count Utrecht broke in. Her cool, appraising face above quiet, clapping hands held an almost sincere smile of welcome to the city of Utrecht.

"Well played, Prince. Your retinue has increased. The City of Utrecht and County Vendink extend you their congratulations. Good day." She and footman Joop remounted and rode toward the market square, when she whirled her horse around. "Prince," she called to him.

"Utrecht?" he replied.

"Forgive my inattention to your goal. This city always wishes its visitors to achieve whatever good they seek. You said something about a community of religious scholars?"

"Yes, I did. It is very courteous of you to discuss that."

"Discussions are what you may have with the priests in the Cathedral of Saint Martin, on the square. They're very good at that sort of thing." She turned again and departed.

Ordowahl wondered, not at the sheer oddness nor the physical beauty of a clean-limbed woman with an athletic, erect seat on her horse, but at the half-smile she'd given him. *Lucky man? I think not. No man who sees that smile ever finds the happiness it may hint at. That much I take as a truth.*

Sir Torwulf is a precious find—an ass,

but one who knows the people here—Prince Ord

has had a chance to demonstrate the class

of Nordwesh ho-hum childs-play with the sword.

   A simple hothead errant knight now turned

   defender, Torwulf has a purpose: find

   his lord Prince Ordowahl, soft-subtly-spurned,

   a noble Haus where he'll be wined-and-dined.

Perhaps a purpose for the prince's wit

will see him when he comes—or less than that,

mere company, as boredom's opposite.

Wish nothing, let the knight be bureaucrat.

   So, what's the upshot? What will happen next?

   Relax, the prince is only thinking, "Text!"

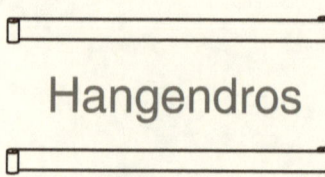

Hangendros

Sobered by his ordeal, Torwulf watched the vice-count depart. He sighed. "No man ever sat a saddle quite as beautifully as she."

"Indeed." Ordowahl had also watched her go. He turned back to speak to his new knight. "Sir Torwulf, I expect to take up residence in this city. Where might I find a fit companion?" *Among the nobility* went without saying.

"Prince, twin brothers will soon inherit Barony Hangendro, or one of them will. It isn't far from here. I know the brothers and have met their mother. You'll find a warm welcome. Along the way I'll explain their situation. Baron Hangendro died not long ago in mid-life, leaving a wife and twin sons. Only one will inherit, but which one isn't yet known."

"I'm already fascinated, Sir Torwulf. I expect Vice-Count Utrecht will make herself part of the discussion, since it involves the county."

*__*__*__*

The prince and knight traveled half a league further west in the modest warmth of late afternoon under a sky festooned with mottling clouds. Smells of hay harvest and smokehouses curing hams for the winter emphasized the season.

They reached a gateway into a courtyard lined with rose bushes, many colors still in bloom. The mansion's massive foundation gave it a look of ponderous dignity.

Hangendros

Ordowahl had not broken out his "polite" set of garments, and Torwulf, scant hours into his new role pledged to Nordweg and to Ordowahl, still wore everyday clothing.

They dismounted. While Klarenz tended their animals, a large door opened beneath a portico inscribed with the Hangendro name.

A tall, slender woman in widow's black velvet half-ran onto the porch past a stiff elderly servant, who held the door open. Her sprite-like manner contrasted with the black of mourning. Her level gaze met Ordowahl eye to eye while he stood two steps below her. She drew her hands up to her ears and looked at him with wide eyes. "Good day, gentle guests. I knew you were traveling westward, but even so my wonder sinks beneath my happiness."

Torwulf answered, "Baroness, lately widow of Gendowert, Baron Hangendro, this is Prince Ordowahl, youngest son of Stegnwahl, King of Nordweg."

"And allow me," said Ordowahl, "to introduce Sir Torwulf of Tannhaueffig. He has entered my service and holds allegiance to me and to Nordweg."

No one even glanced at Klarenz. A personal servant carried his master's secrets. Yet, even by convention his liege's walking handbag, Klarenz received neither notice nor address except when necessary. His humble dun-gray tunic, well-worn leggings, and beaten-down shoes, plus the brass loop through one earlobe, marked him a bondman.

The baroness paused to examine her visitors. She took a close look at Ordowahl and asked for a moment's grace. She turned back toward the inner part of the mansion and told a servant to prepare to house two guests, "and not just for the night." Turning back to them, she invited her guests to ascend the steps and come into a large entry hall. Its plum-colored drapery, tiled floor, and ancestral portraits might have belonged to a count.

"Prince Ordowahl, to you I am Fretheldin, and Sir Torwulf, to you I remain Baroness Hangendro. Yes, Prince, I am widowed. Your notice honors me, also your presence in my Haus."

She paused and gestured with her eyes toward Klarenz to be sure she had permission. "Please excuse me again, for just a moment," then instructed him to guide the stallion, horse, and mules around to the back.

"Prince and Knight, please come with me to a more comfortable room." She led them through a side door into a parlor with a fireplace, plush upholstered furniture, and a central table.

A small fire pulled air into the room. Peach colored velvet draped the walls to help keep out the weather's current warmth. A servant brought three lit candlesticks to add to the fire's flickering light.

Taking a seat near the low fire, Widow Fretheldin turned to Ordowahl and asked, "Prince, and Sir Torwulf, I haven't enjoyed such company in too long a time. Please sit here with me."

They sank into the parlor's overstuffed armchairs. She asked, "My dear Prince, I take it that Vice-Count Utrecht has told you about my twins. It is too much to expect, but can you help the unhappy woman before you, and speak to them?"

"Fretheldin, the vice-count said nothing about them. But the title of Baron won't split between brothers, will it? What instructions did your husband leave?"

Her brow wrinkled and she looked down at her wringing hands. They appeared to wrestle each other. "He died suddenly and left no instructions. Indeed we loved, I love both our sons equally, and I grieve at having to disappoint one to settle the future of the barony. Let me tell the story.

'Twas an icy midwinter day in late January of the Year of Our Lord one thousand six and forty. (1046 CE) An elderly, honored midwife found herself summoned to the Hangendro estate.

The baron's daughter-in-law, a woman (myself) of twenty-four years, was about to give birth. She felt certain it would be twins.

Wilfbur, my Wils, came first from the womb. His mother was ever certain of this in her heart (my heart): "A mother knows."

As the aged midwife bent over to pull that first babe from the new mother's loins, she shuddered, drooled, slumped to the floor, exhaled one gurgling breath, and became still.

Which twin would succeed their father as baron then lapsed into mystery when the servants assisting her ignored the death rattle. They huddled around the gradually cooling body, anxious to revive her, long enough for the other twin to emerge beside his moments-older brother.

Each child in his first fitful breaths blew the mucus out of his own throat and nose. Two unhappy newborn sons lay squalling on the birthing bed. Two afterbirths lay beside them. Their mother shivered, supine, naked, and blue, a mess between her thighs and not even the strength to speak, before her servants surrendered the midwife to the tender arms of death.

Wils and his brother Herrobur, my Heri, received their names that evening when they were carried, by custom, into the family chapel to receive the Sacrament of Baptism.

The priest applied the names based on which infant first came to hand when lifted from the carrying cradle.

While different, they were alike in shrieking at being immersed in the baptismal font's near-freezing water to make certain that, live or die, they would be Christian.

The boys differed in many ways: build, face, hair, and demeanor. But life was too chancy to expect that they would both be healthy, or esteemed, or even living, when the time came to settle the barony on one or the other.

"Baroness, thank you for the story. Yet I've heard that Vice-Count Utrecht owns this decision. What have you seen of her?"

"Prince, she visits often, but aside from quiet chats with my sons has done nothing consequential."

"I see," said Ordowahl. "So Vice-Count Utrecht is showing no preference and has shown no judgment. Do I understand it rightly?"

"I would not say a lack of judgment, for Vice-Count Utrecht is very sound in that regard—just the lack of stating one. Besides that, to be sure you understand, the sons are mine and while neither is chosen, this barony is mine. I fully intend to decide and have not given the vice-count any encouragement."

"Yet the vice-count is, as you say, already handling the issue of succession. What help can I offer?"

"You can, Prince, be my guest here for whatever time is convenient. As a guest you will make the acquaintance of my sons. After you have gotten to know them, I ask you to make a frank assessment of each to me, in private."

I must guess that Utrecht takes a very proprietary view here. This will cause certain trouble. Ordowahl's face looked dubious.

She restated her request. "You seem to carry a great mystery, and God only knows what lies ahead. Sir Torwulf, didn't you say that the prince chose Utrecht as a fixed destination? Please honor me by accepting the hospitality of this Haus, and as you see fit educate a mother's understanding of her sons, to help her see whether her firstborn—and my heart knows which that is—finds your approval. Vice-Count Utrecht has told me she plans to bestow their father's title upon one of them, but I don't want her to ignore me. Despite your having fewer years even than the vice-count, something tells me that your understanding will be accurate."

Klarenz had returned and stood against the wall behind his liege.

"Fretheldin, when a Christian traveler finds welcome, it is by God's grace, and I am happy to begin my time in Utrecht under this roof. As to your sons, when might I meet them? I imagine them to be very busy during the day, competing to manage the barony."

"Indeed, Prince. I see them each evening at supper. I hope that you will use the afternoon to find your way around the grounds, and find comfort here."

*__*__*__*

"Wils, Heri, come meet our new guests." Baroness Fretheldin beckoned her sons into the parlor off the front entry.

The table held mugs, dishes, and flatware for five, several candles, a tureen of beef-and-barley soup, and platters with pickled beets, rolls, walnuts, a cheese, and slabs of butter.

Heri said, "Prince, we've heard of your coming." Long strides brought him to Ordowahl, and he welcomed the prince with a strong handclasp.

Heri had sandy hair and an air of command. He stood two hands taller than Klarenz, thus a hand taller than Torwulf. He looked solid, of good weight with little fat. In bright blue tunic, hose, and shoes, he looked like and had the poise of a dandy. He also took an almost impolite interest in the prince.

Wils said, "We understand that you're to be a guest in our house this winter. Welcome." He had a more sedate pace and gave the prince a decent handclasp. He also nodded welcome at Sir Torwulf.

He had darker hair and an aura of studious intelligence, height about the same as Heri, but a lighter body. Wils wore an olive green tunic, dark green hose, and black shoes, more of a scholar's kit. He stood well but carried thoughtful calm almost to an extreme.

"And you may not know this," said Ordowahl, "but Sir Torwulf of Tannhaueffig is now sworn to my service."

Torwulf and the twins exchanged formal nods. The knight and prince both wore calmer colors—brown with belt and footwear of tan and orange.

"Now, new friends," said Heri, "let us begin all our stories over supper."

Baroness Fretheldin took a seat at one end of the table, Prince Ordowahl to her right with Torwulf next to him. The brothers sat along the other side.

Klarenz maintained both a straight face and attentive, but anonymous posture, standing behind his liege. Footmen also stood behind the baroness and her sons. A serving maid set out two pitchers of ale.

"Let me guess," began Ordowahl. "Each of you has had long knowledge of Vice-Count Utrecht, beginning when you were young lads of five years, I think—and the count's daughter just a toddler?"

"That is so," said Wils. "She has changed much, wouldn't you say, Mother?"

"Indeed," said Fretheldin with a smile. "We doted on her, and my sons gave her many pick-a-back rides when they were children. Their ages are somewhat close. Utrecht will reach twenty-two years next spring, while Wils and Heri already have twenty-four years and a birthday during the coming winter."

She paused, as if to reminisce. "But those days are gone into fond memory. Since then, my sons, you have become men and the count's daughter has become a, well, an adult. You have all grown well past childhood."

She turned to face Ordowahl directly. "Now, we have much to learn of you, Prince, and you may have some curiosity about us. If it please you, show us yourself in conversation while we eat."

Heri and Wils looked at him as though anticipating a great tale.

Their mother said, "Tell us about Nordweg and your father the king. Acquaint us with your brothers and sisters and the adventures that have brought you here from such a distant place." The baroness and her sons settled back, looking comfortable and expectant, while nibbling at supper.

Ordowahl replied, "After getting eight children, all sons, and burying two wives who had each given him a newborn heir, Father married a third time. That woman is my mother, and her first child sits with you. Mother then daughtered him three times before reaching the age of barrenness."

"Such homely details," said the baroness. "I see in you a mother's firstborn yet can believe that you came to your father after many other sons."

Ordowahl nodded. Being likened to a firstborn was novel, and he put it aside. "Baroness, Heri, Wils, it is good that we have the winter before us. Your guest could bore you with a thousand details."

"No, never boring," said Heri.

"So let me begin with a sketch. When I finish, please ask any questions that you like."

The baroness sneaked a glance at Klarenz, who was standing very, very straight and trying to hide a grin. She felt an odd curiosity toward him and smiled before turning back to the story.

When the prince's tale finished, the twins stood and bade their mother a good night, but Wils and Heri were eager to hear more.

A servant brought pitchers of wine and water, strained out the grape fragments and other lumps, then poured the thick, yeasty liquid into their cups. When she stirred in water, the result was drinkable, alcoholic, and even pleasing to the taste. Yeast in both ale and wine was part of the drink and a valued nutritional gift.

"This may be even more difficult to believe," said Ordowahl, "but over the past sixteen years Klarenz has mastered so many skills and crafts that were he to go into any workshop in Utrecht, he'd find something to teach the owner."

At this point Wils and Heri both gave Klarenz direct stares. Wils didn't challenge Ordowahl's strange boast, but Heri had to address it. "Truly he is a bag of tricks. He looks very unlike any smith I've ever seen, yet you credit him with gaining mastery of near a dozen trades in the time a good man takes to set himself up in one?"

Ordowahl nodded yes.

"And then to learn iron, turn iron into steel, and the steel into a very fine sword, all in the span of a year? Prince, I don't doubt you, even though experience begs me to."

"Just so," said Ordowahl. "Work my bondman had done in Nordweg, at a time before I became a man, marked him when I encountered him after the battle with the Vikings. I recognized him from that alone, plus the fact that he could use flawless Nordwesh."

"But," asked Heri, "Klarenz aside, when you slew the Black Knight, was it in any manner simple? If you had but one good arm, and he with a sword, even a stumble wouldn't bring death to the knight. Please open this to us, Prince."

He spoke again of upending the Black Knight and opening his throat. They gaped for a moment.

Heri shook his head. "The way you put it in such simple words, Prince—I try to picture that in my imagination."

"Well, Heri, it was what it was. I picked up his sword. It smelled of poison, you know? A hundred ravens swooped in, from who-knows-where."

"Ravens?" the twins asked.

"I knew one could get through at any moment and revive the bastard a second time. So I opened his throat. A thousand biting flies blew out of him. Only rot-sodden clothing and maggoty bones remained. I had never before endured such a stench. Getting to the point of opening that wretch's throat wasn't simple, but the death stroke was a flick of the wrist."

He pantomimed the action. The speed of his wrist, flicking back and forth, left them staring. And it had looked so casual.

The humble Klarenz, wearing bondman's weeds,

holds mysteries much duller than, less bold

than Ordowahl's. E'en so the prince's needs

for weapons? Wit? He's worth his weight in gold.

    His travels done, the prince and retinue

    have come to rest. His purpose should be clear.

    Not Lady Janalei nor Utrecht drew

    him hence—this city's priestly atmosphere.

A man of nineteen years, so young his beard

is fuzz at best, yet tried beyond the weight

of heavier men. His scholarship unpeered,

feels called to seminar, to cogitate.

    No entrée should he need to join the class—

    good Father Ewald let him say the Mass.

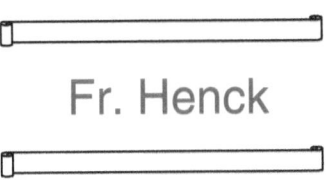

Fr. Henck

The Lowlands lay very close to a cold sea, making the weather not just damp, but chillier than inland areas farther east. Even in September, early mornings wore blankets of cloud so low they often met the ground as fog.

Before first light Ordowahl, Torwulf and Klarenz returned to the center of Utrecht to attend dawn Mass at St. Martin's Church. Afterward they went around to the rectory door. Klarenz began to shiver in the foggy gloom of the hour after dawn. Ordowahl knocked.

A slender, middle-sized, middle-aged priest clad in the black robe of his office opened the door at once. "I be Father Danelagh. I needn't ask who *ye* be, now, do I? And as to yer purpose for travelin' here, we've been told ye are on a mission God the Father has set fer ye?"

He gazed up into Ordowahl's face and invited them in. "Up the step, Prince—mind yer head comin' through the door—and welcome." An Irish brogue complicated understanding him, but a sweep of his arm made the message clear.

"Thank you, Father Danelagh. Did God send me here? If so He kept it from me. The idea seemed to spring up within my own thick skull. I've had the privilege of reading St. Jerome's Vulgate, and wish to continue doing so in good company. I am Prince Ordowahl, son of Stegnwahl, King of Nordweg. But I don't stand on titles. Please use my given name. This is my knight attendant, Sir Torwulf, and my bondman, Klarenz. In the eye of God we are the same."

"And ye can call me Father Dan. In God's eyes I can't get away from the title, but after that, Prince, just Dan will do. Come in and take bread with me, if it please ye."

They stood in a small room with a table, several short stools, a platter with a few pan-fried biscuits remaining on it, a jug of water, a slab of butter, and a few cups. "Please, break bread with me."

"I accept your invitation to a morning meal, Father Dan. Your biscuits look very good, so thank you."

"I was just finishin' me own breakfast—I've taught the good fathers here that in Ireland we call it the breakin' o' the night's fast, or break fast."

Ordowahl smiled. "It's good to learn something every day, and now my day is complete."

"Not so fast, young Prince Ordowahl, not so fast. Ye came here fer a reason, and I haven't yet heard it. What brings ye to the Rectory now?"

"I journeyed to Utrecht because of its reputation for Christian scholarship. While I haven't trained for the priesthood or taken holy vows, I find the Word of God a rich source of answers."

Father Danelagh smiled. "Yes, Ordowahl, all who have the privilege of readin' from it should look there."

"Father Dan, I came here to learn how to ask it better questions."

"Did ye now?" he answered with a raised eyebrow. "I'll be back in just a moment." He rose from his stool and dashed out of the room.

Ordowahl raised an eyebrow at Klarenz to ask what he thought of the priest but got back a quiet shake of the head. Father Dan returned to the doorway. He beckoned to someone down the hall. "Father Henck, I found ye a curious one," he said.

In moments an old man, also wearing a priest's robe, came in and took an empty stool. Looking at Fr. Dan he said, "I see that your wild story, for once, misses truth for taking the modest side."

Father Henck turned to Ordowahl and extended his hand to let the prince kiss his ring of office. "The peace of God be with you, my son," he said, then turned and did the same for Torwulf and Klarenz.

"Thank you, Father," said Ordowahl. "And also with you. I am

Ordow—" but was interrupted.

"I know about you, my son. I am Abbot of Utrecht, but in private please call me Father Henck. Now, in a few words, explain to me how you became familiar with Holy Writ." His eyes held no smile, nor threat, but Ordowahl thought he heard a loaded question.

"I am a son of Stegnwahl, king of Nordweg. Father encouraged his priest, Father Ewald, to instruct us in Latin at first. Later he added Greek."

"Yes?" asked Fr. Henck.

"To the classics of Latin and Greek literature, plays, essays, philosophy, et cetera, Father Ewald added the Greek Septuagint and the Vulgate of Saint Jerome."

An upward twitch of Fr. Henck's eyebrows betrayed his surprise.

"I fear, however, that my older brothers didn't embrace the study of Christian faith, or Greek plays, or Livy, or Plato."

"Really?" said Fr. Henck. "I believe I've seen one or two of those texts myself."

"My brothers thought it a chore to trot out some tidbit at supper to satisfy Father. He demanded that we recite new knowledge, in Greek, every midweek evening."

"I see." Father Henck paused for a moment. "Then tell me, Prince, how often did Father Ewald ask you to enter holy orders?"

Ordowahl's blank look told him that hadn't happened.

"The Church's mission can be compromised when the Word of God falls into unschooled hands. I mean in specific, those which haven't been disciplined to the priesthood and nursed on the milk of Church doctrine."

"That, Father Henck, is something Father Ewald mentioned often enough. Without trying to dismiss your meaning, I've been tutored at length by, and a time or two been tutor to, my beloved Father Ewald."

Father Henck raised an eyebrow and gave back a stiff smile. "Tutored *him*?"

"According to him, so I suppose yes."

Father Danelagh broke in then. "I propose, Father Henck, that

Brother Ordowahl, if I am bold to say it, might add to some of our discussions."

Father Henck showed Fr. Danelagh a look of blank surprise but said nothing.

"I'm told he silenced this recently arrived knight, Sir Torwulf here present, by referring to Saint Paulus's 'through a glass darkly.' I overheard and hoped my own application of the Holy Word of God could be as ready and as appropriate." Torwulf crossed himself but said nothing.

"Ready and appropriate? Father Danelagh, you haven't lost the ability to astonish me." He turned to Ordowahl. "As God gives peace to each of His children, I would like to hear your confession, Prince. In doing so I may receive some of that same peace myself." He crossed himself.

Father Danelagh didn't surrender the floor. "Father Henck, what was it we were reviewin' most recently?"

Father Henck turned toward the prince. "Ordowahl, do you have any understanding of the topic of predestination? We were about to spend an hour on that."

Ordowahl's face relaxed. His gaze wandered to a spot high on the wall. After a moment he asked, "Do you mean one's salvation and God's Hand in the matter?"

Father Henck nodded. That eyebrow raised a third time, betraying mild surprise. "Brother Danelagh," he said, "I am intrigued. This once, let us convene our study session with laymen present."

In moments three additional priests entered the room. Klarenz rose to stand behind his liege's stool. But Fr. Danelagh head-wagged a slight "no" and left the room. In a moment he reappeared with a stool.

Klarenz tried to find a word of thanks but stood mute with surprise. Another tiny head-wag told him to sit down as though he were any other child of God, so he did that.

When all had settled in, Fr. Henck made a formal introduction, omitting mention of Torwulf and Klarenz. "Brothers, greet Prince Ordowahl, ninth son of Stegnwahl, king of Nordweg. And yes, he is from far away to the north, and no, Vice-Count Utrecht suffers no peril."

He smiled as though making a private reference that they would understand but not the prince.

Ordowahl suspected that local lore had tied him to the vice-count in some unguessable way. But the "no peril" part was at least soothing. He replied, "What are your names?"

In addition to Fathers Henck and Danelagh came Fathers Petur, Jemck, and Kerk. Each stood, gave a name and a polite smile, and sat down. Each had shaved the top of his head to indicate disavowal of worldly aspirations.

Ordowahl noticed that both Fr. Danelagh's mop of unruly brown hair and Fr. Henck's speckled near white remained intact. Such things didn't deserve comment.

"We reached an impasse, it seems, Ordowahl, and we hope that you can tutor us." Father Henck made no attempt to sound ironic, but one or two tiny snickers seemed to contort the sealed lips of Frs. Jemck and Petur. Father Kerk frowned for a moment.

Ordowahl answered, "Whatever God has allowed me to understand, Fathers, I doubt will add to your own wisdom. But your competing ideas prick my curiosity."

Father Kerk brightened. "Ordowahl, we have two views of how souls are predestined either to heaven or to hell."

The statement hung in the air, so Ordowahl jumped in as though invited. "Jesus told his disciples that some were given to Him by God the Father, and that He had not lost a single one of them, *because* they were given to Him."

He scanned their faces to see if he was even close to their prior discussion.

"Yes, that is so," said Fr. Danelagh. "There be souls which be destined beforehand to finish their earthly journey, win the race as Saint Paulus has it, and reach heaven. This is true."

The other priests nodded their agreement. Father Henck asked, "Ordowahl, can you speak of souls which are destined to hell?"

At once he said, "Scripture names a few. Among them are Judas Iscariot, Pharaoh opposing Moses, and the High Priest Caiaphas who, condemning Jesus, said, 'Because it is better for the One to die for the many.'"

He'd told them nothing new.

Ordowahl continued, "In the Gospel of Matthew, Jesus gives the parable of the talents. The poor fellow who failed to use the talent he was trusted with begins, 'Master, I knew you to be a hard man, reaping where you did not sow, and gathering where you scattered no seed.' If you invert this, God is a loving master who does not sow evil, but reaps good from it. For example, that high priest, whom we presume to be a damned soul, still speaks prophecy that states the reason for our Lord needing to die on the Cross."

Father Henck replied, "One thief on the cross believed on the final day of his life, and the other did not. Explain that in your own words."

"Surely, Father. Many find doom by honoring themselves above the creation. If they do not change, hell is their fate."

Seeing agreement, he went on. "The other thief on the cross honored Christ. That day he entered into heaven with Christ Jesus, and whether or not he also honored creation, it was his belief in Christ that saved his soul."

"But," interjected Fr. Kerk, "explain whether or not, in your mind, all who are not predestined for heaven are therefore predestined for hell."

"You ask for a guess, Father Kerk, but to me it seems evident that, since Jesus called us to go out to all nations and teach all people, the fates of those souls must depend in part on how many we reach."

"Ah," said Fr. Kerk. "God can intercede. He does choose to allow some to reject Him. But since He knows in advance they'll do that, those He doesn't choose to rescue are therefore inverted to be chosen, predestined, to hell."

"In which case, Father, if we have free will to choose and God honors a man's choice to reject Him, predestination itself is moot. I find no way to believe these two things at the same time, first that God chooses, and second that we do."

Father Henck peered at Ordowahl, lowered his head, and sighed.

"Yes, brothers, we have someone who aspires to tutor us."

Ordowahl looked around the group, trying to read their expressions, but with the exception of Kerk, each kept his expression guarded. He sensed they felt challenged, so he changed the subject.

"Fathers, I am relieved that I pose no peril to the vice-count. Is she under some threat I should know about?"

Five soft chuckles fondled the mood.

"Ordowahl," said Fr. Kerk, "Vice-Count Utrecht has made it plain that she intends to die very old, very happy, and never wed. Her real person, Lady Janalei, is difficult to read but does show affection for men. None, however, have gotten her to set aside the office of vice-count. We see many men come here from far away and at first not understand Lady Janalei's smiles. I presume that you've seen a smile from her already?"

"Yes," said Ordowahl. "But you mentioned her 'peril.' Why?"

Fr. Dan tried to explain it: "Ye can understand that being wooed will reassure any unmarried woman, and fer that matter many that are. But her actions as an adult always come down on the side of 'old, happy, and unwed.' She seems to hold the prospect of a marriage as some kind of doom."

Ordowahl found nothing in that answer to aid his understanding. "No suitor ever threatens Lady Janalei's blessed singleness?"

Fr. Danelagh nodded. "Ordowahl, ye be nobody's boy who may have once rolled a girl in the hayloft. Ye be a man who's had women in his bed."

Ordowahl frowned. "Stories grow, Father."

"From seed, no doubt." His eye twinkled at the pun. "But we merely judge that yer chances with Lady Janalei be nil. What's more to the point, if ye seek her hand, ye'll not find it. And if ye persist, she'll banish ye."

"Ordowahl," added Fr. Henck, "I am her confessor. I betray none of what I hear, but mark this: as her confessor I know her far better than anyone else, even her parents. She will never marry."

"Thank you, Fathers. I foresee taking a wife far in the future and not here. Nonetheless"—he bowed his head—"even in costume as

Vice-Count Utrecht, she leaves a man very desirous of her company."

"The importance of it is," said Fr. Henck, "we pray that your presence among us will be peaceful. That peace will vanish if you approach her on any basis beyond happenstance."

He paused for a moment. *Are these old men jealous of a young man's sins? I think they are telling me that Lady Janalei, both with and without her daytime mask of Vice-Count Utrecht, is a trap. This only deepens the puzzle.*

Returning to polite conversation, Ordowahl said, "I see, Father. I have come here because from time to time I feel God's small finger on my ear, if you take the image. He sends me to places I haven't planned."

"So, did you choose this destination, or our Lord Almighty?" asked Fr. Henck.

"This time it felt to me that I did the choosing. I seek to learn better how to shape the questions that His Word answers. Your company is what I came for, even though when I met the vice-count I somehow felt a gentle caress on my ear."

Father Kerk reacted to that: "So you feel predestined to be here, then? And what purpose might God's small finger have announced?"

Ordowahl's mouth fell open for a second, and he composed his answer with some care. "Father Kerk, in his letter to the church at Ephesus Saint Paulus says that we are His workmanship. And moreover, each of us has works to perform, set out before us in advance."

"Yes. Works are proof of faith."

"My greatest hope is to understand what my assigned works are when they appear, lest I pass one by."

"So you may mistake the tasks God has set before you? You may confuse a young man's desire with a mission from God?"

"Father Kerk, I am a sinful and unreliable partner in God's work. Even so. He makes all things work to the good of those who love Him."

"I see you bending several scriptures to support your

conclusion."

"Yes. Even when I mistake His purpose, He produces good from it. That too is a promise, hence also predestined. And yes, I have learned to my deep regret that desire is not destiny."

Father Henck interrupted. "All well and good. Now, Ordowahl, please set aside a time to tell me more about your encounters with Black Magery, or black magic."

"They puzzled me at the time, Father, but God seems loath to let me fall."

"Something in the pit of my stomach abhors such matters," said Fr. Henck. "And in any event we will select a later time, and not discuss them now. But I want very much to connect your surviving those encounters to the purity of your Christian faith."

I sense Father Henck struggling to choose between the safety of his flock and his duty to care for a troubled sinner. And my discussing predestination after warning me against trying to tutor them. Ordowahl bowed his head and left, with Torwulf and Klarenz in tow.

He's not a threat to Utrecht: she to him?

her smile has come already and it felt

like God's small finger's touch. What seraphim

were sent to help him play the hand he's dealt?

    His only aim appears to be a fond

    attempt to study with a priestly Scribe.

    It hasn't dawned just yet how far beyond

    his grasp he's reached, Church wisdom to imbibe.

Not only that, but demon practices

he'd turned against their users—magic, if

you will? And latched him fair? Like face-kisses

with Satan, in their deepest fears? A whiff.

    So far he doesn't know that war is on.

    First face is Utrecht, of a polygon.

Sparring

After the morning meal with the family, servants removed the pot of porridge, dish of honey, plates of bread rolls, butter, slices of mild cheese, and the jug of fresh, warm milk. *Less austere than biscuits and butter with the fathers,* he noted.

After two weeks of just getting acquainted, Ordowahl decided to learn more directly. "Heri, help me observe how a Vendinker baron handles Vendinker problems."

Heri was just rising from the table. He turned a genuine smile on Ordowahl. "You do see a baron before you, do you not? The very flesh and soul of one. Stay close by me. This may turn auspicious at any moment. I feel it in my bones. Wils and I compare daily what we each hear from our various stewards' reports so that nothing gets lost. Today I am the one to hear reports."

"Kings do this," said Ordowahl, "and I'm sure dukes and counts do so as well."

"Vice-Counts, too," Heri reminded him.

Indeed, and I hear an echo in that: "Stay out of Utrecht's way!" But he said only, "Acquaint me with Barony Hangendro's various aspects."

They reached a side door, the one reserved for servants, couriers, and the like. Heri introduced the man standing there. "Prince, this is majordomo Fettur. Fettur, Prince Ordowahl."

A grave-looking man of perhaps forty-five years bowed to

Ordowahl. "Prince," he said in a soft, respectful purr.

"Who's first in line today, Fettur?" Heri got down to business.

The majordomo opened the exterior door and ushered in a half-dozen men in various levels of dress. "Baron, it is exchequer." He didn't bother naming the man, just his function, for Ordowahl's benefit.

"I won a nice wager yesterday," Heri said. "Let's start with that account then proceed to your regular accounts."

The man was dressed in drab but still tailored clothing. It was clear that he did much less manual labor than the others. "Baron," he said, "it has brought us to even for the year. Very good."

Heri smiled. "Even, eh? Who says I don't know a good wager when I see one?"

"Silver on hand for buying goods is low, but, considering that harvests are nearly in, our funds will expand soon."

"Go on."

"Household expenses are slightly below where we expect them to be but will need adjusting to house and feed your highly esteemed guest. I trust your mother will also be wanting to celebrate more than usual this winter." He eyed Ordowahl.

"Excellent. Set aside a twentieth of this month's revenues for the purpose. We'll adjust as needed by and by." After several other accounts, especially including arms and training, Heri released the man with a simple nod.

More prosaic reports regarding livestock and feed, haying, and bulk crops sent by cart to a shipping dock on the Neder Rijn concluded the business of the day.

"Heri?" asked Ordowahl.

"What do you think?" Heri asked back.

"Beyond budgeted expenses, I noticed nothing regarding actual troops, and their current training."

"That, my friend Prince Ordowahl, is where we go next."

Heri's manner suggests that Barony Hangendro has a very special fightmaster.

*__*__*__*

Heri introduced Ordo to the fightmaster. "Roneult, please greet

Sparring

Prince Ordowahl of Nordweg."

The man had above-average height and decent bulk. When he examined Ordowahl then held out his hand to the prince, there was no doubt in any mind. Roneult's realm was the armory and exercise yard. To access and use it one first had to persuade Roneult that he had a worthy purpose. The extended hand meant that Ordowahl had passed a cursory initial inspection.

"Roneult," said Heri, "how are our current trainees doing?"

"My lord," the man replied, and *lord* in his mouth mixed the perfunctory with actual respect. Ordowahl surmised that Heri had trained with the fightmaster and gained his approval as a qualified man at arms.

"These men are now ten weeks in my care. Twenty began, eleven sent back, nine remain. Among them I may find seven or eight with the hands and eyes, the stamina, and the brains as could make them worth further training."

Heri looked happy to hear that and turned aside to Ordowahl. "Roneult is so hard on this county's young men that they arrive trembling."

Ordowahl smiled. "It's the same everywhere. A good fightmaster presses awe into youngsters, and some become hard, like a smith hardens steel."

"Aye, but he is also a fair man, and those he keeps to the end of the quarter-year will stay proud of that for the rest of their lives. For that matter, I am one such myself." He turned back to the fightmaster. "This is good. Now I ask for a sparring area and basic practice weapons. Today I wish to work with Prince Ordowahl. And he, in his own way and his own yard, will extend the training of the nobles hereabout, beginning with me."

Roneult couldn't keep a smile from lighting up his face. "Lord, Prince, I'd like my trainees to observe. I trust this will not be an inconvenience."

"Where shall we work?"

"The west corner is free, Lord Heri."

Nine young men stood close behind him. The fightmaster led them in a march at a steady pace, arms swinging. They and the two nobles went to the west corner of a large flattened area devoted to arms training and practice.

"Jaan, two swords and bucklers." One of the young men sprinted toward a small stone building in the middle of the practice area.

Heri and Ordowahl posed themselves in the standard ready position, left leg back and right leg forward, weight centered, both arms held away from the body. The youngster slapped sword hilts into their right hands and the enarmes, or hand straps, of small round shields over their lefts without seeming to break stride.

Heri said, "At least our swords and bucklers are the same sizes." At the word *sizes* he leapt at Ordowahl.

The prince had been watching Heri. One hip showed past the edge of his shield. He sidestepped Heri and sword-slapped his shield as Heri pulled back.

This was Heri's first introduction to Ordowahl as a sparring partner, but his impetuous nature refused to show awe or defer to the prince's apparent ease.

But a quiet "stop" came from Roneult. Prince and lord, from long training as youths, stood where they were and adopted the ready posture.

"Lads," said the fightmaster, turning to his trainees. "Who can tell the prince's secret?"

Their thoughtful looks showed them ready for the question. After no more than three or four seconds one of them raised a hand and said, "Sir! Permission to speak, sir!"

The fightmaster looked him in the eye, raised his eyebrow in invitation, and the young fellow spoke.

"Sir! The prince's eyes were on the lord's center. I believe that he keyed off the movement there, even though the lord's sword moved first. Sir!"

The fightmaster twitched his head up-down, to show he agreed. The speaker relaxed. A small downward motion with the fightmaster's left hand and the word "twenty" dropped the other eight trainees at once onto their bellies.

They pushed themselves up, body straight, shoulders as high off the ground as their arms could get them then lowered to touch nose to dirt, and raised—lowered—raised stiffened bodies a total of twenty times. The fightmaster kept the rapid count.

At twenty they drew their knees forward to touch their shoulders and leapt erect. The fightmaster paused for a moment then gave them a grunt of acceptance. Each one relaxed a bit, as though he might have had to do it again.

"With your leave, my lord and prince, these lads still need a lot of careful attention." Without waiting for a response he gave them a pro forma nod, turned to his young men, and flicked his right hand in a "that way" gesture.

The men sprinted back to where they had been a few moments before and resumed the regimen that Heri and Ordowahl had interrupted.

After a period of time sparring, Heri tired and stopped to rest. "Prince, your size makes you almost impossible to contend with, but also your speed! Tell me how to train for that."

Ordowahl didn't smile. The question was old and never had a comfortable answer. "Heri, you've seen some of my exercises, and I believe I've seen you exercising as well. So what did you see me doing that looked unusual?"

"Truth to tell, Prince, we have little to teach one another. So, you've hidden nothing? You've already displayed all your moves and stretches, lunges, lifts, leaps, spins, sprints, what-have-you?"

"Yes, Heri. Perhaps there is a secret in the time spent on each one, or how hard I exert myself in doing each, or when and how much I rest. To proceed through the complete repetitions may take the rest of the morning. If you like, we can do that now."

"Yes, of course, my friend. Let me shake my right arm to relieve its weariness and drink some water. Then let's go, and Wils take the hindmost."

"Wils? I'll spar a while with him too. For now, rest and water are very important, but not overmuch of either at one time."

*__*__*__*

The next day Wils spoke as they were leaving the morning meal. "A word, Prince, if I may. I have already heard reports and would like to speak with you."

Torwulf took this as a cue to leave, and went to the training yard. Klarenz remained the invisible servant.

"Hello, Wils. We haven't gotten to know each other well, yet. What's on your mind?"

"I would like you to know more of the contest between my brother Heri and myself. You've heard the story of our birth, and only one can replace our father as Baron Hangendro."

The prince paused for a moment. "Your mother claims that you were born first and seems set on passing the barony to you."

"Yes, Heri and I have known it ever since father died. But she hasn't forced the issue."

"So Heri continues to forward his own right to inherit as somehow natural. Further, I know that Vice-Count Utrecht disallows my own participation in your contest. So what help can I give you?"

"Yes, Prince, well said. The vice-count's interest in working without interference defines her in almost everything. She has said nothing about asking Prince Ordowahl for insight."

"Then, aside from your mother's belief that you were born first, what qualifications have you advanced to Vice-Count Utrecht to sway her choice?" He looked for a response but got none. He continued, "And, to be sure, wooing for the right to take the count's daughter to wife is an obvious qualification."

"Ahem, you haven't yet tried wooing her yourself," Wils said. "Attempting that is like scaling a hundred-foot wall of smiling ice."

"A chilly image."

"Well, there's nothing either cold or discordant about her. But each new suitor seems to discover a core of something immovable just beneath her smile and find himself dismissed."

"I've been warned off by the good fathers of Saint Martin's Cathedral. They said much the same," replied Ordowahl.

"Indeed. She tells every suitor, a short while after he announces himself, that his time is up."

"Wils, I pray none of us ever endures such a peril."

"As usual you see with clarity and purpose. But to my original point. Heri and I bring different gifts. We will each stand the barony, and the county, in good stead."

Sparring

"You both appear to believe this. So, tell me what these differences are, as you see them."

"Only one that matters. I make decisions after careful thought. Heri decides quickly. While he often chooses rightly, he can be too quick and too emphatic. This creates unhappiness and distrust."

"And what about yourself? Are you slow to make up your mind?"

"That, Prince, is in the eye of the beholder. But when I reach a decision, it seldom needs to be revisited."

"And does Heri choose well often enough that he has confidence in his own judgment?"

"I dread those moments when it's apparent that he failed to consider something. Heri's mistakes show themselves chiefly when he blames someone else for his poor choice."

"Can you give me examples?"

"He bought a fine-looking mare, but she was barren. Or one spring he bought a baronet's crop of wheat. At harvest time it turned out to be withered, and the agreement lacked a clause to split the loss."

"Such things happen, Wils. What of it?"

"Once, a horse race included an unannounced horse which had never yet lost, and of course did not lose that time, either."

"I see. But from time to time Heri does find that it's the other fellow who guessed badly?"

Wils had to grin. "From time to time. Often enough to keep him out of debt, thus proud of his own judgment."

"Do I hear you say your brother Heri is decisive but not thoughtful, whilst you take thought but can be slow to decide?"

"He often says so and brings it up each time he sees Vice-Count Utrecht."

"This vice-count of yours is very canny. How many times does Heri have to make his point before the vice-count answers him?"

"That I'm not sure, but she never divulges a decision before its time."

"How like you, Wils. That seems a good sign. So, how often have you advanced your own points? What does she say when you describe the sad outcomes of Heri's more rash decisions?"

They found Roneult, got his salute, and reached the far end of the exercise yard.

"Well, Prince, it is as though she spars with me, and nothing I say seems to move the vice-count's opinion one way or the other."

"I've observed that Vice-Count Utrecht can't, or doesn't, keep a smoky wisp of female presence out of her conversations."

"Indeed this is true, and it's maddening. You mustn't use her Christian name when she wears male clothing, for at such times she is Vice-Count Utrecht and abhors any reference to lady Janalei."

"I see. She holds her counsel, acts on her father's behalf, and brooks no interference."

"It is so. But a smile from Vice-Count Utrecht always brings Lady Janalei to mind."

"And when you visit the county castle and she dresses as a woman?"

"She attends each new entry into her field of wooers like a maid cultivating, or cutting, a flower in her garden. Moreover, she will hear nothing of some business that she may have conducted in pantaloons just an hour before."

"So in other words, by day the vice-count is a calm negotiator who reveals nothing, and in the evening the count's daughter controls her conversations with equal firmness."

"Yes, Prince, that is the case. You begin to understand."

"Then tell me again, Wils, what can I do? My interest is to help the barony. You make the clearer case, without evident bias, while your brother insists it's his by right."

"Prince, I think a baron must deliver more accurate and more thoughtful judgment than what Heri has produced. And he, of course, says timeliness is a baron's first concern."

"Yet Heri hasn't given me his own opinion."

"I ask you, Prince, to help Utrecht see who is better prepared to serve."

"Would she even listen? But for the sake of the barony, Wils, I will try to do that."

"As seems fair to you, Prince."

Sparring

Again in the morning, Ordowahl and Torwulf paused from light training in the exercise yard when they heard someone gallop their way.

"Halloo, Prince!"

They looked around and saw Heri riding across the exercise yard and without pausing to consult Roneult.

"Yes, Heri?"

"I believe, Prince," he said while dismounting, "that you're speaking behind my back regarding my right to this barony. What say you?"

"Your right, Heri? No, I have not, yet you curl the lip. What's wrong?"

Heri stood, nostrils flaring, taking several large, even breaths. "Is it right, Prince, to discuss a man behind his back?"

"Well, Heri, aside from dismissing your brother as a serious candidate, you've said nothing else about him to me. I know you and he both claim the barony. Does your right overmaster his, if that is your grief?"

"So you've taken sides. I knew it, and you haven't denied speaking against me with my brother."

"My friend, if you weren't present, how can you know what we said or didn't say? I hear an accusation with nothing behind it."

"Do you tempt me now into my brother's sin? Have no doubt, Prince, it will be an arrogant error to assume the right to intrude into matters that have nothing to do with you."

They said he was rash, and it shows. "Your views seem fixed and beyond discussion, Heri. Nothing I can say will change your mind. That rigidity, my friend, is a sad trait for any noble, much less a baron."

"Now you offer insult to my face?"

"I offer you a criticism, not a judgment. I will continue to speak with whomever I please, and concerning whatever I am asked, beholden to my own judgment."

Heri jumped back onto his mount and left with a shouted warning: "Judgment, you say? Bah! What judgment is there in taking sides in a matter that doesn't concern you? Be wary, Prince."

Torwulf looked askance at Ordowahl, as if to ask what could be troubling Heri. Ordowahl just shook his head, and they returned to training.

*__*__*__*

"Halloo, Prince!"

Ordowahl was walking Hammerfoot in the stable yard, as no groom had yet gained the stallion's trust. *Where have I heard that voice before? Like Heri, she sounds furious.*

"What did I fail to tell you, Nordweg? Why have you stepped into my domain?"

"You must be referring to the succession of Barony Hangendro. In fact, I would like to discuss the brothers with you, but not until you are so inclined."

"Prince or not, it would be impertinent for you to confess an interest."

"I have no interest. But I feel entitled to speak with either brother from time to time just to form an acquaintance. For that matter, one of them did ask me to form an independent opinion."

Utrecht bared her teeth while dismounting from her lathered horse. "Nordweg, you show interest far beyond mere acquaintance and ask leave to disturb affairs to which you have no entry."

"Can Mother Baroness Fretheldin participate in the choice between her two sons?"

"Since you ask, Prince, she can. But I pray she hasn't insulted the county by inviting counsel or advice from you. Now, have you discussed Heri with Wils?"

"No, although the subject did come up. No more. I have also formed no judgment, Vice-Count Vendink, although I am prepared for any thoughtful discussion."

Utrecht's eyes were like green stone. "No matter the baroness's naïve invitation, you have no right and therefore no reason to intrude."

"Even when asked?"

"By no means on your own merit. While you allege yourself royal, you are also a newcomer to the affairs of County Vendink. I insist that you disengage from the county's internal concern."

"While I understand the count's right to oversee the decision, Vice-Count, as well as your duty to defend it, the best interests of both the county and the barony still move me to discuss the twins with you."

Utrecht counted all the way to ten, her breathing slow and deep, her pulsing fingers betraying the way she checked her anger. "Prince, I may have accosted you more than you warranted. But do not think for a minute that you have redeemed yourself." Her frown betrayed some inner turmoil.

Ordowahl asked, "Am I now a sinner? I wish not to offend you, Vice-Count."

"Be at peace. I accept your intent to act with modesty. But do not be fooled. I did not invite you into this business, and your offer to take part is unwelcome. Good day, Prince." She turned and in one smooth leaping motion remounted her horse and spurred it away. Her ribboned red-to-orange-to-gold hair trailed behind her like a pennant lifted in flowing air. She may have seen her mount's lather, because at once she slowed it to a walk, and her braid fell down the length of her firm, trim back.

Lord Heri's hand of fellowship holds out

a righteous thorn of ownership and blame.

His minutes-elder brother Wils, devouter

than his twin, stops short of counterclaim.

    Their natures seem so opposite. The vice-

    count seems like both: she races in with rash

    reaction, yet she turns from fire to ice

    when reason interposes, calms the clash.

That polygon's first face is hot, "Don't touch!"

In short, his unpreparedness is plain.

His naïveté proves this: he needs a crutch.

Adulthood's polish? More like scatterbrain.

    Withal, the prince is never prey to doubt.

    Just struggle on; if need, he'll do without.

Inquiry

Another grim Dutch morning. During the ride from Haus Hangendro to St. Martin's Cathedral a light mist collected like dew on the three men's cloaks. They arrived prior to the dawn Mass to stand in line to confess.

Confession in theory was anonymous, but one could soon distinguish one priest from another. And while whispering made it more difficult for the priest to understand who had come to confess, they learned to tell one parishioner from another.

Theory vanished among the upper ranks. By custom the nobility had their own priests close at hand. Lady Janalei / Vice-Count Utrecht often made her way to confession at the Cathedral prior to the dawn Mass, sending word the prior evening to alert Fr. Henck, who insisted on confessing her.

Father Henck was not in the booth, which helped Ordowahl relax. *I want to avoid Utrecht after her angry words yesterday.* The priest turned out to have a heavy brogue, which gave him away as Fr. Dan.

Ordowahl's first whisper told Fr. Dan who had come to him. He waited through a wan litany of harbored animosity, irritation with someone who must be the vice-count, inevitable lust rising from nineteen-year-old loins, and a rudeness detected in hindsight which, in Fr. Dan's ears, could seem rude to no other person than the prince.

Fr. Dan issued an audible sigh, which caused Ordowahl to stumble. "Me boy, there's a line of actual sins waitin' behind ye, so next time please confess to Father Henck. Three rosaries and four Hail Mary's: done. Bless ye me son, yer sins be fergiven."

*__*__*__*

As the Mass ended Fr. Henck came down the aisle to bless the small congregation. When he reached Ordowahl he said, "If you have time, Prince, please break bread with me in the rectory."

"Thank you, Father. I hope to begin to study God's Word under guidance, and I recall your interest in my encounters with black mages and their works."

"Yes, Prince, that is, in fact, what I have in mind. All of the brothers are likely to join us, but we've ample room for you, your knight, and your man Klarenz."

When all found seats, they filled the room. After each one had opened and buttered a bread roll, Fr. Henck said, "We have a matter of grave concern. Do you, Prince, think yourself entitled to read from Scripture while you stand outside the Church? Can we, in good faith, accept you into any discussion of appropriate teaching? In short, do you submit your mind to the Church?"

A direct challenge. "Father Henck, of course I do. Can I ask a question in return?"

"If it shows proper respect for the primacy of the Church, certainly."

"Well then. From my earliest life the Church has been present to me in the form of Father Ewald, priest to the royal family. He required all dozen of his charges, my brothers and sisters, to read the Latin Scripture of Saint Jerome. We discussed what we read in close detail. So, since the Church has many official teachings on sin, salvation, duty, and the like, and has developed them across a thousand years of diligent scholarship, does it have a library that traces and defines these teachings?"

"Better than that, Prince. We possess, as priests, the full teaching of the Church on all matters that bear on those who aren't in the priesthood. Just ask a question of a priest, and he'll have the answer."

Inquiry

"To be sure I understand, Father, you were gracious to admit me to your discussion a few days ago. Since the topic remains under debate, it therefore can have no application to anyone who isn't a priest, and the Church's teaching on the subject, if there is one, applies to common folk, but not at all to priests?"

Father Henck's face froze. He stared at Ordowahl, eye to eye and neither blinking, for the best part of a minute.

I'd better blink, or he will declare me disrespectful and defiant. Ordowahl blinked.

"Took you an entire minute to submit your mind, did it? Prince, please leave us now. I find your conduct unbecoming and disrespectful. When you arrived you said that you were comfortable finding answers in Scripture but wanted to know more about which questions to ask."

"Yes, Father."

"You place your soul at risk, young man, by asking an impertinent question of a priest."

"Father, I—"

"Silence. Prince you are, Ordowahl, in your own country. But the keys of the Kingdom are not in your hands and, until you become a member of the priesthood, never will be. This hand holds the keys to your soul. Guard yourself from disturbing it further. Now go."

Klarenz whispered in Ordowahl's ear, "Liege, I know your nature abhors giving challenge. I fear that Father Henck hasn't learned that yet." Torwulf looked at the ground, crossed himself, and said nothing.

*_*_*_*

Another dawn Mass ended in an invitation to breakfast and further interrogation. *Father God in heaven, let me speak truth, and then let them hear it as honest. Did good Father Ewald spoil me, to think I could converse with clergy about what is in God's Word?*

"Prince," said Fr. Henck, "I and my brother priests are very concerned about you and have more questions. Answer them for us, to help us care for your soul."

"Of course, Father. Your attention flatters me."

Father Dan shot him a private look, a warning, as if to say, "Boyo, don't ye be sarcastic now."

"So," Fr. Henck said, "we heard you speak of being drugged by the Viking mage-king Ingvik. This we comprehend as the power of plants and herbs. While mysterious, it is something we encounter from time to time. He drugged your drink, following which you dreamed a contest, correct?"

"Yes, Father, I did dream it."

"And in your dream your own white mage briefly took part before Ingvik's image in the dream banished him?"

"Again, yes. That happened in the dream."

"Then your mage's single sentence gave you the key to resolve the puzzle and to drive off Ingvik's image."

"Yes."

"What of the actual Ingvik the next morning?"

"He would not look me in the eye but showed a passing, small curiosity as to my experience the night before. It seemed as if he knew I had dreamed and would not discuss something that I felt to be my victory."

"So, Prince, you credited him with magery, after a single dream? You read tiny clues as proof that your dream was in some way real under God's heaven?"

"Father, his behavior seemed consistent with the talking jackdaws. While Vikings demand that their chiefs prove right by might in battle, Ingvik was pudgy. He was slow and in all things cautious. Yet everyone around him feared his smallest whim."

"That much, at least, is consistent with this world." The other priests chuckled.

Your refusal to acknowledge my version is your own, Father. You weren't there, and you haven't encountered Heorald.

"So," continued Fr. Henck, "from that point he was an odd sort of Viking ruler, but fooled you into not just going on a raid against a Christian town, but also guarding his longboats during the raid?"

"For a time." *You are a skeptic, Father Henck, but you also seem to relish the diminution, that I look foolish. Well, so be it. I was, and very much still am.*

Inquiry

"Yes, then we learn that you sat down to break bread with them. So you waited long enough for half the town to burn before plucking up your nerve to slay your captors, and did so while they were lulled."

"Exactly, Father. I murdered them."

"And your confession of that murder?"

"The priest I confessed it to disagreed and gave me a penance for thinking it murder."

"I see. The way you tell it, I would do the same. Yet I also see you hold fast to the charge your priest disputed."

Yet you don't believe me. But then I might not believe such a story myself. "Yes, Father." *Here I trade insincerities with a priest! Father God in heaven, keep me on the path of truth and light.*

Father Dan interrupted. "Prince, be ye certain in yer heart that it began as murder? Given that their job was to keep ye from yer Christian duty?"

"Thank you, Father Dan. Slaying two unsuspecting men felt like murder, but the rest found that in keeping with Viking ways. Yet, Father, I am not a Viking and do not endorse Viking morality."

Father Henck took back control. "Prince, we aren't here to explore the finer points of a Viking's conscience. Explain to us again how Ingvik died."

"All during the battle Ingvik sat in the basin of a fountain at the center of the square. He dabbled his feet like a child at play. He saw his men fall all around him. He knew he had lost."

"How odd that a mage can have a child's sense of play." It wasn't a question. The image seemed to fascinate Fr. Henck.

"Indeed, Father, I saw it the same. As did Klarenz." He looked at his bondman, sitting at the next spot around the table.

"Then he gave his soul away?"

"Father, his image in the dream said that he had no heart left, hence no soul. It had fled him long since as a consequence of using magery to control the loyalties and lives of all his subjects."

Father Henck mumbled something to himself. Ordowahl's ears picked it up as, "Part of the burden of all who lead."

Ordowahl continued. "Ingvik stood and applauded as though

congratulating children for singing a simple rhyme. Then he slit his own throat. You might have thought he was about to shave, but of course he nicked himself to the full depth."

"Polluting the fountain with his feet was bad enough," said Fr. Kerk. "Did he bleed into it as well?"

Ordowahl smiled a wry half-smile. "He lacked the grace to fall forward, fathers. His blood turned out to be a stream of flies, which flew away and were gone within seconds."

The priests' faces froze, like stone. Klarenz, who had seen it, blanched.

"His body consisted of crusted pus and maggoty bones. The stench was foul, and so strange that I can find nothing in my experience to describe it."

Father Henck paused. "Prince, in all the confessions I have ever heard, nothing like this has ever arisen. Brothers," he said looking from side to side, "we must spend time in prayer now, to find cleansing and peace, before resuming this day's regimen." He nodded at Ordowahl, ending the audience.

The next morning held another dewy, grim pre-dawn ride to the Cathedral of St. Martin. For a second time Ordowahl had sent Klarenz the prior afternoon to notify Fr. Henck that he would attend dawn Mass. This time Klarenz reported that Utrecht would be there, also, but by the time they arrived she had already come and gone. Her absence left him disappointed, although he couldn't say why.

After the Mass, and after breaking bread with the group of priests, Fr. Henck continued the interrogation. "Prince, we've heard divers recountings of the joust with the Black Knight. Summarize it for us." Ordowahl began:

Klarenz's breakfast porridge held a poison. The Black Knight sent a substitute to assist me in the joust. I noticed an odd thing he did, and the Black Knight's own second did the same. During the run the lance behaved oddly. I did the same odd thing in time to meet him lance to lance and shield to shield.

He crumpled on the ground, his head bleeding. His emblem was the raven One flew down to his body. Its touch restored him.

After a mid-day meal I found Klarenz under that spell. A

nearby raven governed his actions. I managed to rouse him, by smiting the raven.

He looked aside at Klarenz and got a quiet nod.

Klarenz revealed the Black Knight's plan to lay a spell of frost. By a ruse we reversed cold to heat. In the second run my shield failed. The Black Knight's lance gored me but instead of blood, honey poured out.

Reversing cold to heat made the gout of honey a lubricant not a prison. I dumped the honeyed mail over my head and he slipped on it. When I cut his throat his stench far outdid Ingvik's.

During a week abed and two months convalescing, Ingvik's totem bird, a jackdaw, kept constant watch outside the house. No scar marks the injury today.

Father Henck looked a question at Klarenz. "Bondman," he said, "answer the Church with your soul at stake. What did you see of these things, and what do you know to be truth and fact?"

Klarenz didn't hesitate. "Father, I saw Ingvik die. Under the Black Knight's spell I heard boasts of cold and honey. I regret that I didn't hear about my liege's shield becoming shavings and pinfeathers."

He drew a remorseful hand over his face and continued. "I saw him kill the Black Knight. The stench made my belly revolt. A jackdaw pecked once at Ordowahl after he fell, and one was always present during the time of his healing. Fathers, on my soul, everything my liege said is true to my own witness of it."

*__*__*__*

Father Henck convened the priests half an hour before final prayers. "Brothers, Ordowahl understands that black magic is evil. But did he when he turned it against the Black Knight? Does that use compromise his soul?"

Father Kerk spoke first. "Yes, of course he used it. He knew that the Black Knight was a black mage, same as Ingvik the Viking king. Yet we live in a world full of everyday evil."

Father Petur asked, "Do we use evil, knowing it is evil?"

Father Jemck replied, "Do we purposely use it, or only inadvertently? More to the point, do we believe that the end justifies the means?"

Father Dan spoke last. "When a man in battle loses his weapon, or in the prince's case is attacked naked of any weapon, do we not bless him if he foils his opponent by seizin' and wieldin' the enemy's own weapon? Let me ask whether the prince chose evil, or merely seized what God let come to hand then either reversed its effect, as in the heated mail, or used it for his own? And that fer Christ's purpose?"

The brothers looked at Fr. Henck. Could he sort out their arguments this time? None of them realized they were holding their breath until Fr. Henck spoke.

"All God has made is pure and good, and He reaps where He did not sow."

No one pointed out that Ordowahl had opened that interpretation of the parable in Matthew's gospel.

"We in our fallen state are so familiar with our own evil that handling someone else's to reap a godly outcome is easy to believe in. I tremble that the prince's possible debt to Ingvik's jackdaw, for healing him, may come due. I hope that God shields him. King David's bloody hands kept him from building the Temple, but like David, may the prince always have a heart for God."

Slow smiles of relief showed on their faces.

"However," said Fr. Henck, "we still have the matter of whether the prince thinks himself entitled to read from Scripture while yet uninstructed by Church training. Can we, in good faith, accept him into any discussion of appropriate teaching? Will he master his untidy youthfulness and hasten to submit his mind to the Church?"

"The prince has a voracious mind," said Fr. Dan. "A week ago he asked for lessons in reading runes. I asked him why, and he simply said, 'I can't read them. They may be old, but I won't be able to rest until I've learned them well enough to be sure what they say.' So I sent him to Willem Friis."

Father Jemck nodded. "He has several students at the moment."

Father Henck looked at them. "We still have the matter of the prince's idea of his own importance. He may be royal. But he's not trained! Consider that we have, just now, narrowly avoided ordering

58

a heretic's cleansing death by fire. Is his holding holy conversation alongside us, brothers," he asked while scanning their faces, "something to speak of lightly? So soon after hearing him speak of deflecting a power that came from Satan, and of being healed by another such?"

The other priests echoed the deep concern that creased Fr. Henck's face.

It really doesn't look good for the prince

to study any further with the priests.

Can't introduce a novel thought, evince

an argument of any sort? No "yeasts?"

    To date he doesn't realize this much.

    Discredited as "Just a warring child,"

    they talk behind his back in fluent "Dutch."

    His prior learning? Here, unreconciled.

Unready to retreat, he'd better find

another focus for his energies.

A puzzle now confronts him; what new kind

of trouble, what newfound antitheses?

    His time in town is looking short. His cause

    for coming masticates in churchly jaws.

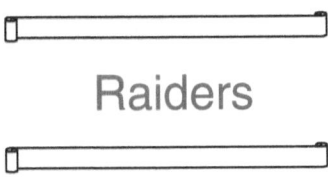

Raiders

Leaving the Rectory that same morning, Ordowahl saw a large number of armed men proceeding across the square toward Castle Vendink. "As good a time as any to see the castle, Torwulf." He followed the train of men to and through the great drawbridge gate.

Fightmaster Roneult from the Hangendro household caught his eye. "I notice several of your own pupils are present. Are they learning ways to defeat black knights?" The man's smile was frank. He had the fearless calm of someone who read men well and had taught war to hundreds.

"Yes, Fightmaster, they are learning to pray." Ordowahl smiled. "What best use do you have for me?"

"The vice-count will be covering that later. She has already made herself clear."

Vice-Count Utrecht came over to them. "Prince," she said, in a voice of command. "Today you have an opportunity to aid County Vendink. Count Marvistjen has appealed for armed assistance. I even invite your observations as we proceed. All decisions are mine, but your thoughts as a man who has seen battle should be useful." She gave "should" a dubious accent. "I've accompanied Father many such a time. Do not think me a novice in war."

He gave her a polite smile. "Vice-Count, I do not think of you as a novice at anything a vice-count needs to do, including armed combat. But allow me to stay near you when there is fighting, for my own peace of mind."

She gave him a cold look. "I will permit that. It will be important to keep Roneult present, so also you. I'll want the eyes and thoughts of you both."

"Thank you, Vice-Count. What is the tale?"

"Mother married a count. Her sister likewise married a count, Marvistjen. His lands lie west of here along the seacoast. He reports that Viking longboats came, near the height of the moon. It rose an hour after sunset; they arrived in middle night and pillaged a fishing village. They carried away both dried fish and a hundred bushels of grain, which will be precious by the end of winter when the granaries have emptied."

"Starving peasants are poor sources of revenue. Did the raiding party go beyond theft?"

"Not so far, but they left scraps of paper written with old Viking runes. Warnings, no doubt. Your presence may be useful, Nordweg, though not required."

*__*__*__*

A large troop of mounted nobility, each noble bringing several dozen armed men, filled the grounds of Castle Marvistjen. The hour was mid-morning; the distance had required them to camp along the way. Men and horses crammed the yard when the count emerged to greet Utrecht and Ordowahl.

Marvistjen bloomed with muscle and had a brusque manner. "My best to your father, Vice-Count. How is he?" The count stood eye to eye with his niece. While she stood man-tall, he could have made two of her.

"Thank you, Uncle Petur. He cannot make even a half-day's ride in a carriage but of course was furious at staying behind. Please tell Aunt Marte that Mother is doing well and sends her love."

"Yes, of course. Now, Ja—Utrecht, who do you know with access to drawings of the old Viking runes, and who knows where to find longboats?"

"Uncle, you have the shore and numerous fishing villages. They will know more about longboats than I. But the city is home to a great variety of scholars. In fact, one stands here with me."

She gave Ordowahl a backhand slap, trying to keep the blow above his belt, and hard enough to bruise her hand when she hit the top of the buckle. She suppressed a sudden wince.

"Prince, I have heard of you," said the count with an open smile, and looked up into a big-jawed face that might have been smiling back at him.

"I am pleased to meet you, too," said Ordowahl and held out his hand.

The count shook it as best he could and turned back to Utrecht. "Niece, we have no idea who in this county has any access to longboats, and we don't believe that Norsemen exist anywhere near this coast."

"Yes, Uncle, the bodiless don't carry away plunder."

"Instead someone has tried to impersonate them. I hoped you might have heard something about longboats and can tell me who in your city knew runes or recent attempts to learn them."

Ordowahl broke in. "I have. The fellow would not give his true name, but from his accent I place him south of here."

Utrecht scoffed. "Your own mouth can't make decent language, but you can hear that small a difference? You never cease to exceed some boundary or another, Prince." She craned her neck to look him in the eye, thus be sure he took the double meaning.

"The fellow stood a hand taller than either of you," he continued, "a slender man of forty years. He tucked his half-brown hair up under a hat, with eyebrows and beard dyed dark."

"That helps, but there are a hundred men of that height, age, hair, and build. What else do you have, Nordweg?"

"He has two warts on his left eyebrow and is missing the bottom bit of his right ear. He walks with a long stride—"

"Enough," burst in Utrecht. "Uncle, doesn't this sound familiar?"

Count Marvistjen chuckled. "Thank you, Prince. I feared you were about to ask for paints and a brush. Yes, Niece, we know the man. He is a tricky devil with ambitions that drive him far beyond plain dealing."

"Then, Uncle, what keeps this man safe from a sword's point?"

"Four men have died on his sword's point. He also enjoys the good will of his count and all the lesser nobility."

"Is he also noble?" asked Ordowahl.

"His grandfather was a craftsman, and his father a wealthy merchant. He is a landed knight. His ambition is to marry off his children above his own station. His firstborn, a daughter, is betrothed to a man set to inherit a baronetcy."

Ordowahl asked, "Vice-Count, can you describe how you would, in his shoes, set up these raids?"

"I would search far and wide for a longboat, learn runish characters as he seems to have done, and man the boats with the dregs of cutthroat bastards."

"Sailors?" asked her uncle. "Many of them go to sea because they've made themselves unwelcome on land."

"Hmmm," mused Ordowahl. "Sailors might not know how to operate a longboat, but if a craft is to be found, then its owner could teach them its ways and riggings. What, by the way, is the fellow's name? He called himself Johanus Johanus, but it felt false when he said it."

"He makes up a new name when he doesn't want to get himself attached to something, and that one is new to me. He was born Willum Weverzoon. How did you meet?"

"I too like to expand on what I know. Runic characters are of historical interest, and by chance we shared a teacher the day after I arrived."

"Please bring yourself into the present, Prince," said Utrecht. "We have a weaver's son to catch in our loom."

The count looked disapproval at her. "Niece, such liberty. You seem very casual in this man's presence."

"Uncle, casual is as casual does. In truth I find him hard to manage."

Her uncle Petur chuckled at the idea of a woman needing to manage a visiting prince, but Utrecht didn't share his amusement.

"Uncle," she said, "we've brought you one hundred fifty men at arms, ten mounted knights, five baronets, and three barons. You may have heard this from the courier I sent ahead. Tell me the best use of these men."

Roneult and the Marvistjen fightmaster settled the visiting barons, baronets, knights, and armed men into camps, using the exercise yard. The barons sat down with count, vice-count, and prince around a large table in the main hall. No sweetmeats or even water distracted them from the business at hand.

Marvistjen began. "Forty miles of coastline as the crow flies, much of it little more than reeds and mud at high tide and quarter-mile-wide mud flats at low tide. That, plus many long and narrow inlets. Such is my shore. Stationing four hundred men at even intervals would put them beyond shouting distance from each other. While hard to defend, the mud will impede any attack. Just a dozen sandy beaches with gentle slopes interrupt that barrier. Five of these are fishing villages, each with a rudimentary pier."

He waited for the picture to form on the visitors' minds. "My friends," said the count, "The raiders so far have struck two villages, the first one four days ago and the second last night. This time ten villagers died, and one raider left a bloody track." He paused to suppress his emotions. "Half the village burnt. Both raids came at night, near high tide. A full moon's tides are near midday and middle night, and each day the moon falls behind by a bit less than an hour. Please forgive me for stating the obvious, but not all of you live near the sea."

Ordowahl added to that. "The present moon is half-waned and reaches the top of the sky perhaps three hours before dawn."

Petur said, "They'll soon have to raid during the day to have any light."

"If three unraided villages remain, plus seven empty beaches, forty men at each one might give them a fight," Ordowahl said, "and we know when raiders are likeliest to appear. Petur?"

"You speak with the kind of knowledge Utrecht said you might have," Count Marvistjen said with approval. "Niece, what he says makes sense. Fishing villages use the moon as their clock, because the tides follow the moon."

Ordowahl showed modesty. "Even peasants know the moon

well."

"The fishing boats are at sea until a while after high tide. They set out on the tide's ebb and return when it is full, to fish as long as possible."

"Then," said Utrecht, "the raiders appear when at least some of the men are out fishing." She thought for a moment and glanced at Roneult. "Fightmaster, how are our armed men?"

"Tired, to be sure, but far from exhausted. Our horses will need a day of rest, though. Since the second raid was last night, tonight may be less likely. How far to the other villages?"

Petur answered, "Half a day's walk, or more, from here. Niece, does that give you any ideas?"

"With your permission, Uncle, separate your men into three sets and ours the same. Tomorrow we'll form three troops and travel to those villages."

"Fightmaster," asked Petur, "what do you anticipate?"

Roneult answered, "The raiders will do one of two things. Since they know or at least expect that by now you will be guarding the other villages, they will wait until our attention wanes."

"Yes, that's one. What's the other?"

"Because they took an injury, they may come back tonight. Do you have anyone guarding those villages now? And what of those other sandy beaches? Do any of them have stores that can attract a raid?"

"Bowmen guard each village. They are hidden and will use fire arrows on any longboat that comes ashore, once the raiders have left it."

"In other words," said Ordowahl, "don't provoke the raiders when they land. What about the raiders' sentries? And a second question: Did anyone examine their footprints, their tracks, to see if they had someone along who knew how to reach the food stores without wasted time searching?"

"Utrecht, the prince asks good questions. Please listen to my answer and give me your thoughts."

She looked at Ordowahl with an unreadable expression then turned to listen to her uncle.

Raiders

"First, yes I do not want to risk deaths. Peasants live hard lives but breed well, yet there is no excuse to ignore their safety. So, yes, my aim is to trap the raiders when they are burdened with plunder."

"Uncle, their sentries?"

"My bowmen have good sight of the piers, so the raiders' sentries should be no problem."

She considered this for a moment. "I concur, Uncle. But the raiders will be numerous. How do a few bowmen handle a longboat's-worth of armed men?"

"At night, bowmen firing from cover will be difficult to spot. Once they have set the boat afire they will kill all they can before vanishing into the dark."

"Without a way back, the raiders will take flight rather than exact revenge. Is that it?"

"Yes. Now to the prince's second question. From the disturbance of the ground they seemed very familiar with each village. Also, we think they number about twenty-five."

Ordowahl asked, "Is it probable that they have perfect knowledge of all these villages? Did they choose ones they knew well, for instance?"

"We don't have an answer to that. All things considered, they may not return for many months, or they may return tonight. Bear with me for a time. If they haven't returned in a week, I will not object if my niece's men return to County Vendink."

On cold probation, Ordowahl and Torwulf

go with Roneult, as Hangendro men.

That animus the vice-count splays before

him, right out loud, is just his regimen.

He knows, in fact, while she asserts control,

that he's immune. His easy-going smile

is not derision, but a full parole

that he will walk the codependent mile.

His work as royal is of course to fight.

Marvistjen's call to Vendink means, him too.

Is this atonement? Does he deem it right-

atoning, more than just a deed to do?

He's casual t'ward risk; he volunteers

to scout ahead. Of course, he disappears.

Asea

Torwulf, Klarenz, Roneult, and Ordowahl sat beneath the stick-bare branches of a cherry tree. "Well," said Ordowahl, "may I compare this war we've come to help fight to a tree in October? Many little twigs, but no promise of next year's fruit. Three days gone by without the smallest news."

"Prince," said Roneult, "several hundred men at arms grow restless. Some are bored, while others seem to show a sense of foreboding. A mystery does them no good. Our numbers swamp the raiders, but the idea of a sudden attack by night, when all good men should be sleeping, makes them uneasy."

Vice-Count Utrecht and Count Marvistjen joined them.

"Prince," said Utrecht, "I haven't seen you in some time. Good of you to drop by."

Ordowahl nodded at them. "After a good night's sleep I surveyed the village defenses these past two nights. I return with no better idea than I had when we arrived. If the raiders are familiar with each village, they will also know by now that we have archers set up in blinds. Think like a raider. What will you do to turn that into a disadvantage?"

Torwulf sat silent. Klarenz almost dared to speak but realized that the strategy of war wasn't a craft he knew nor cared to learn.

Ordowahl continued, "Three days without news also means that the moon sits at the top of the sky just half an hour before dawn.

What will that mean?"

Utrecht spoke. "Let me answer that. The prince has a mind that can turn shadows into daylight. Perhaps some of the black magic he managed to foil has rubbed off on him." Whether or not she meant the remark was her secret. Her smile appeared, but her face was turned at her uncle.

The count gave back an odd look, as though he might be disappointed in her, but answered the question himself. "The raiders will anticipate archers to stage an ambush. Thus they'll land at one of the other beaches and find their way overland in daylight."

"Land at daylight, attack, and carry the plunder away at dusk?"

"Aye, Prince. The best beach lies halfway between two ripe villages. I've asked Roneult to place archers and armed men near each of the empty beaches—fifty men or so at each one, and fifty at each of the remaining villages."

"Do you expect this to surprise Weverzoon or his men?"

"No. They will think twice about any attack, since we'll be ready to repel them."

"Utrecht?" asked Ordowahl. "Does Weverzoon often show sober patience? After two afternoons spent learning runes with him I think he owns a fierce will and a sharp mind. What might this sort of man do to counter our defenses?"

"Uncle Petur, the prince may have guessed well. What can he do to flank our men? How can he approach them unseen? And what is the possibility that he's done this already?"

The count looked at them and went silent for a few moments. Then, "Roneult has watchmen overlooking all five empty beaches. They know to watch closely near high tide."

Ordowahl asked, "What keeps Weverzoon from stranding a few boats on one of the many a mud flats and marching around to take our men from behind?"

Utrecht answered first. "You got seasick on that little day trip when the Vikings landed far to the north from Hammaborg, did you not?"

Ordowahl nodded. "Yes, that is so. Your careful attention to my limits is an asset."

"Uncle, let him starve. Tomorrow morning let him go out from the northernmost village, sailing south to look for boats abandoned on a mud flat. He is formidable, or so his friends claim. Send a few men with him and see what they find."

The count looked at the ground for a moment. He looked up and said, "Prince, my friend, do as you see fit. If you wish, I have a handful of archers able to kill at fifty yards while standing on a moving boat. I will send them with you, sailing along the shore to find the raiders."

Ordowahl said, "Done. I like it." He went to find food and ate a hearty meal.

*__*__*__*

That afternoon Ordowahl returned to the northernmost fishing village. At the end of the ride Hammerfoot was sore, overheated, and becoming lame. As soon as they arrived Ordowahl took him to the village thane and asked for very careful treatment of his stallion.

Petur's courier arrived at about the same hour, confirming that Ordowahl wanted to set out when the tide was high enough for a boat to leave the dock then sail southward along the coast, pretending to fish.

Half an hour before dawn the village headman led him to a small, fat-beamed, deep-hulled boat. It had room to hold five men, plus himself, plus fishing nets. The boat could sail several miles out into the sea and ride ordinary waves, but if the wind came up it also might roll and make him even more nauseous.

He told the archer-boatmen, "Ignore me if I become seasick. It won't be the first time. We need to look over all of the mudflats from here south to the next county. If anyone has stranded a few or even one boat we need to respond to it."

"Prince," one of them asked, "what kind of response?"

"Go back north to the first place this boat can land safely. Secure it, then all of you help me locate the men who left that boat. We have to make them understand their terrible misfortune."

His hard-eyed grin put a spirit of grand adventure into them, and for an extra time the archers checked their bows and store of arrows, plus knives and hand-axes for close fighting.

Keeping as straight a track as they could, by noon they had sailed about twenty miles of undulating coastline, covered fifteen linear miles, and scanned at least one hundred miles of convoluted shore.

Ordowahl had eaten nothing that morning and did his best to keep eyes focused on the unmoving shoreline. They told him that a stationary reference would help prevent becoming seasick.

The farther south the fishermen-archers went, the more encouraged they became. No raiders appeared, and success felt imminent. Then a watcher in the prow said in a hushed but urgent voice, "There! I see a longboat on the horizon."

They flung some fishing nets out to the sides. This made the little boat more stable in the water and gave the impression that the party were in fact "fishing." They angled a bit away from the shore. The longboat had someone perched atop its tall mast and fifteen oars on a side. As it came nearer, one of the men recognized a sailor leaning over the longboat's port side, trying to get a close look at them.

He turned his back, hoping to keep the sailor from recognizing his face, and asked the others to keep a sharp eye. That wasn't necessary. The longboat veered toward them, four archers standing erect with bows raised.

Ordowahl commanded, "Three of you stay in the boat and take cover behind the hull. Fire without exposing much of yourself."

The three closest to the longboat said, "Aye."

"The rest of us go over the side away from the longboat, hang on, and I hope you know how to swim. Keep your knives and fighting gear with you. *Now.*"

He flung himself overboard, keeping one hand on the boat. The other two archers didn't consider this a good idea until an arrow thudded into the boat between them. The first three flopped below the boat's wale and eased back up to send three arrows back.

The longboat archers hadn't thought to protect themselves from mere fishermen, and two of them fell. The other two crouched low. More "fisherman" arrows found sailors farther back, and a roar of battle rage rose up. The longboat turned to ram the smaller fishing boat, and the tops of men's heads appeared. They were getting ready to board, unless they managed to sink the fishing boat.

"Now back in the boat," Ordowahl called out. "Kill the archers first, then the closest man."

Two wet, shivering archers clambered back, each with help from a giant arm. They stood just in time to see arrows from the two remaining Viking archers. One hit an arm and the other creased a man's skull. Four archers fired back. Two enemy archers and one seaman fell, to a cacophony of screams and yells.

The two boats collided. The fishing boat was making minor headway, but the longboat was traveling faster than a man can walk and struck at an oblique angle. The men in the smaller boat lost their footing when the fishing boat tipped and began to slip under the longboat's hull. Its other side rose, catapulting Ordowahl back aboard.

For a moment it seemed that the longboat would drive the fishing boat under, but its deep, sturdy hull rebounded and came back up to float beside the moving longboat, a foot of water sloshing in the bottom. Nobody noticed.

Three attackers jumped into the boat before realizing that Ordowahl had gotten back aboard. With a hatchet in one hand and a knife in the other, he moved with greater speed than they could anticipate. While he was pulling knife and hatchet from two limp bodies an archer put a shaft through the third man.

The longboat rode a yard or so higher from the water than the fishing boat. Ordowahl left the archers to pick their targets, at quarters so close there wasn't time to aim. He leapt up onto the longboat deck, grabbed an oar, and began to mow men down.

In no more than a minute, perhaps two, the fight ran out of the few raiders still able to move.

In the fishing boat one Marvistjen archer lay dead, and one had that first arrow through his arm. Three battered Marvistjen men remained standing amid a clot of raiders who had lost their final bet with fortune. In the longboat many had bleeding wounds, several nursed broken bones, and all the rest but one were either dead or drowning in the sea.

Ordowahl looked again. The one man still standing was Willum. "I will write your name in runes, Weverzoon," he said, as cool and even as a racing heart and heaving lungs would allow. Over his shoulder he called to the archers. "Get into the longboat and bind this man. Willum, these men will bring you to Count Marvistjen." He looked at his arms and beheld three cuts, two of them deep. "And then we will bind up each other's wounds."

*__*__*__*

Utrecht had asked her uncle to come to the southernmost village. She told him she believed they would encounter the prince there. The two nobles stood in chill air looking west at the dimming sun. The ebbing tide took the sea lower until the pier came near to being unusable. When the longboat landed, its greater height and lesser depth proved important. The fishing boat was in tow and beginning to drag on the bottom mud. Ordowahl stood in the longboat's prow.

"You got blood on yourself, Prince, but you carry yourself as though little of it is yours," Utrecht said. It came closer to praise than he anticipated. It felt odd to be glad that she didn't smile, but showed actual concern. He saw her look at his bandaged arm, as though taking stock.

"Prince, are you now a sea captain?" asked the count.

"Thank you, Petur. Quite an interesting view from there. One of the archers has died, and one has an arrow through his arm, so he doesn't look good at all. The other three hold an interesting fellow who has won a number of sword battles but alas found no chance to use his sword today. I'm sure you will enjoy speaking with him."

The prince stepped down onto the pier. "Count, I claim this boat as plunder. I trust you to offer a fair price. You see in the boat a few men who have survived the fight. They are pirates and deserve death."

"Just like that, Prince?" The count looked surprised.

Utrecht couldn't hide her sudden displeasure. "Prince," she said with hands on hips, "what came over you? Why make *us* hang them?"

"My friends," he answered, "I ask the vice-count to rescind her block on the count's hospitality. I haven't eaten since last night and

74

didn't want to delay my return."

The count ordered the surviving raiders slain at once and their bodies dumped out at sea on the morrow. Without a word the weary archers re-boarded the longboat and cut the throats of whichever pirates remained alive. Weverzoon endured the night on the ground, bound and unable to move.

Ordowahl, Utrecht, and the count traveled by starlight and reached Marvistjen Keep in middle night.

The following morning the Vendink men saluted Count Marvistjen and set out for home. Torwulf and Roneult went with them while Utrecht and Ordowahl remained behind.

Weverzoon arrived at noon—unfed, soiled, and now held erect by two of the count's bulkier footmen. He stank, and the count's hearing took place in the courtyard, with everyone standing.

"Weverzoon, I have testimony from several good and trustworthy sources. It regards your depredations on my lands and your unprovoked attack on a fishing vessel just offshore from my lands. Your crimes require death. Speak now, if you believe you can persuade me to make it merciful."

Weverzoon's stoic unconcern showed the toughness that had made him indispensable to the nobility he served. He said only, "Count, I do what I do. I take lives as I see fit. I knew that a day like this might come. So it is here. Do you expect me to snivel?"

That was all the count could get out of him. He spoke to one of the footmen. "Cut him into a dozen pieces, head last. Bury them in my orchard, to feed the trees."

Utrecht turned toward Ordowahl and spoke in a low voice, meant for him alone to hear. "Nordweg, you have gained some of my trust. But you must not involve yourself in the business of County Vendink."

He smiled, but inwardly. The simple fact of her saying something private, for his ears only, felt like warmth.

At least the vice-count used faint damns as praise.

Her uncle Count Marvistjen let it slide—

he'd didn't see the need to turn a phrase.

The villain's boat was booty; then he died.

 Both Wils and Heri stayed at home to run

 in joint their father's large estate. The twins

 stayed back, each eyed the other's half-begun

 maneuvers, counterpoising two chagrins.

With Ordowahl apparently returned

to Utrecht's trust, his isolation from

their conflict might as well be unadjourned.

Of course, he doesn't think he's "meddlesome."

 The polygon of trouble swings around;

 another facet slaps him down to ground.

Celebration

"Prince," said Heri, late one morning a week after Weverzoon had been dealt with. They were in a shady alcove off Roneult's exercise yard, resting between endurance drills of leaping and gyrating while holding weights.

"Yes, Heri, what is it?"

"My friend, I admire what I hear about the way you defeated that jack-hole Weverzoon, and I hope that no ill will remains between us. I do consider you to be a man with a fair and gentle mind."

"Thank you, Heri. I had begun to feel concern."

"Let me show you my good will. Landed knight Sir Ehrbijn was born on this day thirty years ago. My friends are providing a celebration to honor him. Can you join us?"

"Heri, of course. Tell me where, and I will be very happy to attend. In fact, let us go together."

"We won't need footmen, Prince. Sir Torwulf told me he has some other matter on his mind, so he won't accompany us."

Ordowahl thought it a little unusual but took Heri at his word.

The autumn sunset became moonless darkness when Heri and Ordowahl set out for Ehrbijn's manor. Ordowahl asked, "Heri, where is Wils?"

"Prince, I'm sad to say that Sir Ehrbijn doesn't have Wils's friendship. My brother is at home this evening—of all things, I think he plans to read a book."

Ordowahl chuckled. "Heri, you should try a book more often yourself. A book is like a wise stranger you invite to sit with you, to supply a one-sided conversation."

"Prince? How can there be a conversation with just one side? Two hands clap, but with only one nothing happens. A conversation is the same."

"A lecture then. While he cannot reply when you rebut his claims, you will also not offend him if you dispute what he says. The fellow who wrote the book is often thoughtful, even wise."

"As you will, Prince, as you will. I find that sitting still too long plagues my joints."

They had gone at most a quarter mile from the Hangendro gateway when a noise from overhead spooked Hammerfoot. The stallion reared up in fright. A great net fell onto horse and rider as they went under a huge tree. Ordowahl heard Heri yell "Flee!" then gallop away.

The net was made of massive ropes. It bore Ordowahl low in the saddle. Five men sprang out on one side and their weight, perhaps with the help of a horse or two, toppled rider and stallion.

Ordowahl had no time to ponder. On instinct, he pulled one leg up to keep his stallion's ribs from crushing it. Hammerfoot squealed and thrashed in rage.

Their attackers had strung draw-ropes through the hem of the net. Now they pulled them to close it into a makeshift bag that trapped the horse's legs and flailing hooves. The giant stallion could not rear up to fight back.

Ordowahl crooned in Hammerfoot's ear while five clubs began to beat him. In moments the prince lost consciousness.

Time passed before Ordowahl could see, hear, and think again. *I may have been here for a minute, or an hour. I am glad my attackers ran away, just like Heri. His friends knew his mood, and I was careless not to. What will the fascinating Utrecht think? A troublemaker has come? And Fretheldin? No matter, I won't stay here like an ass in a snare.*

He took stock; at first everything hurt, and the heavy net pressed him against the stallion's body. He couldn't move his hands enough to search for wounds, so struggled to reach his knife. After several moments of agonizing effort one hand reached the sheath at his belt. More effort, and he drew the knife then began to cut through the net, one heavy rope at a time. He marveled at its toughness and wondered what sort of fish this was meant to catch.

Ah—a cargo net like they use in Hammaborg: I am finished goods to be shipped out. Ha. Once free of the net, he worked to expand the opening along Hammerfoot's body from tail to head. All the while he crooned soothing words to the animal, caressing him as he severed ropes, one by heavy one.

He wondered whether the clubs had hit some part of his horse, too. When the net no longer confined Hammerfoot the prince went to the other side, where huge hooves lay quiet, and cut the hembinding rope.

The giant stallion lumbered up, back onto its feet. Ordowahl forgot his own agony and dizziness until the animal was again standing by him. He leaned on the warm flank. Mounting Hammerfoot was beyond what his aching, bleeding head and face, bruised limbs, and battered joints could do, so they walked, side by side, back to the Hangendro estate.

In the morning he awoke to find Klarenz changing the dressing on his scalp: another scar, among several, but the first real scar on the top of his head.

"Thank you, Klarenz. You put me to bed like an infant. You'll make a fine father when the day comes that you have a wife and she bears you children."

"Liege, tell me where it doesn't hurt," Klarenz replied, in a wry voice. "Did you see your attackers?"

"No, but the celebration had an obvious planner. I'm going to take meals here for a week. Tell the household I've come down with a contagious fever."

"Yes, liege, in fact you are feverish now."

"I will use the time to recover from the bruised flesh and sprained joints."

"And your cracked rib and bone bruises? Liege, they will take much longer to heal."

"That's true, my good nurse, but I can deal with them once the cuts knit and the flesh recovers from its sprains and bruises."

"Liege, I have long experience with the healing arts. I will bring you hot and cold compresses, healing poultices, willow bark tea, and soft foods. You're in very good hands, if I say so myself."

"Be modest or immodest as you like, Klarenz. I've learned never to doubt you."

*__*__*__*

Half a week passed, when a visitor arrived from Castle Vendink around midday. The vice-count had learned that the prince was ill and wanted to reassure herself that he would recover. She knocked at the door and entered, as a man might go into a man's bedchamber, without hiding her eyes.

Ordowahl had been napping, but the knock awoke him. The door opened about the same time his eyes did. *Who comes now? She's bold as a badger.*

"Prince," said Utrecht. "Liar, I had feared you sick, but you're not sick at all. Here I felt worry, but I see only slings and bandages. What have you done to earn such a beating?" She pulled up a chair beside his bed.

"Thank you, Utrecht. It's good to see you, too. How have you been?"

"So, Prince, tell me about your enemy."

"Do flies land on meat?"

Utrecht continued to inspect the damage, even lifting the coverlet to find any other bandages.

"I ask you to remain and visit." Ordowahl pressed the issue. "I take it that you knew no reason to suspect I wasn't feverish and vomiting?"

"Prince, a fever I would believe, but to see you sored and lamed strains belief. Where is your prowess now, O man of speed and strength, pirate killer and slayer of black mages? And I repeat, who is your enemy? I need peace in my county, and I see it doesn't protect you."

"In business terms, it was a net loss."

"Please explain that."

Celebration

"No one has reported seeing a ship's cargo net, have they? One found on the road a quarter mile from here and ruined by a series of cuts? The clever fellows who dropped it on me while I passed under a tree knew better than to leave it to be found. At least Hammerfoot is well recovered after being laid on his side with his hooves hobbled."

"I see. So from this I see anger splaying out against you. Tell me your state of mind, Prince."

"You know the source yourself, and you know that his acts are rash. Do you follow me so far?"

"I hear an accusation against Heri."

"Do you imagine a different attacker?"

"Prince, your story leaves little room for doubt, but aside from being embarrassed, what? Do you plan to demand a noble's life over a prank?"

Prank? "My wounds are demoted from ambush to prank? The injury is mine, Vice-Count, not yours. So also is a response. An ambush demeans the one who laid it. That doesn't sound like anyone with Heri's upbringing, so I'll give him the formal benefit of the doubt. Now, Utrecht, this visit is done. I yearn to nap."

She laid a hand on his forehead for a moment. It was pleasant and calmed his mood. The novelty of it kept Ordowahl from mentioning that he enjoyed her touch.

"I came to offer a get-well wish. Now I learn that Heri might need an even greater one. Tell me, what should be County Vendink's official view?"

"Your father would understand what I've said and without my needing to say it. So why does the vice-count ask?"

"Give me an answer first."

This one is determined either to see Heri's boon or my bane, or even both. A pity that her smile can also make one forget to breathe. "Heri chose his act and dissembled friendship to bring it about. I did not threaten him and do not, but your choice of a next baron looks interesting."

Utrecht frowned. "Prince, while you speak frankly, I find no answer to it. You may even be correct."

He looked at her, raising the one good eyebrow to challenge the "may even be."

Another caress to his forehead. "But true strength is always gentle, my friend, like this. I'm sure you know that. Show me that you do."

"Rash acts often incur a cost."

"And what was the cost to you, Prince?"

"I am inconvenienced, but will not ignore a base insult. Does the county plan to involve itself in Heri's sin?"

"Actions speak louder than words. Once you act I'll tell you how County Vendink will respond. Good day, Prince."

As she left the room he thought he could hear her mutter under her breath, something about men and fragile vanity.

At least I believe in her discretion. She will not divulge what I have told her. In a way I pray that she does. It would free me from her power, and she would stop being mysterious if she revealed herself as, for instance, meddlesome.

*__*__*__*

Ordowahl's rumpled bed and stuffy room oppressed his mood and offended Klarenz.

"Liege," he said, delivering a ninth supper, "Everyone keeps asking about you. A five- or six-day illness isn't unusual, but the robust health you always enjoy has them asking. Especially Sir Torwulf."

"Sir Torwulf would challenge Heri to a duel of honor, which means to the death, or at minimum the loser's exile. I can't allow him to discover Heri's act until I've spoken to him myself."

"Yes, liege. I expect the bone bruises to persist another two or three months, and the cracked rib several weeks. But the discolorations have faded, and the split lip is healing well."

"Good. Tomorrow I will take the morning meal with the family. So, what is the fare this evening? Some appetite is returning."

Klarenz left with empty soup bowl, mug, and plate.

Tomorrow Heri will confront me. He'll ignore my injury, or pass it off as well earned. He will not show dismay, because in his eyes, his own acts are always reasonable. He shows himself to be the sort who assigns all blame to others, none to himself. Bringing him to accept his fault will be difficult, but far more satisfying than killing the county's evident favorite to become Baron Hangendro—also half the sons of the righteous and good Baroness Fretheldin.

That night Ordowahl sent Klarenz to notify Fr. Henck that he was well enough to come to confession before the dawn Mass.

Father Henck sat in the confessional when Ordowahl entered his half of the booth to begin his confession.

"Prince, it's impossible not to know who I am hearing, both from the color of your voice and the distance above my ear. It is good to know that you are well."

"Thank you, Father. I have many sins that burden my conscience."

Father Henck sighed loudly. "Prince, your time is your own, but here it is also mine. Please do not abuse it with the sort of minutiae you generally bring. Have you lusted in your heart, be it for sex, revenge, or the like?"

"Yes, Father."

"Please qualify that."

"While I was still sick abed Utrecht paid a visit, and when I felt her hand on my head, I yearned for much more than that."

"I see. That's temptation, Prince. Jesus Himself was tempted. Revenge?"

"No, Father. I was, as you say, very tempted, but haven't pictured any such thing in my mind. Yet, back on my feet, I have felt a continual judging anger against Heri, and I fear that I may not yet have found a way to forgive him."

"In time, Prince. Three Hail Mary's and one Our Father. Your sins are forgiven. Peace go with you."

He backed out of the confessional and bumped into Utrecht. She retreated a sudden step, looked him in the eye, and whispered, "Never mistake pity for affection, Prince," as she stepped around him and into the booth.

After the Mass he and Fr. Henck sat down for a breakfast plate of rolls and butter—one never came to Mass with food in his belly—to find that the other priests had left the two of them to hold a private conversation.

"Prince, I learned that you've been recovering from a beating not a fever."

He's not one to beat around the bush. "Father, this is so."

"Prince, I'm all too aware of the people in this county and how they might behave. And of course all of them talk about everyone else. I learn everything in the confessional, to the point where I ignore whatever I hear outside it."

Ordowahl had to smile. *Careful here, he can't be in the habit of sharing intimate details with anyone yet rise to his position in the local hierarchy.* "Indeed, Father."

"As the count and vice-count must be, so also I am curious to understand your mind with respect to Heri."

Here it comes. "Father, the vice-count lectured me on the idea that true strength expresses itself gently. I take the inevitable comparison to the true strength of Christ, who died on the Cross for all sins of all men everywhere."

"Yet, Prince, I doubt you'll bare your chest for Heri to strike a second time."

It was said with gentle humor. Again, Ordowahl had to smile. He was disarmed.

"I may emulate Christ but still have to honor God's use of me, which I believe has only begun to unfold. But I won't put Heri under my foot such as to bare *his* chest, thus wring a surrender and confession from him. While I entered manhood only two and one-half years ago, this much I have known from early on."

It was Fr. Henck's turn to say, "Indeed." He paused, "I know the difficulties this contest presents. I have stood ready to offer counsel, but so far all I hear is a polite 'No, thank you.' Here is my own opinion, to be shared with no one. Because you are a prince, Ordowahl, and based on my experience with you, I give you my trust that what I disclose will go no further. I hope that Wils becomes baron."

"Thank you, Father. Trust is always a burden, so thank you for bringing me into your confidence. Like you, I believe that Wils deserves a high place in the nobility. Since Count Jakop has no male heir, he could do worse than to invite Wils into his family."

Father Henck raised his head to the ceiling and tried to swallow a belly laugh. "Excuse me, Prince, but that idea is both sublime and ridiculous. Watching Lady Janalei grow from precocious toddler through a childhood like no other then split herself into a second persona, a vice-count who brooks no interference and intends to rule the county to the end of her life, well, my son, you have no idea. You've seen her, I know, but even so you have *no* idea."

He enjoyed a moment's chuckle then straightened his face. "Please do not tempt Utrecht to hate you, Prince. By drawing a rash assault from Heri, I imagine her confident that it has ejected you from the issue. So you should by no means rejoin the contest between Heri and Wils."

I need to take care. But I'm incapable of spending time in this city yet not be moth to her candle. He recalled the first such candle, Gnade Grace – her flame nearly ended his freedom. *Utrecht is a fascinating challenge, and I must solve her. But I can't tell Father Henck that.* "I hear your warning, Father. If not hateful, she seemed more than just annoyed behind her formal mask of vice-count the day I arrived. But she also seemed merciful for a moment, when she saw the bandages."

Father Henck's look of understanding told Ordowahl that was something Utrecht had shared during confession.

But in what tone of voice and with what underlying significance? I can't read the abbot's face, so I don't know. Some day I will.

When he returned to Haus Hangendro he went straight to his accustomed area in the exercise yard. The cracked rib pained him, but with Klarenz's tight wrap, he worked to rebuild his strength and stamina. While he was there, Heri came into the west corner as well. He kept a simple countenance, as though playing at riddles.

Ordowahl ignored Heri as though he didn't exist. *I'll play him my own riddle.*

That evening for the first time in many days Ordowahl took a meal with his hosts. He was looking forward to a hot and complete meal, so began to fill his plate without waiting for Klarenz to serve him.

"Prince," said Heri, with banal calm. "How good that your illness has passed and you are well enough to join us for the evening meal."

Wils and their mother were also at table, as well as Sir Torwulf, but Heri spoke freely. He seemed not to care what they might hear or how they might interpret his exchange with the prince. His expression showed no condolence, rather the cold eye of a repeated threat. Ordowahl's face showed vague discoloration and a new scar on his lip.

Torwulf understood Heri's calculated indifference as soon as he saw what remained of the damage to Ordowahl's face. He was halfway up onto his feet, wearing a dark scowl.

"Sir Torwulf," said Ordowahl, "I need your patience. I disguised my injury because I needed, and still need, to handle the matter myself." He turned to Heri. "My friend, someone close to you gave no thought to the reputation of Barony Hangendro. The birthday story appears to have been a falsehood; I hope you've been able to find the liar and deal with him."

Heri looked back at him with head tilted to the side as though curious.

Ordowahl continued. "I expect you, as host, to uphold the honor of your mother's guest. I will tell you what little I know of my attackers, and I hope you can bring them here to face me."

Heri's expression still didn't change. "Prince, I've heard you spin a tale of killing a powerful knight by slicing his throat while he lay at your feet. First show me that your own honor is real."

Ordowahl, exercising a patience founded on pity not fury, turned back to eating. He ignored Heri, who rose from the table.

"Heri!" barked Torwulf.

Ordowahl raised his head and said, "Heri, you have a guardian angel who wants you to discover that true strength is best shown through mercy. We will discuss this again, but not over a meal."

Fretheldin's face crumpled. She struggled to find her voice. "Heri, you shame me more than if you had slapped my face. Your father would have disinherited you, or worse."

Wils spoke: "Had you but asked, brother, I could have told you in that moment both that your gambit would fail, and that it had no point in the first place."

Heri's face melted into a sneer. "You have no grounds to criticize a brother whom you have discussed behind his back."

Wils's face froze. "Heri, has desire to become baron corrupted you this much?"

Heri left.

A week passed while Ordowahl divided his time between the exercise yard, reading and re-reading every book he could find in the Hangendro manor, stretching his injured limbs and body with slow and tentative movements, and sleeping.

He'd needed jackdaws' help the first time 'round.

Lord Heri's gross attack had left him sore,

and for a second time Prince Ordo wound

up flat in bed, on his posterior.

    Another price was holding back from Torwulf

    news of Heri's insult. 'Twould have meant

    dismissal from the county, if not more.

    The vice-count tells him "Strength should never vent."

Can twenty stone mince like a faerie queen?

He'll heal, at least. His dignity is marred

but little marks on lip and scalp don't mean

a thing—a fighter's face is often scarred.

    Just nineteen years, constrained to nobleness,

    how spin up vengeance, done with politesse?

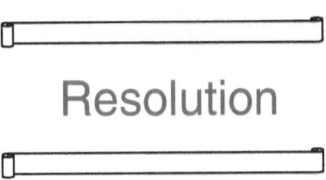

Resolution

Halfway through a crisp mid-November morning Ordowahl worked up a rolling sweat in Arneult's drill yard. *A fortnight ago I doubted that I could do much, but increasing work has eased my dismay. Losing so much strength and endurance shocked me, but things are coming around a bit.*

Wils came over to speak to him. Ordowahl welcomed the chance to breathe and rest.

"Prince?" Wils asked.

Too few days have passed to hold a real conversation with Wils, but courtesy demands a reply. "Yes, what is it?"

"You have not confided in me. I have tried to draw you out into conversation, but you appear distracted. Please speak to me with candor. What have you let pass?"

"It is both foolish and rude to come between brothers, Wils. Your contest remains in Utrecht's hands. If your mother made any protest she hasn't mentioned it to me, and I have no insight into Utrecht's view regarding Heri's accusation."

"Prince, I don't understand how a simple conversation can do harm."

"Wils, your brother misconstrued a conversation just like this one into a belief that we plot against him."

"I see. Thank you, Prince. You always wind up giving me more than I ask. Yes, it would be wrong to hold a real conversation."

Just as Wils turned to walk away Heri came upon them. "Why, Prince, do you persist in this shameful pretense?"

Still? "Heri? Who are you afraid of? I won't ask you to defend your remark in combat, as your loss would be inevitable. It would prove nothing."

Heri's face remained frozen in a sneer.

Ordowahl saw that denials were, to Heri, like last fall's leaves in the wind. "Let it be like this: I challenge you to call your five friends to meet me here this evening so that we can resume our discussions regarding honor and strength."

The sneer didn't shift so much as fade.

"At least your heart is strong, Heri. I will face all six of you at once. The outcome will not be a simple death. I challenge all of you. All at once." The prince's voice sounded casual, but his face was not. Heri looked, to Ordowahl, as though he felt the challenge was insincere.

"Prince, be careful what you ask for. I know, for instance, that both you and Wils secretly lust after Utrecht. Don't deny it! If one good beating didn't persuade you do stop interfering in Vendink business, come get another!" Then he spun on his heel and left at a near jog-trot.

Ordowahl threw Wils a questioning glance, but got nothing much in return. Wils mumbled a hasty apology and left.

The day proceeded without event, well into the dark of evening. A ring of two dozen lit torches surrounded the lawn next to the Hangendro manor house, making enough light to read by. Heri and his five friends stood in the center making uncomfortable small talk, each looking over the others' shoulders to guard against a sudden attack from any quarter.

"Baron," said Ehrbijn, "how able can he be? Giant or not, we pounded the fear of God into him. We left him bleeding and unconscious."

Heri asked back, "And what did you find the next morning? A bloody prince or a ruined net?"

No one answered him. All six kept their eyes moving to spot any sign of an approaching form or moving shadow.

Resolution

Ordowahl sat a dozen feet above them on a large tree limb. October's end had stripped its leaves. He wore soft, black garments that made no noise and blended with the night sky behind him, and aimed his gaze at the ground below the tree, looking out the tops of his eyes. *Let's see how long it takes them to drop their guard, just a little bit.* He waited for the moment when no gaze pointed his way.

With a hand on his perch the prince yelled, "NOW," dropped to grab a limb below him, swung down to the ground, and made a panther's fluid rush. While they were spinning around to react, he bowled over the closest one. He also grabbed the man's sword.

Heri and his remaining friends saw the threat, the stolen sword, and stood still.

Ehrbijn was next man on the right; Ordowahl held the sword just behind the shoulder. Its point penetrated cloth and skin. A trickle of blood slid down the inside of Ehrbijn's tunic. The landed knight refused to flinch.

"A net fell on me a few weeks ago," Ordowahl said in a calm voice as though he were making small talk.

No one said a word.

"I wanted to see just how effective it might be to attack from above. Acknowledge, my friends, that I shouted a warning at you." His face was sober, his expression flat.

The pushed-over fellow crawled around to get behind Ordowahl. Before he could take position Ordowahl backed up a step and half kicked, half thrust the man into a heap at the base of the tree.

An extended arm kept the sword point close to Ehrbijn's upper ribs. Again, the man didn't flinch.

"My friends," Ordowahl asked them, "what might a man do to regain his honor when it is scorned? For one man to treat another with contempt, the simple answer begs for attention." He looked around the group. They seemed to sense that Ehrbijn's life hung in the balance. Heri and the others didn't move.

Ordowahl continued. "Let me hear your own thoughts, without the use of iron. Place your swords against that tree." He flung the sword backward so it rotated once then stuck in the tree trunk. It quivered there, half a foot above the huddled, cringing form.

Heri clapped slowly. "So, an ambush is a sorry tactic indeed. Thank you for your little demonstration, Nordweg. Do speak to us of honor."

"Thank you, Heri. I say that you are of no account. Do you shame me for using your own trick? Do you demand loyalty from these men despite acting without honor?"

Heri said nothing. He looked at his friends, four standing and all still armed, including Ehrbijn. They turned to look at the prince as though for guidance.

Ordowahl lowered his head in feigned disappointment. "Fellows, Goliath had his David. Where are your five slings and your many smooth stones?" He turned beetled brows on Heri and said, "Defend your honor or be known forever as liar and coward."

"I am no fool, either, Prince. You have said it yourself, that any trial by combat would reveal no truth other than your greater force of arms." Heri looked around the circle of his friends. Their quick gasps and widened eyes accused him of cowardice. They wanted the honorable fight they sensed Ordowahl was about to offer them.

"Prince, *you* still stand accused of a secret plot and of lying about it. You chose sides and have no answer. No, you are the liar and the blackguard." His face added to the snarl in his voice.

"Heri, it is one thing to make an accusation, and another to be correct. Your slur isn't just wrong, it is transparently wrong."

Wils had seen the gathering and knew its purpose. He stood in a shadow on the manor porch and stepped into the ring of lights.

Ordowahl was the only one who noticed. "Wils, come forward. If your brother accuses you of conspiracy, I demand that he and all his friends combat me here on this ground, now. There can be no certain outcome, other than multiple deaths."

"Heri," said Wils, "I engaged the prince in conversation and asked him to form his own opinion. You, on the other hand, feared that I might have tried open persuasion, which you have worked on everyone else." It was clear to Ordowahl that Wils was referring to Utrecht; he could see shocked recognition flit across Heri's face.

Heri looked at his brother, whom he once loved, and said nothing.

Resolution

"You judged me, twin brother, according to your own inclinations. If that makes you the Hangendro then I am not. Go in peace, Heri. I resign, to keep my own head high."

Ehrbijn, having been poked and made to bleed, was about to draw his sword.

Wils stopped him. "Friend, he can reach that sword in the tree and run it through your belly before you can say your mother's name. Heri, if you keep your sword, I will use mine on you."

Ehrbijn wasn't convinced, "The five of us, even without swords, should be able to prune this vulture's wings. I for one am ready to risk myself to uphold your succession to your father's barony."

"Uphold it, Ehrbijn?" Wils's voice held recognition, not resignation. "I just surrendered it."

Heri stood, mute and trembling, while his friends waited. His gaze went distant, as though he saw possibilities, hazards, consequences, as though he looked at them with new understanding. After a time he said, "Prince, my brother's sense of truth moves my own. Wils speaks with a brother's heart. I withdraw my accusation, Prince. I ask your forgiveness."

Heri's friends stood speechless. They looked back and forth at each other. "Heri," said Ehrbijn. "Please, my friend, my baron!"

Ordowahl looked at Ehrbijn for several moments. "It would be a petty justice to return bruise for bruise and cracked rib for cracked rib. All of you might dwell on that." *I suppose this is mercy. I have already made one bleed and broken another's ribs. How can I add injury to the central figure and still think myself merciful?* He turned to Heri. "Here is my hand in forgiveness. I forgive any wrong you have done me."

Wet cheeks showed a contrite heart. He wiped them with a sleeve and came forward.

Ordowahl took Heri's extended hand and clasped his other hand on top to show Heri that he was appeased, and once again his friend. Ordowahl drew him into a quiet hug.

Heri turned to face his brother.

Wils said, "Heri, I repeat my quitclaim. Even a wrong decision can be better at forcing a conclusion than a slow one."

Heri had no words to reply.

"But, brother, promise me that, when a baron, you will discuss your thinking with me before committing to a decision. Must I attend alongside you like a second footman? So be it. Barony Hangendro needs both of us."

Heri canted his head to one side and replied, "Wils, my actions and yours, taken together, prove you right. Brother, I pledge to ask your counsel before I give voice to an impulse."

The four standing friends picked up the one still in a heap beneath the tree. They pulled his sword from the trunk, slid it back into its scabbard, and helped him to limp away. None of them said a word.

*__*__*__*

Utrecht came the next day, again at noon. She wasted no time in small talk but spoke as soon as Fretheldin, her sons, and Ordowahl could be brought together.

"Wils, you quitclaimed the right to succeed your father. Thank you for easing my burden. The choice was very difficult."

Wils made a slight bow of the head.

She said, "But the difficulty itself wasn't as important as the peace of not offending one or the other of you. To me you are like brothers. I believed you, Heri, in part because you accused the prince but not your brother." She looked at Ordowahl for a second, but said nothing.

He answered her stare with a straight face.

Utrecht turned to Fretheldin. "Baroness Mother, your difficulty was mine, too." She turned to Heri. "We will set up celebration in the spring, to afford time to gather the neighboring counts and all my barons. Heri, Count Jakop is pleased to name you Baron Hangendro."

Ordowahl looked at the relieved family. He asked, "Utrecht, is your problem now resolved?"

"Yes, Prince, and thank you. I find myself grateful for your odd but instrumental presence.

Heri asked her, "Vice-Count, is my honor restored?"

"Prince, is Heri's?"

Resolution

Ordowahl gave each brother a close look, "Wils, Heri, Fretheldin, Utrecht, no one is without flaw. I believe that everyone, and each of us, is God's child. We are redeemed by Christ's blood."

They looked puzzled, as though he had revealed himself to be a priest.

"I cannot carry a grudge. God requires each sinner to forgive. I hold each of you in high esteem. Will that do, Utrecht?"

Utrecht's wrinkled brow betrayed her concern, but she said nothing.

I see the look on your face, Vice-Count. Yes, you know that forgiveness is one thing and honor another. Heri's own acts will see to that, in time, or they will not. His own acts must restore his honor.

The vice-count names him instrumental in

a County matter (does that change his mind?)

yet tells him often-times he's not to peek within

the County's purview, not the smallest kind.

    It's hard enough to work the details out

    of how to deal with Heri and his twin,

    yet it's gone well past time to pay devout

    attention to the count: "May I come in?"

The count, of course, knows quite a bit about

Prince Ordowahl. He'll want to know his purpose:

he came in—so when, at last, go out

and on his way? We wish to sit, confer.

    So young and slowly growing less naïve,

    What novel trouble might the prince conceive?

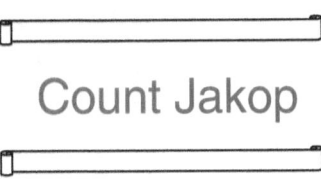

Count Jakop

Two days passed when, after supper, Torwulf upbraided his liege. "Prince, you visited Saint Martin's the morning after you arrived. Father Danelagh introduced you to Father Henck and the brothers there."

"Yes, Sir Torwulf, that is true. They were the reason I came to this place."

"And I understand that you wanted them to discuss some odd piece of Church doctrine."

"That is also true, although if the subject we discussed seemed odd, you might do well to spend more time with them yourself. What bothers you?"

"It's long past a polite interval to present yourself to the count."

He's right, but the count must know through his daughter that I've been preoccupied. Yet I can only guess at what she's told him. Did she cast me in a kind light, or perhaps a fair one, or something else? "I see. You and I shall go tomorrow to enquire after his health."

Riding toward the City, after the morning meal and just as the sun gave first light, Ordowahl and Torwulf went over the protocols of visiting a personage such as Count Vendink.

"Prince, when we meet the count you should introduce me first—I know it may seem odd, but our custom is to start with the most junior member of a group and proceed upward."

"Yes, it is the same in Nordweg."

"Klarenz must not accompany you as footman, servant, or what-have-you, since it might appear that you depend on the special talent of your own man."

"Must I impose my needs on my host's footmen?"

"Trust me on this. Someone's 'talented man' has, from time to time, caused real mischief. Just so you know the reason."

Ordowahl thought for a brief moment. "Right, Sir Torwulf, that's a small surprise, but I'm glad you mentioned it."

Half a league at a light canter meant that dawn Mass was well in progress when Prince and Knight guided their mounts at a sedate walk through the imposing gateway of Castle Vendink. They entered an extensive walled compound and saw it empty.

The last time they had gone in it had been full of men assembled to assist Count Marvistjen. The castle's tree-lined courtyard grouped a hundred rose bushes, some surrounding a central fountain and some in a long rank around the edge, by the trees. They stood barren in the middle of a cold autumn.

Torwulf set the example and Ordowahl copied him, as though pairing steps on a dance floor. They ascended flagstone steps and paused on a covered porch large enough to shelter twenty or more.

Torwulf stepped to one side. "Prince, I must stand to your right," and stepped behind the prince to take the correct position. He whispered, "You should lift the metal weight that is hung on the door, and let it drop. Once."

As soon as the weight struck the use-polished brass target below it, the door opened.

The man at the door was ancient, dignified, majordomo or a senior butler. "Honored guests, to whom is it my pleasure to speak?"

"We are Sir Torwulf of Haus Tannhaueffig, now sworn to me, and Prince Ordowahl, son of Stegnwahl, King of Nordweg."

Torwulf relaxed when he saw that Ordowahl asked nothing, volunteered nothing, just gave the asked-for reply.

The butler seemed to brighten a bit behind his leather-stiff professional decorum, as though he had suspected the huge man might be socially clumsy.

Count Jakop

"This way if you please, Prince Ordowahl of Nordweg and Sir Torwulf of Tannhaueffig."

He led them into a large front parlor with a wide fireplace and a roaring fire. The room held several large chairs with woven-leather backs and seats. Tapestries depicted various scenes of hunting and one of Venus and Adonis in intimate embrace. Three multi-tiered candelabra hung from a high ceiling. A pair of padded benches sat against one wall.

Count Jakop Vendink sat near the fire at a large oak table. He struggled to raise his ancient, stiffening body to greet them.

"Welcome, Prince, and Sir Tannhaueffig, welcome. I understand that you've acquitted yourself in an interesting fashion, as well as assisting Vice-Count Utrecht in rescuing her aunt Marte's husband, Count Marvistjen. Please sit with me. I hope to hear an account of your travels."

Age had compressed the count to medium size, though that was hard to gauge once he sat again, enfolded in an overstuffed chair. His face would never again be called handsome. Blasted by wind and age, it also housed a remarkable collection of fading scars—a wart would draw notice on that face by its darker color. His wispy hair was pure white.

He seems to have fought often, thought Ordowahl, *and hand-to-hand many times. He survived those, hence he was formidable. Does he still have strong will and a ready mind?*

"I've received gossip, Prince Nordweg, concerning what took place earlier this year in Ermsleben, in the Harz mountains of Saxony. It's told that you detected some kind of fraud there and settled a black magician's mischief."

Ordowahl gave the count a modest smile. "That's one way to put it."

"I find it remarkable for one so young to achieve so much. My own domain has its share of small frauds, and larger ones—the life of a count is never simple."

Ordowahl nodded. *The count may have forgotten more stories than I've had time to hear.*

"If it please you, Prince, let me hear your own version. If I find you as capable as a prince should be, I may ask you to spend time here among us."

Implying that my visit here is disturbing someone and will continue at the count's pleasure, else not.

"Sir Torwulf," the count continued, "first answer me this: what do you know of Prince Ordowahl's ability to distinguish truth from fiction and work out the right judgment in a complicated matter?"

Torwulf shifted in his chair, ready to get up.

The count asked him, "What, that is, can you say from the time you've spent with him? What is your own experience?"

Torwulf rose, bowed to the count, and made himself sound as much the diplomat as he could. "With the leave of my liege Prince Ordowahl, I will be plain. It was my misfortune to impugn his character, but the prince's modesty and nobility instructed me in my fault and how to expunge it."

The count's brows raised in surprise. Sir Torwulf's first appearance in the city had marked him a hothead. His set-to with the prince and subsequent behavior had become common gossip.

"I understand him, now, as a subtle, wise, and patient man, a most virtuous man. He has turned aside more attacks than my own, and each time with grace." He turned to face Ordowahl. "My Prince, I beg your patience, but this is my truest, fairest answer to the count."

"Well now," said the count. "I've been curious to see a giant, which is you, Prince, with the ability both to tumble like an acrobat and to fling yourself down from a tree as though imitating a squirrel."

The count released Torwulf with a nod, and the knight sat down.

Ordowahl remained seated and spoke with the count as a man to an honorable host. "Count, do you believe that there could be such a thing as black wizardry? I am a praying man and a follower of Christ and His gospel."

"Aren't we all?" asked the count. "How do you combine reverence for God with the filth of black magic?"

"Israel's first king, Saul, summoned the spirit of the dead prophet Samuel. That failure to obey God cost him his throne, his life, and his family. Scripture condemns traffic with spirits other than the Holy Spirit in the Trinity. All the rest is black magic."

The count looked at his hands for a moment then said, "I see a possible connection between spirits and magic."

"The Black Knight had an ability to make a thing change and become something else. He could so capture men's hearts with a false bliss that they were, in body and in fate, his to dispose like pieces on a game board."

"Tell me then, whether those men partnered in that."

"The villain swept my bondman Klarenz into his web. I know that Klarenz's heart is clean. The sin belonged to the Black Knight."

"So you can judge men's hearts?" The count raised an eyebrow.

"Before Klarenz, I also experienced that kind of attack. But suffering the assault of a man throwing petals doesn't make one a flower, eh?"

The count had to laugh at the incongruous image, while Torwulf rubbed his chin in confusion.

"But I retrieved Klarenz, survived the Black Knight's worst, and released the rot within him. This required God's grace; without it I wouldn't be here to tell the tale."

Reference to "rot within him" got one of the count's bushy white brows to rise. "Prince, there may come a time for you to tell the specifics of that. But continue."

Like all others who'd heard Ordowahl tell of Black Knights, mages, gouts of flies, ripe stench, and maggoty bones, the count could not help being impressed.

"And that's why there is no scar to this day? Prince, I find myself tempted to ask you to remove your clothing." But the count's soft smile gave the lie to that.

"Count, that healing might also have put me in debt to a black mage. Payment may come due when I most need it not to. Yet I trust in Christ and in God our Father. Amen."

The count asked, "Sir Torwulf, what have you heard and seen of this matter? Compare the story you first heard to what he has told you since?"

Torwulf stood, again. "Count Vendink, I had heard what must be the same gossip, but I find no way to doubt him."

"Hmmm." The count mused. He looked back and forth at the two men's faces. "Prince, I've also heard it said that the city of Hammaborg cast you out for abandoning a woman, much-beloved by all, both pregnant and daughter to a wealthy merchant."

"Yes." Ordowahl admitted it without a qualm. It guarded the real reason—the shiny, razor-sharp, unbreakable swords Klarenz had made.

"But observing you, hearing you speak—albeit with a most distressing mixture of accents. You must spend time learning to converse with more grace—I find nothing callous or deceitful in you."

The count paused in thought. He gave Ordowahl a direct but not unkind glance and said, "You seem a man in more ways than size. I invite you, Prince Ordowahl of Nordweg, to make an extended visit here."

Ordowahl tilted his head at this, as though to ask the count to say more.

"No doubt there is much of life and governance that you don't yet know. My barons have a certain energy that I welcome, but from time to time it expands into conflict."

Ordowahl had to grin.

"For instance, Wils and Heri Hangendro—that pair made a perfect puzzle. With no invitation from my heir, Vice-Count Utrecht, yet at a personal cost, you managed to precipitate her decision," the count said with cocked head.

Precipitate? Fall from a precipice, perhaps, but few gains come without cost. "Count, I have come today with more than the simple desire for a courtesy and the chance to make your acquaintance. With your patience, I also came to ask a favor."

"I will be happy to consider whatever favor you might ask, Prince."

"Vice-Count or no, I sense that your daughter's company enlivens any event she is party to. Those few times we've spoken together already anchor me here."

"Anchor? That is a strong term, Prince. You came to sit at the feet of our religious scholars, did you not?"

The narrowed eyes show his concern. Speak truth. "I came to this city to spend time with your religious scholars, but my interests have multiplied."

The count considered this for a time then answered the request. "My daughter has, from the time she could speak the words, rebelled at the thought of taking a husband. She is so strong-willed I despair of a son-in-law to become count when I die."

"Husband? Please do not misjudge me. Rather than a spouse I seek the simple company of one of the most challenging people I have ever met."

The count pursed skeptical lips: "You value her not for her beauty or her estate, but only because she is difficult?"

"She presents a fascinating puzzle, and one I may in time manage to understand, if not 'solve.' But soon enough I will return to Nordweg. My future is there. Hers will be here."

"It is important that you know this as truth, Prince."

"Count, if your daughter marries, her husband will not be Nordwesh. But I find her company stimulating and enjoy the intelligence, wit, and sheer vigor of her presence. And I also find a happy sense that each day has its own importance, in and of itself."

The count nodded and paused briefly. "Throughout her childhood my daughter said two things in particular, to those who asked and many who didn't: she would never leave the county, and she would never marry."

"Yes, she makes that very clear to me as well."

"So I've done what I can, while I yet live, to prepare my daughter. I have named her Vice-Count and deputized her as regent in my stead for all matters that arise within the county."

"She does so with a firmness that most men of her rank would long to achieve."

"Without a moment's pause she took the city's name as her given name, Vice-Count Utrecht. She is for all intents and purposes her father, thus in effect a man, when she acts as my vice-count."

"But what is the vice-count's record in battle? Your face bears testimony to many battles of your own. Will County Vendink be at risk?"

"Hardly. Each of our barons fights well and has a good number of men-at-arms, not to mention our own company of permanent soldiers."

"I can see her holding the loyalty of a thousand, or ten thousand men, without needing to wield a sword."

"If in fact Countess Janalei were to be challenged to single combat, the outcome would be in some doubt." The count smiled at the thought.

Ordowahl kept a straight face. *She might be quick and deadly, even untiring, but has no bodily strength compared to a man.*

"Nobody I know has the stones, the manhood, to risk becoming my heir's victim. In a recent battle our barons had no trouble, and she played her role well."

That I can believe. She has the stones of a warrior.

The count continued. "Don't think for a moment that your spending time in my daughter's company will bear anything like the usual fruit."

"I don't seek such, er, fruit, Count."

"As you will. I will instruct her regarding your right to treat this county as though you were, say, a younger brother not yet come of age."

"I see."

"She will accept your right to accompany her, at first silently, and after a time invited to make an occasional comment. Will this do?"

"Yes, certainly."

"Then, Prince, you have the correct frame of mind to accept my kindness in this matter. That pleases me. I predict that the vice-count will be very cross with her father, but I invite you to take up residence in this city and commit yourself to this county's ultimate well-being. That may prepare you for your next trial, wherever it may be." He gave "next trial" an odd squint that suggested, "which will be the one after keeping my daughter company."

The count beckoned to a servant, who brought a tray loaded with candied nuts, slices of cheese and sausage, small pickles, crackers, mugs, water, and mulled wine.

They made small talk for the final hour of the morning. The subject of Vice-Count Utrecht did not come up.

Those pow'rs that be have made it plain that she

who is to be obeyed, the vice-count, must

remain inviolate from swainish plea.

The joy of all who've tried it? Gone to dust.

     Her father says the same, with quiet smile

     but goes so far as bind her to this man

     since she can teach him politic, and guile,

     while he can be her test, "rule if you can."

Her father's known her mind from early on,

for instance that she fears a northern prince.

This oblique face of her own polygon

now ties her pious duty to the prince.

     So Ord tempts fate, his mind yet unaware.

     Who can persuade this youth to take good care?

A Death

An hour past a late, chilly dawn, Vice-Count Utrecht stood at the castle gate. She wore lavender breeches and a tan, fur-lined coat. Her lady-in-waiting Emluyn had tied lady Janalei's hair into a ponytail, this time with a blue ribbon to complement the vice-count's lavender garb.

Middle-aged Joop accompanied her, wearing formal footman's clothing in the county's green and gold. As always he seemed more like a devoted nanny playing dress-up for his beloved girl, whether little or not. The vice-count's costume varied day by day, but her schedule did not. Ordinary messages arriving at any later hour would receive her attention no sooner than the afternoon, and usually on the morrow.

Ordowahl, Klarenz, and Torwulf approached the castle gate on horseback. Torwulf chose to isolate himself by staying up alongside Klarenz while Ordowahl dismounted.

Utrecht looked up. Her face fell at once into a polite grimace. "Prince Ordowahl, you may observe while I oversee the affairs of the nobility insofar as they affect my father Jakop, Count Vendink."

He noted the cold formality of her tone then examined her clothing. Above the glossy leather breeches a sheepskin fleece-lined coat, buttoned upward from waist to bottom rib, curled open up past her throat. From there it flared into a collar ending high behind the neck. Where the coat gapped open a tunic of white lace appeared over a luminous gray satin shirt. The lace and satin dared the incautious to guess, in error, that the vice-count had a feminine aspect.

"Prince, may I ask your intentions with regard to the business of County Vendink?"

Ordowahl stared into tawny-green eyes.

She began to scowl. "An answer, Prince, if you please. I am inferior to you in title, if indeed a prince of Nordweg has standing, but I have business to conduct. Please reply."

"Vice-Count, I have no mission. But I am intrigued by the way County Vendink governs itself. I wish to observe and perhaps learn."

She gave him a rude stare. "Your reputation, Nordweg, reached this place long before you did. Taking up residence at Haus Hangendro led to your involvement with their issue of succession. I welcome challenges, but whoever opposes me comes to realize his mistake."

"I see."

"By sheer happenstance, your interference precipitated a solution. But your request to inject yourself into the affairs of County Vendink is something I strive both to understand and to remain unmoved by."

"I have no wish to move you, Vice-Count."

"We are bemused by the reputation which has preceded you—willingness to indulge women of any age whatsoever, as well as to dabble in black magic. But my father the count has insisted that you be made welcome. I recall him using the term 'baby brother,' a relationship that is at best novel"

"Thank him, please."

"Be alert to this, Nordweg. The welcome isn't mine and may be withdrawn. Do not make your presence in any way an obstacle to the primacy of the count, such as by interfering with his administration."

"I understand your primacy in handling the affairs of County Vendink. Yet I may make observations, as I see the need."

"You will avoid becoming party to any of County Vendink

affairs. Is this clear?"

"It is obvious that I'm required to be circumspect."

"Do not imagine, Nordweg, that you may come to regard Lady Janalei as a plaything. Your odd behavior in Hammaborg is part of what encourages her to doubt whatever pose you may adopt."

"As you will, Utrecht. I am disposed to serve you in whatever capacity you find useful."

"Then you are free to go, Nordweg, for I have no use for you."

"And to serve your father in whatever capacity he finds useful."

"Then you may go in to wait upon him."

She is tart, but I feel something other than ordinary ill will. In fact this feels like sport. I even enjoy the exchange. "Let's not spar. I will observe and, to whatever extent my thoughts and observations seem useful, advise you of them. Your father believes that I can provide an advantage."

She glared again for a moment then relented. "I am his get, he is my father. I obey my father in all things, and no one else in anything. Please distinguish between making pertinent observations and advising, which I disallow."

"As you will, Utrecht. What is our—er, your goal for this day?"

"Today I have a death to resolve." She mounted her horse and cantered away without a backward look.

Klarenz and Joop fell in behind their two masters and stifled grins. Torwulf smiled enough for all three.

At a light canter the trip took half an hour. Their conversation stayed terse. Ordowahl might say, "This scenery is much more pastoral than where I grew up," and receive in reply, "Are you sure you've finished doing that, baby brother?"

Or he'd ask, "Do you have a wealthy set of merchants in County Vendink?" and get back a snide "Planning a change in livelihood? I'll be happy to introduce you around."

Each time a twitch of smile curved one corner of Ordowahl's mouth. Male office or no, Utrecht's presence, wit, sense of purpose—her carriage, her voice, her face—each made her curtness sparkle. Just the strength, the self-possession of her gave him a belly-deep sense of happy wonder.

After a few minutes' silence Utrecht remarked, "Prince, you're still here. Do you pursue me?"

Aha. She doesn't ignore me; she may want more conversation. "Utrecht, do you interpret my action as other than professional interest? I accompany you and leave pursuit to others."

"You reserve your pursuit for the young women of County Vendink? Your prior adventures in that regard are legend."

Ordowahl smiled. "I reserve it to their own volition." *No I don't—it would alter something important between us, but I can't put my finger on it.*

She gave him a harsh squint. "Do not mock me, Nordweg. I don't care how many women of whatever age you may dally with, Lady Janalei won't be one. Maintain decorum by keeping women out of our conversation."

"Instead of pursuit I ride alongside you and at least an arm's length away. Your dignity is secure, and I will refrain from discussing either of our successes with the desirable young folk of County Vendink."

"Hmmph. Nordweg, you can be very boring. But I've had too much experience with insipid people to be put off by them."

That didn't sparkle. I note the limit of her humor. They fell silent for a time.

"Today we visit a baronetcy that has suffered a death. You may learn that such matters are never simple."

"Never simple, and most often with hidden parts."

"Please do not distract me. I don't want a stranger making jokes of my subjects' stories. Am I clear?"

He ignored the latent insult. "Perfectly."

"The deceased is a son of a baronet whose holding is part of County Vendink with no baron to come between him and my father. I am to judge whether the son died by fair or foul means."

"What details do you have?"

"Baronet Percevalle's youngest son, Lord Ergen, who is old enough to sport a full beard"—a sarcastic smile at the inch-deep fuzz on Ordowahl's cheeks and chin—"went out of the manor house between first and second sleep."

A Death

"Nothing out of the ordinary there."

"Last night was cloudy and moonless. In the darkness he stumbled and wound up head-down in a well behind the manor."

"Did he have any help in stumbling?"

"Ergen's bed warmer, a scullery maid, had tried to follow him. She heard him rise and go out. Then there was swearing, a sound like a fist hitting a face, then a sound like a mallet brought down on a log, and a splash."

"The well, then, isn't dry."

Utrecht rolled her eyes and went on. "The butler and his wife, alleged to be coupling and deep into their passion, heard someone outside. The scullery maid heard swearing while the butler and his wife heard 'someone.' Lord Ergen appeared to have encountered an unexpected person, argued, fallen, and struck his head on the stone casing of the well. He could have stood up, lost his balance, and gone in head-first."

She gave Ordowahl a questioning look. "Well, Prince, my uninvited reader of hearts and souls, what comes to your mind? Tell us how a man can couple—with ardor, we're told—while following a discussion outside his window."

Ordowahl answered, "Without explaining the finer points of coupling, Utrecht, let me ask whether we've ruled out an attempt by the dead son to attract the butler's wife into a nighttime dalliance?"

"Something akin to your own nature, no doubt." She set her mouth in a mocking twist.

No trace of smile appeared, so Ordowahl ignored it. "Let's suppose that the butler went out to intercept him, made an angry attack with something heavy, then pushed the body of his master's son down the well."

"I suppose we could, but what standing would a servant have to object to his master's son? The act might be ugly, but only in the butler's eyes."

"True," he admitted.

"The baronet might have shaken his head at his son's odd tastes. To say nothing of yours," she purred.

"In other words, the old fellow wouldn't have chosen to

intercept the son. I can follow that. So, Utrecht, who else would have a reason to be out there?"

"Any of a hundred people."

"That many. Do you know Lord Ergen by reputation? Personally?"

"We played together often as children, Prince. Being youngest son seemed to have spoiled him, and he might have become a landed knight at best. His father doted on him rather than train him up to right behavior."

"That's a frank assessment. It explains your estimate of a hundred enemies. How would you separate them into categories?"

"Categories? Which sins did he favor, and who were the victims of each?" She shook her head at him.

"That's one way to view it. Cuckolded husbands, displaced lovers, bad gambling debts, slights both intentional and unintentional—I think those could begin the list."

"Prince, you have such a background in sins. But then, alas, so does anyone trying to maintain order in an area the size of this county."

"Here and in Nordweg alike. People are the same everywhere."

"Lord Ergen went from a pigtail-pulling boy to a practiced, frequent skirt-lifter. He wanted to push his male part into anything he could take from behind or make to lie beneath him. Is that a category you have personal experience with?"

"Tsk, Utrecht, that topic is not permitted between us."

"*You* may not introduce it. But no matter. In his case, there were a number of so-called 'love' conflicts, but in the past half-year he seems to have let that habit die."

"So we can ignore that one. Gambling debts? Did his father stop doting on him long enough to stop paying those?"

She turned to look at him. "Tell me more about gambling. I have learned much about men from my father, but this isn't something we've had to deal with before."

"Then it doesn't matter here, does it? But to answer your question, among some men wagers can be commonplace and may cover anything you can imagine—"

A Death

"I can imagine a lot."

"—from whether the next dog either man sees is bitch or cur, whether the next bird will have an attractive song or just caw, up to the outcome of a horse race or who can turn the head of the next girl they see. Torwulf, can you add to the list?"

"Liege? While trying not to eavesdrop, I recall pastimes involving dice and some game called pacheesi, played out on a marked board. Games such as that can fill hours on end."

"Men's pastimes seem very weighty," Utrecht said. "How do men make their way in the world if they consider their time to be of no account, spend it idly risking idle money on random events?"

"So we can avoid that cause. Did he tend to give insult?"

"No, Prince, Lord Ergen was prone to be petulant and could find insult where one may not have been intended, but he offered no insult to anyone. He was almost likeable."

"What then, was his weakness?"

"I, Prince, will find it. If you discover anything more pertinent than cuckoldry, debt, or insults, ask yourself first whether it could be worth my time."

Ahh, Utrecht, that is a high bar. But getting words out of you is worth any effort. Hearing you say anything at all is worth my time. It's a pity I can't show you that, but your evident distaste for friendlier conversation seals my lips.

Reversed-sense smiles emblossom Ordowahl.

That is to say, he smiles from backward joy.

She jibes at him with sharpened verbal gall

yet, in his ear, her catty snarls sound coy.

     Of course, few royals ever hear the scorn

     of any woman of a fertile age.

     At least not Ordo, he so recent-born,

     and circumspect (save Gnade Grace's rage.)

He knows no reason why the vice-count shows

such open spite. The contradictions mount—

while men line up to court, and kiss her nose

and lips, the prince is sure he'll never Count.

     No idle thoughts, they have a death to parse.

     He's here on trial, cannot yield to farce.

Murder?

When they arrived, a well-dressed, slender man of perhaps fifty years stood at the door, waiting to greet them. "Ahh, Vice-Count, please come in, and your guest is my guest also." She gave the baronet a consoling hug. "Percevalle, my heart breaks to know that Lord Ergen is gone."

He dried a tear, bowed his head, and swept his arm for Utrecht, Torwulf, and Ordowahl to enter. Ordowahl noticed that the manor was old, genteel, and while smaller than the Hangendro mansion, well tended inside. He turned to see who else would come with them, but so far just the baronet accompanied them. He led them into a parlor.

"Percevalle," said Utrecht when they were seated, "Ergen and I took first communion together. Did he receive Last Rites?"

"Dear Utrecht, yes, this morning when he was pulled from the well. Just a few hours ago, and he looked blue-white. The sight of him broke my heart." The baronet was too stricken to say more for several minutes. At last he stood and went to the doorway. He turned to one side and said, "You may enter and speak, one at a time." He beckoned at someone.

He left the room to give each member of his household freedom to speak with at least a little candor. Witnesses, one by one, starting with the lowliest, paraded into the parlor to answer the vice-count's questions.

First in line was scullery maid Ornje, who had warmed Ergen's bed in the night. "Please, highnesses, forgive me, for I am about to faint."

Ordowahl's face was difficult to read. He held silence, as did Torwulf. They were outsiders where the vice-count knew many of the particulars.

Utrecht did her best to soothe the girl. "Ornje, please help us. You have nothing to fear. We need to discover how Lord Ergen came to plunge down that well. Any smallest thing you can tell us will be a big help. You do want to help us understand what happened, don't you?"

The trembling girl nodded, still in terror.

"Take a few deep breaths, calm yourself, and tell us about an ordinary night with him."

Ornje clasped and unclasped her hands several times then spoke. "Lieges, on nights when Lord Ergen calls me to his bed, he puts himself in me, and when he's done he even cuddles for a short time before he goes asleep." She looked around to see if they understood. "Most nights," she continued, "he gets up and goes out a side door to piss in the yard. Sometimes I go with him, sometimes I piss in the chamber pot, and sometimes I only lie waiting for him."

She looked around, her shyness returning. The awe she might feel for the son of a noble father surprised no one. "Last night I went out after him, but when I was in the doorway I heard something awful. Lord Ergen wasn't nowhere. I was bad scairt, so I went back to bed and buried myself under the covers."

Utrecht asked, "Can you describe the awful sound?"

"He an' another man was talking low. I heard two sounds of something smacking something. The second time was like nothing I can name. Then a groan, a splash, and another deep groan."

"Did you recognize either of the groaning sounds?"

"The first was Lord Ergen. The second I don't know."

Utrecht had no more questions. Several other staff came in but had nothing to add. The butler and his wife came in together.

"Butler, tell us what you heard." Utrecht's direct look and commanding tone told him nothing would suffice short of clear truth.

"Vice-Count," he said, with welcome self-assurance, "Lord Ergen was confronted by a young man who asked him a question."

"And what question was that?"

"The fellow apologized for lying in wait for Lord Ergen in the dark of night but wanted to ask for the hand of Ornje, and could the lord leave off from calling her to warm his bed?"

Startled, Ordowahl broke in. "Can you identify the swain? Was his voice familiar to you?"

Utrecht added, "And more to the point, what did Ergen say?"

"Nothing, Vice-Count. Instead I heard a fist strike a face and a body fall to the ground."

"Anything else? What put Ergen into the well?"

"Please forgive an old man's speculation, but I heard what sounded like a stumble, as though a second blow went out, hit nothing, then a second body fell to the ground."

"Could the other person have tripped Ergen?"

"That I cannot say, but the second fellow's head made an odd, hollow sound when he fell, like a small log striking a larger one."

"Yes, his head struck something hard. Go on."

"Someone, which had to be Lord Ergen, got back to his feet. I heard a groan and a splash. The other fellow made noises of deep anguish. Then he must have gone away. I heard nothing after that."

"Prince?" asked Utrecht. "Before I commit to a version, tell me what you think may have happened." Her face gave him no clue as to why she included him in the discussion

Ordowahl said, "In my estimation Ergen struck the first blow but was the second one to fall. The part I find difficult to define is what made Ergen fall onto the well casing."

"Sir Torwulf?" She deigned to acknowledge the knight. "I should have asked you first."

"I've seen someone rise from sleep, Vice-Count. Such a one is seldom steady on his feet. Suppose Lord Ergen makes a lucky guess, strikes the swain full on, and the swain falls insensate."

"This much is plain."

"He doesn't realize the fellow is down. He puts everything he has into a second strike. Nothing checks Lord Ergen's swing, so he stumbles."

"So he fell," Utrecht said to keep the narrative going.

"Something hard, such as stone, nearly knocked him senseless. He rose, groaned, could not keep himself erect, and tumbled into the well."

"And the swain?"

"He regained his wits, realized a fearful wrong had happened, and went away."

"Yes, and thank you, Torwulf, you have gone beyond what the very astute prince said." Utrecht made a face on "very astute."

"Prince, who should our next witness be?"

"The first, Ornje," said Ordowahl.

"My, you are good with the names of women. Yes, let us see what she has to say about her swain. Missus, what can you add to your husband the butler's tale?"

"Vice-Count, I also recognized the swain's voice. And as I was closest the window, I did manage to see by dim starlight. It was Ergen who swung twice and fell against the well."

"Poor fellow," said the butler.

"As a woman," she continued, "I can have no opinion, but if asked I would fault the swain for his arrogance at even asking Ergen to free the scullery maid."

"You both may leave."

As the couple filed out, the aged baronet and his wife came in, eager to know what the vice-count had learned.

The bereaved father's first question was, "If I understand you fully, Vice-Count, Ergen managed to cause his own death, but only after being spurred to anger by this villein. Is that as you see it?"

"Yes, baronet, it is."

"Guide me then in how to punish what amounts to murder. Shall I give him the death of a thousand lashes, have him broken on the wheel, what?"

"First, baronet, consider your Christian duty."

"My what? Liege, Vice-Count, please tell me what I am supposed to learn from you. My duty to Christ is to Christ, and my duty to Ergen is to avenge his death."

"Yes, Baronet, your duty to Christ is to Christ," Utrecht replied. "Also let me question your duty to a son whose own fit of anger escaped his control and caused him to die—and by his own act, at that."

"My beloved son! I cannot replace him, Vice-Count. This arrogant worm sinned against my son, so also against me. His act precipitated Ergen's death. His own must balance the scales."

"We will discuss this again, my friend Percevalle. Leave us."

Banished from his own parlor, the baronet turned and with fluttering hands went back the way he came in. His wife stood still.

"Baronetess, what have you to say?" Utrecht used a kind voice.

"Vice-Count, Ergen had become attached to the girl. The swain imagined that he loved her, and in time would have given her children. Ergen set about doing the same. That is what I have to say." She looked for permission to leave, got it, and left the room, as near tears as her husband had been.

The three sat in silence for several minutes. Utrecht did not move, Ordowahl shifted his weight, and Torwulf sat back further into his chair.

"Utrecht," said Ordowahl, "the girl looks to have the same guilt as the boy."

"Are you serious?" she shot back. "Two men fight over a woman, and it's her fault? What tripe!"

"Why didn't she tell Ergen about her swain? Who was she trying to protect?"

"Turd wash, Prince. Piss and shit. It is *so* the sin of a man to impose himself on a woman then hold her accountable for the trouble that befalls him. Please forgive my male vulgarities, *Prince*, but you mark yourself as one of the lesser lights in all the dullness of manhood."

He held her gaze for a moment, saying nothing. Then, "I understand your outrage. Let's ask the girl back, to question her about the swain and his reasons for coming here in the night."

"I suppose that you expect her to say that she asked him to appear so the two of them could dash back to their village?"

"No. They would be found out and their banishment, or worse, would be certain."

"Then what do you expect to learn from her?"

"Please give me your patience, Utrecht. What you want most is a just resolution, no? I hope that you will take the time to gather even more information than we have now."

She sighed. "It's bad enough, Prince, to lose someone I grew up with, regardless that he had his flaws. To hear a bald insult, followed by yet another request for my patience, and from you, takes me near a limit."

She rose and stalked to the doorway. "We wish to question the scullery maid further." Utrecht, her face closed and stoic, waited for the girl to return. Ordowahl seemed to expect something special. Torwulf did his best to remain silent and unseen.

Ornje crept back into the parlor. She trembled and clutched at a chair just to stand erect. Ordowahl lifted an eyebrow at Utrecht, as though asking permission to proceed. She shrugged.

Ordowahl sat on the floor in front of her, to be less threatening, and she sat on the chair. Even so he was taller.

He opened one hand and placed the girl's two hands on his palm. He asked in a quiet voice, "Dear girl, tell me about your swain whom Lord Ergen struck last night."

She blinked, closed her eyes, sighed, and began to breathe deeply. She lifted her head and looked up into Ordowahl's unreadable face.

"Giant, him an' me once loved. But when I came here, I believed he'd find someone else. For me the chance to work in this Haus was wonderful."

"Did you see him after that?"

"No. After half a year Lord Ergen started takin' me to his bed. He was gentle an' I hoped he'd get me with child. It was better'n I coulda hoped for with Timothun."

"Did you recognize Timothun's voice last night?"

She had wrapped four fingers around one of his, and it seemed to calm her. Utrecht's eyes widened to see it.

"Prince, yes. Iss bin a year since him an' I spoke, and 'twas a surprise when he come 'round here. Oncet or twicet I thought I could see him ahint a tree or a bush, and one o' those times he waved at me, but I ignored him."

"Then, if you can find the words, tell me why that wasn't something you could share with Lord Ergen."

"Indeed? If I say a word to Lord Ergen, Timothun is banished or worse."

"Tell me again what you heard them saying, outside the doorway."

"Timothun apologized for comin' in the middle of the night, but said this'd be the only way he could speak with Lord Ergen. Then the lord told him to ask his favor, but Timothun sounded angered."

"So, dear girl," he asked, "what was the favor?"

"When he asked for my hand, me an' Lord Ergen was shocked, both alike, and I was sad."

"You knew it wouldn't end well."

"Almost before Timothun was done talkin' the lord clopped him, and he dropped like a dead man. The lord tried to kick him, but Timothun rolled and the lord missed. That made him fall, and you know the rest."

"What about Timothun? Did you say anything to him?"

"He sat up, hurtin' real bad. Then I whispered at him that Lord Ergen was down the well. I could tell his jaw musta bin broke. He groaned like doom, and went back toward the village we come from."

"Thank you, dear girl. I know that you have loved two men and lost them both on the same night. Ask the priest for comfort. I am sure he will find something in God's Holy Word to ease your soul's anguish." He looked at Utrecht. "Do you have any other questions you want the girl to answer?"

"No," said Utrecht. "Ornje, we are satisfied with what you have said. Fear nothing from us. Go, and be at peace."

With Ordowahl's help Ornje stood erect, teetered for a moment, and left the room.

"Fate!" said Utrecht. "Her yearning swain enters the lion's den, and the lion dies. Percevalle demands the swain's death, and I for one curse at fulsome fate."

"Utrecht, I sympathize," said Ordowahl.

"This broken-jawed Timothun cannot remain here, and perhaps not remain living. Having a commoner ask his liege for a favor is seldom appropriate, but having him ask so much and in such a way, and trigger such a result, demands a penalty."

Perhaps a slight nudge will help her choose an action. Am I a fool, here? But she seems torn. "So, Utrecht, show me the gentleness of true strength."

She glared at him. "Prince, tell me how your father would have handled this. I will tell you what my father would have done. Then I'll tell you what I'll do."

Ordowahl spent several seconds searching his memory for a like circumstance under his father's hand, and one came. "Father judged between a lower member of Nordwesh nobility and a peasant, where the peasant had interrupted the nobleman at twilight and in a rush."

"So far we are the same."

"The noble's hunting dogs had killed and eaten the peasant's goat. The peasant asked for its replacement, and the noble responded by breaking the peasant's arm."

"So he suffered a broken bone, but this noble lived."

"No one died, but father had the noble's arm broken and gave the poor man two of the noble's goats."

She gave him a condescending smile but said nothing.

Ordowahl continued. "All the nobility showed Father their anger. He told them that we are all the same, slave and free, in God's eyes. The nobility reigns by God's will but must love all of God's subjects alike."

"Love? For a peasant?"

"Yes, and an eye for an eye, a tooth for a tooth, noble and peasant alike. They hated that, but Father as king reminded them that a damaged peasant does no one any good, so it was an appropriate reminder."

"I see. So would your father have broken Ergen's jaw?"

"I suppose he might have, if Ergen's dogs had eaten a goat and Ergen still took that first swing."

A Death

"But in this case Ergen's death complicates matters."

"Father would have paid, from his own purse, the man price for Ergen, to Ergen's father, and have done with it."

"The *man* price?" she asked in shock.

"There is no equivalent man price for a baronet's son, but it is far beyond what a peasant can hope to afford."

"And from his own pocket?"

"Yes. Father knew the peasant would be unable to work for a while and showed him compassion. He would have told Percevalle to be happy that he did not make him pay the man price to himself."

"Indeed. I would almost hope to meet your father, if not for the fact that my future is tied with bonds of love and duty to County Vendink."

"So, Utrecht, what would your father have done?"

"I believe he would have had Timothun hanged, as a mercy killing, and consoled Percevalle as best he could."

"And the vice-count? What will she do?"

"Vice-Count Utrecht has shifted her view, Prince. At first she would have banished Timothun and considered it mercy"

"No surprise there."

"But hearing your father's style of judgment"—she looked at Ordowahl—"I will not insult Percevalle by offering him the man price for his son. Faults and all, Ergen was a decent nobleman's son."

"If you say so."

Another frown. "I will have Timothun receive ten lashes for impertinent behavior, assign Ornje to care for him while his jaw heals, and provide half a year's peasant income for their wedding. So they had better turn out to be suitable for each other."

Then she looked askance at Torwulf, who had been quiet the whole time. "Sir Torwulf, you are welcome in the same sense as any other resident of the county, but please do not feel invited. We will do well enough in future without your presence."

Torwulf nodded and kept silent on the way back.

Prince Ordo models "strength through gentleness."

He shows it as he comforts Ornje's mind.

The vice-count adds her own, that it may bless

a broken jaw and blunt those left behind.

     But then she drops retainer Torwulf from

     his master's side—no allies: come alone.

     Knight plunders up his mind ad libitum:

     distracted, Ord's as useless as a stone.

Her father gasps in shock. A noble line

abides a peasant's wrong? Turns law on'ts head!

She loves her father, also scorns the shining

"men own you" life-rule all women dread.

     Don't think you have the vice-count figured out.

     T'ward privacy of mind she is devout.

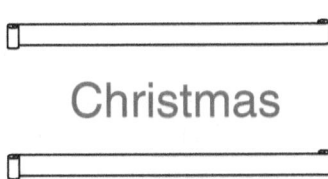

Christmas

Breakfast at Haus Hangendro always included some variety of meat, be it ham, bacon, sausage, goat, sheep, beef, or game. But in the season of Advent, preparing for the Savior's arrival, all abstained from such. They ate only fish, and perhaps eggs, but nothing that drew breath.

"My hostess!" said Ordowahl at breakfast on December first, "I sense the time of lean meals. Nordweg does the same. I think all Christendom avoids eating meat from now until the Mass of Christ. I have come to appreciate fish, especially as in the Haus of my host Sir Egeno in Ermsleben just a year ago."

Fretheldin struck a saucy pose and waved a serving fork at him. "Prince, I'll hear no comparisons! Yet I'll also guess that you've never had fish like what we serve here in Utrecht. The sea is our neighbor, and seafood is our strength."

*__*__*__*

The entire Hangendro party emerged from St. Martin's Cathedral following the Mass of Christ.

"Sons, Prince," said Fretheldin, "take small steps and small bites. Today is only the first feast day of twelve, and Count Jakop is sure to host a grand one. Just bear in mind that your stomachs aren't in the best of condition for rich meats!"

The three men laughed about that and "reminded" each other to have a care, all the way across the square, down the lane along the castle wall, and through the main gate.

The door to the main hall stood open to the weather. Crowds milled in and out. Roaring fire filled each fireplace and the crowd added their own heat. While not cozy, it wasn't all that cold. Winter wear made everyone who could afford it rosy-cheeked and happy.

Every pocket or handbag held small bulges. By custom, each person attending the party brought a trinket to give to one other guest, and the long-anticipated meat presented by Count Jakop consisted of four great beef carcasses, dry aged since the middle of November. They had been roasting over spits since the evening before. Great ceremony and a meat-filled but otherwise plain meal ended the time of penance, thus releasing everyone to celebrate the Savior's arrival.

Celebration is as celebration does, and everyone looked forward to Twelveday. This year the giant's arrival heightened that.

Lady Janalei began the first day's festivity by saying, "Let us elect a young boy to be Master of the Feast, someone naïve to our ways and willing to become the subject of many japes. Let it be the vice-count's younger brother, Prince Nordweg."

Maid-in-waiting Emluyn, standing behind her, patted her lady on the shoulder, as if to congratulate her.

Janalei turned a mocking version of her smile—the one that she knew entrapped most men's hearts—on Ordowahl. Heretofore he and she had made believe he was a nonentity to her. The full brightness of that smile, turned on him, stung.

The idea of an adult who was also a mysterious outsider, instead of a nine-year-old, got a roar of happy approval. As soon as the noise subsided Ordowahl sat down and said, "In the case that I am chosen, my first command as Master shall be that all unmarried noble ladies here, and as many married as may choose, shall, in order of their rank, highest first, seat themselves upon my lap and give me no less than five earnest kisses, full upon my face."

Janalei paled and threw him a stony look. "In that case, childish man, I withdraw the suggestion."

However, Lady Ariana, marriageable niece of neighboring

Count Breihoff and second only to Janalei in beauty, hadn't waited. Attired in Breihoff colors of oak and silver and standing very near the prince, she stepped toward him. Before Janalei had finished her unhappy reply, she seated her prim self in Ordowahl's lap. She proceeded to put her arms up around his neck, press herself to him, and deliver at least six ardent kisses.

Cheers and ribald catcalls drowned out the rest of Lady Janalei's remark. It took minutes for them to subside. All the time Lady Ariana beamed her adoration up at Ordowahl. When the noise faded she, looking happy and smug, stood up and walked toward the fireplace. She spun around and made a sweeping curtsey. "My noble friends, this fire is less warm than kisses from Prince Nordweg. Please pardon me while I remove my jacket, the better to shed heat."

This took the mood too far. It was only the first day, after all, and early in the afternoon. Further into Twelveday clothing might become less restricting, but the look on Lady Janalei's face brought everyone down to smug snickers. Alter ego Vice-Count Utrecht had spent considerable time with the prince. It set tongues wagging.

After rounds of song came the time to present gifts. Being of royal birth, the prince stood first. He beckoned to his footman Klarenz. "Bring me what you have made," he said. "My man has made small silver bells which a lady may sew to the end of a sleeve. They make charming little noises to alert the household staff when the mistress approaches. He shows concern more for his fellow servants than for me."

The ladies tittered and waited for an invitation to receive the gift. Janalei tried to find a spot out of his line of sight. Ariana, on the other hand, struck a very pretty pose and kept her eye on the giant prince.

"Fretheldin, my hostess, you have known that Klarenz made these. The first must be yours."

She approached, gave him a fond smile and a caress on the cheek, and held out her hand. When Ordowahl dropped the trinket into her palm she picked it up and jiggled it. The sound was bright and joyous; she smiled. "My household will be the happier," she said, and on impulse stood on tiptoe to give him a peck on the cheek—it required him to bend down, and he did.

Janalei saw that and rolled her eyes.

"He made two dozen of these," Ordowahl said. "I will present two on each day of Twelveday. Lady Janalei, I doubt you are eager to receive one of these, but I beg you to take your gift now."

She crossed her arms and looked bored.

Ariana came up to him then and whispered something private in his ear. She pulled back, gave him an intimate, flirtatious smile, and held out her hand. Then she took the little bell, rang it, and as Fretheldin had done, she kissed him yet again. Each of the next eleven days the tiny bell came with her, sewn at her left shoulder, "the one nearest my heart."

Days two, three, four, and five passed. Each morning when Ordowahl appeared at the castle gate to accompany Utrecht, a servant appeared to tell him that she had no business for the day, it being Twelveday and all. Most of those days found Lady Janalei attending the dinner. On the sixth day Joop told Klarenz that Utrecht had gone off to handle a nuisance; she appeared in the middle of the afternoon.

No one ever seemed to have anything to settle during Twelveday because it was a time of peace, joy, and giving gifts. Ordowahl suspected the vice-count received the distraction as a windfall, an excuse to be absent. But for the rest of that afternoon Vice-Count Utrecht's cold eye followed the prince. Ordowahl found it very easy to sense that Lady Ariana's open fondness toward him irritated both personae—vice-count and lady—almost beyond their ability to be civil.

Father God in heaven, what am I to do? While Lady Ariana behaves toward me with overt familiarity, she can't help sense that Lady Janalei finds it painful to watch. The last thing I want to abet is imposing that irritation on someone I'm growing fond of.

Yet when I attempt to dissuade Lady Ariana, it reminds me of telling Klarenz to pick his nose when some amorous spark is about to pass between him and a new female. Nobles don't pick their noses. When I asked Joop for a polite equivalent it seemed to amuse him. Sly devil that he is, it made him giggle. A mystery.

Christmas

It borders on defiance toward my unreasonable daytime friend, but for the life of me I won't pass up a kiss from a pretty girl. Even celibate as a priest, I enjoy kisses.

Each day's dinner began at noon. Hosting rotated around to each of the Vendink baronies in descending order of seniority. There were twelve: Hangendros stood thirteenth, since the first day always belonged to the count.

Day eight belonged to Baron Vlinck. The Vlinck household gave Ordowahl an odd feeling. Their eldest son had a comely wife with a suckling infant. But she couldn't hide her dislike of the younger son's very pretty wife, who while very pregnant also looked morose. Moreover the elder brother seemed happy that his sister-in-law, his younger brother's wife, was great with child, while the younger brother, husband to the prettily pregnant one, showed indifference. Everyone pretended not to notice, but it laid an odd feeling over the day.

Each hostess, in this case Vrau Baron Vlinck, got a silver bell. The second went to Katrinka, the unhappy-looking pregnant wife.

__*__*__*

Epiphany arrived, the twelfth day. Baron Jophan Maihoff hosted, and Karyn Vrau Maihoff would get the first bell. Ordowahl asked Ariana to intercede with Lady Janalei to accept the twenty-fourth and final bell and tried not to eavesdrop that conversation.

He saw the two women in chat, their heads together and faces down, for privacy. Ariana appeared to attempt explaining something to Janalei, who at first shook her head as though scoffing, but Ariana dipped her head as if in apology. At end they twined fingers in a woman's equivalent of a man's handclasp. Ariana walked way and appeared to leave the party.

Janalei looked baffled and unconvinced. Challenging the crisis, a tried-and-true military strategy, Ordowahl went over to her. "Lady Janalei, please pardon the interruption."

She turned a blank, polite face toward him. "What is it, Prince Ordowahl?"

"I have one bell left. I've felt open rebuff from you for the entire Twelveday, which I know is only just. Nonetheless let me make this request. Will you accept the last of Klarenz's beautiful bells?"

She looked at him as though still puzzled but at least no longer burdened by aggravation. "Yes, Prince, I will. And thank you. You can also clear up a mystery for me."

"If I can. What question do you have?"

"Why on earth did you give Lady Ariana the impression that you and I were connected in any way? She seemed much taken with you, which you did *nothing* to deflect." She gave him an accusing look. "Just now she came to undo what she feared might be her theft of your attentions. Yes, don't deny it; you gave her a great deal of your attention."

Women are such a puzzle; she refuses to be wooed yet accuses me of wooing Lady Ariana. "What is your question, my lady? Whether my attentions to Lady Ariana were in fact illicit, or perhaps not?"

"Oh, forget it! Just don't make too much of it when you present that damned bell."

I dare not look smug—and should I feel that way? Courting Lady Janalei is fatal to those who attempt it. Father God, help me avoid that death.

(Ordowahl)

'Twas very foolish to respond in kind

to Lady Janalei's small jest. She made

me out a little boy. I tried to find,

in turn, a ploy to kiss her as a maid.

> Why do I long for company like hers?

> Why don't I pine for Ariana's kiss?

> It puffed me up to see them both rehearse

> the ways each set the other one amiss.

Relief awaits me in the Fathers' den,

to study more on GOD's most holy Word.

They I can count on to behave like men.

Adult decorum—temper's seldom heard.

> I full intend to listen, then to grow,

> beyond the twigs my childhood priest could throw.

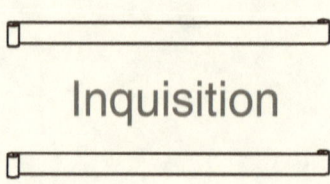

Inquisition

The Christmas Twelveday passed. The winter weather remained dank, foggy, and full of clouds. Everyone yearned for some bright sunshine. Ordowahl's sunshine took the form of regular sessions with the Fathers, and occasional County business to transact with Utrecht. After the tense not-quite-hilarity that Lady Janalei unleashed during Twelveday, returning to the usual, if never normal, restored the prince's sense of place.

Even at the approach of spring, Ordowahl, Torwulf and Klarenz dressed in wool to shield them from the dense lowland fog. Vague shapes could close in to lend sounds a mystical air. One day in particular as the entered the sanctuary for dawn Mass the prince encountered Vice-Count Utrecht as she left the confessional. She treated them as though their presence was mundane. Lady Janalei's grudging acceptance of a bell had long since fallen beneath Vice-Count Utrecht's notice.

Father Henck sighed to himself when Ordowahl began his whispered confession. Tiny matters lamed the prince's conscience, things others wouldn't notice. At all.

The priest revered the sanctity of the confessional and so gave the prince three uninterrupted minutes before checking him. "Prince," he said, "you've said nothing so far regarding the vice-count. Are your interest and interaction with her beyond reproach? I sense that she's always of divided mind toward you."

Inquisition

"Father, I am shamed by her unhappiness. But while I feel the same pull she exerts on any man with eyes and a mind, I abstain from behavior that is other than pure and polite."

"We all," intoned Fr. Henck, "mistake intentions for successes. Four Hail Mary's and one full rosary, during which you will focus primarily on the discomfort your presence inflicts on the vice-count."

At the breaking of bread after the Mass, Fr. Henck asked Ordowahl, "Prince, which is your patron saint?"

"Father, I was born on a day without saints. My tutor Father Ewald, who also baptized me, selected Bede the Venerable to be my patron. Like King Stegnwahl my earthly father, Saint Bede was a scholar well versed in both Greek and Latin. While on earth he translated much of the Christian Greek Scripture into his native tongue."

"Is that so? While he is a saint, I wasn't aware he'd done that. And I'm sure Rome isn't anxious for another such doing."

"I see. Well then, Father, please tell me more about my patron saint as you know him."

"He was instrumental in persuading the Irish," he said with a smile for Fr. Danelagh, "to adopt Rome's method for finding each year's date for Easter, and in so doing altered the entire path of faith in England by placing it under Rome's headship. He also wrote an extensive history of the Church in Britain, up to his time."

"Guide me then, Father, in understanding him as my own patron saint. What lessons may I take, and what kinds of protection may he grant me? How should I understand my patron saint's influence or gift? And moreover, Fathers, how did Christians born on Bede's day, but before Bede was canonized, find a patron?"

Father Henck looked around the small room. "Brothers? I seem to have taken all of our student's time this morning. Can anyone enlighten him?"

Torwulf and Klarenz edged back slightly from the table and looked at the floor.

Father Petur answered. "When baptizing a babe whose birth falls on an empty day in the calendar of saints—which hasn't happened here in many years—the priest would consult its parents, look for a saint who cares for that town or province, or whose day is nearest, and may consider the father's occupation. He will find many good choices. We don't, brothers, happen to have any bad saints, do we?"

He got a small chuckle for the ancient truism.

"To answer the prince's earlier question, let me try," said Fr. Dan. "As ye're well aware, saints in heaven devote their time to special works. Some saints are known by their profession in life. They tend to matters of that profession, others for where they come from. And each has a day. All infants born on that day become part of tasks of the saints of that day, so to speak. We've bin through all that. So what be yer question again, lad?"

"I suppose, since Saint Bede was a man of the Word of God, I can trust in his guidance as I study. But on a deeper level, Fathers, how do we know these things to be truths? I've been through the entire Word, from Genesis to Revelation, and many times at that. But nowhere did I find anything to explain the powers we presume for saints."

Father Henck steered the discussion back toward established Church teaching. "Prince, it has been over a thousand years since the first Christians walked the earth. In that time the Holy Spirit has been working, constantly."

"Yes, Father. That is true. Jesus promised us a Comforter, who guides and heals us."

"In fact, the Spirit intercedes between earth and heaven with, as it says in Scripture, 'groans too deep to utter.'"

"Yes, Father. I ponder on that from time to time."

"So if the Spirit doesn't use words, nonetheless He does communicate."

"Yes, Father."

"And without words, when the Holy Spirit communicates with us here below, we have no further Scriptures. We know that there will be no more prophets."

"Again, yes." *I wonder where this is going.*

"So when we learn a thing via the Spirit, there is no written passage. We merely receive these clear truths in our own understandings. When many people receive the same truth, it becomes established and over time becomes a Holy Tradition."

"Yet, Father, wouldn't learning something via the Spirit make one into a prophet? If you see the dilemma, such a teaching may simply have arisen as a tradition of men. And the few times Scripture speaks of tradition it always refers to traditions of men, and condemns those."

"Prince, when many passages give one meaning, the few which appear to contradict them merely demonstrate that we have failed to understand it, or perhaps haven't found the necessary exception in the other ones."

"I see. Father, allow me to gather up all the passages which touch on tradition, both for and against. Then I might have the understanding I seek."

"One thing is yet lacking, Prince. Do you mean to jeopardize a thousand years of collected spiritual truth and, in effect, undo the entire work of the Holy Spirit? These are traditions of the Church, after all, and not traditions of men."

"Yet if they were not present in Scripture when the canon was chosen, we face the likelihood that they weren't necessary to Salvation then, hence not now."

"Actually, no, whether or not they were necessary for Salvation is not a matter you are prepared to contemplate. Moreover, they were part of Church teaching all along. What we call 'tradition' is simply unwritten teachings which arrived in oral form through the apostles and have been lovingly maintained ever since. But if I had said yes, what would you infer?"

"That they appeared in one place at one time, and spread, therefore likely came not from Christ's apostles, but from mere men."

"Prince, you must take care. For one who has broad knowledge of the text to take up an issue with a Church teaching suggests that your knowledge, if broad, is also shallow. A small ripple on the sea of your understanding seems ready to swamp your little boat. Do you take my meaning?"

"Father, I do. Please forgive my temerity."

"Is this your confession?"

"Yes."

"Then this is your penance. For the next year you may not quote from Scripture, even so much as to allege your understanding or insight, without first seeking advice from a priest. And for the next six months you are not to join in any of our discussions. I am being tender, young prince. I admire your ardor for God's Word. But I am beyond dismayed at your willingness to venture conflict with Church teachings of such long standing. In your defense I grant that this was not your intent."

Ordowahl bowed his head.

"I didn't hear a response."

Ordowahl nodded his head further downward for a moment.

"Because I have not yet had a spoken response, Prince, here is a third part to your penance. You must isolate yourself from this city and all its inhabitants for one month, nor speak to anyone from this city during that time."

Ordowahl raised his head, looked Fr. Henck in the eye, and said, "I accept your penance, Father, but cannot bind my conscience. I cannot shirk my duty to Christ our Lord by not speaking a truth."

Father Henck stood and waved him away. He shouted, "It is I who instruct your conscience, so it is also I who bind it, not the unguided mind of a youth. Now leave before I lose my temper!"

Our earnest prince can't keep from causing fright.

His penchant is advice; he isn't meek.

He volunteers to think, mistakes polite

rhetorical remarks for cues to speak.

> So now he's cast adrift, in terror of

> good Father Henck. Resumed patrol with Vice-

> Count Utrecht must descend from God above,

> else prince winds up conversing with the mice.

To give up now when peace is near at hand—

e'en though the bishop thinks he goads her sore—

say what you will, the vice-count's mind is grand

enough to out-think Henck—a minor chore.

> Yet confidence becomes a headlong fall;

> the leaping runner's race becomes a crawl.

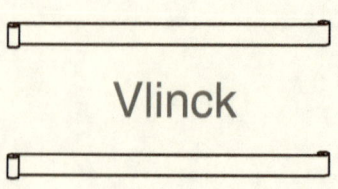

Vlinck

Ordowahl had returned at once to Haus Hangendro. Klarenz went to the gate of Vendink Keep. Arrayed this morning in brilliant green leggings, tunic, and coat, Vice-Count Utrecht gave him a puzzled stare. "What message do you carry from the problem prince?" she asked. Her face held the deadpan look which, to a bondman, counted as friendly acceptance.

"I learned that my liege has been forbidden to speak with any resident of this city for the span of a month."

"If he sent this message, he in effect is speaking with me. Isn't that so?" Her look showed Klarenz that she was testing the prince. Had he thought this through, or not?

"My liege showed curiosity, Vice-Count, regarding where you might appear this morning, if outside the city." He waited for her response.

She turned away from him and examined some linen sheets in her lap desk. They bore many inky squiggles She handed the top two to Joop, by custom standing beside her.

He slid them into one of her saddlebags and took the lap desk back inside one of the gate's anterooms. When he returned, Klarenz had not moved.

Utrecht nodded at Joop, muttered under her breath something about following her father's will, and rode away. In a loud voice she told Joop, "I hope that Baron Vlinck will be glad to see us. This will be a long day, so we'll need a moderate pace.

Klarenz threw Joop a happy look and returned to Haus Hangendro at a brisk canter.

*__*__*__*

As Utrecht and Joop entered the Vlinck gateway they noticed a Hangendro footman just leaving. She said nothing to the fellow, who must have guided Ordowahl and Klarenz there, and not at a slow pace.

Shaking her head to dispel the mood, Utrecht took one of the linen pages from her saddlebag. "Joop, this is today's pressing matter. How ironic that it involves a rogue's sexual misdeeds." She turned a direct stare on Ordowahl, as though putting him in his place.

She turned back to Joop. "I also stipulate that while we are outside the city all of the prince's and my remarks are directed respectively to Klarenz and to you." She held the linen out for no one in particular, until Ordowahl accepted it.

Mixed feelings of amused insult and fond gratitude helped Ordowahl keep a plain face. "I see Baron Lengdepflum pressing suit against one of Baron Vlinck's sons. He claims that the fellow took Lengdepflum's daughter Katrinka by force, and she has now born his child. But isn't she already married to a Vlinck son?"

"The other one, *Klarenz*. There are two."

"Ah. How is it that Baron Vlinck isn't the one to pursue the interest of the cuckolded son against the brother?"

"Because, ahem, the first son is not entertained by his wife's or by any woman's body. He would, on the other hand, be happy to find you in his bed, Joop." She gave her footman and former nanny a fond smile. She turned toward the prince and gave him more of a smirk than a smile.

Ordowahl pretended not to notice. "What is Lengdepflum's interest here?"

"You can't see it? Lengdepflum laments his very unhappy daughter, wedded to a man who disdains her while also *observing* his older brother's forcible attempts to produce an heir."

Ordowahl looked at Utrecht to read some expression on her face.

"Is there more to the story than this? It's been said of the distressed wife that she flirts, doesn't hide the fact, and delivered twins."

She seemed to pounce: "And one of the twins might be your master's, *Klarenz*?" Another turn-and-smirk.

Ordowahl gave her a look of patient innocence. "I haven't been here long enough, but in any case, no." He shook his head. "And it has nothing to do with the impotent husband's vigilant protection of his wife's extramural virtue."

"I don't care! Stop talking about whose virtue is whose when a poor woman's body isn't her own. For pity's sake. You men. Focus, Prince," she said, dismissing the subterfuge of names.

He watched her face, as though waiting for a surprise.

She ignored the direct eye contact. "The infants are four days old. One is female and resembles her mother's Catholic husband in face, hair, and skin. The other is a son and resembles a landed knight known to have flirted often with the mother."

"I see, Utrecht. Two children, two fathers. Vigilant attempts to bar contact with the son's adventurous father have failed."

She shook her head. "Please hold your tongue until I finish the story. No one can place them together during the months leading up to the first signs of pregnancy."

"So they mounted a dutiful effort to prevent the fellow, and he broke the chastity of their barrier anyway?"

A snort. "All parties agree that relaxed attention occurred no sooner than four months prior to birth, which came at full term. Now both Lengdepflum and Vlinck are involved."

"Yet the bride's father, Lengdepflum, sues her supposed brother-in-law the elder Vlinck son. Shouldn't both barons assail the landed knight?"

"No."

"There is more to this than you've said thus far, Vice-Count."

"Lengdepflum wants Vlinck to bear the expense of raising Lengdepflum's natural grandson, both to include the child's education as a gentleman and to endow him with a landed knight's estate when he reaches maturity."

"I see. Lengdepflum sues Vlinck for the costs of raising a

bastard son born to Vlinck's daughter-in-law, on grounds of failure to protect the woman's virtue."

"In this case, protect it against her wishes, and given her situation I dare you to blame her. But, yes."

"Her father-in-law Baron Vlinck, on the other hand, wants to hire a wet-nurse for the infant girl and raise her as a Vlinck while sending its mother back, with her bastard son. So why doesn't Lengdepflum also sue for the return of his daughter's dowry?"

Utrecht looked at him for a long moment. "Prince, is this a fool's jest? The dowry covers the Vlinck family's shame and loss of respect."

"That was not in jest, Vice-Count. Lengdepflum expected Vlinck to care for the bride. He cannot be responsible for their lax oversight."

"Men! As if a woman's sole act is to achieve then sustain a pregnancy and in all other ways assert no judgment nor have a right to choose for herself."

"I take your point, but in this case what word would you use to describe Katrinka's judgment?"

"No one is perfect, Prince. One woman's evident poor use of her ability to choose should not blame all of her sex. And beside that, I forbid you to blame her for the repeated torment of rape by her brother-in-law."

"That was ugly indeed, Utrecht." He showed appropriate disappointment. "Then let us think of the landed knight. Does he have any voice in the raising of his son?"

"Again, men! No man will hold him guilty for the simple act of bedding a willing woman. And few men would take an interest in raising a bastard, even their own."

"What then, Janalei," he said, daring to use her birth name, "of declaring the landed knight's estate forfeit to Lengdepflum? The son is his. Either do that, or require the landed knight to raise the child."

"My birth name is *not something for you to speak,* Prince. To you I am Vice-Count Utrecht. How have I failed to make that clear?"

"I apologize, Utrecht, Vice-Count Vendink. But my question is worth answering."

"The choice to raise the son was made by its mother's family, and the landed knight has had the tact to pretend to go on a journey."

"So Lengdepflum wants the privilege of raising the bastard son as a Lengdepflum, yet wants the cuckolded family Vlinck to reward him for this sacrifice. Men's choices are often as hard to defend as women's."

She glared hard at him. "Flatulence. Men's choices are always based on their feelings, foremost those of their dicks. Most women's choices run to the practical, Prince. I will not debate a topic you're so ill-prepared to discuss."

"Stipulated. What will I observe when we go into the Haus?"

"You'll find a warm welcome, Prince. As to what else may transpire, you will have to prepare yourself with a guess. You'll learn better that way, rather than chirping like a nestling bird anxious to receive every smallest worm of information."

As though on cue the massive front door opened wide and Baron Vlinck stepped out. Medium-sized, dressed in deep grays and not quite ugly, he wore a sad look, as though life haunted him.

He welcomed the vice-count in person, beckoned Ordowahl to come in, and shooed Joop and Klarenz around to the stables.

They sat in a front parlor, just a tad bigger than Count Jakop's dayroom. Five small chairs sat against the walls, light enough to reposition around a modest circular table.

"Thank you, Vice-Count Utrecht. I am blessed by your visit to hear my sad story."

"I am sure that it is sad, Baron Vlinck. Please tell me the story as you have it, and include everything you can think of."

He sighed in evident woe. "Vice-Count, my younger son took the hand of Katrinka, daughter of Baron Lengdepflum, but he failed to produce an heir upon her body."

"Is this the result of failure even to attempt it?"

"Yes. After several failures to so much as touch her nakedness his older brother produced the heir himself."

"Brother took brother's place in the marital bed?"

"In fact our priest blessed the attempt by citing something from the Old Testament regarding one brother getting a dead brother's wife with child to keep the man's name living. My younger son is, alas, dead to women."

"No pretence, no ruse, no—"

"Nothing worked. Once she became pregnant we began preparing to bless a new grandchild but find that we have two. The granddaughter can only be a Vlinck, but the other, a boy, clearly has a different father."

"I see. What has Lengdepflum to say about this?"

"You may ask him that. I cannot use Christian language to describe his demands. It is sufficient to say that he wants his daughter back, alleges that her marriage is void, further that the infant daughter is a bastard because she was conceived out of wedlock—" He paused for breath.

"Go on, Baron. I'm sure you have more to tell me."

"Yes, Vice-Count. Lengdepflum is happy that I keep and raise my, our, granddaughter, but insists that I bear the entire expense of raising and educating the bastard boy, and at his maturity endow him as a landed knight."

Ordowahl and Utrecht exchanged glances. Barons were hard bargainers, or they didn't remain wealthy.

"Baron, what else will I learn when I visit Lengdepflum?"

"He, Vice-Count, will slander the Vlinck family name for permitting, or enabling, or even facilitating his daughter's wild promiscuity. We are to bear the shame of her wretched conduct."

"I understand your pain."

"I will be overjoyed to have his daughter absent herself and her sluttish manners from this Haus. We will be rid of the stain of her strumpet self and her fornication."

"You will retain her dowry." She had not made it a question.

The baron stated a simple fact: "I have it, I possess it, and it is poor compensation now for the wreckage she has made of the Vlinck family and the Vlinck name. Prince, do you have pertinent questions or observations?"

Utrecht stifled a frown; in the baron's Haus his right to engage anyone in conversation stood beyond challenge.

"Baron," began Ordowahl, "tell me about the means you used to keep Katrinka chaste. I'm sure you were vigilant, but it's always instructive to hear another man's solution to an old problem."

"Thank you, Prince. The woman was always in the company of two maids, or her husband, or, ahem, both her husband and at times his concerned, well-meaning elder brother."

"Did she sleep alone?" Ordowahl asked.

"Yes, now that you say it, she insisted on privacy. None but she and her supposed husband were in their bedchamber during the night."

"I see. And how deep a sleeper is he? Do they sleep in the same bed?"

The Baron hung his head. "My son, Prince, became so disdainful of his wife's flesh that he slept on a couch in their chamber."

Ordowahl looked over to see Utrecht's expression. "Vice-Count, have we heard enough?"

"Yes, we have. Thank you, Baron. We are concerned for your good name, so this discussion will remain private. Just you, the prince, and I will ever know what was said here."

"Thank you, Vice-Count. And thank you, Prince. I pray that the Lengdepflum cunt runs home to her mama, takes the bastard boy with her, and we'll hear nothing about them, ever again."

Utrecht rose and said, "Please don't bother setting out anything scrumptious to eat. We still have far to go. We'll show ourselves out."

(Vice-Count Utrecht)

I have to hear the shame of womankind?

In this young woman's life the men are wrong.

The baron surely knew his son's slack mind.

The elder son stood up to stud. "Be strong!"

    They knew beforehand that Katrinka swived.

    She did her part to bear a child 'mid scorns.

    Now all the men look on her twins, unshrived,

    and whine that righteous brothers both wear horns.

What's more the oafish prince thinks only of

refunding money. What an ass! I can't

count up the diff'rent ways he shows self-love

in counting his poor stock. So arrogant!

    For now I spend a dreary horseback day

    while hearing that one noise he makes—a bray!

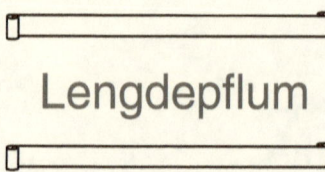

Lengdepflum

Vice-count and prince stood near a patch of winter ice in the shaded part of the Vlinck courtyard, waiting for Joop and Klarenz to bring their horses around from the stables. Over half a day's ride lay ahead of them to reach Barony Lengdepflum on the far edge of County Vendink. Hunger and thirst overtook them when the noontime sun stood high overhead.

While Joop and Klarenz spread a blanket and set out a cold meal, Ordowahl and Utrecht went over to stand by a leafing-out tree, dappled by descending bangles of light.

The need to converse out of earshot of servants, even those as loyal and discreet as Joop and Klarenz, kept them chatting in whispers.

"Utrecht, we didn't ask about a lusty man's ease of access to Katrinka's windowsill."

"Before we set out this morning I asked Joop to see what he and Klarenz could learn. Your bondman Klarenz has a singular talent for gaining a woman's trust."

"Talent, yes—often enough also a curse."

"You would do well to learn from that." She shot him an arch glance.

"I will guess that they now have useful information."

"Let's go find out," said Utrecht, and the pair rejoined their footmen.

Lengdepflum

The meal began in silence. Then Utrecht asked, "Klarenz?"

"Yes, noble lady?"

"Did you find Joop a way into the baron's manor, one usable while lit by starlight only?"

Joop elbowed Klarenz in the ribs. "This rogue had to pry his face away from Katrinka's maid's middle part to wave at me out her window."

"Not just near a window, but also near enough to wave?"

"Ha! I don't think the maid even knew he'd done that. And yes, the spot to scale the wall and a highway up the trellis are both well worn by shod feet."

Utrecht gave a hearty guffaw and slapped Klarenz on the back. "Congratulations, bondman. Prince, you boasted about his powers of persuasion, and now I believe."

She gave Klarenz a saucy smile. "Klarenz, please take care never to make your special smile at Lady Janalei, eh, my good fellow?"

Ordowahl enjoyed her bawdy bonhomie. She saw it, looked for his hand, and gave it a hard slap. "Don't. That smile wasn't for you, Nordweg."

Soon enough the make-do meal was done. They went on and reached Haus Lengdepflum in late afternoon. The Lengdepflum parlor held an evening meal already laid out, so they ate at once.

"I beg you, stay the night," asked the baron.

Utrecht replied, "We will stay two nights to give our mounts a day's rest."

Lengdepflum sent a courier to Castle Vendink to say the vice-count would be delayed.

During the supper their daughter didn't arise in conversation, but their days-old grandson did; somehow they'd seen him and were overjoyed. An impromptu songfest followed dinner. Many of the household staff joined in and seemed eager to lighten the difficult mood.

At evening's end prince and vice-count went separately upstairs to find sleeping arrangements. Joop and Klarenz found bedding among the household servants.

At the morning meal Katrinka did come up for discussion. Baron

Lengdepflum asked, "Vice-Count, did you have a chance to speak with my daughter? How did she look? When you saw her babes, what did she say to you?"

"So much!" said Utrecht. "First of all, she's still weak from the ordeal of a first birth and gives thanks to God that, being twins, each was small."

The baron nodded enthusiastically. "Her mother and I were very concerned when we learned that her belly had grown so large. So, please tell us more."

"The daughter is precious, and has the unmistakable look of a Vlinck father. The son has a different face, complexion—beyond the right number of toes and noses, just about everything separates him from his sister."

Lengdepflum shook his head sadly. "Poor Katrinka, so abused by that wretched family. She sent us many letters. You know, her husband did not even consummate the marriage? I am saddened to say this: those innocents are both bastards."

Ordowahl repeated his question from the day before. "Why don't you also demand the return of the dowry if their treatment of Katrinka was so cruel?"

Utrecht put a restraining hand on his shoulder. She turned to him and said, in a stage whisper, "Observations only. No advice." Then she turned a sweet smile back at Katrinka's parents. "Please ignore him. His grasp of social customs can be so unformed."

Lengdepflum gave Ordowahl a brief look of sympathy and shrugged. "They have possession of the dowry. I made a round-about demand for its return in the form of their paying the expenses of raising the son and endowing him at his majority with a landed knight's estate."

Utrecht looked curious. "Round-about?"

"We haggled much of this out day before yesterday. Each of us, Vice-Count, hopes to persuade you to intercede with the other to expand his concession." He shrugged again, as though he didn't expect anything like that to happen. They had decided as men, and that made it all but a formality.

Utrecht's face went cold for a moment. "There's one side of this that neither of you have mentioned."

"And what is that?" The baron succeeded in looking puzzled.

"Her lover, Baron. Who was it that found his way into her bedchamber to father the male child, and within the same day or two that the brother-in-law seeded her daughter?"

Vrau Baron Lengdepflum spoke up. She had been her daughter's confidant through a difficult time of waiting to receive a proposal of marriage. "I know a certain landed knight, living near the center of County Vendink. He was my daughter's lover before her marriage to that Vlinck sissy-boy. Nobody was supposed to know that she was not a virgin, but many young women come to their marriage bed with more than a little experience of what happens there."

No one showed surprise.

"Her lover didn't give up. His name is Sir Gebaustaadt, and he lives ten miles from here, halfway to Vlincks'. He never tired of making the journey to continue swiving with her."

Ordowahl began to involve himself more. "Do the Vlincks have any acquaintance with Sir Gebaustaadt? Do they know where he lives?"

"Prince, I am sure they do not. They accuse no one other than our poor daughter."

"Then, Baron, has anyone spoken with the landed knight?"

Father, mother, and Utrecht all erupted at once. "What kind of idea is that?"

Utrecht then turned to Ordowahl. Speaking one slow word at a time as though he were just learning to read, she said, "We discuss a matter that involves two noble families. Both are baronies."

Ordowahl kept patient silence and tried to look humble, although a beetled brow and huge jaw made that difficult.

Utrecht tried small words. "A searching dick filled an open cunt. Neither one matters here."

Both Lengdepflums nodded vigorously.

"On the other hand," Ordowahl replied, "Katrinka won't receive a second proposal of marriage."

Utrecht drew her answer out to emphasize it as another "small" word: "Riiiight."

149

"So she will come to live here in an embarrassed and unwed state. Or she can make a life with the man she wants in her bed and who wants at least that much from her."

All three of them frowned.

"Have you asked her about the rest of her life, or does your concern begin and end with your current wealth and standing?" Ordowahl sounded as quiet and respectful as he could but turned his questioning face on Utrecht.

Such impudence. But, damn him, he may have a point.

"Vrau Baron Lengdepflum?" he asked. "Does your daughter Katrinka have any weight on your scales at all?"

Utrecht broke an awkward silence. "I like pertinent questions, Nordweg. That one felt very impertinent. Katrinka's father has the right to make all major decisions for her. Am I right, Baron?"

Vrau Baron dug an elbow into her husband's ribs, wearing a deep frown.

Damn. When will the pushy prince stop asking meddlesome questions?

Once the baron's position became clear, a relaxing day ensued. Ordowahl devoted his morning to martial training.

Lady Janalei had brought no suitable clothing but managed to borrow a flowing dress left behind by Katrinka, which let her resume being a woman in a woman's world. She and Vrau Lengdepflum mulled over the special touches given to Katrinka's trousseau, now neglected, and the little differences of details of managing noble manors, the homely gossip of two women passing the time of day. She found Vrau Lengdepflum boring but in the most amiable way.

The baron rested in the exercise yard to enjoy Ordowahl's company during the morning but declined an offer to walk with him through the woods in the afternoon. For an old man of more than fifty years, exploring the unarable parts of his estate, its hummocks and fens, held no value.

"Prince," called out Lady Janalei when he returned late in the day. His clothing carried bits of new leaves from the spring growth, and he brought her a tiny basket woven from fresh grass.

Lengdepflum

Such rumpled contentment. I could strike him. She fell into Utrecht's persona without realizing it, and spoke to him. "Where have you been all afternoon, what is in the basket, and what complaisant woman wove it for you?"

Smiling, he sat down next to her, being careful to leave a hand's-width between them for courtesy's sake, and put the basket into her outstretched hand.

"A mother bird is unhappy now, and her eggs will not hatch. But the nest and eggs were so charming I had to bring them back. The sight of nature's perfect simplicity restores something in me."

Lady Janalei stared into the basket.

"I see that some little boy must have retrieved the nest. Yet his use of a knife, so delicate, is beyond the skill of a child small enough to have done this."

Ordowahl showed humor on his face but said nothing.

"And the basket. Tell me more about the maiden who did this." She glared up into his eyes. "And I am sure that Vice-Count Utrecht will have words with you regarding how close you sit, Nordweg."

He looked at the tiny gap between his hip and hers. He found himself staring at sleek perfection, vivid and firm and delicately curved—he jumped to his feet. "Pardon, my lady. If the vice-count were here I could take her out to find another just like this, retrieve it, and weave another basket, except that it might require half a morning tomorrow. Either that, or take the word of Prince Nordweg as honest and true."

Simpleton or otherwise, his straight face forced her to take him at his word. "You are a true woodland sprite, Prince, and always find some new way to astonish me. I dub thee Prince Fairy Toes of Vendink." She even let him see a tiny smile.

The lady Janalei has dropped her guard

to speak with Ordowahl, albeit brief.

It must have been for Lengdepflum's regard

she dressed and acted 'lady,' for relief.

> How ladylike, you ask? She knows he'll see

> her as a woman. When he might she cues

> him on, encourages the prince to be

> himself. Her spite then makes him pay his dues.

How do we read this giant, lethal man

with fingers that can nimble up wee grass

into a basket for a bird's nest? Ban

him from her fertile hip, "Too close! How crass."

> But wait and see him nudge her judgment. Vice-

> Count does what's upside-down, near over-nice.

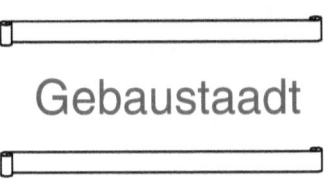

Gebaustaadt

Another trek from one side of the county to the other, which ended after the pale sun had crossed the zenith. A lavish midday meal awaited them in Haus Vlinck, and they ate with just small talk to pass the time.

The servants cleared away the dishes and serving platters, leaving goblets and a fresh pitcher of watered wine.

"Vice-Count," began Vlinck, "what news do you bring me from Lengdepflum?"

She favored him with a kind, level gaze for long enough to make him uneasy. "Baron," she said at last, "I must weigh what few facts I have on hand. For one, the groom did not consummate his union."

He stared into her calm, motionless face and at last gave her a shrug. "Despite the priest's permission, my beautiful granddaughter is a bastard?"

She nodded. "Your son may be dead to a woman's body, but he is not dead. For this reason County Vendink does not condone one brother standing in stud to his presumed sister-in-law."

"The grandson is a bastard in any case. I won't give Lengdepflum so much as a copper coin toward the raising of his, but not my, grandson."

"I accept that. But there is the matter of separating a mother from her child."

"What of it? Our granddaughter will have a wet nurse and the

153

very best of care. I will add that we will raise a much more ladylike and modest young woman than the one we received in marriage."

Ordowahl looked on, fascinated to see it play out. Utrecht showed such polish, she might have been her father's pupil all her life, not just the last four-plus years.

"No," she said, "you will not. Her natural mother will raise her, and not in the company of her natural father."

Vlinck stared in astonishment, beginning to protest, when she silenced him.

"Your upbringing produced one son who cannot even push dick into cunt to become husband much less father, and another capable of rape upon a sister-in-law."

"With all due respect, Vice-Count, this is too much." A red face and quivering hands punctuated his protest.

"I will not discuss it further. This matter is closed."

Vlinck's anger began to get the best of him when a small vocal click from Ordowahl stopped him.

Vlinck swallowed. "Vice-Count," he pleaded, "I must be part of my granddaughter's life!"

"That, Baron, is up to you. In a week or so, when Katrinka is ready to take her twins to their new home, I will guarantee you a welcome there. But you must guarantee me something in return."

"And what is that, Vice-Count?"

"You will guard your welcome by good conduct toward the man and woman who will raise your granddaughter. You will treat them with kindness for the rest of your lives."

He swallowed again. "Vrau Vlinck!" he said, his voice faint and scratchy. "Call *mijn vrau* in here," he said, and a servant went to fetch his wife.

"What is it, *Mijnheer*?" she said, and came to sit beside her husband.

"We are to lose the babe." He could say no more. She sat down and they wept on each other's shoulders.

Utrecht gave the prince a nod, and they left.

*__*__*__*

In late afternoon the small party reached the estate of landed knight Gebaustaadt, father of the boy. His reported absence had been a pro forma fiction, but the knight had not expected them. He was out inspecting his serfs doing spring tilling. A servant ran to find him, and in a short time (it was a tiny estate) he returned to welcome them.

"Vice-Count! And Prince!" He could not contain his surprise. "Surely you will stay the night with me?" He couldn't presume but knew that they would need food and lodging.

"Sir Gebaustaadt," said Utrecht. "We will return to Vendink Castle yet tonight. I have business there each morning and have been away two nights already."

"Please take a meal with me. How can you not be hungry and thirsty?"

"Thank you. You will prepare a basket of bread, dried fruit and meats, rest our four mounts, and send us home on spares. You'll get them back after ours have had a day to rest."

He nodded and let his face ask the next question.

She turned to Ordowahl and said, "Prince, stay with your stallion if that pleases you, or return tonight, whatever you wish." It was a fact, not a request.

As they were eating, Utrecht laid out for Gebaustaadt his future in the county. "Knight," she said between bites of bread and cheese, "your lascivious conduct with a woman wedded to a Vlinck son is noted."

He looked chastened but said nothing.

"Your silence is correct. There is nothing you can say. But by a stroke of good fortune far above any you may ever merit, Lady Katrinka's marriage was never consummated."

He showed no surprise. Katrinka had held nothing back from him.

"You continued to fill her bed as though she remained unwed. In the eyes of God and the Church she stayed single."

He nodded again, mute and shamed.

"So here is my grace to you. She and you appear to be married in spirit. Therefore you will marry her in the Church and raise all of her children." She looked into his eyes to see if he had absorbed the consequences of his acts, and he nodded.

"Vlincks will be welcome here, and you will allow them to visit their granddaughter."

He made a cautious nod.

"Freely."

"Th—thank you, Vice-Count," he stammered.

"You will raise their granddaughter to whatever standard they ask, and I'm sure they will be overeager to help you with that. The son is your own. Several years from now Vlincks will demand that your daughter live in their Haus to facilitate her training. *Resist.*"

His face set. "Certainly, Highness."

"Lengdepflums will have free access to your son and may assist you in providing well for him. They may suffer the same temptation. Again, resist it."

"Thank you, Vice-Count."

"Don't thank me, Sir Gebaustaadt. Thank two baronies and two sets of noble grandparents whom you have insulted." She rose to return to Castle Vendink.

Ordowahl chose to return with her, astride Gebaustaadt's freshest plow horse. Along the way she gave him an odd command. "Prince, I realize that while my own judgment has decided the matter, it sprang from your unusual, or untutored, or naïve thoughts. In future, please restrict your remarks to topics that have only a passing interest." She said nothing else on the journey home.

Now comes the vice-count into father's court.

She acted on Ord's "gentle strength" advice—

she bade the prince be gentle in retort

to Heri's base attack: "Make peace, be nice."

    Forgetting that she told him she would choose

    her own responses to each matter, she

    fell into honest chat, not prince's ruse,

    reflecting on his father's polity.

But then the prince returns to hornet's nest.

He's openly conversed, for sev'ral days

with, not "a" Utrecht dweller, but the best.

Confession? He'll submit, without self-praise.

    Is this the arrogance of plastic youth?

    Forgiveness not permission? How uncouth.

Influence

After a quiet morning meal Vice-Count Utrecht found her father in his dayroom. He wore a thoughtful look, staring at nothing while whittling on a small object. He looked up when she came in, unannounced, and sat in front of him.

"Daughter, you seem troubled."

"Daddy, it's that horrible giant, Nordweg."

He gave her a sharp look. "What has he done?"

"He got Father Henck mad at him."

"And? How did he manage that?"

"I'm not sure, but I learned it from Klarenz three mornings ago when I set out to handle the Lengdepflum–Vlinck twins. For the next month Ordowahl is to have no direct conversation with any resident of the City."

"Very strange. He must have found some way to twist the good father's tail indeed." The hint of a smile crossed his ancient face. "I see you have a lot on your mind. Lay it all out, daughter. I will listen until you have run out of things to say."

"Well. All I could get out of him was that he's under a heavy penance that keeps him from so much as admitting he knows any single thing from Scripture, cannot study with the fathers for half a year, and for proposing that he should be ruled by his own conscience, must also refrain from speaking with anyone residing in this City."

158

Influence

"I can tell you feel his insult. Yet, daughter, you don't sound happy that he won't bother you for the next month. Why is that? I'm glad that you mentioned this before I found some other way to free you from him." He smiled at her. "Filial piety?"

She looked at him, stumped for an answer. Finally she said, "Daddy, what can I say? But consider what happened the past few days. She began with her choice that each would speak to his own footman, loud enough to be overheard . . .

". . . And to cap it off, Daddy, he persuaded me to deliver, as the official judgment of County Vendink, the most outlandish thing. Marry off Katrinka to Gebaustaadt and set them up to raise *both* infants to adulthood. Moreover, each pair of natural grandparents must court the favor of the Gebaustaadt couple for the right to provide special gifts and training to their respective grandchildren."

Jakop threw his head back and, silently, laughed until his sides hurt. She stared at him, at first concerned that he was in the grip of something fatal, then took insult when she saw that he was laughing, and doubtless at her, not with her.

When he stopped the silent guffaws, he lapsed into several low chuckles, wiped his eyes, and gasped for breath. "Daughter, we have to do something about the prince. Indeed, he is a rogue, but tell me why you found his strange suggestion worth adopting."

She came back to good humor and relaxed. "Yes, Daddy, he is a rogue. But despite the complete upside down-ness of having grandparent barons woo a knavish free knight's favor to attend to their own precious grandchildren, it resolved so much. Vlincks and Lengdepflums aren't yet at peace with each other but are on much easier terms, and the daughter's lot as raped mother is salvaged once she becomes a Christian wife. Both her babes wind up raised by their natural mother, yet each will be trained as a baron's grandchild."

Jakop's face sobered. "Still, Jana, a free knight upends two barons. How do you plan to explain this to ten other barons?"

"That, Daddy, looks difficult."

"I recall you finding ways to handle many other difficulties. It's my pleasure, here, to handle the dispute between Henck and

Nordweg." He did not say, "Father" Henck.

*__*__*__*

Jakop sat in his day parlor, as usual. In another half-hour or so he would rise, take a bite of lunch, and go upstairs on the arm of a sturdy servant to nap. He sat staring into space, as though contemplating something very difficult. It seemed to absorb his whole mind. Either that, or he was reliving some bit of old history. The servants could never be sure.

A knock at the doorway alerted him. "Yes, what is it?"

"Sire, the right honorable Abbot Henck hopes to speak with you."

A servant ushered in the priest, then helped Jakop struggle to his feet. "Abbot, thank you for calling on me. It is difficult for an old man to travel about. I wanted to speak with someone less tiresome than Father Danelagh." His smile made it into a jest. The count's high regard for Fr. Danelagh was no secret.

"Count, you are always welcome to use our time and service." The abbot took the chair opposite the count, across the small worktable. "What is it that I can assist you with, Jakop?"

"Hanryk, my good friend, it has to do with a most unusual stricture that has come to my notice."

Father Henck raised an eyebrow, feigning ignorance.

Jakop refused to take the bait. "As you know, I have decided to take the Nordwesh lad at face value while he trains for his future life as a royal. To date I've found him a clever and engaging young man."

"Clever? Yes, he is, but sometimes I'm afraid he lets his imagination outrun his judgment."

Jakop let a chuckle leak out. "Hanryk, his imagination can also be a great asset. Some other time I may amuse you with one or two of the outlandish, yet also just and effective, ideas he has put forward."

"Outlandish is as outlandish does, Jakop."

Jakop gave the priest a frank gaze on. "Indeed, my friend, outlandish is as outlandish does."

"Why, Jakop, what do you mean by that?"

160

Influence

"Hanryk, you hold the keys to the Kingdom."

"Yes, of course, by laying on of hands down from Saint Peter." He crossed himself.

"I, my friend, hold the keys to County Vendink and, by extension, to this City."

They locked eyes for several tense moments.

After a lengthy pause Fr. Henck stammered out, "Far be it from me to bind anyone's presence or absence from your demesne, Count."

"You instruct the consciences of everyone in your see, Abbot."

Another tense moment. Father Henck broke the silence. "Jakop, I haven't bound anyone's presence here."

"Removing God's gift of speech within my city from one of your souls, Hanryk, in effect bars him from it."

At length Fr. Henck dropped his eyes. "Count, I take your meaning," he said, and left the room.

*__*__*__*

At the end of the afternoon Klarenz appeared at the confessional just before the evening Mass. It was the custom for Joop, Klarenz, and other servants to mark, in chalk, a symbol for their respective masters, to announce that they would be present to confess in the morning.

Ordowahl had long since taught him the alphabet. It was a shock to discover that Klarenz had difficulty learning to read. Writing wasn't difficult as long as the prince gave him the spellings, so Ordowahl's mark on the slate board consisted of beautiful letters OPN, for Ordowahl, Prince Nordweg. But this afternoon he stood there until the Mass was about to begin and a priest emerged from his side of the booth.

"Father Petur, a word, please," he said.

"Yes, my son, what is it?" The priest had just moments before he would begin the Mass but took the time to hear Klarenz's question.

"My master the prince cannot speak with anyone from the city for a month. Does that include the confessional?"

Father Petur smiled as though he knew a secret. He whispered, "Tell the prince that whispers in the confessional are never

161

disallowed," and turned to go up toward the altar to begin the Mass.

Klarenz caught the man's kind humor and lettered the prince's mark onto the announcements slate. Not having confessed yet himself, he didn't stay for the Mass. He looked for the vice-count's mark. Joop made a kind of numeral 8 laid on its side and said that at her first communion the lady Janalei had told him what it meant. But he would never divulge its meaning.

Klarenz saw the mark and took that bit of information back to Haus Hangendro.

*__*__*__*

Dawn came late in winter. For those attending dawn Mass, receiving the Host into an unsullied stomach also meant a late breakfast. By the start of spring that problem receded. Still hungry, but feeling expectant, Ordowahl, Torwulf and Klarenz reached St. Martin's well before dawn to prevent contact with anyone in line for confession.

Father Henck was in the booth, waiting to hear his two primary penitents, inter alia. Ordowahl entered his half of the booth, and Fr. Henck was waiting. He knew it was the giant prince when the overburdened kneeling bench creaked under his weight.

"Good morning, Prince. We may dispense with anonymity. I have a word for you before you begin."

"Yes, Father, what is it?" Out of force of habit he whispered his question.

"I've given thought to your penance, and have decided that the third part has been met. I will dispense with the rest of the month, lest you stumble here or there."

So he knows I've been in conversation with Utrecht. So be it. "Forgive me, Father, for I have sinned. My first sin was in honoring the letter, but not the spirit of the third part of my penance. I am heartily sorry for it."

"Sometimes, Prince, even the letter is better than one can expect. One Hail Mary. Continue your confession."

Leaving the booth, Ordowahl found Utrecht waiting. He gave her a quiet nod and saw a trace of expectation on her face, as though she were curious about something. *My goodness—she and Jakop must have intervened with Father Henck.* He mumbled "Thank you," and went to stand near the pulpit at the cathedral's center, to hear Fr. Henck's homily during the Mass.

He often found coded messages buried in what the priest said and in what he didn't say. Some of them were personal and unmistakable. Some had to be for other members of Fr. Henck's noble flock. It felt too much like snooping, but in the case of Vice-Count Utrecht, he couldn't keep his curious mind in check.

Where she was concerned, nothing ever came, beyond tantalizing hints. Today was different. He watched the vice-count out of the corner of his eye. *Aha. The count, as lay authority, took a risk in challenging Church authority and was fortunate.* This time. *That old fox. And Jakop is another. I can learn so much from both of them. I wonder just how far I can push Father Henck on the traditions of men.*

Regardless that a "friendship" won't occur,

the prince appears to stand on solid ground.

Less often does he see her manner blur

from clear to icy, arch-smiled runaround.

 The difference is small, but dignified

 to deal with Utrecht when, if with ill will,

 she brief unbars approach to'er female side,

 e'en goes so far as tease him for a skill.

The greater skill belongs to Jakop, Count,

who counters Bishop Henck re Ordowahl.

The prince aspires some future day to mount

up half that heft of wit, sly wherewithal.

 Where is he now? What new thing happens next?

 Whatever it may be, he's lesser vexed.

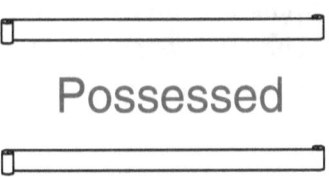

Possessed

One overcast morning in early April Ordowahl found Utrecht at the castle gate, but dressed in rough leather. She even wore a fleece-lined jacket, the sort a wealthy peasant might wear while cutting wood on a hillside.

He arrived, in time to see maid-in-waiting Emluyn slink back into the castle, still carrying a handful of ribbons. Before he could say anything, Utrecht hailed him. "Prince! There are reports of a dangerous interloper who has journeyed up from the south. Have you heard anything?"

"My lady Utrecht—"

"Vice-Count!"

"My lady Vice-Count Utrecht," he said, winking at her expression of distaste, "last night Heri and Wils were discussing a story like that, but their details were few. What do you know?"

"My lord Prince Nordweg, he has come up from County Breihoff through Barony Zollhuysen, and appeared yesterday afternoon in Barony Maihoff. I'm sure you met Baron Maihoff at one of the Christmas events"—her eyebrow went up—"while you were so enamored of Breihoff's niece, the lady Ariana."

He ignored the side topic and dismounted, handing the reins to Klarenz. He asked, "Has Jophan given you anything more specific?"

"I'm afraid not. The fellow is reported to be demon-possessed, ruthless and violent. *Like* the devil, he's also difficult to track down.

He shows up, takes what he can carry away, and disappears."

"Hmmm. Barony Maihoff is broken up by patches of marsh and unarable woodlands. This fellow sounds like someone who has found the ability to stay hidden except for short forays. What about hunting dogs?"

"Brilliant as always, Nordweg. The fellow knows ways to avoid leaving much of a scent trail—"

"A good dog, Utrecht, can recognize and follow almost any novel scent."

"—and is adept at disguising himself with peppered shoes then leaping into water to wash the pepper off."

"So by looking for partial trails of peppered shoes—and it strikes me that pepper is a very expensive disguise for a man's scent—there must be a pattern in where and whom he robs."

"Again, brilliant. How else did we know that he was going to come through Maihoff next?" She gave him a skeptical leer.

"The trail of theft would tell as much. What sort of small camps has he left? He must sleep from time to time."

"You managed to find a tiny bird's nest."

"As can any boy of five or six years."

"This time let us hope you can find a man's nest."

Ordowahl laughed. "So often dismissed with a sarcasm, and able to do things no one else can?"

"No other adult, at least."

They reached Haus Maihoff at noon and shared a light meal with Jophan and his wife Karyn. Two small children, perhaps three and five years old, were too curious to leave them alone and too cautious to come very close. They lifted Ordowahl's mood. Utrecht wrinkled her brow but smiled.

Over warmed wine they got down to the details of the latest place the fellow had appeared.

Jophan answered. "From what Zollhuysen says—my neighbor baron in County Breihoff—the fellow has only one trait. He waits until no one is looking, just at dusk. He coats the bottoms of his shoes with pepper. If the village has dogs, they smell the pepper on his feet and for some reason ignore him."

Utrecht looked askance at that. "Really? Do they think he is a servant from the Count's kitchen and should not be challenged?"

Jophan chuckled at that one. "Jani—er, Utrecht, your guess is the best I've heard. But he is quiet, dashes in to seize whatever looks easy to carry, and is gone before anyone can tell where he went."

Ordowahl asked, "If he is such a small and moving nuisance, why does he need a baron and a vice-count to put a stop to him?"

Utrecht answered that. "Because if he is seen, he also kills the one who sees him. No one can tell whether he's three feet tall or seven." She jerked her head at Ordowahl.

In early afternoon the party found the prior night's aftermath. A fresh grave showed that the "possessed one" had killed a young wife who tried to guard her pan of supper biscuits. Her weeping husband said the man had run his knife into the lower part of her torso and sawed upward to her ribs.

A collection of huts—shelters of branches and reeds plastered with annual layers of mud mixed with straw—surrounded a dirt common area and a small well. A priest was there praying over the fresh grave. He tried to console the husband, who cradled a son just old enough to wean. Both wept. A woman who happened to have a nursing infant of her own took the toddler to give him the comfort of a teat.

Ordowahl waited while Jophan conferred in hushed tones with the village elder. He returned with a story about seeing the fellow disappear in the direction of a nearby marsh. A few trees grew on a bit of dry ground out in its middle.

"Prince," he said, "it is simple to deduce where the man has gone to ground, but how do you propose to confront him? Your weight alone could well bury you knee deep in a muddy spot."

"Utrecht? What are your thoughts?" asked Ordowahl.

"It wouldn't do to make wooden plates to go under your boots to keep you atop that wet stuff," she muttered.

"Let me look for the fellow's footprints. While the people in the village have destroyed his trail where it leaves the village, I may be able to pick it up farther on. If he can trek the marsh, perhaps I can, too."

Without saying more, the prince looked in the direction toward the marsh, went to the victim's hut, and began to walk with slow, deliberate steps. He took a step, then looked up to scan the ground for several feet in front of him and choose where to step next.

Utrecht and Jophan had been consoling the villagers, who had gathered to absorb both their baron's good will and his strength of heart. They stared in awe at the huge, ominous prince.

Ordowahl studied the ground the way a woman might study a garment, looking for that last flea. He made a slow zigzag, taking a quarter hour to go fifty yards toward the distant marsh.

Utrecht turned to gauge his progress. Rather than send him a jibe, she considered his diligence in poring over the ground and how much reverence the villagers showed all three of their noble visitors. She nudged Jophan, who took his own look at the prince.

Jophan turned to the villagers then and told all of them it was time to return to their labors. He didn't care to have them starve, after all. He and Utrecht stood side by side, watching Ordowahl for another quarter hour. By this time he seemed to have a better idea of where the intruder may have walked.

He stopped, turned back to look, and waved at them. "Come see this," he said. He didn't seem excited, but they trotted over to where he was.

"Look." He pointed at a small depression surrounded by bent grass. "What does this tell you about our possessed man? What sort of foot, and what weight?" He was squatting on one foot with the other leg stretched out, looking casual.

They bent down for a close look. "You tell us, Ordowahl. Why should we have to provide all your answers?" said Utrecht, with a serious look bordering on scorn.

"I believe he is of ordinary size, a few inches above five feet tall, well muscled but with little fat, and has an average-sized foot."

They looked at him as if he had made that up on the spot.

He expected as much and warned them to maintain silence "If I can hear you, I'll have to stop until you've gone back to the village."

Utrecht frowned at that, both out of concern that the prince might find himself in trouble with the demonic fellow, and because she didn't appreciate anyone giving her instructions. She and Jophan stood up.

"What's your wish, Baron?" she asked.

"Vice-Count, I will arm myself with sword and knife and try to keep him in sight. What will you do?"

With her usual stare of command she said, "I'll keep you in sight and carry a weapon of my own."

Ordowahl frowned at that but knew better than to object. "Very well then," he said. He turned to peer at the ground in front of the footstep. He guessed that it was the man's right foot, so he looked one running step ahead and a bit to the left.

Finding it, he had an example of the man's stride and looked ahead on the right. Within minutes had reached a patch of bushes. He scanned for, and found, a broken twig to project where the man would have headed next.

In moments Utrecht reached that bush, trying to keep Jophan in sight. Her heart was in her mouth. Her voice quiet, she uttered a prayer. "Almighty God, please keep Jophan safe, and for that matter the prince. I've seen him come back from danger with others' blood on him. Let it be so again. Do not tempt me to cringe, Lord, but please keep these eyes and ears open and sharp."

By mid-afternoon Ordowahl knew that he was closing in on the madman. *He should have traveled away from here after killing the woman. He is crazed but not foolish.* He took care to be silent and listened both forward and behind to be sure Jophan didn't alert their prey. He also needed to keep Jophan in sight. He had instructed the baron to avoid letting the man flank them, and to keep Utrecht in mind as well.

Then he found it, and not in the marsh. *A natural glen, bushes cut with a knife, not a hatchet. Green for a day or two, so good cover. He is a clever fellow, give him that.*

He recognized the bones of a rabbit and perhaps a robin. Both fur and feathers had gone with the fellow, explaining why he had come back to the camp instead of fleeing. He saw the pan that had held the biscuits, probably deemed less useful.

"Halloo!" he called at Jophan. "He ran away last night." When they reached him he showed them the abandoned camp

After returning to the village with Jophan and Utrecht he released the entire party and rode Hammerfoot out to the abandoned campsite. The fellow hadn't taken care to hide his footprints as he fled across the moist spring grasses and not-yet-plowed fields. Ordowahl atop Hammerfoot covered several miles in about an hour. The track seemed likely to pass near Haus Maihoff, and he would reach that point about the time Utrecht and Jophan reached the Haus. It gave him some worry.

The fellow's tracks took Ordowahl into a marshy area. This one had bushes, out near the middle. Trekking under yesterday evening's patchy light of a few stars and a moon low in the sky, the fellow must have stumbled across this place and used it, knowing he'd traversed a watery bog.

"Well, Hammerfoot old stud, this is where you need to stay behind for a bit." *And this is where I need to endure being soaked. At least his dunking spot or spots may tell me where not to tread. And I hope he has decided to spend the day resting.*

A splashing sound marked each time a foot came out of the water or went in. Rapid motions of submerged feet generated their own sloshing noises. Bending as low as possible to avoid making much of a profile in the still-bright late afternoon, the giant prince waded through the sopping marsh with all the slow stealth he had.

A quarter hour elapsed before he reached some bushes, still in wet muck, that bordered the tiny island. Pulling himself up onto wet ground would make noise, so he paused. A look back at Hammerfoot, fifty yards distant, showed him placid and grazing.

The prince turned back to cup his ears forward. He detected quiet mumbling, A sudden shout froze him in place. He heard a madman interrogating his devils.

"Why does the world lave shyte upon me? I work and slave and what happens? I am tied at the neck, an animal. No one respects me. In fact the whole damn village is one nest of lies! They torture me with their slack-mouthed filth and untruth. But is anyone else any different? Hah? NO! No one gives a damn, and when I try to let them help me what happens? HAH? Damn jackass bastards try to stop me. They need killing. It's a great pity I didn't kill the whole damn lot of them when I left."

The voice subsided into vague mutters, and Ordowahl stood up. The poor tormented soul had some kind of devil riding him, and he strained his prayer ear toward Heaven, trying to hear a Word telling him, giving him the power to drive the demon out.

He heard none. Evidently that spiritual gift wasn't his to have. The only choice was to confront the man, face to face. If he could carry the fellow back while still living, he would only die at once for his crimes, and not with any mercy. This changed the afternoon from hunting, to haunting, to bleak.

The fellow fell back to muttering against his demons.

In as few strides as he could, Ordowahl went over the bush and through whatever greenery blocked his sight of the madman. He began his own monologue: "I never met a fellow as damnable as one valuing others' lives lower than his own." He repeated it as though memorizing a litany. Ordowahl hoped the fellow's mood would get him to reply the same way he might to anyone so unwise as to dispute a plain truth.

In moments the madman did appear, a young fellow of average height and body, gripping a bloody knife and yelling. "*You shut your Satan-serving arse mouth* whoreson pig swiver God *commands* me to carve your *curdled* face and stop up your dung-smeared *prick hole mouth...*" When perhaps twenty feet away the fellow noticed that Ordowahl would make two of him, with muscle and bone left over.

His jaw dropped, but he saw that his accuser carried no weapon. "YAAAHHHH!" he screamed while lunging forward with his knife held straight out. The madman had no hesitation anywhere in him. He was accustomed to using the knife to kill and was about to drive it into any of several vulnerable spots—liver, gut, groin, leg.

The prince had planted his feet in the soft ground. He relaxed and focused on the knife. At the last split second he twitched right, spun left, and grabbed the man's fist. The struggle was brief, and Ordowahl felt less regret than sadness when he drove the attacking arm, and knife, back into the madman's belly. He pressed it deep

171

and sawed a long slice.

He waited for the bleeding to stop. With gentleness toward something that once held a soul God loved, he lifted the corpse by the rope that had served as a belt. He carried the mortal remains through the marsh back to Hammerfoot. On the way he washed the knife and did what he could to splash clotted blood off both the man's torso and his own pantaloons.

Afternoon had gone to dusk when Ordowahl appeared at the Haus Maihoff gate. Klarenz met him in the stable to curry and feed Hammerfoot. Ordowahl dropped the madman's body at the side entrance, where a servant could handle it

He went in and gave Jophan and Utrecht a brief account. She stared at his blood-smeared groin, but said nothing.

Alone, he traced the madman's hasty track.

Alone, he faced the dregs of damaged mind.

Alone, he brought the vacant body back.

Alone, he got to "done" from "undefined."

     The baron and the vice-count knew full well

     the depth of human pain, the lonely muck

     a soul contrives when life's a wretched shell.

     The prince's task was simply his bad luck.

The prince and vice-count each were worried sore

that harm would fall on 'tother, yet without

a conscious thought of whether any more

than common human kindness had peeked out.

     So how do prince and vice-count do tomorrow?

     Wait and see. Let fortune field its sorrow.

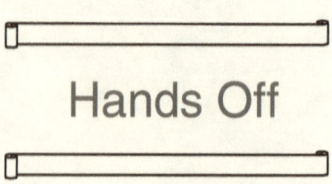

Hands Off

Bustling preparation filled the month of April. Barony Hangendro's grand festival would unroll across County Vendink's social scene on the celebratory first day of May. Klarenz seemed hard to find, but when Ordowahl had asked Fretheldin several times during the month, she just smiled.

Guests began arriving one or more days ahead of the event. Through it all, Fretheldin, Heri and Wils provided gracious attention plus much food and drink.

At dawn on the great day Prince Ordowahl stood watching the commotion. *Last night I am certain that I drank overmuch. It's been too long and I lost the ability to judge when to stop. I certainly hope that Lady Janalei has had time to recover her pique.*

Heri stood in the main hall amid servants making last-minute preparations. He chortled to himself, "Today, the first day of May in the year of our Lord one thousand one-and-seventy, Count Jakop, in the person of Vice-Count Utrecht as his agent, invests me as Baron Hangendro."

The day would begin with a mime show acting out, in the most reverent and dignified manner, the story of Jesus' miracles, culminating with the Feeding of the Five Thousand. That one would unfold into the midday feast.

Heri had gone down early to greet his guests, most of whom had arrived the prior night.

"Prince!" he said, when he saw Ordowahl. "What a magnificent gift, Klarenz's very large, many-colored woven tapestry. When it was unrolled yesterday, you saw me at once give it a place of honor in the main hall. I am very, very happy to have it, Prince."

"Baron," said Ordowahl. "I felt awe when I saw what Klarenz had helped to make. When it was complete he tried to describe the changes he wrought to widen the weavers' loom and strengthen it to bear the extra weight of yarn." He gave Heri's back a tap.

"Prince, you still have much to teach me," he said with a smile. He turned and addressed the next to come down. "Vice-Count. I hope that you are well this morning."

Utrecht gave him a formal smile, paused to clasp hands, and walked past Ordowahl without a glance. She made a "come with me" signal via a finger-wag hidden from Heri's view. Torwulf and Klarenz were occupied elsewhere. Ordowahl followed her out into the courtyard to a spot among the near-herd of horses filling the yard. She stopped and turned toward him, looking at him with the accusatory disgust she might use to discipline a footman caught having sex in an upstairs bedchamber.

How drunk was I, and how drunk was she, and I know what I did.

"How many times have I told you not to make yourself part of Lady Janalei's social life?" She poked him in the chest as hard as she could.

"Utrecht, my friend, I'm sorry if I—"

Another poke. "Sorry, my arse! You were clearly drunk. If I can't trust you at all when you are tipsy, Nordweg, I can't trust you enough at other times."

"I do remember Lord Iosefus putting his hands on—"

A third poke. "So? Has no one ever tried to lay hands on a woman before? And is Lady Janalei so hateful that no one has ever laid hands on her?"

If I say she's tempting, she will take it badly, and if not, she will feel insulted. "Is there a safe answer to that?"

"Men! So bold, yet so worried about a safe answer to a *rhetorical* question. But, *Prince*, there is much more at stake than intruding on Lady Janalei's endurance of a fawning sixteen-year-old boy. Or do you find a perverse joy in telling someone else's child what to do?"

This isn't the same as defending my sister Ruta against an unwanted approach. OH! And as Janalei is now, Ruta was also loudly angry then.

"Yes, it's best you keep silent. Dismissing poor Iosefus was despicable, but Lady Janalei would have overlooked it."

"What offense did I commit?" *I* know *what it was. I laid a hand on Lady Janalei myself, a simple reassuring hand on her hip—ohhh, my hand fit there as though her hip were created just for my touch.*

"Always the innocent! You are so transparent and were so very inappropriate. You took possession of Lady Janalei as though she were your betrothed."

"I, ahh, um—"

"Do I listen now to a fumbling oaf? By all the saints and scoundrels, Nordweg, if you had wanted to court Lady Janalei you knew the answer. *No!* So instead you pretend protection just to stage a sly assault on her person. The outrage, Lady Janalei's body being pawed *by you,* is fresh in her memory."

"Utrecht, I apologize. Please forgive me. I confess, the gesture wasn't one I thought through."

"Gesture! Hah! Fondle, yes. Take your illicit protection and your condescending fakery away from here."

"How—"

"While you remain Hangendro's guest, your presence in their Haus is secure. My own presence and Lady Janalei's, to honor Heri, is required, although now also disgusting. From this point onward you can no longer inflict yourself on me, much less Lady Janalei."

She turned on her heel and stalked back into Haus Hangendro. Over her shoulder she said, "Just stay away!"

Ordowahl felt incapable of moving, so he simply stood there in the slanted early morning sunlight. *Father God in heaven, existing in this city without Utrecht's companionship makes me like a bush of thorns growing in the middle of the town square—better yet, in the most dry, stony place there is. I know she is beyond courting yet I treated her as a familiar woman. Would that she were! Guide me, Father. I am bereft.*

*__*__*__*

Heri had persuaded Wils to don a simple but majestic white robe and play Jesus. He was in every scene, surrounded by players in costumes that covered the rainbow.

Romans wore red tunics, Pharisees and Sadducees shades of blue, tax collectors pied in conflicting shades of green, merchants brown. Peasants wore gray sackcloth and went barefoot, even given that the season remained cold. A clear sky blessed the day.

Wils showed no fear of anyone's suspicion of impiety. His Jesus was serene, and Wils mum. An actor behind the painted scene spoke Jesus' lines. Wils had coached the man to be sure that his Jesus was elevated and reverable.

At the feeding of the five thousand, instead of trying to break loaves and fishes, Wils stood at the main hall doors and beckoned in all the guests.

Utrecht was among the first to arrive, with Joop in tow. Heri held places at the head table for his mother, on his left, with Ordowahl next to her. He sat Wils to his right, with Vice-Count Utrecht next to Wils.

All servants hugged the wall behind their masters. A maid and two footmen separated Klarenz and Joop. The two shared brief snatches of conversation as first one, then the other stepped forward to assist his master.

When it was Klarenz's turn to serve his master wine, he whispered into the prince's ear. "Utrecht is on the verge of asking her father to send you away but will let things cool a bit first."

Ordowahl whispered a quiet "Good job" but did not allow his face to betray that he or Klarenz had exchanged anything more than the customary "More wine, Prince?"

At length Heri rose from the meal to head a reception line for his baronets and landed knights. Each knelt to kiss his signature ring. Ordowahl already knew most of them.

While Heri was accepting these tributes, a second line formed behind him. He knew the protocol; after receiving tributes and loyalties, he turned around. In ascending order of seniority he went down the line of his fellow barons. Each greeted him with warmth and spent time letting him know that the Vendink barons had assembled to include him as its newest brother. Each also told one of the myriad embarrassing stories of Heri's exploits and excesses. Jophan, Baron Maihoff, told the first and best one.

Making a long story short, Jophan had just come of age at seventeen years. He and the eight-year-old twins were hiking in the woods, in springtime, and came across a bear with tiny cubs. Heri rushed forward and leaped onto a rock shielded by brush. The bear perceived a being six feet tall. Heri waved his arms and shouted, the bear ran away, and Jophan caught him like a sack of potatoes when he jumped back down from the rock.

The story was well known, but the listeners took it seriously. Heri, Wils, and Jophan might all have died there. But the eight-year-old Heri had claimed that he wanted the bear to fear him.

Utrecht stood at the end of the line, senior to her barons. Jophan stood at the other end, before today the junior-most. Utrecht said, "Fear? More like bore the poor thing to tears," but the jibe was old so everyone laughed politely. No one noticed that Utrecht was far less ebullient than usual. She saw Ordowahl and Jophan exchange greetings and pledge to meet later to become better acquainted. Her smile vanished, leaving a flat line for a mouth.

Before Heri could reach her to receive the count's deputized and formal welcome, she turned and walked away. Everyone was so taken by the effect of Ordowahl's presence that no one noticed her snub of Heri. Half an hour passed before anyone noticed.

*__*__*__*

At morning Mass Utrecht left the confessional booth as Ordowahl approached it. Her immobile features reminded him of frost. In the booth Fr. Henck cautioned him. "Please be sure to include your sin of assault, Prince."

After the Mass and breakfast with the fathers, he spent time learning their views on the early parts of the Book of Revelation before he excused himself. He found Utrecht and Joop gone from the castle and went in alone to call on Jakop. The head butler

178

showed no surprise. The count must have told him to expect the prince.

He went into the small dayroom, got the count's attention, and took a seat across the small worktable. "Count—"

"Prince." Count Jakop's quick, cold tone stopped him. "You have managed to throw my daughter into some kind of state. I anticipated that this might happen, and of course she asked me to cut off your access to her. But when I said that it would be no problem, she did something odd."

"Count, I—"

"No matter, Ordowahl. I heard that you were drunk, that after you took it on yourself to send away the clumsy sixteen-year-old Lord Iosefus you put an arm around Lady Janalei and let your hand fall onto her hip."

Ordowahl hung his head. "Yes, Count. I did do that."

Jakop chuckled. "Who would not? She makes every man a moth to her candle. If I had been there and seen a need to send someone away from her, I would have put a father's hand on her, and she would have leaned into me, because we adore each other. Not as man and woman, but as father and child."

"Yes, I'm aware of the feeling that passes between you."

"And, come to think of it, she's now a grown woman. She'd turn and wag a finger at me for thinking she needed the help. But in your case, that wasn't a father's hand."

"I take your point."

"This morning she came to me and did much more than wag a finger, Prince." Jakop's expression had gone serious.

Ordowahl dropped his head farther then turned his face up toward the Count. Being so tall, this amounted to a token gesture. He knew a second shoe would drop.

"Shall I go on?"

Ordowahl's face went white.

"I am very protective of my daughter." The count's face looked unforgiving. "Whatever is going on between you two, it troubles her. Very much. As I told you, this morning she wanted me to banish you, and I agreed as though to a simple request, not deserving a second thought."

Jakop gave Ordowahl a hard look. "She showed a level of helpless anger that I have never seen before. You have an odd power to affect her. Yet when I agreed, she seemed flustered. Something is going on, young man, and while it's due more to her than to you, I don't like the effect. You, and Klarenz, will absent yourselves from this city for a month. Find a confessor nearer to Haus Hangendro and attend Mass there."

Ordowahl sat there, mute.

"You may show yourself out," said Jakop, and he went back to what he had been doing.

Ordowahl didn't hear the count's faint chuckle.

That afternoon found Ordowahl making his own journey into springtime woods. He delegated the task of leading his pupils through martial drill to Torwulf. *Even though the trees and bushes and grasses are all different, woods are woods. What injustice it is to say I am alone, when the birds and animals God created surround me? Adam named them and didn't know that, except for the Presence of God, he was as alone as anyone, ever. Would that I felt that Presence now, in fact. At least Adam didn't rue the lack of a companion he'd never had.*

Do I dismiss Heri, Wils, Fretheldin, Torwulf, and Klarenz from the company of men, to call myself "alone"? Truly I am not. Yet I am cast out. Utrecht can be in base terms aggressive, abrasive, always ready to poke at something. Yet there seems a hidden twinkle behind every jape, every arch-browed insult. Father in heaven, I miss her company.

Why is that? It's not as though we are sweethearts, or even smile at each other. But, night before last, while I could tell that she was at least as annoyed at me as she was at Iosefus, for the briefest moment she did lean into me, before she rebounded and drove an elbow into my rib. I only hope she didn't add to my sin by bruising her elbow.

Father, help me understand what is happening. In Nordweg I could speak frankly with Elspet, daughter of the village thane. She was like an aunt to me. I had a female friend. And I, even as one of twelve children, would have felt alone without that!

When I found Klarenz and realized he had broken Elspet's heart, I made him expiate that guilt by binding himself to me. Yet despite my sin in doing that to a half-innocent man, you gave me him a as wonderful gift.

Since coming of age I've had women in my bed many times, yet just one met me there in friendship. She didn't want something from me first. Well—the rest, we exchanged favors, if you will. My body longs for more of that, yet because I know it would upset Utrecht, I forbear.

Ha! As if anything could harm her. She shows both the tender vulnerability of a fifty-foot oak and the soft mystery of a summer's night. How can I compare her to Gelde, a grandmother, who taught me so much about simple friendship, companionship along with her bedtime intimacy? When the candle is out, a woman is a woman is a woman. Too few understand that. And most young people have no idea of the depth of that woman's soul.

For the first time, Father, I had both a woman to couple with freely and a close friend. That made becoming one flesh so, in a word, significant. So what now? I act the old man trapped in a young man's body, reminiscing past joys now held unavailable, as though more may never be. How can this stand?!

Beneath Utrecht's jibes and harsh looks, I find a friendship that goes to my bones. I know it by the way I feel whenever we are in the same place. In the brief moment when my hand lay on her hip, it seemed to complete something. It was as though a barrier between us had fallen.

Now, the friendship is gone to frozen mud, and the count turns me away. Yet, heavenly Father, just as a Christian has the sure hope of salvation, I feel the sure hope that You will help me endure this. Amen.

For the ensuing month Ordowahl said nothing more than simple politeness required. He remained present to his martial arts pupils. Everyone else understood that his banishment dropped a net of grief over him that weighed on him far more than Heri's cargo net, and no knife to sever its ropes. They left him to his private misery.

Daily exercise and martial drills became fierce, sweat flying. Ordowahl stopped only when all strength was gone. Exhausting the body brought balm for the soul. The one companion he turned to was Hammerfoot, a stallion who at least had been to stud—a lot. They sometimes ranged far and returned late. Each night the prince's exhaustion gave him sleep without dreams.

The month ended. He tried to imagine an encounter with Utrecht, on the morrow. *Father, in the Psalms I find this:* "Let my soul praise Thee, and let Thy judgments help me. I have gone astray like a lost sheep: seek your servant, for I do not forget your commandments." *Surely by offending Lady Janalei I offended You. Please comfort me now and help me give You praise.*

They've been apart, but Ordo only knows

that he has suffered, guesses Utrecht's been

at peace. So should he move away? Suppose

he leaves without a word? Lord, no! Amen.

    Unfailing comes the prince, his welcome—what?

    But as a man he knows the crisis must

    be met, else he is not a man. Clear-cut

    his duty—life is short, and dust to dust.

He's purged his soul and expiated guilt,

at least in his own eyes. So, what of her?

Might stab him with hard anger, to the hilt?

His inner sense has told him, don't demur.

    His exile done, his thirty days elapse.

    The next part of his life ? Who knows? Perhaps.

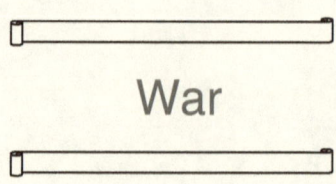

War

Spring expanded into frequent rains and heat. Each muggy day began with a dewy, humid dawn. Ordowahl felt trepidation at his return to the city and to Utrecht. On the second day of June, the day his exile ended, Prince Ordowahl arrived to find her in a sour mood.

When he dismounted she said nothing. Mute and frowning, she handed him a parchment bearing a wax seal. The seal belonged to adjoining County Jaagrmur, to the northeast. "What do you make of this?" he asked, after reading it. "Its date is five days ago. When did it arrive?"

"Last night, an hour after sunset. That pleasant-seeming county hides a man whose habit is to push against his neighbors with one aim, to expand his holdings. Can you guess why he would do this now?"

"Vice-Count, a very aged count with a daughter ruling in his stead? The question is less 'why now' than 'why not.' Do you take insult in being assessed as daughter?"

"I'm inured to it." Her flat face didn't say "accommodated."

The prince nodded. "But I take insult from his evident failure to include a huge obstacle in his planning. And no, not you—me."

She appeared to ignore the blasé assessment that he had even greater cause to take offense. "When you read his letter of demand, name the strengths and weaknesses you find."

"Point by point, he writes: First, that your father Jakop confess to lechery."

"Not an issue."

"Second, that your father's taste in debauch runs to ten-year-old baronets' daughters."

"I can think of a baronet whose habits stray there, but otherwise a bare-faced lie."

"That he pay damages for the alleged offenses by ceding three baronies which happen to abut County Jaagrmur."

"Never."

"Of course. Fourth, he alleges that lines of inheritance over the past half-dozen generations include so much of his County's bloodlines that these three baronies should already be part of County Jaagrmur."

"Marriage across county lines is common. By his token County Vendink has a greater claim to his than he to mine."

"And last, he demands back-payment of revenues from those three baronies, the sum being enormous."

"Yes, Prince, it would take all of what County Vendink has on hand in coin, gold, silver, and gems."

"He concludes his demands with a date certain. You must answer him by settling this debt no later than tomorrow at noon, including the formal ownership of the three baronies and many abject apologies."

"Again, *never*. I have spent enough time with Count Jakop to intuit what Jaagrmur is doing. I expect him to be in full trespass of at least one of those three baronies already. So, my friend, ask how you can help."

My friend? By comparison Jaagrmur is a simple man. "Utrecht, you need information on the disposition and numbers of his armed men. The Hangendro estates lie at an angle to the path toward Jaagrmur. I will go there to bring Sir Torwulf with me."

"And?"

"It will help if you send someone with me who knows the county lanes and roads, to find the best route to the baronies he mentions."

"Joop."

"Then, Vice-Count, I would leave the barons' degrees of loyalty for later. One is easy for many to overpower, thus one or more of them may already have surrendered in principal."

"Prince, it's never pleasant to have a volunteer give himself orders, but in this case, you've only stated the obvious. Go, and I expect your return by noon."

Traveling at a steady canter brought Joop, Klarenz, and Ordowahl to Haus Hangendro in half an hour. After giving the horses half a brief rest they set out again.

Torwulf exulted that he would be giving his liege active service. Joop led them to the middle barony of the three, the likeliest place Count Jaagrmur might be. Ninety minutes' travel, varied between canter and walk, brought them to a nondescript junction of two lanes.

"Masters, County Jaagrmur lies northeast. This lane runs northwest to southeast along the inner side of the three baronies that abut County Jaagrmur, also the ones he claims."

"Joop, visit the barony northwest of here. Klarenz and Torwulf, see to the barony southeastward." They parted company, and Ordowahl went forward to examine the center.

Within minutes Hammerfoot showed excitement. *I can't tell much yet, but he seems to scent other horses, oiled metal, and leather. He scents action.* He let the horse pick its way but held to a slow walk until he could sense something himself. He found a copse of saplings, which would at least break up his outline. He halted Hammerfoot behind it to wait for Jaagrmur's men to become more distinct. Soon enough he could make out someone who had to be Jaagrmur, flanked by two barons on either side and, counting carefully, seven more behind them.

That number seems too small. County Jaagrmur consists of seventeen baronies, at last count. He could already have flanking groups, before he's even spotted anyone.

Ordowahl rode out. Wordless, he stopped when fifty feet from them. The count advanced to within a horse's length, as though that were a safe distance. They eyed each other for a moment.

Ordowahl broke the silence. "Today is Monday, my noble friend."

"Do you challenge me?"

"I state a fact, Count. Do facts challenge you?"

"Impudent wretch. I will have a brace of archers send a dozen arrows into you before you manage to fall off your horse."

"I think not, since your declaration of war upon County Vendink is alleged to begin tomorrow, and you stand today on the lands of Jakop Count Vendink."

Jaagrmur spat on the ground. "That scoundrel."

"I, Ordowahl, Prince of Nordweg, challenge you to fight here to establish which of us has better right to stand on this ground."

"I've heard of your supposed prowess, Prince. I believe you capable of going into the woods of an afternoon and returning with a bird's nest slung in a tiny basket of woven grass. What else can you do that may surprise me?"

"I am ready to answer your curiosity, but I bid you retreat to your own border, now, and await an embassy from Count Jakop at noon tomorrow."

"You bid me? Yes, Prince, you surprise me, but only for your poor taste in threats."

"I bid you, Count, without speaking a threat. Consider your position. You are under a challenge and cannot, with any shred of honor, attempt—"

An arrow whistled by Ordowahl's ear, so close that he felt lucky not to have it bleed. In the moment he spurred Hammerfoot and charged the count, who shied away. As he passed by, his sword came out, flew up, and slashed Jaagrmur's mount at the throat. The horse reared up in panic then faltered from the mortal wound.

Ordowahl spun Hammerfoot around, leapt off, and grabbed the astonished count around the midsection with his free arm, yanking him off the failing steed. He turned the count to face his barons.

"Count Jaagrmur," he called out in his best bass roar, "bring me the archer who loosed that shaft." In a conversational voice he added, "Having such a bad marksman in your company has put you at personal risk. I suggest you bring him here now."

The count tried at first to struggle but lacked a foot in height and eight stone in weight. One enormous bicep, forearm, and hand pinned him to a hard chest. His feet dangled above the sod. Ordowahl's other arm still wielded a dripping sword. Pressure on the count's midsection made it impossible to breathe, and his flailing arms began to sag.

Ordowahl eased the pressure. *If the count goes inert, he'll stop being a shield and become the reason for a massed charge.* "Tell them."

Careful to draw a full breath, the count called out his archery master. "Blenck! Send me the fool who loosed that shaft."

"Do I have your parole, Count? I will place you on your feet when you pledge safety to me and free passage away from this field."

The count paused for a moment, unready to yield, but also unwilling to stay to be crushed by Ordowahl's arm.

"You're taking too long, Count. Now I add the demand that you return now to your titled lands. Jakop Count Vendink will send an envoy to meet you at the boundary between this barony and its neighbor in your county, tomorrow at noon."

He kept his grip loose enough for the count to breathe lightly but making sure the count knew he was still helpless.

"Blenck!" shouted the count. "Send me the fool, lest I judge you to be the greater one!" He spoke over his shoulder to Ordowahl, in a quiet voice.

"Yes, Prince, I grant you safe passage between here and whatever road you took to come here. You and I will settle the cost of my stallion another day."

"And the parlay tomorrow at noon." Ordowahl made it a statement of fact.

"Yes."

"Here comes your archer. You may stand on your own feet." He lowered the count, with genteel courtesy after the manhandling, and added, "Your life depends on your army's calm. I applaud their discipline."

Count Jaagrmur turned around to look up into young but stony eyes. He looked over his shoulder to see the archer, who stopped in front of him. "Blenck!" he shouted. "Put this man on half rations." He waved the terrified archer away then turned to look with some pity at the carcass of his neck-slashed horse. It had bled out.

He stepped closer to look at what Ordowahl's sword had done. "I want a thousand swords like that one. You may go now." He turned to face his barons again and told them, "Safe passage for Prince Ordowahl from this spot. Someone get me a horse."

Ordowahl remounted Hammerfoot and looked at the Jaagrmur barons. "After you," he said, and waited for them to leave.

Joop and Torwulf had heard faint echoes of Ordowahl shouting. Each went back to where they had parted company and waited for him to return. No voice but his could have made those sounds, or the dire threat they conveyed. Almost as soon as they met they could see Ordowahl coming toward them through a pasture.

"Hail, Prince," said Torwulf. "What news?"

"Sir Torwulf, Joop, I made the acquaintance of the count, not far from here, and we had a small exchange of unpleasantries."

Torwulf beamed and said, "Jests upon returning from possible death."

"One of their archers lost an arrow, and the count seems to have suffered the death of his mount. A most pitiable sight." He paused. A droop in his shoulder proved that he felt the horse's death as a personal slip.

"The count will meet Count Jakop's envoy tomorrow, at noon, at the boundary between his lands and County Vendink, perhaps three miles that way," and he waved back the way he had come. "I pray the vice-count finds this development encouraging."

*__*__*__*

At noon of the still chilly spring day four riders returned on tired horses. Joop and Klarenz walked them back to the stables. Utrecht met them at the castle gate.

"Sir Torwulf, Prince, please come to table. Cook has hot food, which I imagine you'll enjoy." *They seem to have worked hard. Learning what they've discovered can wait until after we've broken bread together.*

Once their hunger had fallen, she asked, "So, Prince, what did you discover?"

"The feet of the count, plus nine of his barons and a host of armed men, on the soil of Barony Fleischgeber."

"Did they see you?"

"I showed myself to them and discussed their trespass. They saw reason and await an envoy from County Vendink at noon tomorrow, on the boundary between Barony Fleischgeber and the Jaagrmur barony which abuts it."

She looked at him for a moment. "Prince? The aggressive Count Jaagrmur, in company with nine of his barons and hundreds of armed men, turned around and left. What did you do, sing them a lullaby?"

"Not quite a song, Utrecht. I did raise my voice. Also, after one of their archers sent a shaft past my head, I managed to unhorse the count and wrap him in a close and embrace."

I know what Mother thinks of close embraces. Enough! Nothing to think about there! "Hmmph. Close, indeed."

"Simple diplomacy and tact brought about your appointment tomorrow. I do believe that you plan to be your father's envoy?"

Giving him a cold, annoyed stare, she said, "You dare to arrange a meeting in the name of County Vendink?"

"I expected you to see the advantage this confers and show at least a small thanks to Almighty God that the arrow didn't strike me."

"Would have been simpler, Prince, if it had."

"Yet Vice-Count Utrecht is never given to the simple, is she? If I ever find forgiveness for today's sin, Utrecht, you may also thank me for halting a large invading force."

"Prince, how do you manage to make plain statements of fact sound like arrogant brags?"

"Facts speak for themselves. The tale of Jaagrmur's retreat is one man's word, which you may choose to treat as fact, or not."

"Do you fancy I'll invite you take part in County Vendink's embassy to County Jaagrmur?"

"That, Vice-Count, is yours to decide. I will pray for your safety if I am not there to guard it."

"We're not done, Prince. Last night I sent a courier to Count Marvistjen. He has replied and will have four of his barons at our parlay tomorrow, with all their men."

"It will be good to see them again."

"While it was beyond impertinent to arrange it on your own, I anticipated that you would do as much without consulting me. Yes, Prince, I invite you to observe the talks tomorrow."

"Thank you, Vice-Count."

"I'm sure you will find other men to chat with among Marvistjen's barons. I ask you to wait for an invitation before you speak."

"You always surprise me." She saw his face relax. "I will hold my tongue but may speak if the right questions don't find a voice."

There is no way to silence him! But at times he does see a thing that no one else has, which can be a consolation.

The prince has gone from lout to thorn, but has

at least done all that she expected, and

he ought to understand that she is—as

he hoped for—counting on his steady hand.

    He knows his footing rests on thin, slick ice.

    Her steel confines his "help" to "speak when asked."

    She also has him raised to "making nice"—

    qua male. She's female but that's always masked.

She mentioned Uncle Petur's barons' men;

but counting noses, Jaagrmur has more.

What other shoe will drop? Has Utrecht been

unwise? She's known as Wisdom's metaphor.

    So what has Utrecht done to stabilize?

    Just how has Ordowahl been cut to size?

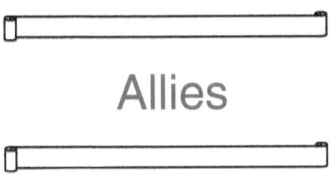

Allies

A simple lane along one edge of Barony Fleischgeber divided County Vendink from County Jaagrmur. Utrecht emerged onto that lane at noon. Four Marvistjen barons came out on her immediate left, five more from County Naechstofen on her right, and interspersed between them eleven of her own. Many, but not all, of their men at arms stood behind them. They appeared to overmatch Jaagrmur's now-fifteen barons' full complement, arrayed behind him.

Jaagrmur had posted scouts along the lane, as had Utrecht, to choose a spot for count and vice-count to meet. Utrecht let her horse take one step forward. Jaagrmur did the same. Each horse took a second step, and they stopped, a horse-length apart.

Ordowahl had been behind her and took her center spot in the line of barons. Prince or not, the Vendink barons ceded it to him without a murmur. He peered into the array of armed men gathered in a cluster behind Jaagrmur. The count had brought knights on armored steeds, and behind them pikemen and swordsmen on foot, but no bowmen that Ordowahl could see.

Ordowahl's heart sank. *Idiot that I am, I made him look the fool before his men. Now he will try to assassinate Utrecht! He has too few bowmen to post one or two in the trees at every spot along two miles of lane, without knowing which spot they'd choose to meet.*

But just a handful of archers can make a fearful difference if he has managed to hide them close by.

Ordowahl listened with half an ear to the formalities passing between Utrecht and Jaagrmur while he peered at each evergreen tree within sight. Fields and half-leaved deciduous trees lined this part of the lane, but two small clusters of yew trees held his attention. *I hope my eyes are on the right one. Murder simplifies so many conflicts!*

Utrecht and Jaagrmur wheeled their mounts around and returned to their respective sets of barons. An arrow flew out of a tree forty yards to Ordowahl's right. Its short flight would be difficult to intercept, but he spurred Hammerfoot forward and thrust his shield out to guard Utrecht. The arrow pierced his shield. Its head almost grazed her neck.

Ordowahl threw the shield on the grass and tried to repeat his move from the prior day, but Jaagrmur had anticipated that. The moment Ordowahl charged to intercept the arrow, four barons, two on either side of Jaagrmur, also charged and shielded their count. Eight more came up behind them.

Ordowahl pulled back on the reins, but not in time for Hammerfoot to collide, chest to chest, with one of those mounts. That horse reared and fell, but an even dozen barons now hemmed him in.

"Now your ransom, *Prince*," sneered Jaagrmur, "will be your mount. I believe his name is Hammerfoot, is it not? I will accept him as fair exchange for the steed you hacked apart yesterday."

Behind the prince's back several volleys of arrows shredded each tree in the group that the arrow had come from. Two archers fell, and a third leapt down and ran to the protection of the nearest group of armed men. At the same moment volleys from the Marvistjen side went into the other knot of trees, and three more bowmen fell. Forty archers strode out onto the lane and trained their bows on Jaagrmur and his knights.

"I am surrounded, Count," said Ordowahl, "but I believe an attack on me, if quick, would still be costly." He wheeled Hammerfoot around and returned to the Vendink lines at a deliberate walk. As he passed Utrecht he muttered, "I saved your life, and you mine. We're even."

She snorted back at him, "Your fault both times!"

He dismounted to retrieve the shield and pulled the arrow from it. The act amazed those who saw it. It cost him visible exertion but still left jaws agape.

Joop accepted the arrow with a small nod of respect and put it into a saddlebag. Utrecht wouldn't break her concentration to deal with so useless a thing as a battered arrow.

She commanded both Ordowahl and her barons. "Come with me. Twenty barons and I will discuss the situation. Prince, yours will be a twenty-second voice. I want your counsel to come last."

Ordowahl cleared his expression and followed behind her. The barons gathered behind the few trees nearby. Utrecht began with a nod at Ordowahl. "Describe yesterday's meeting with Jaagrmur."

"Yesterday the count and I exchanged formalities, and I rebuffed his claims. He expected as much, reasserted them, and came here today to speak with Vice-Count Utrecht."

"Thank you, Prince. Jaagrmur is known to walk over weaker opponents or conquer by direct use of arms, and any of us might do the same."

The barons took this as obvious.

"Naechstofen and Marvistjen barons, try to recall a time when Vendink was not involved and you had encounters with Jaagrmur."

After a moment a Marvistjen baron spoke up. "Vice-Count, when he is well matched he does his best to confuse his opponent, but when bluster and other such tactics fail, he becomes cautious."

Another seconded that idea: "Vice-Count, he's adept at hiding his forces, flanking moves, and ambush such as today's damned archers."

A third added, "But if subterfuge and trickery fail, he adopts a more conciliatory tone, lessens his demands, and once in a while retreats without achieving any of his demands. Even then he seizes some small prize to claim a victory."

"My father's experiences are the same. He has recounted all of them to me, in good detail. It is time to send Jaagrmur home a lesser man." She looked around the group of barons. "Give me your counsel on the material gains we can extort from this asshole."

Ordowahl observed them discussing the idea. His turn came; he asked, "What sort of prizes has he grasped from others? What do your memories tell you?"

Twenty-one pairs of eyes looked at him.

"A man understands his own game. Demand much from him for the needless trouble he has imposed on you, also for his twin assaults on me and on the vice-count."

The ideas began to take root. He looked at Utrecht with a raised eyebrow, as if to ask her the same. She shook her head and turned to the grouped barons.

"Since we have more available to us than the men here, and he has brought all but two of his own barons, we need to discover what he might have in reserve."

Smug faces indicated that their enemy had no neighboring counts or barons he could call on, and that with fifteen of seventeen barons on the field, he'd already deployed all available troops.

"At this stage Count Jakop would think he was bluffing." said Utrecht, "and so do I. At any rate he is not betraying whatever weakness he may have."

A Naechstofen baron said, "At best his two weakest barons stand in reserve. Is he willing to gamble that we have our own reserves hidden nearby?"

"For instance," added Ordowahl, "he could have kept some men out of sight, a mile or so to either side. Where are our reserves, and how long before we can bring them here?"

She scanned all the barons' faces. "I would like you two Marvistjen barons to scout in your direction, and you three nearest Naechstofen barons in your direction. We have agreed to meet again at dawn, which will mean a fight. Try to return before night falls." The five barons she had pointed out left the gathering.

Ordowahl marveled that powerful men twice her age obeyed at once. She had garnered much from her time with her father, to make direct orders and have them received as though her father were speaking. *Watching her, it's as though the old man's younger face has been right here and speaking through her.*

"All of us need to eat well. Prepare food, with enough for tomorrow also. Then get good sleep. Barons, please meet me here at sunset to reevaluate our prospects."

Utrecht pulled Ordowahl aside for a private chat. "Prince," she said in a quiet voice, "Remind me of all the subtleties and misdirections that an unprincipled man such as Jaagrmur, or yourself," she said with a wrinkled smile, "might indulge."

"You are not simple, Utrecht, so at least give yourself credit for basic insight. Imagine a lie that he could invent to make you think something which wasn't true."

"There are so many."

"The lie will contradict his real mood, the readiness of his forces, their numbers and types of weapons, even the spoils he may have promised them. Each answer will appear as its false opposite."

"In other words, reverse what he says and that will be a better idea of the truth."

"He will also lay traps and pitfalls well in advance to delay or injure unwary men rushing into battle, and those are just the first that came to mind. And of course he will present some truths amid the falsehoods. Misbelieve a truth and he will have you there as well."

"As usual, Prince, I ask for information and you provide fog." She sighed. "If you are expert at nighttime strolls you might decide to look for those pitfalls and traps, but not until dark."

"The night makes many things easier."

Damn seducer! But keep your wits, girl. You need him close by. "Jaagrmur will post sentries. In fact, they may flag his traps. Are you ready to play Fairy Toes for me?"

He gave a happy grin, which contorted his oversized face into a devilish mask. He saw her make a tiny cringe.

"My friend Utrecht, if a grin can do that to a brave woman who knows my heart, think what it will do to a stranger, in near-darkness."

Do I know that heart? One moment he seems the cad, the next he terrifies me, then he sees my fear and calms me. Damn damn damn.

How can I stand my ground as Vice-Count when he has such a powerful effect? Damn!

__*__*__*__*

The first-line sentries had positioned themselves within shrubs or under a group of trees, making it possible to circle around and approach from the rear. In the partial moonlight, the grin worked almost too well. He had to clap his hands on men's mouths to muffle inevitable cries of panic.

Each one received a simple gut-punch. A bone-breaking fist slamming into the center of a man's body just beneath the ribs doubled the man over, unable to breathe. The prince hobbled each man's legs with his own belt, stripped the jacket off, muffled his voice with a mouthful of sleeve, and tied his arms.

While it would be simple and effective to break their necks, leave that for daytimes and as a very last resort. I cannot slay a man whose crime is owing service to the wrong count.

Quiet words delivered from inches away swore each one to silence. To make noise would be to die. All of them understood.

Just two watched the Naechstofen end; there were no more. With too much bare ground to cross without being visible, he strolled through the Vendink side and back out to survey the sentries on the Marvistjen section of the line.

After silencing two there, the prince found enough cover to make his way to a nearby Jaagrmur camp. A group of men sat around a fire exchanging the mood-raising banter of men about to face combat. They gave the impression of being ready to fight at dawn—not hours before.

Ordowahl returned near a Marvistjen sentry, scuffled his feet to be heard, and gave the password. The man had heard that the prince had mastered stealth but still jumped at the unexpected noise.

"Good evening, sentry. You will find little traffic coming this way," and walked away without explaining the remark. Before entering Utrecht's command tent he coughed and announced. He found Joop and Emluyn with her, so he was brief.

"No sentries remain near the lane. Inward from there men sit around fires encouraging themselves into a fight-happy mood. They should take position at dawn."

"We, the barons and I, decided that you might have the good fortune to tell us about their preparedness. The disabled sentries, Prince, will be a problem."

"Indeed they will. Sentries watch for part of a night, so when their relief comes there will be great consternation, and the camp will be alerted."

"Why on earth do you want to alert them?" She was aghast.

"It is to be hoped for. The men will lose confidence, then lose more sentries the same way."

"So, Fairy Toes, you'll go back again, maybe dance all night?"

"Yes. It should be simple for the Vendink forces just to march into their camps while the Jaagrmur men are beginning to wake up."

"The moon sets about three hours past midnight, Prince."

"Even so the sky should stay cloudless, so there will be starlight. Walking with careful steps will slow our men, but they have at most a quarter-mile to reach the first set of camps. Do you recall Gideon?"

"Who is he, one of the Norse gods?"

"As written in the Jewish Testament, he led a key battle. It took place long after the Israelites entered the Holy Land, when they were oppressed by the Midianites."

"Midianites."

"The army of Midian lay encamped before Jerusalem, ready to attack in the morning. God chose Gideon and by means of signs He told Gideon to use, Gideon winnowed his ten thousand down to three hundred men. He sent them out to stand in a ring around the enemy camp."

"Three hundred? Against an oppressing nation's might?"

"Gideon blew a horn. At once all three hundred men blew their own horns and broke clay pots in which they had hidden lamps. Surrounded by three hundred lights and three hundred horns sounding attack, the Midianites fell into blind panic and killed each other. Gideon didn't lose a man."

"I won't bring death to all of Jaagrmur's armed men. What more practical alternative can you suggest?"

"The final sentries will be bound and gagged. Our men can use torches to help them walk in silence. When they reach a camp, let them tread through with shouts and clubs, and drive the Jaagrmur men ahead of them."

"The other camps will be alerted by that."

"Precisely. You see the value in driving one throng of barefoot, sleepy men into their fellows, and all of them disorganized. You should be proud of yourself."

She snorted. "Prince, I did ask them to sleep early and rise early. I didn't think to have them make clubs, but there may be time for that when they are awake and dressed."

"You asked me to think dishonest, devious thoughts."

"Yes, Prince. Not so much devious as irregular. Is that the sort of thing a devout and reverent man considers devious?" Her face showed annoyance and a defensive mood.

He tempered his answer. "No, just unexpected. Ponder what your enemy is prone to do, and from that guess what he believes you will do. He will prepare an unexpected defense against your standard attack."

"Why doesn't Roneult ever tell me such things as this? He said once that when an unexpected defense succeeds, it becomes lore and over time becomes the new standard defense. Same for novel attacks. Tried-and-true wins too often to replace it with a gamble."

"Still, do something different. Get there before he does, for instance. Attack under cover of dark."

"I see. His troops are only falling asleep now, so it's probable that they won't be ready any sooner than dawn."

"Just so, Utrecht. His tricks, ruses, flanking maneuvers, and so on will be for nothing if his men come under attack while still in their bedding."

"That is reprehensible! Honor demands a certain degree of decorum, Prince."

"The same decorum that Jaagrmur shows by bringing false charges and outlandish demands? If that is so, my good friend, decorum sounds willfully improvident."

"Here I was ready to credit the panic of bound-up sentries as enough to dishearten the enemy."

"Utrecht, it may mean that they are up, and armed, halfway through the night. They will not attack us while it is still dark, just waste themselves in fretting."

"You think so, do you?"

"I do. Ask what I will do next."

"Tell me. There seems never to be a way to stop that mouth of yours."

"When I silence the second watch of sentries I will go back to see what the camp is doing. When I return our men will be waking up, and we can refine our tactics then."

"We? Our?"

I am too familiar. She hates that. "Your, my lady."

Utrecht frowned. *Damn! He pushes too hard.* She nodded. "Sleep. A sentry will wake you. At what hour?"

"I'll do that on my own. Good night, Utrecht."

At four hours before dawn the middle-watch sentry stepped close to Ordowahl, who was in deep sleep. The sentry bent down to shake his shoulder and leapt back when Ordowahl rolled over and stood up.

"Migod, man, have a care!" said the sentry.

Ordowahl enjoyed a luxurious stretch. "Thank you, my good yeoman sentry."

Still dressed in dark and soft, hence noiseless, clothing and wearing soft black shoes, Ordowahl spent five minutes doing wakeup exercises and ate some of last night's travel ration. He washed it down with a flagon of water he'd set under a cloth beside a tree, and set out.

The setting moon's shadows are treacherous. A simple tuft of grass or bush can make a long sliver of shadow. Every molehill waves a tiny flag when it loses the moonlight for just a moment.

Ordowahl knew that it would take longer, but he still knew where the first sentries sat. He still found them bound, and for the most part asleep.

Bastards. Leaving men out for the entire night. But if Jaagrmur is as clever as a man would have to be to get away with his many aggressions, he will have set new guards in new places.

A second, slower, approach led Ordowahl to discover the second quartet of sentries. They had chosen similar spots, and he found them with no more difficulty than the first set. From the Marvistjen end of the line he again crept in toward the Jaagrmur camps and found an inner ring of three sentries.

The man is a fox. Ordowahl marveled at his cunning. *No one has warned the sleeping men. The count expects the inner ring to sound the warning.*

The inner ring might have been there all along, and he regretted not making more certain of that on the first visit. One by one he scouted them out, and it was much later than he had planned when he had silenced the last of them. He went back to the middle sentry and again ventured away from the lane until he found a camp. Its fires smoldered, and the men all slept. A dog barked, but he left doing his best imitation of a deer fleeing through the grasses and thickets, and the dog didn't follow.

Very bright, and bold, but he forgot that whatever can take out one ring of sentries can also take whatever other sentries he has. But what lie have I told him, and what lie does his response tell me? The actions a man doesn't take can reveal as much as those he does.

He returned to the Vendink camp as promised; Joop and Emmi both slumbered. Utrecht's candle had nearly guttered, but she awoke from a light doze when he entered the tent.

"We've waited on you!" said Utrecht. "Our whole plan was about to come apart, just because we needed to know what you found."

"I worried about you, too."

"Focus! What did you learn?"

"This time there were two rings of sentries, and the outer ring was in different hiding places. Jaagrmur has to know that the outer ring was compromised, even though the second watch let all the first watch stay bound up as they were."

"What do you think he did about it?"

"Not enough. All in the camp I came up to were sleeping."

"And the other camps?"

"We may not find them asleep, Utrecht, but in the night sounds carry well, and I heard nothing. At least one camp, but near the middle of the line, had snoring men. That sound is impossible to imitate."

"So one camp out of a hundred still sleeps."

"They may have interviewed the first ring of downed sentries and discovered which direction I had taken. They would then assume that if I came back I would either take the same direction, or the reverse."

"That seems logical."

"They are also resolute, Vice-Count. Anything capable of disabling all their sentries should have terrified them."

"Go on."

"The camp I looked in on this time was near the middle of the line."

"So in other words, they appear not to suspect anything."

"Perhaps. A dog sensed me, but I was able to pass as a forest animal fleeing from the dogs."

"Fairy Toes is dead. Long live our forest animal."

"As you will. I'll sleep until I hear the noise of fighting, then Hammerfoot and I will join in the fun." He left, went to where the horses were tethered, and slept between Hammerfoot's huge hooves.

The vice-count bears the onus. She must win,

and therefore needs to hold control. And he

who follows his own counsel? It's a sin

each time he acts in ways she cannot see.

He's yet a youngster, hasn't led this kind

of war. He's learning: was a bound-up guard

too simple for Count Jaagrmur's seasoned mind?

He found a camp asleep; they slumbered hard.

So back he goes, to slumber like to them—

he's gone forth twice, and knows for sure he's known.

The second set of guards are down. Ahem—

That pre-dawn march? As set as cornerstone.

Our prince thinks he's God's newest gift to war—

he'll waken when they fight but, 'til then, snore.

Stalemate

An hour after dawn a strong female hand pushed on his shoulder. He rolled over, by good fortune away from her, and sprang to his feet. Utrecht fell back in surprise and watched him rub his face.

"Alas, Prince, they forbore to fight."

"And what concessions did you wring from him?"

"Concessions?"

"I see there is a story here. Please tell it."

"I will. Can you listen without interrupting, until I am done telling it?"

"Please tell it in a coherent sequence, and indicate when you reach the end."

"You are so easy to please, first thing in the morning."

"As you will."

A tiny smirk. "We captured all twenty-five of them. The other eight hundred seventy-five got up about the time we did and flanked our Vendinkers. Then the Marvistjen and Naechstofen men flanked Jaagrmur. He did his best to placate them and pry them away from our defense. They held firm, the Marvistjen barons because they owed us a debt of defense, and the Naechstofen men for another reason." She blushed a little, and the morning light let him see it.

"No need to guess, there, Utrecht. Your face tells the story. I pity the poor fool who tries to woo a steep mountain of wet ice."

"What? I have no idea where you heard *that*. Lady Janalei is not one of your concerns, and still you fling an insult. You deal with Vice-Count Utrecht, Prince. Me only. Are you always cranky and insulting in the morning?"

"I tender a humble apology but do not withdraw my estimate of Lord Naechstofen's sorry prospects."

"Hmmmph. Our seven hundred troops mingled with twenty-five of Jaagrmur's barefoot, furious men. His other eight hundred seventy-five troops ringed us, while two hundred Marvistjen troops on one side and two hundred fifty Naechstofen men on the other side hemmed them in."

"An 'onion' formation."

"It has a name?"

"It does now. I can see why Jaagrmur has so many victories. When the time comes that you are Count, Vice-Count, get him drunk and have him describe each one."

"You may have talent as a scout, but planning battle isn't yet a strength." She sneered at him. "Now focus."

"Me? I feel your story has more to it."

"Thank you for your patience, chatty one. After a long parlay in which Jaagrmur returned again and again to the horse you killed, we agreed to a brief truce."

"So the fight is at noon?"

"He also says that no power on heaven or earth will ever again disturb so many sentries. In fact he seemed insulted."

"Done?"

"No. He wants damages for disturbing Jaagrmur lands."

"Done?"

"Yes."

"What damages will he award you for disturbing Vendink lands, and what damages will he award you for the unnecessary expense and burden of meeting him and turning him away?"

"I didn't bother asking."

"What other damages and expense will he pay for the ugly lies and slander against your father? And, from your long dealings with your father, what would *he* add to the list?"

"Prince, just this. He would demand blood."

"Very well. I will draw whatever blood your father would feel is appropriate."

"Not by your hand, Prince. *Mine.*"

"You just stopped making sense and have gone down a leafy lane, a mad dash toward your tomb. Tell me how you stand a sparrow's chance against him."

"Because I will carry your curved sword."

"How will you become accustomed to its weight, its length, its feel, the way it swings, what sort of cuts it can make, the fact that it has but one edge, and I'll find a dozen other things you'll need to know with a moment's thought."

She tapped her foot. "Done?"

"Not even both your arms could wield it with any grace whatsoever."

"I will account for half as many edges with twice as many hands, Prince. I may be slender, but I am very fast."

"You are very fast with your wits, Utrecht, but in this case they've far outrun your common sense."

"I saw your maneuver that first day, against Sir Torwulf."

"Speaking of him, he is suffocating with the need to do noble service. What if he uses the sword as your champion?"

"You may teach me." She looked him in the eye. "You may withhold your sword. Those two choices I give you. I suppose a third would be to lend me the sword but not teach me."

"I would feel better with an archer poised to put a shaft through Jaagrmur's neck. I know just the shaft to use."

"Why are you being obstinate about this, Prince?"

"Why are you? As vice-count you have the exact same abilities with a sword as does Lady Janalei. Is it she who will go out to meet Jaagrmur? It might disconcert him enough to give her half a chance."

"Got you! You are so easy to outmaneuver." She laughed at him and waited for that half-mobile, stoic face to shift.

"I suppose you feel more in control now. That's good, my lady.

Now, if I have the privilege of hearing truth, tell me what *did* happen this morning."

"He asked to meet Sir Torwulf, one on one, and while not required to go to the death, the winner's claim is supported against the loser."

"And Jaagrmur's claim remains vast."

"No, we narrowed it to about a ten-to-one ratio."

"In Vendink's favor, I hope. I doubt your father would ever stoop so low." He scowled.

"We aren't going to lose, Prince. I am leading him on. So, tell me how good Sir Torwulf is. How well can he fight?"

Her cunning must be great. My own man, Torwulf? Jaagrmur dangles him to bait me, and likely she knew it at once. "Do you ask me that now, after letting the county's fate hinge on him?"

"Not so fast, Prince. I said nothing of the sort."

"Then please repeat yourself. What actual terms have you agreed to?"

"These: he wants you weighed on a scale, and he will provide two men whose combined weight matches yours. Sir Torwulf insisted that he become part, so they will have three men to our two."

"I like that much more. Did you know I taught Sir Torwulf the drop-and-roll? He's quite good at it, and three people know the move. You make a fourth."

"Mhmm. I hope he has learned it well—you got away with it when he was drunk."

"Yes. But at the right moment it may serve to cut a man's legs out from under him. Sir Torwulf will wield a sword that will let him do that."

"One of yours, or Klarenz's? That is a good idea."

"Please tell me the stakes that will attract five men willing to die for their count."

"Three hundred pounds of gold if Jaagrmur wins, against the same in silver if Vendink wins."

Ordowahl stared at her in dismay. "You need me to take part. I will do combat for equal terms. There isn't a way that Jaagrmur can pose as the more righteous. If he does, I refuse to dignify the contest."

"You hesitate?"

"No, Vice-Count, I refuse. Either an equal wager, or I will just observe."

"Even at two to three, you are certain to prevail."

"I do not count the ten-to-one likelihood of my victory as a justification for his ten-to-one difference in the result."

"I see." She looked skeptical. "Jaagrmur would never bet with an equal outcome."

Ordowahl continued. "Their three have mass equal to our two, and carry three swords."

"Yes, of course."

"The wager must be equal value, three hundred pounds silver, for instance. They will also add the weight of my sword, in gold, if they lose, or accept my sword as plunder if they win."

"Once again, Prince, do you elevate yourself to full stature in negotiating Vendink's outcome?"

"Vice-Count, those are the conditions under which I will risk myself and the damage I cannot fail to inflict on those three poor men Jaagrmur sends me."

They had been standing beside Hammerfoot while men-at-arms took the other horses toward the lane. Utrecht looked around, sweeping the area from behind, to the left, ahead, and back around to the right. She turned back to Ordowahl and said, "We are alone. What I say will go no further. You will meet Jaagrmur and present your demands."

"Good."

"He will expect you to do this. He will also have the balance beam prepared."

"I will examine it myself, of course."

"From there, Prince, the fate of five men, the treasuries of two counties, and the reputation of my father will rest on you alone." Her face didn't ask, it spoke a fact as plain as a mud pie

"I, as Prince Nordweg, will take Count Jaagrmur to the edge of whatever precipice he likes. But he and I will go there on my terms."

Do I sense some internal joy hiding behind that masked but captivating face?

"Blessed Prince, I could kiss you." She swung her bright smile around and went to the command tent.

*__*__*__*

Ordowahl stood at the curtain guarding the command tent's opening and intercepted Torwulf when he emerged.

"Sir Torwulf, you and I together will do armed combat, to surrender or to death, with their best three swordsmen."

"Yes, Prince!" He rejoiced. "I learned the same just moments ago from the vice-count. Tell me more about the way they will select their best three."

"By weight. A balance beam rests on a narrow fulcrum. A broad, level fulcrum is inaccurate, so we will not give them a way to cheat."

"I saw you inspecting it."

"You and I will stand on a cross-piece at one end of the beam, and their three on a cross-piece at the other end. When the beam stays level, their three will have been selected."

"And if our end has been weighted, how do we discover it?"

"You and I will try the beam both ways—you at one end and I somewhere that makes us balance, mark that spot, then test the other end. The beam will be fair if those marks are the same distance from the center."

The moment arrived. Noonday sun heated the helmets and mail of many, specifically including Vice-Count Utrecht, Count Jaagrmur, and Prince Nordweg.

"Count," said Ordowahl, "you allege that I owe you for the horse you rode onto Vendink land, which I killed in answer to your man's unwarranted arrow. You also remain under my personal challenge."

Jaagrmur said nothing. Ordowahl's voice hadn't carried to the count's men, who stood a respectful distance away. The Vendink men and Vice-Count Utrecht likewise gave the conversation privacy. Soft voices couldn't be overheard.

"Further, Count, your terms are not acceptable. If Sir Torwulf and I manage to defeat your three men, you will pay to Count Jakop the weight, in gold, of my battle sword."

He raised his sword, the one Klarenz had made from the two mirror-bright, single-edged, curved swords that Egeno's sons Hans und Franz had called "girly strips of shiny metal." When Klarenz finished, it was fit for the prince's hand and no other, too long and too heavy for anyone else. Since then Klarenz had polished just the edges to deadly razor sharpness.

"Let me see that, if I may," said the Count. When he had judged its weight he said, " I marvel more at its unwieldiness than its weight. Risking five pounds of gold means far less than the fact that with a regular sword you might be fast enough to overwhelm a troop. If you lose, the sword will be mine." He raised an eyebrow to hear the rest of Ordowahl's demands.

"Last, Count, if your side suffers the loss, you will pay three hundred pounds in silver, as agreed. But this will be the outcome no matter who loses."

"Vendink gold is too good for me? Are they impoverished?"

Ordowahl continued. "If by some fluke your men should defeat Torwulf and me, Vendink will pay three hundred pounds silver. But when you accept these terms I will also withdraw my challenge."

"I fully expect Vendink to lose, so the matter of gold against a metal that is eleven or twelve times less valuable insults me."

"This is not open to negotiation. But because I will at the same time lift my challenge against you, your life will be safe once I win."

"And my horse?" the count asked, stone faced.

"And the fact that your man attacked me without warning or challenge?" asked Ordowahl.

The count sat for a full minute. His gaze never left Ordowahl's unmoving, sober face. Stone and carved root burl would each have been as stolid as that too-young visage. Jaagrmur sighed and turned back toward his men. He signaled one baron to join them, and Utrecht approached Ordowahl.

"The terms are struck. If Vendink succeeds, I will pay the weight of this sword—he pointed to the prince's oversized weapon—"in gold, else the sword will become mine. And whichever count loses will pay three hundred pounds silver to the other. Do you all understand?" and he looked hard at his baron. The man's eyes widened, but he nodded affirmation. Utrecht kept a sober face and gave a solemn nod.

"One hour." Jaagrmur and his baron went back to their lines. Utrecht went back to hers, with Ordowahl following.

(Vice-Count Utrecht)

I need his sword and strength, but can't believe
the pow'r he wields around me, as if king.
I shield myself against his pull, achieve
a shield with Markus, small-beer sweetie thing.

> So many handsome men that come to court—
>
> what's one more, when I'll marry not a one!
>
> To keep me safe from falling, guard my fort,
>
> I kiss the face of one more "Honey-bun."

So do I now rejoice that Ordowahl
has softened Jaagrmur, where I would fail?
He guards my lands through simple impulse; all
he'll earn from me's a placid fairy tale.

> I mourn the deaths he'll bring, as though by right.
>
> How can I feel his pull, against that blight?

Fini

Noon. Ordowahl and Jaagrmur sat on their mounts in the middle of the boundary lane separating two counties. Too many men to count stood dozens of rows deep along both sides

"Thank you for doubting me, Prince. You have managed to demonstrate that I am scrupulously fair in all that I do."

The count waved at three waiting men, who went over and stood on one end of the sturdy crossbeam. They drove a dent into the moist sod of late spring.

Ordowahl and Torwulf went to the other end, four feet in the air. Ordowahl climbed onto it and gave Torwulf a hand up. When they stood erect on the crossbeam the other end rose up, paused, then went to full height. Ordowahl and Torwulf's end came to rest on the ground.

The count barked out a command, and the smallest man jumped off. Another fellow came out. He mounted at the center and walked up the beam to the end. That end descended, overshot for a moment, then returned to level.

"Jump!" commanded Ordowahl, and all five men hopped off.

Jaagrmur took it on himself to act as master of combat. "Arm yourselves and advance to accept the challenge!"

Five men came to stand in the lane, swords held vertical at the waist in the form of a salute. The count started them with a simple nod. They each stepped back two large paces, bowed, and dropped into fighting stances. Shouting to be heard over the roar of two massed camps of fighting men, Jaggrmur said, "Now!"

At once the three Jaagrmur swordsmen attempted to make a ring around Torwulf and Ordowahl. One man had to get behind Torwulf, who lunged at him while he was in full stride. He, the medium-sized fellow who made the beam balance, was very fast, but Torwulf's sword flicked out and broke through the man's mail at the wrist. "Thank you, Klarenz!" he shouted, and tried to engage the closest other man.

Torwulf didn't have time to look behind him to see what the injured man was doing.

Ordowahl saw out of the corner of his eye that the fellow, his wrist still spurting blood, held a knife in his good hand and ran toward Torwulf.

"Behind you!" the prince shouted, and Torwulf whirled to face the wounded man, his dagger just inches from the knight's belly.

Torwulf couldn't avoid the dagger entirely. Its point penetrated one of the rings of his mail shirt and drew a nasty slice across his abdomen. He wielded Klarenz's razor-death sword to half-sever the man's good arm through his mail then spun around to intercept his other opponent. That fellow now had Torwulf from the side and lunged, sword out at arm's length.

Torwulf managed to use the flat of his blade to deflect the thrust. Ordowahl uttered a bass roar, "Remove your man," while turning to confront the largest opponent. Jaagrmur motioned to a baron, who darted in to drag the double amputee to safety.

Torwulf's man also wound up close to Ordowahl and off behind him. In a movement too quick to follow, the prince used his sword to swat the second man's blade and knocked it from his grip.

While Ordowahl clashed swords with his own man, Torwulf's opponent ducked back to pluck up his sword before Torwulf closed on him.

"Charge him," shouted Ordowahl as he drove his own opponent backward several steps. Torwulf lunged at the second man, and the two of them stood clanging swords together, neither man moving.

At that moment Ordowahl saw his man's attention shift for an eye blink to note his companion's status. The prince feinted a duck-and-roll to the right while the man divided his attention. The fellow went sideways to follow the prince, who had moved the other way—feint right, dip left.

Rising, he shoved his man, already off-balance, into Torwulf's foe. The two Jaagrmur men collided back to back and wound up flatfooted, each with a sword pricking his throat.

"Yield," demanded Torwulf, and "Yield," demanded Ordowahl.

Torwulf's man might have got free but knew that Ordowahl's much longer sword and lightning reflexes meant that his partner's life would be forfeit, thus his own with it. He dropped his sword and lowered his arms.

Ordowahl's opponent saw that he would be helpless against two men and did the same. They stepped away from each other as Torwulf and Ordowahl pulled their sword points back, bit by bit. The two defeated Jaagrmur men turned to face their count. They knelt in apology.

Nobody paid attention to the blood scattered about by the first man's two injuries. Jaagrmur trod upon it, on foot and fuming, while his troops tried to console the defeated men.

A host of Vendinker troops had seen the fight; now they produced a cacophony of the exultant noises men make when they face a known danger and emerge with a victory.

Utrecht went out into the roadway. She took Ordowahl's sword from him and stood face to face with Jaagrmur. "The weight of this sword is five pounds," she said. "I know this already. Do you care to dispute the weight with me?"

Jaagrmur looked at the sword. "May I weigh it in my hand?" he asked.

Ordowahl found Jaagrmur eyeing him. He stared back and made a tiny head-wag to warn Jaagrmur that if he stepped out of line, he would die.

Utrecht had turned to look at him also, saw Jaagrmur's glance, and caught the head-wag. "He knows you too well, Jaagrmur. Here, but don't cut yourself. It's razor sharp." She dangled the sword by its pommel to let the count grasp it in his hand.

"Five, eh?" he said. "More like five and a half, but your number is good. Three hundred pounds silver and five pounds gold. Will a week do?"

"I will bring my army to Jaagrmur Keep a week from today to collect it. Will that do?" She took back the sword.

"Here. Tomorrow. Bring your scales." Jaagrmur turned and went back to his men. "Camp tonight," he told them.

*__*__*__*

Roneult came to Ordowahl to discuss what he had seen. They sat on the trunk of a large fallen tree. "Prince," he said, "what was the point of such a risky move? That man could have spitted you."

"You are right, Roneult, there was a small chance that he might have. But why didn't he?"

"You were closer, Prince," he said. "You tell me."

"I saw his gaze shift to the other fellow's fight with Torwulf, and I managed to give him a feint. A man's gaze flickers quickly, but he can miss much before he reacts to something happening below him."

"Big as you are, you got below him? I did see you duck a shoulder. Is that what you mean?"

"Just that, Roneult. It helps if God has made you quick, but I would never try it on a man who wasn't drunk or distracted."

"So I shouldn't try it against you, eh?"

"You are Fightmaster for many good reasons. But in this case, my friend, you speak truth. Considering that you are no longer a youth, it wouldn't work well in general, and not at all with me."

The fightmaster had come to accept Ordowahl as a peer in the arts of war. He showed him the same smile of respect that he would a much older man.

Utrecht saw them conversing. *They look and act so calm in the presence of dismemberment and blood!* She went over to them. "Are we having a good time, after smiting the enemy? Is our vanity of triumph well-fed?" she asked. "God help me, I have seen blood spilled, but never in so tidy yet off-hand a way." No one dared acknowledge her accidental pun.

Roneult rose, excused himself, and left.

Ordowahl stayed seated and looked Utrecht in the eye for a short moment. "Yes, Klarenz sharpened Sir Torwulf's sword, which he used to shorten each of a man's two arms. We ground his blood into the earth with our boots. Yet he lives, and the others remain whole."

He continued to look her in the eye. "All three wear the embarrassment of losing, albeit to a giant. In time their exploit and the fact they survived will spin tales of courage. Years from now they will brag about this. On the other hand, the count's daughter Lady Janalei spurns the men who come to court her. They have no protective coat of mail to shield them. A different giant defeats them, one with a softer but deadlier weapon. Like the fellow who lost both hands, some will never be the same."

She drew back in shock then rage, daring him to finish.

Ordowahl ignored her reaction and finished his statement. "But none of those wounded are likely to boast in later years. I am glad their soul's blood doesn't mark the ground where a lady cups it in her hands for a while then releases it into the dust."

Her lips drew back in a snarl. "Do you whine on behalf of the oafish sorts who accost both me and Lady Janalei with their unsolicited and unwanted attention?"

Ordowahl seated and she standing before him, they stared at reach other, her eyes bare inches above his. He struggled for half a blink, then again became patient. "My apologies, my friend. That slipped out in a tired moment. After a battle a variety of fatigue can come over a man. It can mimic death's whisper in a dark night. Please do not tell the lady Janalei that I have made an intemperate remark."

From winner to whiner, and he pleads fatigue? Men! "Hah!" she said. "What sort of obfuscation is that?"

"Your own, man-dressing, man-acting Utrecht. It is your own. But, as in all things, I try to honor you and the things you insist upon."

We are arguing! "Prince, this is much too intimate. Leave me!" She walked away.

(Ordowahl)

She vexes me, and yet I'm bound up tight—
I bless the fool who occupies her mind
because his "manly" presence calms her fright.
Yea, why should I expect we're intertwined?
    Escaping murder was a gift, and still
    she railed at me for lopping off a limb,
    when nothing else would serve 'gainst evil will.
    Her face, upon a time, makes fair look grim.
Must I now bear the deep-undoing sight
of her smiled kisses on another man?
Must I now lie, dissimulate my spite?
Dear God, don't let me view her "courtesan."
    She's all her own, and nothing owes to me;
    I am the fool, and she the hanging tree.

Jumpy Goat

Ordowahl and Klarenz reached the Vendink Castle gate when the sun sat three hours up the sky and the air was nicely warm. Utrecht sat in her fair-weather spot, two hours behind her usual schedule.

Nonetheless, she anticipated that Ordowahl would appear, and he did. He looked happy to see her. She had a secretary-case open in her lap to review notes from the day before and looked up when Hammerfoot approached. She noticed a very relaxed and smiling prince astride the stallion.

"Ahh, Nordweg. I sense the demeanor of a man who had a most satisfying night! Do I know the lucky woman? Rather, please don't tell me." Utrecht's eyebrows arched, and her smile showed teeth. "Don't deny it!"

"Very well."

"You don't deny having taken a lover last night?"

"No, I do not."

"So you don't bother to deny it?"

"You told me not to do that."

Utrecht's face fell into a cold stare. The image of the prince disporting himself assaulted their redeveloping fellowship, and she found herself unwilling to ask why. Regarding him as brother, younger or no, had been complicated and grew more so all the time.

Ordowahl dismounted and sat down next to her. "Forgive my

tardiness," he whispered. "I felt the need for some exercise this morning, and it had a most calming effect."

She threw him a suspicious look. *Smug, isn't he? But why do I care?* "Focus!" She handed Ordowahl a piece of stiff linen. "Yesterday a baron's courier reached me with news of a missing goat. Perhaps you will be able to plumb the mystery: where has it gone, and why, and with whom."

"Whatever question interests you, Utrecht, interests me. Let us go and find an answer."

Ordowahl made a flourish toward the horses already tethered on the inside edge of the gate and noticed two extra. Their riders would make the party six. "So, a baron in this county alleges to have lost a goat and extends to you the burden of finding it?"

"Just so, Prince. The baron's six-year-old daughter Ejmilie bottle-fed the goat when its mother died birthing it. The animal has in all probability been eaten by now."

"From weaning to waffle topping, the goat's life was cut short."

She curled her lip. "Please. Do not make light of this. The poor baron has no way to explain the loss to his grieving daughter, whom he dotes on."

"I know how that would tax me, and I'm not even a father yet."

She snorted, and her smile had teeth in it. "I am sure that will not be soon, and it will not be here," but she softened the smile.

"So, Utrecht, you are called out for much more than your ability to give comfort to a child. Please tell me the rest of the tale."

"A few similar things have happened in an area about a mile across, spilling across a border between baronies Ummerdink and Engern, with Engern the latest target."

"What pattern connects these?" he asked.

Just then someone came out through the gate to join them. He recognized Lord Markus, eldest son of Count Naechstofen.

Markus gave Ordowahl the nod of a man who recognizes an acquaintance. Wrapping an arm around Utrecht's shoulders, he kissed her forehead.

She relaxed into his embrace then turned her face to him. "Hello, Markus." She put a tiny kiss on his lips.

My gracious sake! Keep a straight face lest you show yourself an idiot.

Markus answered Ordowahl's question.

"Each animal was roughly the same size: a newborn calf, a large dog, and now a goat. Carcasses have been accounted for, but without the hide and head."

"Those would be unusual carcasses," said Ordowahl, struggling to keep his face serene.

Markus continued. "Predators often leave the hide and reduce the carcass to skull, bones, and sinew. However, someone found knife marks on the bones." He stepped behind Utrecht, as though to support her, and caressed her shoulders.

With a sinking heart Ordowahl realized this fellow to be the realization of his guess regarding Count Naechstofen's considerable support against Jaagrmur. "Have we been introduced?"

Utrecht disengaged and brought their hands together. "Lord Markus, eldest son of Count Naechstofen, greet Prince Ordowahl of Nordweg."

"Yes, I enjoyed seeing your duel with Jaagrmur's men. Jan— Vice-Count Utrecht," he corrected himself, "has spoken about you. I am very pleased to meet you and hope that you plan to remain a visitor for the foreseeable future."

So he, at least, sees me as his rival. He wants me gone. As I want him gone. Mustering his dignity, Ordowahl replied, "Thank you. Do you know whether either of these baronies does much tanning of hides?"

Utrecht objected. "Yes, of course! They're self-sufficient in a number of ways, Prince. Perhaps this isn't true where you come from." She teased him but withheld the customary half-warm smile. He noticed the lack; it stung.

He answered, "This doesn't rule out one barony or the other, but if we pay close attention to the tanners, we may learn something."

"Markus and I considered that. Nothing resembling goat or dog showed up after he sent men to drag all of the tanning pits."

Ordowahl nodded agreement as soon as she said it. "But taking the head each time suggests the brains have a use. As the wags have it in Nordweg, every animal has just the right amount of brains to keep its hide in a good state."

It was a stale joke. Markus and Utrecht looked at each other and made ho-hum smiles.

"How would you imagine looking for a temporary, half-hide tannery hidden in a nearby copse of trees?"

Utrecht replied, "I wouldn't. Some things are much too difficult to do well. What would you imagine as a reason for doing such a thing?"

"Utrecht, you seldom see the hide of a poached deer, raw or tanned, because that would make the poaching plain. A goat or dog hide is smaller, thus harder to find, but can serve any of a hundred small uses."

"And who," she asked, "would have a reason to take the risk and tax himself the time and work to cure one small piece of contraband leather?"

"Just because a thing eludes my imagination doesn't mean that it couldn't spring up in someone else's. Failure to conceive an idea doesn't rise to proof that the idea has no merit. Do you follow my reasoning?"

"Empty words, Ordowahl. Answer the question. What possible reason might a person have for scraps of contraband leather?"

"Let me answer a question with a question. When was the last time you spent time among peasants? What level of familiarity do you have with a peasant's day, his wants, the things that can make him content?"

"Often enough, Prince."

"Then you are familiar with the hundred uses of leather bindings, patches, reinforcements in the soles of shoes, crude gloves to hold things that are very hot—leather is a key item of peasant life."

"True enough. Our peasants, however, have leather scraps in plenty. Tell me what will drive a man with a good supply of leather scraps to go off and make contraband, with real goods close to hand."

Can I say this? "The one, Utrecht, who has been denied what he seeks. Does that sort of thing occur in County Vendink?"

A puzzled look crossed the vice-count's face, and she shrugged. "Let's go see."

The spring day had become warm by the time they reached the Engern mansion. Six-year-old Ejmilie stood on the porch. She had been waiting there for a while and squealed her distress when she saw the vice-count. She ran down four steps and out into the sunlight with shiny eyes and upraised arms.

Utrecht dismounted, scooped up the girl, and comforted her.

Ejmilie wept and said over and over, "Willy took Jumpy Goat!"

The five men also dismounted. A servant showed the footmen around to the stable yard at the rear, each leading two mounts.

"So, dear one," asked Utrecht, "who is Willy, and why would he do a thing like that?"

Ejmilie answered, between hiccupping sobs, that Willy was her name for one of the servants in the house, but she could not tell which servant that was.

"I know from listening behind doors that one of them hated mopping up Jumpy Goat's pee and poop. I call him Willy," she said, as though that was a sufficient explanation.

Baron Engern walked out just as her tears began to dry. Utrecht turned to give the baron a questioning look. "Vice-Count," he began, "none of my servants would ever do such a thing as deprive my Ejmilie of her pet. My wife passes the cleanup duties around to all of the lower staff."

"I can see how a child's imagination can conjure up an explanation out of wisps," said Utrecht.

"We've also been letting Jumpy Goat run in a closed pasture for much of the day. To me this is a mystery, despite what my daughter tells me."

Utrecht crooned at her, "Ejmilie, when did this happen, dear?"

"Yesterday morning."

Baron Engern explained, "Each night she and the goat make their bed in a pile of straw. She starts wrapped in a blanket with the goat nestled close. She wakes up covered with straw, her arms around the goat, always with a happy smile."

Ejmilie shook her head up and down. "Very happy!"

"Yesterday morning she woke up alone, and that's all anyone can tell me. The goat has vanished."

Utrecht squatted to set down Ejmilie and wiped a last, half-dried tear from her cheek. She stood to rejoin the conversation.

"Vice-Count, getting her another goat or just letting her endure this unhappiness to prepare her for the next one would be expectable."

"Yes, of course, Engern."

"But she is so unhappy, and so remembers the other times you've been here and visited with her, she made it impossible for me not to ask you for help. I apologize to you and your father."

"Baron," she said, "Count Jakop has been through the same thing, and more than once. He asked me to tell you that I am not to rest until there is an answer."

She bent down again. "But, dear one, what will happen if you discover that Jumpy Goat has died? What if he is now dead?"

The girl's face grew pinched then sober. "Aunty Vice-Count— and you're *not* my uncle!—if I will see him again in heaven, that will make me happy."

Utrecht kissed her on the forehead and said, "Ejmilie, I will find out what happened to Jumpy Goat, and then you will know that in your heart."

*__*__*__*

Standing in the sunlight, Utrecht wore a killing look. "Hang and draw the man who can do this to a child. Markus, Prince, we need to find the person who did this and mete out a right punishment."

None of the men wanted to picture that punishment.

The footmen had returned; "Joop," she said, "you know all the household staff everywhere in the county. I want you to go into the Haus and—I know you can do this—get them to share their own suspicions with you."

He went into the Haus, and she continued. "Markus, Prince, we are going in search of a tannery. Whoever or whatever changed that pet goat into a piper's glove, I will have that person's hide removed, tan it, and give it back to him to wear." She looked at Ordowahl's groin. "All of it!" Her meaning was clear.

Utrecht turned to Klarenz and Markus's footman Hubert. "You two, I need your lieges to send you out into the countryside to find any small tanneries."

"Utrecht," began Ordowahl, "tanning with brains makes the leather very soft and supple. But it also takes up to several weeks, all things depending."

"Why is that important?"

"Let me guess that the brains are used to produce small amounts of high quality leather. Then the occasional small hide becomes something simple to use when needed."

"Connect this for me, Prince."

"The brains don't keep well during the time the hide cures to be ready for applying them."

"I've heard a thing or two about that. Markus, do you take his point?"

"I do. The goat's brains will become useful on something that was started some weeks ago. As the prince says, they don't keep well."

"So, Markus, why is that important to know?"

"I would guess, and correct me if I am wrong, Prince, it means the brains of the small animal are as important as its hide, to treat some other piece of hide that is ready to be treated with brains."

"Exactly, Markus," said Ordowahl. "Hides themselves may or may not have special value. We should be looking for quick access to fresh brains. What does that suggest, Utrecht?"

"Two things. First, get Klarenz to ask the local tanner about the recent use of brains, and second, if the goat was taken for its brains, not its hide, the hide may have been discarded; thus searching for it may be futile."

Ordowahl turned this over in his mind for a moment. "Suppose that someone in the Engern household removed the goat while Ejmilie slept and took it somewhere nearby, left the goat behind, and returned, so the act would have taken very little time."

Utrecht added, "In other words, between first and second sleep? Just pretend to take a chamber pot outside and return after enough time to discard the waste in it?"

Markus said, "Something like that. But how does that get the tanner into the puzzle?"

"It's simple," said Ordowahl. "No tanner was involved. The goat is just an accident, and the tanner never found it."

Markus replied, "But since we haven't yet found the goat, we don't know where its hide and head may have gone. We need to find out what we can from the tanners."

"Markus and Prince, you each surprise me with your insistence on having found the actual answer without having found anything. So, go where you think best, and learn what you can. Meanwhile, once Joop has spoken with the household staff, he and I will do our own looking about."

Markus watched Utrecht go into the Haus. He couldn't take his gaze away from her departing figure. When she passed from sight he said, "Hubert, you have wide acquaintance among the folk of this barony, don't you?"

"Lord Markus, I do. I believe that a tanner may have information that will help."

"Then let us go see him. Tell me what you know of this fellow."

Markus and footman Hubert reached the village about ah hour later, before the sun had reached mid-sky. Markus tried to look bored. Hubert walked all around the cluster of houses and returned with news. "Master, I found the fresh skull of a goat in the bone heap behind a hut. It was buried deep."

"But you dug deeper?"

"The son of his neighbor turns out to dislike the tanner. Most of the children there do, too. He was eager to help me with it. I have the empty skull in a bag tied to my horse's saddle; its brains are gone."

"Excellent! Hubert, we need to show that to Utrecht just as soon as we find her."

"Begging Master's pardon, he is old and doesn't get around well. There is no way that he could have stolen the goat, much less found it."

"No matter, Hubert, I was right," Markus said. "Utrecht will be so pleased to know that time spent with me is always to her benefit."

*__*__*__*

Ordowahl also found fascination in that glimpse of Utrecht departing, even after long association. When Markus and Hubert left, he stayed outside while Klarenz chatted with the household servants. When his bondman returned he asked, "What have you discovered?"

"Liege, Joop and I spoke with the senior maid. It is she who removed the goat, since 'No being with uncontrollable bowel and bladder that is also far less precious than a newborn babe may remain in this Haus.'"

"I wonder why Engern didn't know this."

"Liege, masters other than you often know less than they should. Of course it was she who removed the goat, but only to a pen behind the house."

"So I was right. The miscreant is that senior maid. We should tell Utrecht as soon as we see her."

"She had a helper, her husband. He is the butler. He restrained the goat so she could carry the animal to its pen outside. He made sure the pen's gate was fastened."

"Then we need to find which animal killed the goat."

"Liege, a man skulking about in the night would be able to remove the goat without making a noise, and the gate wasn't fastened in the morning."

"Could it be that the gate was left unlatched on purpose?"

"No. An animal such as a wolf would have made noise and left bits of fur and blood, signs of struggle. The pen was empty, but you've seen no marks of struggle remain."

"Even so, if the gate were left unlocked, the goat could have just wandered away."

*__*__*__*

Inside the Haus, Utrecht passed time consoling Ejmilie. When Joop found her she asked, "Where do we start?"

"Mistress Utrecht, we have the prince chasing madly after his idea that the goat was stolen, and certainly it was. Lord Markus believes the goat's body was used by a tanner, and that is also likely the case, but not proven. However, these answers sit well over a mile apart as the crow flies. Each seems to depend on the other, which neither Markus nor the prince appear to relish."

"Just so, Joopi. Markus hasn't explained how the goat crossed such a distance, which appears to give the prince some fond hope! So if a tanner is involved, how did he find a goat in a pen for the night?"

"And, Mistress, if a wolf took it, where is the carcass?"

"So, my wise and knowing old nanny, what does that tell you?"

"Someone saw the goat and took it. What he did with it is less immediate than the theft."

"How sad, Joopi. I have to find a thief and execute justice on him. And neither of those anxious men can see such a simple fact."

Joop was about to defend the prince, who had fixated on the theft, but said nothing.

"Common sense says the goat has become a thief's dinner, That one will meet his end. Surely he had no idea what he stole. He may not have known the goat's high value, yet he disturbed the order of the whole Barony. I must find him and administer due punishment."

"Mistress, I dread that fellow's fate."

"Theft of any kind is offensive. So, let me think how to find him. He will have had a tasty goat stew, I'm thinking. Peasants eat precious little meat, so it will be known to his neighbors."

"Yes, Mistress, but they also shield each other. Now, such a fellow will be a bold conniver. If he will steal a goat from behind the baron's house, he will also trade for its hide, and likely its brains as well."

"Which says he will have gone to the tanners' village. But he won't live there: say he is somewhere between that village and Haus Engern."

"I know just the place. Pardon, Mistress, but in time past I've been in this area guarding Count Jakop's daughter when she was young and would get into climbing trees, picking green apples, and throwing them at her patient nanny-footman."

Utrecht laughed out loud. "So, a young girl of six or seven years can throw. I hope she couldn't throw too hard."

"No," said Joop, "nor well. But that copse of apple trees sits at the edge of a village, and that village houses someone I have long suspected of being a deep scoundrel."

"Then let's make a surprise visit."

Two people on horseback, one of them Vice-Count Utrecht, caused a quick stir in that village. They had emerged from the apple grove onto the hard-packed earth in the village's center. Joop led Utrecht straight to the suspect's hut. Both dismounted, and she went inside.

Joop went to examine a trash midden behind the next hut over. He toed its surface. Several ribs and animal gristle appeared. He also noticed a large dog gnawing on what had to be a goat's leg bone. He found neither skull nor hide.

Inside the hut Utrecht sat down and asked the aging wife what the delicious smell was. "I would like a taste, if you please."

The wife burst into tears. "My Lady Vice-Count, I am a poor and humble woman. Whatever I have is a gift from my baron's hand, and it is yours. But please do not take my husband from me!"

Utrecht kept a stern face, although a lip trembled and her eye moistened. "Old wife, we believe that your husband crept up to the baron's house two nights ago and took a half-grown goat from a latched pen."

The old woman sighed.

"I am sad to remind you that his penalty is death. It can be no other way. The consolation I have for you is that he is old, and you would lose him soon enough anyway. If we find that he took the goat, he will die."

Utrecht got up and went out. "Joop. What have you found?"

"Vice-Count Utrecht," he said in a clear, formal voice, "the remains of a goat are in the village midden. No one here has anything to say, but the odor of goat stew is everywhere."

"We know who has done this thing," she said to the villagers present. "Bring him to me."

Four village men, each of middle age, led a man out to stand before her. The man's head was downcast, and he wore an unrepentant frown.

Jumpy Goat

"You have stolen a living animal from behind your baron's house; you must die. In fact, everyone in this village who has eaten from the goat must pay a price." She cast a firm, level gaze on the gathered villagers.

No one moved.

"But I will spare them their just penalty if you do one thing for me."

He looked up, stoic, and asked, "What is that, Vice-Count?"

"Tell me where you took the animal's hide and skull. I will believe that the tanner had no idea where they came from, but knowing you, he had to guess."

The thief made a distinct effort to look both puzzled and innocent, as if to say, "Who? Me?"

"Name him, and you will be the only penitent for your crime."

He looked her in the eye, as though searching his vice-count's soul for truth, then said, "The tanner."

"Old man, your life is done. Kneel."

He knelt before her and bared his neck.

Like all nobles, Utrecht went armed. Her sword was fit to her size. Even tall as an average knight, Utrecht was far lighter. Thus her sword, while sharp, was also light. She raised it over her head and, despite the weeping and sobs of dismay from the villagers around her, she pronounced justice.

"You have stolen a live animal from the grounds of your own baron. Rejoice that your death is swift."

With all her strength, she brought the sword down on his neck, and the man toppled onto his side. She'd cut his neck to the bone, but he still lived. "Joop, roll him over."

Joop did so, and the man's face showed intense agony. The back of the neck is one of the most sensitive places on a person's body, and her failure to sever the head made her fear she might cry.

She sat on her heels to saw at his neck. On the third stroke she severed an artery and in moments he bled out. She rose to wipe off the blood spatter as much as she could and turned to the new widow. "Old wife, you have known of your husband's life as a thief. Now you are free from that shame."

Utrecht and Joop mounted their horses and left the same way they came in. She found a stream to wash off whatever still-,moist blood she could find. She cleaned her sword, dried it carefully, and placed it back into its scabbard.

Once rejoined, the party returned in silence. Her father Jakop had executed many a thief, and without a second thought, but the act wore on her. It was the third time she had needed to mete out such a final, personal penalty.

At Vendink Keep footmen Hubert, Joop, and Klarenz cared for the animals.

"As far as you each saw it, you were both right," she said to Markus and Ordowahl. "But the answer had two parts that needed to be taken together."

I am well aware that Utrecht solved the puzzle by herself, and I feel empty inside. I tried to outperform Markus but failed, and badly.

"Still, Markus, your tanner did use the goat's hide and brain. And Prince, there was a person in the household who evicted the goat." She gave each a consoling smile.

"And Engern's household?" asked Ordowahl.

"I don't know what Engern has done about his senior maid and butler. At least little Ejmilie has found a peace. She may, after healing from this, become a strong woman."

She looked at Markus and then at Ordowahl. "Thank you, my friends, for your help. It has not been a good day, but at least a successful one." Utrecht went up to Markus to stand belly to belly with him, put hands on his chest, and gave him a kiss. "Until later, sweet man."

I feel obligated to acknowledge her. "Congratulations, Utrecht. You solved the puzzle on your own."

She gave Ordowahl a surprised look, as though his remark was at best extraneous, and went inside.

When she went up to change into a dress her mother stopped her. "Jana, what is all that blood?"

"It was one of those difficult things, Mama. We caught a thief. I tried for a clean death but had to saw at his throat." She made a distasteful grimace. "But those men."

"Jana? Which men, dear?"

"Markus and the prince. Each tried his best to solve the puzzle, but each also wanted to discredit the other, saying his own half-answer was sufficient. Male vanity is so pitiable. They were like roosters! I can't imagine what got into them." Janalei's attempt to account for Markus's and Ordowahl's absurd behavior so absorbed her that she paid no attention to her mother, who just shook her head.

Mother thinks I'm being foolish, that much is plain. But while she played young men against each other and especially against Daddy when he was after her like a bull in rut, what of it? What can she possibly know? How can she possibly compare wanting to be wooed with my situation? And Janalei put it out of her mind.

(Ordowahl)

Once Bishop Henck relinquished his demand

that severed me from Utrecht—first we spent

two days in useful parlay, took in hand

the most salacious mischief—so it went.

    Yet still I labor under his denial

    of my right to sit with him and study

    God. A while I had the pleasure nigh

    of time with Utrecht, yet she's now "with stud."

I know his fate's a folly, yet it galls

me in a private place to see them kiss.

I've no hope, either. Yet her fondness walls

me off—both show and banish me from bliss.

    My Father God in heaven, laugh at me—

    complaining I'm in Eden, w'thout the tree.

Baron's End

Two hours past noon the next day courier Manfrjed, in Maihoff colors of orange and cream, laid his lathered horse's reins across a row of rose bushes onto one of the extravagant carvings of Castle Vendink's courtyard fountain. The horse put its front feet well apart, arched itself over the roses and dipped its muzzle into the cooling waters while the weary courier ran around the castle to the rear entrance and pounded hard.

Senior maid Dolamrys ran to open the door and shush whoever was trying to disturb the count's midafternoon nap. She looked at the stricken, panting Maihoff courier. "Come in, Manfrjed, what is it?"

"Dolamrys, it was horrifying; Baron Maihoff went out on his horse when the horse, we think, reared up. We found the baron fallen, with his head cracked on a large rock."

"You what?"

"Surely he lay there an hour, perhaps two before we found him." He had to stop and heave for breath.

Dolamrys' mouth fell open, and her body went stiff. A baron, a good one, not yet at middle life, and with rich holdings, dying if not already dead. The wretched contests such an event could unleash! She sat the courier down on a chair by the door and went to bring him a basin of water, a cloth, and a mug of ale.

Rutelyn had overheard the story and gone up to Jakop's napping room. It occupied a corner of the Haus, with the shutters on both windows open to catch any breeze. The clattering arrival of the courier had awakened him.

"What is it?" Jakop asked when he saw her. He swung his feet around and tried to rise from the bed. Still emerging from sleep, he could not.

A footman stepped into the cramped room to assist the count. Jakop let the day robe drop. The footman supported him, and they made slow progress down the stairs.

Utrecht had returned to Castle Vendink with Markus, Ordowahl and footmen just half an hour before. This day's remaining business amounted to dictating the details to a clerk, so Utrecht had sent Ordowahl away with a sister's smile. Enjoying a quiet moment as sweethearts, she and Markus sat huddled together when the courier arrived.

His news, Jophan's likely fatal injury, hit hard. Until earlier this year Jophan had been Vendink's newest baron, and more than that, a lifetime close friend. She told Markus, "I'm so sorry. This can't wait, and I'll need to send the prince out there. I may even have to go as well. Are you doing anything this evening? Staying in town anywhere?"

"Of course. You know where to find me if you have the time."

She gave him a peck on the lips and turned to Joop. "Come with me to the stables. I need you to go after the prince. When you find him, say it is urgent that he go in haste to Haus Maihoff."

"Where shall I find him, Mistress?"

"Go first to Haus Hangendro. Tell Baron Heri I need you on a fresh mount whether the prince is there or not. When you find the prince go with him and be sure to arrive as soon as you can. I will go now, and alone."

The stable hands had two mounts already saddled. Their vice-count looked at them with soft eyes to show gratitude.

In the cool of a waning afternoon Utrecht rode into the Haus Maihoff courtyard and handed the horse's reins to a groom. Once inside, a senior maid led her to a small, quiet room. There she found her once-upon-a-time honorary "uncle" Jophan, husband to Karyn and father to two young children. He lay supine on a large padded bench with a bloody bandage under his head.

The children refused to leave their father. Karyn sat on the edge of the bench by her silent husband, softly whispering love words to him.

Utrecht sat down on the floor near his head. For several minutes she placed her hand on Karyn's while both of them shed silent tears. "Dear Karyn, has he spoken to you?"

Blotting her cheeks, Karyn answered. "No, Vice-Count. I'm told he managed one or two animal grunts when he was found, and occasionally one eye would open, but nothing else."

Utrecht rose to one knee and bent over Jophan's head. "Can you reach me a candle?"

Karyn lifted one off a small table at the far end of the bench.

"Help me look into his eyes," she said, holding one eye open while Karyn brought the candle close. "See, this eye is wide, as though the room is very dark, but holding the candle close does not make it shrink."

She let that eye slip closed and pried open the other one. Karyn brought the candle to the other side of Jophan's head. That eye had constricted to a pinpoint. They opened both eyes to compare them. The pupils were very different, and neither changed.

"Karyn, dear Karyn," said Utrecht in a husky voice. "I have seen cracked heads before. Jophan is going to leave us. Stay with him as far into the night as you are able. Get a maid to watch while you nap. If he awakens and speaks, tell me what he said when I return."

Utrecht rose and walked out into fading light. She knew that the prince would arrive, but perhaps not until after the sun had set. The moon already stood well up the eastern sky, four days until full, so Joop and Ordowahl should be able to see well enough to travel safely. A groom stood there holding her horse. Karyn's staff were very well trained.

She said to the groom, "Tonight three men will come—Prince Nordweg and two footmen, perhaps also Sir Torwulf. Expect all of them to stay the night."

'Yes, Highness. I will know the Prince." His face spoke somber volumes.

"Do not let anyone else through these gates without a very good reason. No other noble who comes to the gate this night will have any reason to come in. Be sure they know this."

"Yes, Highness."

"You speak the word of the vice-count in saying so." She rode back to Castle Vendink without a meal.

*__*__*__*

A party of four arrived well into the dark of evening. "Identify yourselves!" said a groom, his voice as gruff as he could make it.

"We are Nordweg, Sir Torwulf and two footmen," said the prince. *He sounds the way I would expect; frightened, but doing his best.* "What news do you have of Baron Maihoff?"

"Prince, the baron is very near death. I will see to your horses. If you please, the main door is open."

Giant stallion Hammerfoot went tamely to hay and water. He did not challenge the unfamiliar groom, who held the reins of four horses and led them toward the stables.

Karyn herself opened the huge door. She had been waiting for the prince while a trusted maid sat with her dying Jophan.

"Thank God you have arrived," she said, and collapsed onto Ordowahl's outstretched arm. Even by the light of a single candle Karyn's face showed puffy eyes and pale cheeks. Everything about her seemed to sag.

With tender care Ordowahl cupped her elbows in his hands and lifted her to stand upright. One huge hand caressed her neck and upper back. *She is beyond merely tired.* She leaned back into it then led them to Jophan's still form.

"Our children fell asleep here, sitting close to their father. We tucked them into bed just the way they were. Now I only have Jophan to look upon to reassure me that there is still a family Maihoff."

Joop and Klarenz stood near the bench, seeing the sad tableau by one flickering candle. Torwulf sat near them, in silence. The maid said, "Mum, he still breathes, but has said nothing," and left the room.

Ordowahl stood by Jophan's head and leaned down. He, too, checked each pupil, holding the candle close, and noted that one was tiny and the other half dilated. *He has hours, at most. God be with you, my friend.*

Karyn said, "They were large and small other way, earlier. But they still disagree. Vice-Count Utrecht told me that he would die."

"He is near death. I've seen men with broken heads before. None looking like this ever returned to life. I am very sorry, Karyn."

He turned to the footmen. "Joop, I will watch for three hours. Come get me then, and after three more hours Klarenz will take your place. You may return to your mistress at daybreak. We will not let *anyone* into this house before then." He went out to stand on the porch, with the door shut tight behind him.

"How may I serve you?" asked Torwulf.

"Watch with me, so that I may stay awake."

(Vice-Count Utrecht)

The drop from happiness to loss can come

more swift than lightning from a cloudless sky.

I've lost my "uncle Jophan"—pendulum

of fate can make the bravest woman cry.

  Dear Karyn has to wield the Haus alone,

  as though her man went off to war and died.

  Her happy life has gone from meat to bone

  and she? Stays present, keeps deep grief inside.

Of course dear Markus hasn't got the stuff

to help me here—his little kisses showed

me that. My brother Ordo, who can bluff

Count Jaagr—no, it wasn't bluff, he's owed!

  Regardless debt of any kind, he's here

  each time I need him. Dare I name him, "dear?"

First Shoe Drops

At a genteel, relaxed hour of midmorning Counts Vendink and Breihoff sat in Vendink's parlor with a pitcher of watered wine on the table between them, and two mugs. The table also bore a platter laden with small honeyed bread rolls, cheese, and slices of summer sausage.

"So, Androlm," said Jakop, "how is the air this morning?"

"Balmy, my friend, and well scented with flowers. Your roses are already wonderful."

They eyed each other, old familiars as well as old combatants. Doings at their level of the nobility tended to have wide affects.

Breihoff broke the momentary silence. "I deeply regret the loss of not one, but two of your barons in as many years. And the most recent tragic loss raises a second issue, one of succession."

Jakop's eyes widened. "Indeed? Please unfold this for me, my friend. I am taken by surprise."

"As am I. Barony Maihoff lies adjacent to the lands of my Baron Zollhuysen. That fellow, whom you know has no wife, has come to me."

"I know him well, but best by his reputation."

"He has testified to me that Jophan Maihoff, in the hours prior to his unfortunate death, begged him to watch over Karyn and their children."

"And, of course, he must have said there wasn't time nor

opportunity to set this down on parchment, have the priest lay his seal on it, nor bring it to you?"

"You have the gist of it, Jakop."

"And of course he has been too busy since then."

"Jakop, it has been only three days."

"Well, my friend, this presents a problem. I can't believe the tale, not at all. But a noble's pledge that his story is truth raises this above the everyday. Share your own thoughts with me, Count Breihoff."

The formal reference moved the mood forward to one of business and turned cordiality into a genteel facade for hard negotiation.

"I am happy to do that, Vendink, but first I would like to hear your feeling on the matter of Maihoff settling her estate in a manner that could diminish your county and expand my own."

"True enough, I suppose—but if there is issue from the marriage, perhaps there could again be two barons, sons of two fathers."

"That might come to pass, Vendink, but is better discussed on a day far in the future. I hope to hear your feelings on the current matter."

Host Vendink hoisted himself to his feet, one aging bone at a time. "Do not get up, Breihoff. Just the aches of a very old man, and one soon enough dead." He turned toward the doorway. "Rutelyn," he called. "Someone bring my wife and daughter."

While they waited, Breihoff couldn't help smiling. "Vendink, if I were a generation younger and your daughter slightly gentler toward men, I would woo her as both a pleasure to me and a duty to my county."

Vendink said, "Her beauty balances my lack."

Rutelyn appeared at the door. "Yes, my husband and liege?" Tall, hale, and very comely, her billowing mane of red hair explaining her daughter's own, she made a small nod to Breihoff, acknowledging a guest in the Haus. "Our daughter is indeed a beauty, and either knows that all too well or cares nothing for it. And both within minutes! She is close at hand, so if you will wait a bit," she said, raising an eyebrow at him, "I will have Emluyn bring her."

Breihoff and Vendink were sipping from refilled mugs when Vice-Count Utrecht strode into the room.

"So, Count Vendink, Count Breihoff, what matter of governance do you call me to complete?" Her pert face did little to soften the impertinence of such a remark from a younger to an older generation, but for her beauty they overlooked it. Because she wasn't male, she had that freedom to tease. She of course had seen and heard all of the particulars through her father's eyes, but guarded that secret from long habit.

"Let Count Breihoff explain this to you."

Count Breihoff stood and faced her. "Vice-Count, my Baron Zollhuysen advances a claim for the hand of your so recently bereaved Baroness Maihoff. Your father and I, and you as his deputy, should reach an understanding on this before I give him a reply."

Utrecht turned a calm look on him while she re-weighed the matter in her mind. "So, Breihoff, the diminution of Vendink and increase to Breihoff hang on the report of an unmarried womanizer whose estate adjoins that of Maihoff. Do you credit him?"

With the same direct gaze Breihoff replied, "No count in my acquaintance could have been more succinct or accurate." Turning to his host he said, "Dear Vendink, I must credit her."

Utrecht reclaimed the discussion. "Then let me rephrase the question. Do you believe him?"

Breihoff turned back to Utrecht. He couldn't hide his near-helplessness as a male in the presence of such a vibrant, beautiful being. He sighed. "A fair question, Vice-Count. Let us suppose for the moment that I am inclined to. You should know that Baron Zollhuysen conducts himself in an honest manner—when he is vertical, that is, not horizontal."

Jakop made a tiny smile, remembering his own behavior as an unmarried man.

Utrecht snickered. "Zollhuysen's story precludes parchment, nor wax seal to validate his claim. He alleges that Maihoff begged in his last hours for a friend to care for his soon-bereaved wife and children. So, Father, from your long knowledge of Baron Zollhuysen, what light can you shed?"

"Vice-Count, what precautions would or did you take yourself?"

"Jophan was found mute. I believe he had no way to converse with anyone, let alone an intruding neighbor. From the moment he was found he could grunt, but not speak. Zollhuysen didn't find him in an injured state, else he would have taken Jophan to receive care. And surely if Jophan were still hale when they spoke last, the request would have been ludicrous."

Jakop could not hold back a small laugh. "Vice-Count," he said, "you and I may need to discuss this again. For now, Breihoff, it seems best that we exchange ideas often." He struggled to his feet again, this time leaning on his daughter's arm, and the meeting ended.

At supper that night Jakop asked Janalei for any thoughts she had gathered across the afternoon.

"Daddy, Zollhuysen is a confirmed bachelor who has cuckolded many who now raise one or more bastard children for him. These often receive odd favors. The baron makes periodic gifts to each of his 'foster' children." She suppressed any references to her father's own past.

"Yes, Jana, this is common knowledge, even customary for such as he."

"In that case, why does he profess a sudden desire to invert his policy and raise someone else's children?" The question was rhetorical. "And why would poor Jophan, intuiting his upcoming death no less, have begged this favor from someone who has shown no particular skill or experience with children, other than sowing bastards by plowing other men's wives?"

"Daughter, his bastards have found their way into several families, fortunately all of them below his rank. So, you don't suspect that either of Karyn's children is his?"

Still in male attire, she managed to stifle a guffaw. "Male manners are rubbing off on me. But as to Ralf Baron Zollhuysen and Karyn Baroness Maihoff, you'll see a butterfly invite the kiss of a

244

hungry bird before you'll see Maihoff consider such a marriage. The idea mocks itself."

Jakop's smile showed a touch of regret. "Yes, that idea is foolish. Ralf has no natural interest in wife nor child, save to lollop small gifts on 'special' children spotted around his barony. His purpose must be to pass his lands on to a true heir, and no doubt he'll set about making one as soon as he can coerce Karyn into a union."

"You're right, Daddy. We should call on Karyn next."

"Yes, and for the rest of the summer your tag-along prince may have to assist her." The count looked at his daughter for her reaction, but she betrayed none.

By all the saints and Blessed Virgin Mary, why does that stick me? Is it a sore spot? Does Daddy see something in me that I don't? Damn.

Karyn waited for the count and vice-count in a parlor draped in black cloth. She wore black herself, relieved by a small glistening brooch in Maihoff colors, orange and cream.

"Please come in. I've been expecting you," she said. Her cheeks were dry, her eyes red. "Jophan is still warm under the earth, his clay now cooling in the closed claw of death. But I knew there might be an urgent matter. Please tell me your news."

Two small faces peered from around a corner. Their mother shook her head at them and smiled. They scooted away.

Utrecht took a seat on the padded bench next to Karyn and clasped the widow's hands in her own. Her father had also come in on the arm of a footman. He limped over to a nearby chair and sank into it with a grateful sigh. Karyn smiled gratitude at the count, who had journeyed out to see her to discuss her prospects in her own house.

"My dear Karyn, please do not think we want you to rise from a fog of grief and conduct complex business with us. But I trust you've heard of the interest your neighbor has shown."

Karyn shuddered. "Count, Vice-Count, at no time has that wretched man ever set foot in this house. I tended Jophan from the time our men carried him in until he passed into our Savior's hands."

Utrecht pressed the point. "Were you awake the entire time?"

"Either I was awake by his side, or a maidservant, to answer any need. Jophan never spoke."

"And in the days leading up to his accident?"

"To my knowledge, since our wedding, and since taking the barony on his father's death, he never said that anyone, much less that damnable Zollhuysen, should assume his role and administer this barony on his passing."

Utrecht added, "And he had no visitor to whom he could utter such an odd thing in the first place?"

Karyn uttered a deep sigh, drew in a breath, and collapsed back onto the bench. The effort to say this much taxed her, and Utrecht wrapped her in a comforting embrace.

The trip to Barony Maihoff had also taxed the count. The three of them spent a silent quarter-hour. Karyn at last sat up and blinked her eyes. She looked refreshed and called for mulled wine and small slices of cheese.

A week passed before Count Vendink sent his vice-count Utrecht to Breihoff with Karyn Baroness Maihoff's denial; she asked that he forward it to Zollhuysen.

She delivered the respectful message in the form of a parchment. She also managed by gesture and voice to communicate Baroness Maihoff's disbelief and vivid disdain, which Breihoff had expected. Protocol would not let him disclose that he agreed with her.

"My dear Vice-Count, it has been good to see you. I will convey your and Maihoff's respects and wishes in this matter to Zollhuysen."

He takes my hand in a way that I have long since grown used to. Men clasp each other's hands but fondle mine. It became a test of composure, and on that basis she returned a calm squeeze that conveyed no intimate interest.

That business completed, she left without making small talk. Doing so bordered on rude, since the journey covered thirty miles each way. "Please forgive my abruptness, Androlm," she said, with a smile far too warm to resist. "I have much to attend to, and cannot delay."

*__*__*__*

A courier stood at the castle's side door—Zollhuysen's courier, a bachelor like his master and resplendent in Zollhuysen colors, blue and vermillion.

Senior maid Dolamrys eyed him with polite disdain. She ushered him in, and led him to the count. Soft rapping knuckles alerted him, and Jakop turned to see the courier.

"Enter. What might Ralf have to say?" His tone was neutral, lacking any warmth.

The courier stiffened to a formal posture. "My master Ralf Baron Zollhuysen asks for the favor of a meeting with the esteemed count." He stood mute, waiting for a reply.

The count considered turning aside to ignore the fellow, letting him stand there until he had to go relieve himself. But pettiness makes one petty.

"Did your baron indicate his concerns?"

"Sire. He wishes to press suit for the hand of Baroness Maihoff."

"Then why must he come through me?" There were of course good reasons for this, but the count wanted to see what explanation Ralf had given his courier.

"Sire. He seeks your counsel, since the lady in question has rebuffed him."

"Then I rebuff him as well," said the count, and turned back to the whittling he had been busy with when the courier arrived. This pastime remained something he could enjoy, stiff hands or no.

The courier left the way he'd come.

(Ordowahl)

I know that Karyn, Jophan's widow, needs

protection and a steady hand. She's trained

from birth to run her Haus, but Utrecht speeds

to keep my smallest actions well restrained.

     No doubt Count Jakop has a diff'rent plan.

     His word is law, no matter what her hope.

     To have a purpose makes each morning an

     abiding joy. She worries I'll elope?

I pray that Jakop sends me far away,

to separate me from that constant rasp.

Her man-toy Markus, all that kissy-play,

moves my childish pride t'ward envy's grasp.

     This place once held a promise, and I came

     to find its opposite—see, I've gone lame.

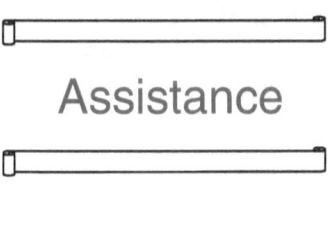

Assistance

\

Glaring overhead, the late June sun dumped heat and light on them as Utrecht, Markus, Ordowahl and respective footmen returned from county business. The sticky heat of an early summer noontime oppressed them, though tempered by a fitful breeze.

A servant met them when they reached the shade of the gateway and dismounted. "My lady and Lord Markus and Prince."

She raised an eyebrow.

"Count Jakop has asked to speak with you, my lady, and with the prince."

Utrecht gave Markus fond pats on the chest. She leaned in close to give him a hug and a soft kiss. "Bye for now, sweet man. I have to go see what's on Count Jakop's mind." She turned her head toward Ordowahl and asked, "Coming, Prince?"

On impulse Ordowahl overstepped a bright line to ask a pointless question. He forced a calm smile: "Vice-Count, before I make some mistaken remark, can I assume that Lord Markus accompanies us each day for a reason beyond his usefulness?"

She wheeled on him. "You choose this moment to ask an impertinent, irrelevant question? The matter doesn't concern you. Actually, I hoped that things wouldn't become awkward between us." She waved her hand as if to shoo a pesky fly and said, "Now let's see what Daddy has to tell us."

They found Jakop in his usual spot, his small dayroom. He said,

249

"I have something to ask of both of you. Daughter, I believe you've been taking Markus along with you from time to time. I pray that Ordowahl's insights and imagination have educated Markus, because I have a favor to ask of the prince."

Utrecht knew what it would be, but out of respect for her father let him name it. Her shoulders slumped for a moment, but she set her face and straightened her posture.

"Prince," said the count, "I ask you to extend the same protection and counsel to Barony Maihoff that you have shown to Vice-Count Utrecht and thus to me." He watched his daughter out the corner of his eye, to see whether acknowledging that the prince had provided exceptional counsel would upset her.

Ordowahl had nothing to say but gave the count a small nod. He didn't bother to look at Utrecht. The open rebuff vis-à-vis Lord Markus made her reaction seem irrelevant. *It's time to accept what she said. I need to go away from here.*

"Karyn Baroness Maihoff will be somewhat less sharp in her treatment of you than the vice-count, whose reported conduct sometimes moves me to ask where I failed in teaching her manners."

Ordowahl found a polite smile. He reflected on his many months of experience with Utrecht. *She and I often enjoy each other's company. But her accepting Markus as wooer has reduced that to a dry bone. Father God, You made dry bones into warriors for Ezekiel, but I am no prophet. Forgive me, but leaving Utrecht's flattened companionship will end a wearying business.*

Utrecht turned her head. She could see Ordowahl visibly relax. Her own expression became pensive. If Ordowahl had been observing her, he might have guessed that something gnawed at her, but the moment passed. He'd actually glimpsed her out of the corner of his eye, but ignored that.

The count waited as each of them abandoned him for a moment, as though in deep thought. Then Ordowahl said, "Count, I will be happy with calmer company, and I am sure that Utrecht will be happy not to have a busybody dog her footsteps."

Jakop looked at his daughter's face. Its immobility made his eyes narrow, as if to read through a mask covering inner confusion.

"I've never seen you this confused, daughter. Ever," he mumbled under his breath.

Ordowahl put the cap on it. "Count, Vice-Count, I will relocate to Barony Maihoff tomorrow. Farewell and thank you for your kindness, Jakop. I have gained much from my time here."

When the rose to leave, Janalei went up to her room. *The prince gives me a feeling I can't name. Lose him? He's the brother I never had. Without him I will like a shoe without its mate, incomplete and not fit for its function. But, incomplete in what way? "Whole" or "safe" or "understood" or—no matter, I have Markus, who at least lets me feel wooed. I can never let prince Fairy Toes find his way down* that *garden path.*

Emluyn and Joop had gone with her. She sat in thought on the edge of her bed, then asked them, "When will the prince return? He said that he had enjoyed his time here, but that he looked forward to residing in Haus Maihoff."

"Jana," said Joop, "Klarenz tells me the prince might look forward to helping Baroness Maihoff acquire control of her lands and holdings. He says the prince hasn't mentioned any other plans."

"Joopi, why on earth won't he just have done with that, then return here?"

Emluyn asked, "Lady Jana, what do you imagine would draw him back?"

"But we've been so effective together. I feel affection for him. He's like an enormous brother to me now. I'm not sure I want to govern without him. I like him, as he says, 'tagging along.'"

Joop supplied the missing piece. "Everyone knows how much you rely on him. But, Jana, why do you think he has spent so much time on your interests, at the expense of his own? I often see you upset at the thought that he might pay attention to another woman. How would it affect him, then, to see you kiss and caress a wooing man?"

Janalei frowned. "What an ugly thought! Leave me now. I have a great deal on my mind."

The next morning Markus appeared at the gate with his usual happy smile and put a kiss on her forehead.

"Markus, my friend, I need to say something."

At the word *friend* he stood straighter and looked suspicious. "Friend?" he asked.

"Yes, dear man. You are a dear, kind man, and my friendship for you is strong."

"I see. Does 'strong' mean that I will never go past friend? I hope that the tender wooing of my beloved hasn't failed? What have I done?"

"Markus, nothing. I like you very much. You have been wonderful company; I enjoy spending time with you."

"Then what, dearest woman? What is the matter? Whatever it is, just tell me, and I will conquer it. Nearness to you is worth any effort, any sacrifice."

I choose between two men I want to keep by me, brother or whatever, versus yet one more wooer whom I'm already close to sending away. "Markus, it has nothing to do with you. There is nothing you need to conquer."

His look switched in a heartbeat from unhappy to vulnerable, even hurt.

"Dear Markus, I am not ready for open wooing. What I want is something else. But I'll always carry your presence in my heart."

His face turned pale. "Then, dearest one, my company has become awkward. Please excuse me for now. I have the patience of Job, but I cannot believe that we will just be 'friends.' What have I done? Please tell me, my love."

Janalei looked at his plaintive face but didn't find words to reply.

Markus sensed his futility and said, "I'll always be ready, as long as you remain unmarried."

"Thank you, Markus. I carry you in my heart, dear one."

He mounted his horse and at a slow walk went back the way he had come.

She let a ray of hope cross her face. *Ordowahl moves himself to Barony Maihoff this day, but I'm sure he'll come by the castle first.* She looked up and saw two men in the near distance, on two horses and leading two mules. The size of one man and his stallion identified the prince, and her pulse quickened. No other traffic on the road held one iota of her interest.

Ordowahl approached the gate and dismounted. Utrecht gave him a smile far kinder and happier than she realized; his answering smile lifted her spirits. He seemed unaware of anyone leaving the castle gateway, which also gave her hope.

"Prince," she said, and laid a hand on his chest. "My friend, I know that I am very hard to get to know well, but there is something I would like to say to you."

"What is it, Utrecht?"

Just then a female voice came through the gateway. "Prince Ordowahl? Are we ready?"

It was Karyn Baroness Maihoff, and she spotted Ordowahl chatting with Utrecht. "Oh, hello, Vice-Count. It is so nice to see you. Baroness Mother Fretheldin was kind enough to invite me to spend a night with her, and now I am beyond happy to have the prince come to stay. The summer could have been an empty hell without a man's presence."

Utrecht replied, "I see. I hope that the two of you establish Karyn's control of the barony."

Ordowahl turned his face back to the vice-count. "Thank you, Utrecht. You had something to say to me?"

"Well, Prince, I hope you that have a fine summer." Her sincerity emerged from a straight, vulnerable face that had forgotten how to smile.

"Thank you, Utrecht. I hope the same for you." He gave her an ordinary smile and remounted Hammerfoot. Then baroness and prince proceeded at the head of a parade of mounted footmen and a carriage full of maids.

Utrecht stood mute. She tried to suppress a feeling of looming emptiness. As they were leaving she called out, "See you in the fall?"

Ordowahl turned to wave back at her. "Yah, see you in the fall."

Rage welled up against Ordowahl's evident ease at leaving her to an empty hell of a summer, alone and barren. Losing his company to the young, attractive baroness doubled that. She fought with a sick feeling of dread. *And what am I to do if he finds in her what I can never let him find in me? Joop and Emmi asked why he would dream of coming back. Damn!*

(Vice-Count Utrecht)

I know that Karyn, Jophan's widow, asks

protection, needs a steady hand. She's trained

from birth to run her Haus, yet here she masks

her lust with innocence, "all scatterbrained."

    I gave him decent chance to hear my mind,

       to clear his misperceptions re Naechstofen—

    did he hear? No, he's so mulish-blind!

    His joy to squire the fertile widow? Oaf!

What ugliness, to think poor Markus daft,

e'en though he is—insipid as a frog.

And kiss him? Did I turn frog prince? I laughed

to see poor Ordowahl go lost in fog.

    So here I am, dry, lonely as a fish

       the summer long, while she's his swiving-wish.

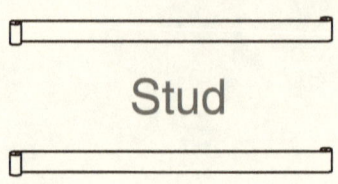

Stud

An hour after dawn, on a crisp day in autumn, the harvest in and yellow-red hues washing over a tree here and there, Ordowahl and Klarenz appeared at the Castle Vendink gate. They came from the direction of Haus Hangendro.

"Klarenz, something about a good breakfast and a pleasant ride sets a man's face into a smile. And this smile can even withstand the sight of Lord Markus receiving sweet kisses from Utrecht."

They dismounted, and Klarenz tied up their horses. Moments later the vice-count and Joop walked their horses out to the gate and tied them in the usual place, beside Klarenz's horse and Hammerfoot.

Utrecht's astonished glare showed immediate anger. She barked at him, "October has begun. Fall came on us over a week ago. Do you tire of plowing the fertile baroness, sowing oats in her ripe field? As well as plowing the daughters of our lower nobility like daisies beneath a bull's hoof? Perhaps some of the prettier peasants as well?"

She turned away from him to calm herself and to review with Joop the sequence of the day's planned events.

Ordowahl looked aside at Klarenz, who only shrugged. "Vice-Count, how do I understand your mood? You know that I have been answering your father's wish by assisting County Vendink."

She kept her back to him.

"And while we're standing here doing nothing, I have to guess at why you would concerned yourself with my supposed attentions to any woman. Haven't you had Lord Markus by your side all summer?"

She turned back to look at him, her face flat and emotionless. "He proved insufficient."

"I see. I pray that in time you find someone who is sufficient. What can I do today to assist County Vendink?"

"Your company honors us," she said. Her expression gave the lie to that. She looked him up and down as if evaluating a farm animal to decide on a price. "Prince, must I offer a welcome, seeing you return from your little Eden at Haus Maihoff? No matter. A landed knight's bull seems to have broken through a fence and serviced a baronet's milk cow."

"Begging your pardon, I fail to understand the gravity of that."

"The baronet is Opdijk. You do recall him?"

"How could I not recall a fine-featured, fussy fellow who refuses to hide his dislike of a woman telling him what to do?"

"He is upset because he was about to breed his cow to a bull with a history of siring cows that produce much milk. Now her calf may be worth nothing much."

Ordowahl paused for a moment. "Vice-Count, without asking why the matter elevates itself to deserve your judgment, let me guess that the bull's owner may be willing to receive half the stud fee his bull should get."

"Half? What 'man' would settle for half of anything?"

"Well put. You remind me, from time to time, that men are less aware of others, besides being less practical than women."

She looked bored.

"Asking the entire fee presumes that his bull's service was stolen. In fact, I will guess that his own carelessness cost him that. I would call that sense, not sensitivity. He can't ask for his full fee. It's simple."

She made a narrow face that spoke disdain for his idea, thus for him as well. "With regard to animal lust, I have a story to illustrate today's problem."

"A story? Thank you. I'm always searching for new stories."
Thank you Father in heaven, her mood seems to have turned.

"Yes. Well, Prince, it is like this: A prosperous baron had a
fenced-in field full of grazing cows. Next to it stood a pen holding
two bulls. A path led past each, and a peasant left both gates open."

Ordowahl clarified, "A baron who pens cows and bulls next to
each other with a simple fence between them, which no bull in rut
would consider an obstacle, and who also puts two bulls in one
small pen."

"So far, so good, Prince."

"They might get along with each other. But if there are cows
nearby then one of them may die—after injuring the other. I think
I'm with you."

She looked at him with surprise. "Are you going to hear the
story or not?"

"Yes, the story. The story is an allegory and doesn't relate to
material truth."

She snorted then said, "Damn. I hate it when a man goads me
into one of the baser male expressions."

He suppressed a smile. *Forgive me, Utrecht, but my own mood
seems to rise along with yours.*

"At any rate, my studious observer of livestock... The younger
bull was the more alert. He noticed that both gates stood open,
assuring a path to the field of cows."

"I suppose, Vice-Count. Beef animals seldom show that much
mental quickness, but for the sake of the story, we can let them."

"Are you going to stop interrupting? Men! And I am one
myself." She cleared her throat and continued the tale.

"So, the young bull rushes up to the old bull, gets his attention,
and explains the open pathway to reach the cows. He blurts out,
'Let's run to the other field and mount some o' them cows.

"The old bull turns his head to the younger and says, 'Lad,
let's *stroll* over there and mount *all* them cows.'"

Ordowahl smiled and said, "I see the purpose of your story. The
lesson is that a slow pace leads to mounting success?" *And, Father*

God in heaven, help me. My own pace makes "slow" look like "sprint."

Behind them Joop and Klarenz stifled outright laughter.

Utrecht frowned at his refusal to enjoy the joke. "Mindless promiscuity marks all bulls, and most men."

"I see, I see. It's plain that the count's daughter has no interest in a man who reminds her of a bull."

"Where did you get that idea?"

"If you will permit any remark regarding the count's daughter, this might dismay her, that no one with the opportunity has ever forgone pursuit."

She gave him a wry look. "Enough of this. We need to adjudicate between a knight and one of my baronets, whose wishes are for the moment more important."

"I agree, my friend. When we revisit the story, though, I hope you'll enlighten me by explaining the role, in your allegory, of those very complaisant cows."

She gave him a mocking smile. "The word *moo* is not something the count's daughter has ever uddered."

At least she smiled, also made a pun. His feeling of satisfaction with the morning rose further.

*__*__*__*

When the group of four arrived, both complainants stood up. Klarenz and Joop handled the horses when the party dismounted.

"Thank you, Vice-Count Utrecht, and thank you, Prince Nordweg," said Baronet Opdijk.

"Opdijk, let me hear your complaint," Utrecht said. "Tell me when you noticed anything amiss, what you saw then, and what your plans were for the cow."

He wore an avuncular expression. "Vice-Count, Rosebud gives half again the milk of any other cow I have, excepting only her own heifer calves. The best bull belongs to Baronet Vornheid."

Aside, Utrecht told Ordowahl, "Not one of my baronets." She thought to herself,. *Something seems very odd here.*

"I lend him my best meat bull to breed up his best meat cow. He keeps the beef-beef mating, and I keep the milk-milk mating."

He stopped to be sure he wasn't wandering too far afield, glared at the knight standing mute beside him, and continued.

"Three nights ago, just as the sun was half-down, I heard a great bawling in my near pasture. I went to see if a wolf or bear had come after one of my animals."

"And what did you find, Baronet?" she asked.

"I saw his bull tuppin' my Rosebud. My pasture gate was open, and this bull must have walked right in like he had no master to mind him."

Out of the corner of his eye Ordowahl noticed Klarenz and Joop elbow each other in the ribs and nod at the prince, who gave them a small grin. Utrecht may have seen that, too, but didn't appear to understand what humor they found in "master to mind him."

What can they see that is funny about a bull without a master?—Oh! "I see," she said. "Knight, give me your side of the story."

"Highness, er, Vice-Count, I was walkin' my bull to serve stud when he suddenly broke free from me by the baronet's gate and ran into his pasture of cows. It is no fault of mine that the gate was left open."

"Yet you failed to control your bull."

"Yes, Highness. But since I didn't get the stud fee I was taking my bull to earn, I claim the right to be compensated for what was clearly the baronet's mistake."

"Who is—" the Baronet Opdijk began, but subsided into an angry sputter when Utrecht held up her hand.

"I'll ask the questions, Opdijk. The owner of a bull has to understand its tendency to charge at just about anything. What control *did* you have over the bull?"

"Well, Highness, it wasn't complete, was it? That's why I offered to split the stud fee half-half, since each of us was at fault."

"And you also didn't give me a straight answer. I took the trouble to travel here, so you must take the trouble to give a complete answer." Her face was calm, but resembled flat stone.

"Yes, Highness. I tied a stout rope to his nose ring, long enough to let me walk behind but out of reach of horn and hoof, which is the only sensible place to be."

"The first sensible thing I've heard so far."

"So I took a look at the baronet's open gate, and it stopped me. The shock, the surprise of it! But I don't have a bull's nose."

"Nor even a bull's sense, either. Why didn't the open gate make you cautious, not careless?"

"Highness, I—"

"Now you, Baronet. Why was your gate open? It's been three days. I expect you to have found a reason by now."

Baronet Opdijk lifted his hand up high, flickered his fingers, slapped it down onto his head to scratch, and looked down at his shoes, as if he were thinking.

"Out with it, Opdijk. A stud fee isn't a valid pretext to bring the vice-count out this far."

Silence.

"What remains of my good will, if anything, brought me here. You play-acted the jolly good uncle for a ten-year-old girl, a dozen years ago. Humor me."

Just then Joop and Klarenz shouted, and the party's horses reared up in alarm. Ordowahl swiveled his head to look in one direction then the other.

Two sets of six rough-looking men rushed at them from opposing parts of the lane. With ropes and knives.

Ordowahl left Joop and Klarenz to fend off the group nearest them, confident the attackers wouldn't have a prayer of doing much to Hammerfoot. The prince drew his knife and sprinted toward the other set. His size, speed, and huge knife made them into rabbits. He chased them until they left the lane to flee in six different directions. One could be heard crying out to another, "Six of us is too few for that damned prince."

At the same time Opdijk stood aside with a look of happy expectation. Ordowahl had left; that was enough. The knight jumped behind Utrecht and pinned her arms back; Opdijk stepped close, almost bumping into her, and fingered the top button of the two on her vest.

Helpless, she sneered into Opdijk's dilated eyes and said in a slow, grating voice, "'Uncle Oppi, we stopped playing games when

I was ten. You do remember why, don't you?" *Rat bastard! God in heaven, smite him!*

"I hear the panic in your voice, Jana. It is delicious. He moved from the now-open vest to her tunic and opened its buttons. He seemed curious to discover how that naïve muscle-chested tomboy had changed to an adult-figured woman. He pulled the tunic down around her shoulders and stared with wonder at a naked pair of teats.

He's never seen a child nursed before, or a woman bathing?

Ordowahl returned at that moment, his knife still out and a bloodthirsty look in his eye. He grabbed Opdijk by the neck and lifted him, leaving noble toes scrabbling for traction. He closed his fist, and the baronet's throat with it.

"Prince!" Utrecht shouted. "He is titled. Do not kill him." Her voice softened. "Thank you, my friend. You played the magnificent bull when I needed one most."

He tried not to stare.

Why do I not cover myself from his gaze? "We will not discuss this event, or the baronet, for a long, long time, if ever. Joop. Klarenz." She shrugged out of the knight's grip, rebuttoned her tunic and vest then turned around to see them bound up in ropes tied with hard knots. "Joop. You child, don't you have a knife?"

Ordowahl noticed the baronet's blue face and put the limp form on the ground, with at least a little care. The man had a title, after all. He cut the footmen out of their bonds then picked up their knives and returned them with solemn grace.

"You did as best you could. Now that you two are free, bind Opdijk and the knight."

The knight, still in shock. hadn't moved. He realized that he had no option. He hadn't let go of the vice-count so much as not resist when she pulled herself free.

She turned to face him. "Lie down by uncle Oppi. Either that or receive the same treatment he did." Her level voice held the edge of death. Tremble?

The knight seemed to know that his life would soon end. He stared at the supine baronet as if at a vapor or apparition.

"Do not run. The prince is much faster than he looks. Just lie still while Joop and Klarenz bind you until you both look like sausages." Nodding at Joop and Klarenz, Utrecht said, "Use all of their rope."

She tugged at the hem of her vest, straightened her shoulders, and took a half-dozen deep, calming breaths.

Two dozen serfs stood where they had emerged from the baronet's house and yard, immobile, their mouths agape. Two still held pitchforks, ready to defend their liege, until someone pointed out the vice-count and Ordowahl.

Utrecht turned to the closest one. "Hitch a horse and wagon and bring them here. Your baronet's footman will transport him and this knight to Castle Vendink."

She turned to Ordowahl, who had his eye on Joop and Klarenz, evaluating their workmanship. He looked ready to help if the need arose. She tapped his elbow.

He turned to her as if spun. "Yes, Vice-Count, what is it?"

A knit brow and squinting eyes underscored the concern on his face. *He looks frightened for me. This is new! I've never seen such depth of feeling on that odd, but always reassuring face.*

"Prince, thank you again." She drew another deep breath, let it out as a slow sigh. For a moment she leaned against him, her face on his chest and hands on his shoulders. Then she pushed back.

"Never a word of this. Not from Klarenz or you." She raised her voice. "I will silence the knight," and she looked at the fellow.

He had heard, and nodded. He would say nothing.

Turning back to Ordowahl, she said, "Opdijk often has a kind of 'play,' but just with his serfs' younger daughters, as far as I'm aware. He has nothing to fear from them."

She turned her attention to the footmen and their bundled cargo. In an outdoor voice she said, "You, Klarenz and Joop, and you, knight and baronet, will speak no word of this to anyone, not even each other. Ever."

Joop and Klarenz rode at the head of a small homeward parade. Utrecht for a time sat on Opdijk's chest where he lay in the wagon bed. Her feet rested on the knight. Her monolog sounded very calm, but firm, not casual.

"Opdijk, you child-diddler, my parents disbelieved me when I told them about playing tickle-under-the-clothes games while sitting on Uncle Oppi's lap."

The baronet's bindings included a loop around his head that forced his jaws open.

"You seemed like such fun. But one visit was enough, you dickless old pervert. Tell me you understand." Utrecht seethed.

The baronet was silent, and the knight lay with his face turned away. Whatever had been in it for him, his fate now dissipated into dust.

"Nnnnhh," said Opdijk at last, through his mouthful of rope.

"Let that be your final word on the subject. In fact, former baronet, let that be your last word on anything."

The cart driver might have picked out the words over the cart's creaking while its wheels bounced without a pause over the very uneven road, but no one else was close enough. Doubtless this was a new form of conveyance for a baronet accustomed to riding on seats in a coach body suspended on sprung leather straps to soak up the shocks of the road.

Ordowahl saw that Utrecht's weight on the baronet's chest made Opdijk gasp for each breath. He did his best not to snoop and rode behind the carriage holding the reins of her horse.

After a time she gestured for Ordowahl to bring her mount alongside. With it adjacent to the wagon bed, athletic grace moved one long, firm leg up and over the saddle. The other left the wagon; she slid onto the saddle and stirrups like a bird of prey coming to roost.

"Sometimes a man in fact *can't* control himself," she said. "That's when you have to reinforce the point."

*__*__*__*

At dawn a spectacle became visible in the main square of the city of Utrecht. Two men, once baronet and knight, stood barefoot and barelegged in stocks. They had teeth, but no tongues. Sleeveless burlap tunics were their sole guard against autumn's chill. Someone other than a barber had shaved their heads, beards, and eyebrows then used soot to make wide black cross-hatching marks that disguised their faces. Leather cords tied behind their necks held heir mouths open.

They could not speak, and no one could recognize either man. A sign above their heads read:

**These have committed grave
offense against County Vendink.
You may give them a slap**.

The men remained there for two full days and nights, without food or water. Their body wastes made a mess of them and their sackcloth tunics. Their faces became bloody pulp. By noon of the first day teeth began to appear on the ground near them.

Stories do find their way out. On the second day they stood exposed as knight and baronet with lands and holdings forfeit.

An hour before the third dawn two Vendink footmen came with carts. They unbound each man. A priest offered them last rites. Each footman hoisted a man onto his cart and drove off in a direction away from that man's kin. The count had taken the forethought to leave a dried-out loaf of bread and a jug of water in each cart. He didn't want them to die too soon.

When either cart crossed out of County Vendink, another cart and driver stood waiting. The first driver used a whip to lash his cargo until the fellow understood that he was to climb into the next cart. The former baronet needed a boost; the drivers combined their boots to launch him.

As before, the cart held a loaf of dried-out bread and a jug of water. No report came back of where either journey ended, or how long it took.

(Ordowahl)

Poor Markus, he a fond but doom-faced lad

was gone—how many weeks, his interlude?

I had no notion what had made her mad,

but speaking slow and homely, healed her mood.

　　She tells a bawdy tale, as man to man,

　　but hasn't found the knack. Then Oppi's joke

　　played out on her, and groped its evil span.

　　Her calm in triumph flung a deathly stroke.

I've never thought her lesser than a man

in any way of war, except for reach.

Her mind is finer than near all I can

recall. Her will can plug the broadest breach.

　　Am I the fool for spending all my days

　　with one whose man-ness chills her beauty's blaze?

Usurper

Ordowahl moved back into Haus Hangendro and resumed instructing his circle of martial arts pupils from his quite able assistant Sir Torwulf. He and Klarenz returned to celebrating dawn Mass and confessing to Fr. Henck.

For a week following Opdijk's fatal mistake, Utrecht stayed inside the castle walls. Emluyn ventured out once to announce that her mistress Utrecht wasn't well disposed. Klarenz guessed that she suffered from unusual menstrual cramps, but not even Joop came forth to provide further word of her mood or health. Each day they appeared at the castle gate and left when Joop came out to tell them that Utrecht would do no business that day.

Just at daybreak, a day or two after Utrecht again came forth to handle county affairs, a troop of fifty armed men had gathered on a lane near Barony Maihoff. Five more were mounted and in mail armor, led by two mailed nobles They paused just around a bend in the lane from Haus Maihoff. The Haus was visible through gaps in the trees, but the armed men were hard to notice.

The nobles proceeded to enter the Maihoff courtyard, dismount, and ascend a small set of steps to reach the porch. The elder, about fifty years of age and beginning to gray, bore a once-handsome face now gone to leather and wrinkles. A bushy beard of mixed brown and white covered the collar of his tunic. Black with gold trim, it identified him as Baron Ferbliet.

The other had to be the baron's son Iosefus, a new man of seventeen years. "Papa, I cannot wait to see the baroness!" he chortled.

"Indeed, Iosefus. But I will speak first. You must listen and stay quiet while I settle the matter at hand."

A senior maid opened the door, and her eyes flew wide in surprise. "Baron Ferbliet, and Iosefus," she said. "Please come in, and if you will, please let me tell my mistress why you have come."

"I will tell her myself. Please summon her."

At the word *summon* the maid stood a little taller, looked askance at the baron, and hurried down a central hallway.

Hushed but dramatic whispering echoed back toward the two visitors, who closed the door behind themselves.

Outside, a watcher had waited for that signal. Five more on horses and forty-five on foot entered the courtyard, making as little noise as they could. The horsemen dismounted. A few armed men led seven mounts around to the stable yard in the rear, while half of the rest crowded onto the porch.

Inside, five male servants emerged from the rear of the mansion. Meeting a baron in such a confrontational way set them very ill at ease. Ferbliet put on the oily expression of a fake uncle.

"Friends," he said, "I bring wonderful news, but it is only for the ears of Karyn, Baroness Maihoff. Please ask her to greet me, then leave us."

The baroness entered the room. "Men, please attend me here. No words that Baron Ferbliet and I care to exchange require privacy."

"My, my." His voice was smooth. "I come with only goodness in my heart, and joy for the safety and protection that is about to be yours, Baroness."

She looked at him, eye to eye. "I seem to recall a series of conflicts between our two baronies, Ferbliet. Have you come to tell me that you and some other baron have exchanged holdings?"

She gave him a sweet smile, joy curdling just below the surface.

"Ahh, I delight in your spirit, dear woman. Having you as a daughter-in-law will make family life fascinating." A hint of menace rode the edge of his voice. "Your Jophan, dear widow, has often mentioned his concern for your future in the event that he should be called home to Almighty God before raising up an adult son."

The baroness had grown hardened to the loss of her husband and stifled a snide retort.

"'What of you, Erneuylt?' he would ask. Each time I would remind him that I have an adult son, and another, now come of age, stands beside me."

He noticed her four-year-old son peeking around a corner, but spoke of his own. "You have seen Iosefus as a boy, but he has attained the age of seventeen years and is counted a man."

She shot Iosefus a grim look. "I offer no disrespect, Iosefus, but what I see, standing beside your father, is one far too inexperienced either to raise Jophan's son and daughter, or to manage a barony."

Iosefus' face, out of his father's line of sight, froze.

She continued. "No matter what conversations are alleged between my husband and you, I find no protection in your offer. None at all."

"Ahhh, dear Karyn, your lord and master warned me about you. He would say, 'Erneuylt, she is very difficult to govern. It is, mind you, one of her most desirable traits. You must, if I were to die suddenly, take a strong hand with her.'"

She drew back in shock. "Rubbish!" she said, with spit flying.

"You prove him so right." He gave her a patronizing look. "Karyn, please submit yourself to reason. It is clear that you will inevitably fail without a man's hand to stabilize and bring order to your lands, your holdings, your baronets—some of them can be very obnoxious, as I am sure you know."

"Baron Ferbliet, I insist that you leave immediately."

He put on a sad face and stepped backward to the door while keeping his eyes on her. He had coached Iosefus not to move until instructed. The baron pulled the door open and stepped aside.

Five men, also in mail, and a crowd of other armed men attempted to enter. As many as would fit stood there, with more behind them clogging the porch and entryway.

"I am sad that it has come to this, dear baroness, but I only do this for your safety, and to honor Jophan's often-repeated request.

He warned me to use a strong hand, and this is what it has come to."

Her stony stare would have cowed many, but not Ferbliet.

"I deeply wish that you had been able to see the reason and generosity of my coming here."

*__*__*__*

When Utrecht came into the Vendink Keep courtyard, Ordowahl responded with a simple smile. "What business do we have this day, Vice-Count?"

"Why do you call me Vice-Count? Between us, Utrecht is much more pleasant to hear."

He looked over at her. "As to calling you by a name not a title, yes. I'll strike Vice-Count from my vocabulary. I hope you will strike both Prince and Nordweg from yours."

"So, you would deprive me of a disciplinary reference, my way of slowing you down?" Her smile held a smallish hope of gentleness.

"Even as I have no authority to apply discipline, I also am not under your own. Parity among friends, my friend, is appropriate, for as long as you tolerate my company."

She smirked and thought for a moment. "Very well, Ordowahl, I will use your given name."

"Thank you, Utrecht."

She handed him a parchment with a broken wax seal. "This came to me at dusk yesterday."

He gave it a brief look. "I see a signature on the reverse side by the hand of Erneuylt Baron Ferbliet, who celebrated a new decade this past spring."

"Read it."

"I trust that the seal is his. He asserts a claim in the name of his son Iosefus to the Maihoff lands and estates—"

"Cautious fellow, isn't he?" said Utrecht.

"—and alleges suit to bind Baroness Maihoff as bride to his son Iosefus. Further he alleges a verbal compact with the departed Jophan, Baron Maihoff. He includes an assertion that, as a point of honor, his word is true."

"And, having had your fling with the lovely baroness, you're ready to abandon her to Ferbliet?"

Ordowahl looked a question at Utrecht and sighed. "No. Instead I am curious why Utrecht has not already appeared to set the baron straight. What have I missed?"

"It helps when you read all of it."

He scanned the rest of the parchment, reading a lengthy text in small script.

"He takes pains to set out his entire relationship with both Jophan and Karyn, over many years and many so-called small adjustments to the boundary between their lands."

Ordowahl looked a question at her: "Many, and many?"

"Yes. But do go on, Ordowahl."

"Over the course of the summer his patience has gone to nothing, waiting for any response to his many pleas that he be allowed to fulfill Jophan's fateful wish, restated for a hundredth time just a week before his most unfortunate death."

"Go on."

"And in conclusion he will appear at Haus Maihoff on today's date. So when did this reach you?"

"A courier delivered it to the palace just after dusk."

"No word of this came to Barony Maihoff while I was there, Utrecht. I looked at all the letters and other messages that came each day."

"Reading her correspondence?"

"Karyn asked me to discuss each one with her and propose a proper response. Ferbliet sent a brief note of condolence, nothing more."

"Regarding Ferbliet, I thought as much."

Utrecht had sent couriers the prior night to every Maihoff baronet plus each of her own—none of Vendink's barons, such as Hangendro. The collection of baronets were to make every possible effort to have their full complement of armed men present at Haus Maihoff no later than noon.

Ordowahl sent Klarenz back to bring Torwulf and set out toward the meeting place, a juncture of lanes a quarter-mile from Haus Maihoff.

Assembly took considerable time. Maihoff's were close, but Utrecht's baronets lived farther away and could not arrive until very late in the morning. As they appeared, Ordowahl began to organize them into a battle order. Utrecht arrived an hour after he did. She wondered whether Ferbliet understood the loyalty of Maihoff's baronets and their armed men. She approached Ordowahl and said, "Please stand down, Ordowahl. I will arrange my troops."

He stepped back but did not cross his arms or lean against something. Instead he walked Hammerfoot forward until Utrecht sent him a loud hiss.

"Ordowahl, just where do you think you're going?" and he halted Hammerfoot.

She continued marshalling troops as they arrived yet never took her eye off him. When the sun looked highest in the sky she declared it noon and gave an instruction.

"Ordowahl, you will move to the rear of the formation. You will keep yourself and Sir Torwulf away from anything to do with Barony Maihoff."

"Utrecht, Count Jakop asked me to protect Haus Maihoff, also to defend the baroness."

Utrecht's face remained a closed mask.

He ignored her cold stare. "I plan to challenge Ferbliet. Since your troops exceed anything Ferbliet can summon, County Vendink's interest is better served if he and I settle this matter without spilling the blood of Ferbliet's men and perhaps a few of your own."

"Do you stand also as her suitor? If not, what possible reason brings you to risk yourself?"

What a convoluted puzzle she is. I've heard many men say that women are beyond all understanding, but then so is the love of God. And in her case, the difference seems small. "Utrecht, I see a problem to be solved and intend to solve it. The baroness will not abandon her lands and follow me when I return to Nordweg, if that might disturb you."

She continued to stare at him, and he held her gaze with as patient a look as he could.

"I give up! Do whatever you want. You always do anyway."

Ordowahl nodded at Torwulf, to hold him in place. He turned Hammerfoot toward Haus Maihoff and ambled forward.

Ferbliet had posted a sentry. The man reported both Ordowahl's movement and the rough size of Utrecht's forces. Before Ordowahl had covered fifty yards three armed men on horseback followed by twenty men at arms surged down the lane toward him. Ferbliet himself held the lead.

Utrecht sent armed men to fan out to either side to prevent being flanked. The fact that Ferbliet had waited for Ordowahl to advance told her several things. The first was that he might hope to reach a gentleman's agreement with Ordowahl.

Second, his apparent carelessness screamed at her to look for some sort of trap, using himself and Ordowahl as bait. And third—well, she hadn't yet thought of a third but was sure Ferbliet had.

Prince and baron halted ten feet apart. "Baron Ferbliet, I challenge you and call you a liar." It was apparent that the baron expected this, and his expression moved from distaste into an open sneer.

"Save your childish theatrics for another day, foreigner. Remove yourself from the private business of County Vendink."

"I have been for some months and do remain Haus Maihoff's champion, by Jakop Count Vendink's invitation."

"Do tell."

"I have seen a letter bearing your seal. In it I find only untruths. State now your purpose in bringing armed men onto the Maihoff estates."

"Ah, but there you are mistaken, foreigner. What I have said is entirely truthful. The baroness invited me here today and has asked me to make my son Iosefus available to her as husband. It is you who trespass."

The baron goaded his horse into a charge. Ordowahl's raised shield deflected the baron's sword strike as man and horse rushed past.

Ordowahl wheeled Hammerfoot around and charged the baron, who had also wheeled his horse around. Their mounts reared up to collide, chest to chest. Ordowahl swung his sword behind the other mount's head to slice Baron Ferbliet's reins, lopping off a swatch of mane as well.

The baron flinched away from the sword stroke and struggled to keep his balance. He fell backward off the rearing horse.

Torwulf galloped near as prince's second while the baron struggled to rise from his butt-sprawl. He signaled for his own second to help him, lest his heavy armor make him go on all fours to stand up. He would not do that while Ordowahl loomed overhead.

Ordowahl glanced back at Baron Ferbliet's troops and shook his head, They didn't move. He dismounted, disarmed Ferbliet, and helped him to his feet. Ordowahl returned the baron's sword, hilt first, and stood back to let him adopt a fighting stance.

"Choose, Baron. You may withdraw your absurd lies with regard to any possible connection between your Barony and Maihoff's. If so I will withdraw my challenge. Otherwise we will prove by arms which of us speaks truth."

Ferbliet was too upset to do other than fight, and lunged at Ordowahl.

Ordowahl pivoted and leaned back to let Ferbliet's sword and arm pass through the place where he had just been. The prince's sword slashed down, faster than an eye blink.

Ferbliet fell to his knees, left hand clutching the stump at his right wrist. He remained silent, though his face contorted into a rictus of pain and rage.

"Baron, you have lost your hand. You may pick up your sword and continue to fight with your other hand, else yield."

The Baron, one hand clamped around the stump of his forearm, shook his head.

Ordowahl turned to Utrecht. "I ask permission to spare this man. His actions sprang from selfish motives, not truth. He is nonetheless a beloved child of God and I would sooner spare his life than require it from him."

"You, Ordowahl, have no standing to take a Vendinker baron's life. I will do that, or not do it, as I and I alone see fit."

She dismounted, drew her sword, and approached Baron

Ferbliet.

"Look up at me. What serves the best interest of County Vendink, Baron? Do you acknowledge your need for penance?"

His face remained a mask, as though he could focus at the moment on his bloody stump, and nothing more.

"And do you renew your obedience to Count Vendink? And do you sacrifice to the Baroness Maihoff, as that penance, the tenth part of all your lands and holdings?"

Baron Ferbliet nodded. Utrecht stepped so close to him that her groin bumped his forehead. She brought the sword hilt down on the back of his head. Three light taps cemented his pledge.

Iosefus elbowed his way through a tight ring of baronets that had gathered around his father. He helped him to stand and used his kerchief as a temporary tourniquet.

"All you armed men!" she shouted. "Everyone. Put away your weapons and return to your homes."

O'er time the way of Vice-Count with the prince

began to fray, to settle, grow remote.

No Markus-kisses needed to convince

him he was neutered, cupid's antidote.

      He asked himself, what might a sweet kiss mean?

      "Would she at length discard me like the rest?"

      A foolish notion—did he dream she'd lean

      again, toward some other, unimpressed?

Why Father God in heaven put him here

was nothing he could glimpse. But naught could shift

him from this velvet prison, so severe,

and yet—to leave her 'd cut him loose, adrift.

      What for it but to stay the course, to see

      each day on day, keep watch upon the sea.

Swapping

In the chilly evening Ordowahl and Utrecht sat with Count Jakop in his formal front parlor, drinking mulled wine. Jakop blessed their resolution of Ferbliet's crime.

"My children, you've accomplished much. A bloody-minded baron is defeated with no loss of life, and he further accepts surrender of a tenth of his lands. I am unsure that I could have done as well."

Utrecht squared her shoulders as though stretching then relaxed. She seemed to have resolved an internal conflict. She asked, "So, Ordowahl, who shall wed Baroness Maihoff?"

"Odd you would ask that, Utrecht."

"Odd? However so? What do you suggest the baroness do, operate her barony without a man's hand?"

"I presume Ferbliet took home the one he lost?"

She snorted.

"Or are you the lone woman in this County who can accomplish such a thing? Do *you* need a man's hand?"

She glared at him. "I do what I must, Ordowahl, and am happy to succeed in it." A sneer flickered across her face, but she let the matter drop.

*__*__*__*

Several days passed with no county business to transact. Out of courtesy Utrecht met Ordowahl each day, just to say she had no need of him. As a rule days with no business outnumbered those with work to do, but this dry spell seemed overlong.

One evening at Haus Hangendro Wils asked Ordowahl to speak with him after supper, in private. Despite the cold weather they went out onto the entry porch and looked up at the stars. The sky was clear and the air very cold.

"My good friend," Wils said, his breath blowing like smoke, "I don't know whether Janalei—er, Utrecht, has mentioned this. We are trying to keep a secret, so she may have said nothing to you."

"Secret? I have no inkling of secrets to keep. What is it?"

"We are beginning to court. Don't you see the simple logic of that?"

Ordowahl could not, but managed to force a look of polite interest.

"I certainly have the wit and foresight one would need in a baron, while Heri has complete confidence he'd make good decisions even though I might not be there."

"Yes, but I still don't see the connection."

"It is so simple, my friend. Utrecht may make use of your wit and skill to handle everyday governance of the county but also declares she will never make her home anywhere but County Vendink."

"I see. So, since you are strong and wise at governance, it makes best sense for you as Janalei's husband to replace Utrecht. Have you and she talked about this?"

"Yes, we have. It is too early to tell how everything will unfold, so we are keeping it secret."

"I haven't heard a whisper of it."

"But since you spend so much time with her as vice-count, you can help me in this. The best way to partner with her when she plays the vice-count, for one. Then upon our marriage I will assume those duties that have sent her out in man's clothing."

"My friend, we could spend the day and perhaps scratch the surface." *For one, she doesn't "play" at anything.* "The count's daughter is two unique and different people, one of whom I know well and one I've seldom spoken with beyond empty chitchat."

Swapping

"Yes, I've noticed. Lady Janalei refuses your company on any but the simplest terms. That cannot be a happy state."

"I get by, Wils. I get along best with Utrecht by doing two very different things. You might take note."

"Please, Prince, tell me!"

"First, I always take care to listen to her. She has a well-developed idea of what she—we—must accomplish, and can become very upset if I—you—disappoint her."

"Don't I know that, Prince. She has always been one to give orders, not obey them."

"The second thing, Wils, is that I never surrender my wit. There are times when I think a thought before she does and go off on my own to prove or discover something."

"Prince, you have a rare gift, from time to time to see the answer before Utrecht."

"When I manage to do that, she always relents. And if I fail, I receive open mockery, even though some of those times I've been right. But she always comes back to a smile."

"I've seen that a time or two, my friend. Yes, you have patience as broad as your back." Wils smiled his thanks and went back inside, trailing happy wisps of vapor.

Father Almighty, please help me to praise You and give thanks, even in my loss of hope.

Yes, Wils is far more suitable to County Vendink than someone from far away and a much better husband for Janalei than anyone else I've seen.

When she set Naechstofen aside, my hope crept back. But that bridge, if it was one, has burned. Father, give me patience to seek Your will. Amen.

——*—*

Markus, Lord Naechstofen, celebrated a birthday. It brought all Naechstofen barons and the counts from neighboring counties, not including Jaagrmur, plus many other nobles of that area. As a courtesy the Hangendros invited Ordowahl to accompany them to the celebration in their coach. He asked Torwulf his opinion. Neither he nor Klarenz expressed anything beyond good will that their liege "get away from County Vendink, and enjoy a festive time."

The journey by coach from Utrecht to Castle Naechstofen began in mid-morning. Arriving after dark, the party took a light supper and retired for the night along with many other guests.

Festivities began the next morning. As always, Ordowahl received full head-to-toe inspections from every man, every unmarried woman, and most of the rest. Karyn Baroness Maihoff had not come, which Ordowahl found comforting.

Being a constant target of stares was seldom easy, but he had grown inured to it. Here it was almost a relief. The prickly competitive response from some of the young men faded when he drank and swore and traded wit with them on arms and hunting. The story of Ferbliet's forced absence amused them all—several times in fact.

Up to the midday meal the celebrants stayed somewhat sober, and young women felt comfortable mixing with all the young men. Despite strict official mores, before the day ended one might discover, here and there, horizontal tangles of legs—male usually clad, female unguarded by skirts.

Ordowahl soon separated from Wils and enjoyed the attention of a few young women he hadn't met before. At one point he noticed Lady Janalei walking toward him with a glorious, happy smile. *Has she come to tell me of her new connection to Wils?* Part of him hoped not, with a desperate intensity.

"Good afternoon, Ordowahl," she said. It was the first time he could remember Lady Janalei using his given name, as though she had chosen to honor the vice-count's pledge to avoid titles.

"Good evening, Janalei." Regardless of her secret with Wils, it felt good to use her first name too.

She started to say something then stepped very close to him and whispered up toward his ear, "Kiss me. Now! And make it look real."

Her forearms went up to rest on his shoulders, and he bent down to kiss her. It was brief and perfunctory, but she drew back and stared at him, slack-jawed, as though she had seen a vision. She leapt up and he lifted her in careful arms. Her hands caressed his cheeks, her toes tapped against his shins.

She kissed him with tenderness but also a fluid passion beyond anything he had experienced before. Her hands kneaded his face and tugged on his ears. Her lips were alive and moved against his.

He stood there, her weight dangling from his shoulders with a liveliness that made her feel as light as feathers, her torso flattened against his chest. He became dizzy from sheer exhilaration. He could not understand what this had to do with Wils and conceded that in the moment he didn't care.

But as she came, so she went. The kiss was over, and before he even noticed putting her down, she was walking away. Then he saw Lord Markus's face. He had seen the kiss, and the prince understood. The man's best chance to reconnect with this once-pursued woman was at his own celebration, and Lady Janalei had warned him off.

Yet her kiss had been fervent, more than just "real." Whether she had meant to use him couldn't matter. The rest of the day and all through the evening she refused to look him in the eye and would say no more than "Oh, hello," when politeness made it necessary, and without politeness's smile.

Some of the young women had seen enough, and soon all of them ignored him. Once Lady Janalei kissed a man, she had pulled him beyond their reach.

Wils and Janalei seemed not to be too concerned with each other. But after that kiss she went to find him; from that moment they were never more than steps apart.

She didn't warn Marcus away by kissing Wils, because they want to keep their courtship private. So on impulse she came to me: a convenient substitute. It was amazing, I'll say that. God help you, Wils, if she comes at you that way.

It was a bittersweet agony to wish Wils well, then endure the endless ride back in the same coach with Janalei's nascent suitor. He didn't connect her having kissed and dismissed so many before with the very different kiss she gave him. He was neither ordinary nor extraordinary, merely assaulted by brief, disturbing bliss.

*__*__*__*

Rome mastered measuring areas of land well before the birth of Christ. That knowledge had not been lost when Rome fell. Even with his stump wrapped in bandages, Baron Ferbliet returned to managing his estates. His land surveyors spent a week going from place to place and spot to spot.

Ferbliet sent couriers to both Haus Maihoff and Vendink Castle with identical messages. He did this on Markus's birthday, though of course he hadn't felt like attending.

The sun still sat on the eastern horizon when Ordowahl appeared at Vendink Keep. Wils "had other business" thus the standard set of prince, vice-count, Joop and Klarenz would prosecute the day's business. Utrecht wore her "every day is the same" face, and handed Ordowahl Ferbliet's message. "It says he holds 3,507 acres. He offers to cede 350 acres along their immediate boundary."

"Utrecht, if I'm not mistaken that land makes a good boundary because most of it is marshy and impassable, thus worthless."

"Brilliant as always, Ordowahl." The wry humor helped her look him in the eye and not blink. Utrecht never conceded that Lady Janalei had any bearing on county business.

They rode together to a designated spot along the boundary. During that two hours no one found anything to say. Even Joop and Klarenz seemed mute. They found Karyn waiting for them.

While waiting for Ferbliet to arrive they made small talk. More than once Karyn looked back and forth at Vice-Count and Prince, as though something between them should be different; she had heard about their double kiss.

A firm set to Utrecht's eyes made it clear that her life did not exist except as Vice-Count. After perhaps fifteen minutes of saying nothing much, the awaited interruption arrived.

"Hello, Baron," said Ordowahl.

"Baron," began Utrecht, even before the baron had dismounted, "the number of acres to cede is three hundred fifty-one. Don't you agree?"

Ferbliet knew it would be petty to counter with three hundred fifty plus seven-tenths, so he shrugged. "You will find these acres to be scenic and a wonderful defensive perimeter, Karyn," he said.

Swapping

"However, Erneuylt," interjected Karyn, "that amount of reeds and bushes has no real worth. I won't need a defensive perimeter between us, will I? And if I ever do, who owns it can't be important."

Baron Ferbliet looked at Janalei, in clear panic that this female could take away good acreage.

"What's sauce for the goose, Baron," said Utrecht. "You will cede to Maihoff good as well as bad, a fair mix of both. You cannot offer her just the marshy parts of a holding which, according to my tax records, produces very well."

Karyn said, "If I may, there is a small rise not half a mile from here. Many times I've stood there and looked over onto perhaps two hundred acres of beautiful fields. May we take a look?"

Utrecht nodded her agreement, and the party proceeded toward the rise at a horse's walk. Ahead of them lay the gem that Karyn had described.

"Baron, your surveyors must have a record of this farmland. To look at it, I believe Karyn's estimate is close."

Baron Ferbliet frowned and looked a plea at Utrecht. "Vice-Count," he begged, "that is the best cropland I have. Please guard me against losing it."

"Tut, Erneuylt, you will keep three thousand one hundred fifty-six acres. A great deal of that is rich and flowing."

His face continued to plead.

"Let us presume that in fact what you say is God's truth, and let us presume that truth is now your permanent friend. Taking perhaps two hundred fifty wonderful acres plus another hundred ordinary ones seems more than fair."

For a second time, he shrugged.

Karyn added, "You must include the manor, fences, barns, livestock, outbuildings, implements, and whatever else is currently situated there." She looked at Baron Ferbliet.

Ferbliet looked glum.

Utrecht delivered her judgment. "Maihoff and Ferbliet, have your surveyors present on this spot at dawn tomorrow. Baroness Maihoff will receive the fields, manor, and everything seen here."

"Yes."

"The arable acres must be at least two hundred, else I will act as needed to bring the total to two hundred before granting any less-productive lands to bring Baroness Maihoff's total to three hundred fifty-one."

"Vice-count, while I your decision brings pain, I accept it."

"Well you should. Ordowahl, have you any comment that you would like to make?"

"Baron Ferbliet, I commend your stamina and presence of mind, so soon after a significant injury. You may rely on Utrecht's sound judgment, because it guards the peace and prosperity of all of County Vendink."

Ferbliet's face didn't budge from fatalistic sadness.

"And, believe it or not, I have no intent to pursue any part of Baroness Maihoff's interest beyond what County Vendink considers just and adequate." He turned to look at Utrecht. *The thing that gives me any consolation is her odd worry that I may take some woman and leave Utrecht behind.* "Be of quiet mind, my friend."

(Ordowahl)

Now this is better, handing Utrecht off

so Wils can have her both, vice-count and bride.

I've had "the kiss" and swum across the trough

of ugly fate—e'en so still can't decide!

    I spend my days with Utrecht, Wils or no,

    and go about the things we've always done.

    Her company, while mute, is balm and so

    I'm staying on though I am not her one.

The days of summer gone, the seasons move

while I am holding calm, and moving not.

Monotony's a thing, much like a groove

that deepens to a rut. 'Tis now my lot.

    Forever and a day in this soft calm—

    is this what God's designed for me? Numb balm?

Dragon

On an early November morning Ordowahl dallied at Haus Hangendro just long enough to miss seeing Utrecht and Wils set out. Despite knowing he would be late, he couldn't hurry.

At the customary one hour past dawn Janalei and Wils set out on the day's business. "Dear Wils," she said, "today I believe us free of that oaf Prince Ordowahl."

Passing through the market square Wils exclaimed, "Look! What is that?" He pointed at something on the western horizon, low in the sky. "Utrecht, is it an eagle? It's far too large—looks much more like a bat, and has a ropy tail. What do you make of it?"

Ordowahl also noticed the creature in the sky. He was close enough to see it fly toward the central square. *Father God in heaven, is this from another black mage?* Terror clutched at him; King Ingvik had been able to accost him in a dream, and the Black Knight had magicked his lance and shield. But this! Ordowahl brought Hammerfoot to a full gallop to do what he could to intercept the demonic thing.

At the same moment Utrecht answered Wils, "Vendink Castle needs us. Collect as many men at arms as you can. I'll find a priest."

Ordowahl saw the dragon turn to follow Wils and Utrecht. Hammerfoot seemed to hang back, when the prince shouted, "Run! Run!" at him, and saw Wils gallop through the castle gate. Janalei stopped to tie up her horse.

Dragon

Ordowahl yanked the reins to drive Hammerfoot into a steep turn into the castle yard. Before the vice-count could run half-way across the yard the creature, as large as she was, crashed onto her back with its talons out.

It knocked her to the ground. She sensed that a huge weight had struck her, and knew she'd heard at least one rib break. She lay there and felt an odd itching in her back, but the shock made her numb to pain.

Ordowahl felt an internal shriek tear at his throat when he saw the dragon strike. Hammerfoot's snort and raised forefeet made the beast abandon her limp form and fly away.

Ordowahl leapt off and bent down to her. "Utrecht! Janalei! Beloved woman, please don't leave this world! Oh, once I could not think, for being so in love with you. Breathe. Live. You must remain here in this world. Please, dear friend, please don't leave."

He slid a forearm beneath her body to pick her up, keeping her prone so that nothing could disturb her wounded back. Cradling her head on his palm and scooping up legs and hips with the other arm he leapt up the steps. A gardener who had seen the attack ran forward to kick at the door. Someone must have heard the noise, for it flew open. He ran into the parlor, laid her face down on a padded bench, and unsheathed his knife. *Dear Father God in heaven help us now. Heal my beloved Utrecht.*

The butler who had opened the door now stood behind the prince, in shock. "What are you doing?"

"Opening her clothing to cleanse her wounds. Bring a basin of water."

He sliced away the vest and tunic to expose her bare back. Eight punctures made by the beast's talons, two pairs on each side of her spine, oozed a pale green substance. He smelled something burnt and looked at her hair. The beast had singed much of it off.

Two maids rushed in and screamed when they saw the frantic giant. Emluyn and Countess Rutelyn ran in behind them. Rutelyn shoved him away as though he were a potted plant, so she could kneel beside her daughter.

"Janalei! Janalei!" she said into the fallen woman's ear, and got back a faint sound, either speech or a deep moan, "Ahhawah, ahhahwah, ahhhhawaaaa," and Janalei's eyes closed. Ordowahl tiptoed back out of the room then ran to the back part of the castle to see how Wils had done rounding up men.

"Prince," said Wils when they found each other, "I am so glad to find you here. What do you know of the flying beast?"

Wils already had enough to worry about. He would not mention Janalei. "Hammerfoot seems to have frightened it, and it flew away. Let's get out there to chase it down. Klarenz, let Torwulf know what we're doing."

Ordowahl ran back out the front entrance without explaining to Wils what had brought him into the castle. He mounted Hammerfoot and trotted around toward the stables.

Wils met him in the side yard. A puzzled look flitted across his face when he noticed Janalei's horse still tied at the gate. "Janalei must have gone on foot to find a priest." He led Ordowahl and three other men, mounted and armed with swords, through the castle gate.

One of them spotted the dragon above the sun in the eastern sky. "Look," he shouted, "off that way."

Ordowahl bid the three men to go toward the southeast. He and Wils would go northeast.

"Wils, keep just behind me," he yelled. "Follow me, and keep your gaze ahead and to the right. I will search the skies to our left."

The two of them set off at a distance-eating canter down a web of intersecting lanes. They kept toward the northeast as best they could, using the sun's low position in the sky.

Twenty minutes passed, and Wils sang out. "I see him, Prince. He is coming toward us and is very near."

"Get your mount under a tree," commanded Ordowahl. He looked where Wils had pointed and saw the plunging dragon, apparently the same one that had flattened Utrecht.

Its body was the size of a hunting dog and either wing could cover Utrecht's horse. It uttered a screech that pained Ordowahl's ears. He pulled his sword, stood in the stirrups, and held the sword close, not showing an upraised arm.

Thank You Father, that I have a straight weapon. The curved sword may serve another time, but right now I need to run the beast through, not slice it.

The dragon flared its wings like a falcon about to take a lamb. Hammerfoot danced on hind legs to splay pawing front hooves toward the approaching beast. Ordowahl clutched a handful of mane to stay upright.

The dragon's front claws spread wide, it spouted flame. Letting go of the mane to shield his eyes Ordowahl extended the sword.

The dragon impaled itself. One claw grazed his shoulder. Fire seared the prince's arm and face. The beast fell off the sword, dead in front of Hammerfoot. The charger smashed down onto it..

Ordowahl bent down to grab the saddle and leapt off the busy horse. Hw held his sword out to the side to keep its razor edge away from the stallion. Hammerfoot reduced the dragon's remains to reeking, green-splattered pulp and ragged wings. He wiped green slime from the blade onto a small kerchief and threw the foul-smelling cloth away from the road before putting the sword back into its scabbard.

"What on God's good earth is, or was, that?" demanded Wils. In unguarded astonishment he ventured close enough to risk a scrape from the pounding hooves. Ordowahl calmed the stallion with pats and whispers. Hammerfoot settled down and sidestepped several paces. Wils and the prince knelt by the steaming remains to get a closer look.

Wings of skin stretched across slender bones accounted for one third of the beast by weight. Its head seemed like that of a lizard, mottled with horns and bumps. Filmy palm-sized scales had covered its head and body. A wisp of steam drifted up from what used to be a mouth. Its overall shape when alive was gone to a splattered mess.

Ordowahl took a rope from a saddlebag and tied the thing's naked, slender tail to his saddle, with slack for it to trail a body length behind Hammerfoot.

"Let's go back, Wils. Can you catch the other men? I'm going to place this in the town square so everyone can see it and no longer be afraid."

Hammerfoot towed the dragon's remains to the city square.

Ordowahl led his stallion to an off-center spot and untied the rope. He went in and found Fr. Kerk just finishing a Mass. He waited until the closing Amen and said, "Father Kerk, please come with me into the square, and do what you can to guard us from evil."

The priest looked puzzled but followed him out to the square.

The reeking remains had drawn a crowd, causing a buzz of consternation. Prince and priest elbowed their way through and stood next to the thing.

"Father, this was seen flying overhead early this morning. It attacked and may have killed an important personage"—he shook his head at the priest to keep him from guessing—"and died when it plunged onto the end of my sword."

"What office can I perform?" asked the priest.

"Father, you can cast out whatever evil may lurk in this corpse, spirit or otherwise. Then bless the spot it lies on. The people of Utrecht will know that this wretched thing has been defeated and its evil purged."

Wordless, Fr. Kerk knelt in front of the carcass and made the sign of the cross. He gathered his thoughts for a few seconds, bowed his head, and began whispering in fervent Latin. The crowd looked on in reverent silence.

Ordowahl didn't stay to watch. He returned to the spot where he had killed the dragon.

Meanwhile a much smaller drama played out in the late morning sky. A solitary raven pursued a much more agile jackdaw, but managed to drive it toward the window of the castle room in which Janalei suffered. A great fever had her sweating through clothing and bedding. She often called out, as if in agony, for someone or something, her voice so muffled no one could be sure it was even speech.

Her mother instructed Emluyn to keep Janalei's face down, to allow her wounds to drain. Green slime came up through every bandage, and she continued to deteriorate. Just raising her up to put water to her lips caused such pain, such anguish, that they feared she would die right then.

Somehow the jackdaw reached a truce with the raven. It stayed nearby, and the jackdaw perched on the ledge just outside the window.

At least once it hopped through the window and pecked at the tortured body. It flew out when Emluyn saw it, but for a full week the jackdaw stayed close, leaving just long enough to find itself a morsel of food before returning to its watch.

——*—*

Ordowahl had killed the dragon in open woods, with no houses around. He found the spot again, dismounted, laid Hammerfoot's reins over a tree branch, and leaned against the tree that had sheltered Wils. "Father in Heaven," he prayed aloud.

Please help Janalei to heal. I am overwhelmed once again with the yearning that mastered my mind and senses. Protect me also, Father, as you protect her. I told her I loved her so much that the earth would be poorer if she weren't part of it. Forgive me for risking insult to Your Creation, but I feel this in my deepest parts. I beseech You, Father God Almighty, minister to her and to me with your Holy Spirit. Help her to heal. Amen.

He scuffed out the odd greenish goo that had dribbled out of the dragon's mangled remains and stayed by that spot until sunset.

A day without joy, also without food or water. Dusk sent him at a slow, slow pace back to Haus Hangendro. When he arrived, the news of Janalei's attack had dropped everyone into deep lament. Fretheldin asked, "Prince, where have you been?"

"Out in the forest."

"We heard that you brought the remains of a dragon into the city square, and we know that Janalei lies near death."

"She lives?" His brows knit, taking him from gloom to desolate hope.

"The count's butler saw you with a knife, and the maids saw Janalei with a bare and wounded back. Then you left and later dragged the battered body of that foul thing here. into the city square. But where have you been all the rest of the day?"

Klarenz knew best what his liege would want to know. "A priest sanctified the spot, drenched it in Holy Water, and covered the dragon's remains with swaths of black lace."

Fretheldin held out her arms, both to give and to receive a hug. "Prince, Wils told us about your taking Janalei into the castle, that you began to tend her wounds. He sends you his gratitude, as do I, and his brotherly love."

"And I him, Fretheldin."

"He is grateful, and prays alongside all of us that Janalei will come through this trial. At the same time, he appears to connect the dragon with you."

Ordowahl nodded. Numbed in spirit, he went to eat something and retired for the night.

——*—*

A second day of Janalei's suffering left its mark on her father. *Almighty God, Father of my Lord Jesus, help me now. Which of the sins of my youth are visited on my daughter? I beg forgiveness.*

I beg You to heal her and bring her back to me. I suspect that her connection to Prince Ordowahl is involved in some way I do not comprehend. Please guide me now, Father. Amen.

After an hour of earnest prayer Jakop dragged his aching body upright and crept down the stairs to the main hall without help. Rutelyn saw him come down from the last step and rushed over to him.

"Jakop," she protested, "What are you thinking?"

"Wife," he said, caressing her hip with his free hand and remembering her body from long ago, "I need an heir."

She felt the caress and remembered once again the numerous, painful miscarriages that had followed Janalei's clean birth.

"You're not going to start over with me, are you?" Her sense of humor, like the rest of her, was still robust and far more fertile than her body.

"No, dear wife," said Jakop when he reached a chair and sat down, "I will steal a son."

"Oh? Don't we have one already? Isn't Wils taking Jani's hand?"

"No. He is not."

"And why is that?"

"Dear one, I read young people better now than when I was one myself, and I was very good at it then."

She remembered his ungovernable womanizing, which had begun before she was born, but stopped so that she could become his wife. To Janalei's and her mother's sadness, those escapades had resumed for a while, after they agreed that she couldn't risk even one more tormenting miscarriage. "So?"

"The prince. She told Joop, long ago, that she would never marry, and Joop passed that along to me. I burdened Joop with the responsibility of constant surveillance, when he first became her nanny."

"You never told me this."

"Joop told me, when she was still very young, that she knew some man would come from far away, marry her, and take her to his land."

"The Prince?" she asked. The idea wasn't a surprise, yet it shocked her to realize that it could be a man so considerate and kind as Ordowahl.

"Indeed so. Many times Joop would ask her, why not marry someone local, and she replied that every local man was insipid."

"What a word!"

"Wife, she has been able to peer into every minute of your life and mine, and from the looks of it can recall each of us from before she was born."

Rutelyn stood silent in shock then asked, "Even in bed?"

"Yes, and I'm sure that includes my bedtimes from before *you* were born. She hides it, but ask yourself how much coaching she needed to learn any skill you taught her."

"None, now that you mention it."

"So, Dear, she knows herself too and has realized that the one sure way to escape her fate is to marry Wils."

"And he's such a fine young man." Rutelyn stood with hands on hips. Wils was her favorite among all possible suitors, including Lord Markus of Naechstofen.

"My Dear, I want that marriage to happen as much as I want anything, anything at all."

She watched him. His face said that he was in mourning.

"We both know our daughter too well to think Wils's spirit wouldn't shrivel once she found herself bound to him for more than a handful of months."

Rutelyn frowned but held silent.

"They wouldn't reach the altar to take their vows before one of them, or both, must refuse to take even one more step toward a slow death."

Rutelyn stared at him, her eyes wide in shock.

"I, Wife, will erase that from her mind by dissolving their betrothal. I will seal it by adopting him to be a Vendink, to become Count on my death."

"This is too much, husband. I need time to think through this."

"No, you don't. You are not your daughter. You always have and will continue to be guided by my decisions. Wils will become count, and Janalei will not spend the rest of her life with someone she finds 'insipid.'"

Rutelyn sat on the floor and buried her face in her hands.

"She will, if what I hope for comes to pass, spend her life instead far from here with someone who possesses, just as I have, a means to work with her wild energies and insights."

Pulling her face up she gasped out, through tears, "You send our daughter far away, forever? What of my grandbabies?"

"I won't be here in time to see them, but they will be mine, too, Wife. I mourn that part almost as much as you do. Our grandbabies will grow up far from County Vendink." A tear leaked down one crumpled cheek.

The fracture of a pile of things has come.

No vice-count role, no Utrecht, even if

she lives. The prince? His conscience beats the drum

of blame, his heart laid on her handkerchief.

>Count Jakop sees what he has always known—

>his daughter never will reign here. She can't.

>Her husband? She'd eat Wils down to the bone.

>The prince sang love to her, his heart's descant.

Has God displayed His will for Ordowahl?

To send him on afresh, to ground untrod?

What strength of mind and heart? What caterwaul

of beat-down hope can help him praise his God?

>We don't have privilege to choose our trial.

>The prince just hopes to skirt the juvenile.

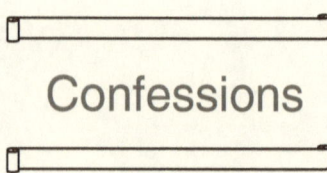

Confessions

That same morning Ordowahl stayed at St. Martin's after Mass to visit with Fr. Danelagh. He hadn't yet heard of the raven's contest with the jackdaw the prior afternoon.

"Father Dan," he called, going in by the rectory's front door.

"Me boy," Fr. Dan replied. From the sound of it he was in the kitchen-shed behind the building. Father Dan came at a run and wrapped his arms around the prince.

"Ordo, laddie, it is *so* good to know ye be well." He stepped back and looked at him, head to foot. "Ye *be* well, bain't ye, lad? I see some singes here and there, and you hold your right arm as though a bandage lies under yer tunic."

"Yes, Father Dan, but considering the dragon's weapons, I am well in body."

"Alas, not in soul. Tell it to me, boyo. What be't that plagues ye now?"

Ordowahl went into the small parlor and beckoned Fr. Dan to sit beside him. The smell of cut onions followed the priest.

"It's shameful, Father. When I learned of Janalei letting Wils seek her hand in betrothal, I studied hard to defeat the small man within me, standing mute below a wall that would not be climbed in this lifetime."

Pungent hands settled onto Ordowahl's tight fists, which released their tension.

296

Confessions

"I believed I had weaned myself from slavery to an unanswered passion. But yesterday I saw Janalei on the ground beneath the dragon, saw what those claws had done, her hair hit by flame . . ."

"'Tis enough, boyo, I understand ye well. D'ye know her state?"

"Father, yesterday she lived. Does she still?"

"I heard quite the tale of a mad giant slicing away at the woman's clothing to bare her back. But her mother managed to push him away same as she might handle a piece of small furniture."

Ordowahl remembered that.

"She's a fine broth of a woman, that one." Father Dan looked up at the ceiling, crossed himself, and said a very quick "Hail, Mary."

"So, lad, ye find yerself once again held in chains forged in the furnaces of Eros and Cupid. I once was the same, in fact. Fer meself, I turned me life around by dedicatin' it to God."

Ordowahl let the remark hang in the air.

"Father, I need to leave this place and go far, far away. Yet, how can I? Something buried within says she still needs me, but in a way I cannot plumb."

"But ye know she needs ye." It wasn't a question.

"It galls me to be an appendage to someone, necessary yet spurned. Do I second the spurning back upon her, by leaving? It would be despicable."

"Then devote yerself to that sacrifice, Ordowahl. 'Tis simple. We are called by Christ to bear torments in His name."

"I have known a few." He recalled a childhood full of continual rough-edged disdain from his brothers. Both his parents' care and later many chats with "Auntie" Elspet made that tolerable. *Here it is again, this time Lady Janalei's unwavering disdain, yet an odd sense of Utrecht's muted fellowship.*

"Bearin' this sorrow, be't in Christ's name or no, is as great a burden as ye've ever plucked up, Ordo me lad, as great a one as ye can imagine. Pray on this, son. Pray on it, and ask the Holy Spirit to speak comfort into yer heart."

"Aye, Father Dan, the comfort that comes when a body surrenders all worldly concerns. Yet I cannot."

"Ye're the bravest man I've come to know, and that's in all

things, not just wavin' a shiny slicer through a horse's neck, or makin' a man's hand fly away into the dirt."

"Thank you, Father Danelagh."

"Dan."

"Thank you, Father Dan. You have shown me where to take my misery and turn it into service to God. Pray with me now that I can do this."

The priest held Ordowahl's two enormous hands between his own. "May the onion scent go with ye as a reminder." He prayed, "Holy Father, mighty God who blesses all suffering, and Lord Jesus Christ, Ye who died fer our sins, and Holy Spirit, promised Comforter, please come now and bless this young prince.

"Open to him the peace that passes all understanding, holy Trinity, and Mother Mary intercede with Lady Janalei on his behalf, that she accept his real worth and the light he may bring her.

"Now help him to make good his pledge of service through care fer his dear mystery, Utrecht Vice-Count Vendink, who is also Lady Janalei. In Yer holy names, God the Father, Jesus our Savior, and Holy Spirit, and with the prayers of Mary, Holy Mother of our Lord God Jesus. Amen."

He pushed Ordowahl's hands away and stood up. "Go now, lad. Me onions be callin' me. Go! Ye've been prayed over, so don't mock it by waitin' here. Go."

*__*__*__*

That evening Wils answered the count's summons. He found his father-in-law-to-be sitting in the small day room with half a dozen lit candles. He wondered why the Count would want so much light.

"Son," said Jakop, "I have something important to tell you. Perhaps the candles let you know that we must see eye to eye, eh?" He didn't smile. "You are to be my son in a different way than we thought."

With a look of quiet surprise Wils took a chair opposite the count. "Sire, what change might that be?" He feared that Jakop would deprive him of fiery, intoxicating Janalei. Inside, fury and panic filled him. He sat, making a fierce effort not to cry out.

"I can see what this brings you, Wils, and it galls me. But for a number of reasons I have concluded this is the correct way forward."

"Count," Wils said. His voice rasped like gravel. He took a deep breath to calm himself. "I love Janalei, and I am pledged to her. She is pledged likewise to me, and I am sure she looks forward, not back. What kind of reason can you conjure up to break a bond so tender, and so beautiful? So made in heaven? I am sure I would die if anything happened to Janalei, and I hope to die if anything separates us. No, Count, I care not that you would, or would not, be father to me. Janalei is the one future I can endure. She is my concern."

His voice reached a high pitch, a squeak of anguish. Without showing any intention he stood and looked down on the count as if on someone who had offered him a true insult.

Count Jakop had known this would be the case. Wils, the quiet and thoughtful one, was behaving more like his irascible twin Heri. A bud of sympathy, sorrow, fondness, respect—what have you, Jakop felt more respect for Wils's humanity than he could remember.

"Wils, do you threaten me?" *He could, and in fact would find admirers, if he throttled me now. But he isn't her father, and he isn't Count. Pray God, Wils, do not slay your chance to succeed me.*

Wils squared his shoulders, tried to quiet his face, trembled, and sat down. "Count, I do not. I refuse, my lord Count, to let anything come between Janalei and me. She is worth any cost, and I will gladly pay it with all my being. Do not try to pull us apart, for if you do I will die a thousand deaths."

For long minutes they stared at each other, expressions fixed as though carved in granite. Count Jakop's face masked so many conflicting emotions that he looked the way someone would when torn by a sudden apparition, half beauty and half wretched ugliness.

Wils nodded and clasped his hands together in his lap. This would be difficult to bear. He steeled himself.

"You are not her father. You are not Count. You are not even Baron. Were I in your shoes, Wils, I might have used a knife on my father-in-law-to-be, dragged my beloved onto a horse, and run to the other side of the world."

Wils did not move a muscle. Anguish made a wrinkled mess of a face that could show judgment, intelligence, good humor. Jakop could see him, by tiny slow degrees, force himself to relax.

The silence stretched to a quarter hour, and the frightened household staff who had come at a run at Wils's first shout saw the count's finger-wave, and went away. Rutelyn stood there, too, out of Wils's line of sight. She waited for the silence to end, to be sure that her Jakop would not suffer a stroke.

When Wils looked close to peaceful, when his breathing had slowed to calm, even breaths, Jakop resumed speaking. "Wils, you will make a wonderful count when you heal from your loss."

Wils's face fell back into a plea for mercy.

"If Janalei were to die, I would adopt you as my son so that you will succeed me as Count Vendink on my death, which will come soon in any case. But I believe she will live, may God grant it!"

"Sire, I pray continually that she will."

"But, Wils, while you would begin with Janalei's formal respect as her husband, you *would* also find her demanding. First she would demand that you share in governance of the county."

Wils's face relaxed for a moment, then he bowed his head to the count. It was so.

"I'm sure you understand that your countess *would* prevent governance by a single mind, if other than her own of course. That would be far worse than having a spinster countess reign."

He looked into Wils's face to see how well his cold remarks had registered. The count waited for the younger man to digest this.

Wils said, "Count, from the day Utrecht saw the prince's condition following Heri's outlandish assault on him, I confess it, I realized that she already cared for him. She was blind to that herself, but since then it has become more and more obvious to me and many others that she won't be able to separate her life from his."

Yes, Wils, and how many fools rush in to pluck a forbidden fruit? In your place I would hope to have the strength to resist.

"I confess myself the fool for having pursued her despite that. But Janalei was too wonderful a prize to let pass, so I persisted."

Confessions

"You confess yourself a fool to the one who will make you Count? But I note your honesty, Wils. God grant that it blossom when I am gone and you succeed me."

"Count, Sire," Wils pleaded. "I will do everything in my power to husband her in a kind but governing way."

"I knew the word would escape you, Wils, but trying to govern her would end her respect. Today I have annulled your betrothal to my daughter."

Wils's face closed into a grimace of both dread and understanding. He twisted half around in his seat to stifle a sob.

Jakop waited for him to regain his composure. "Wils, my son-to-be, I have begun the business of adopting you as my heir. A man cannot marry his sister, and I doubt she would consent to be adopted out herself to come to you as, say, a Hangendro." One eyebrow raised, the count's first wry sign of humor.

The absurdity of that double adoption and Janalei's outraged refusal put a flicker of smile on Wils's face, but the flicker died.

Jakop watched him. *He descends into a numbness like the one that seized Ordowahl when he returned to the spot where the dragon died. I'm told he spent the afternoon in fasting and prayer.*

"Son, your brother as baron is your legal guardian. I have had an answer from him, and he agrees that this action is wise."

"Ahh, Heri must have exulted." Wils knew his twin but made the observation in passing, as though it could take his mind off the real problem.

How quickly he seems to govern his despair. "I have your brother's signature. The two of you have a custom of concurring on all-important matters. But I emphasized my need to have you here, plus his continued favorable access to your advice."

Wils shook his head at that idea. "Heri already chafes at the need to consult and must have shown open joy at handing me off, even to be count above his own barony. Count Jakop, soon to be father, not father-in-law, this will make it more certain that he will accept my advice, and guarantee that he won't seek it."

The count had to smile. *Wils understands Heri as only a close brother can, and already he has regained some presence of mind.*

Wils said, "But that is not to the point. The right course is to accede to you. I pledge to honor this change with my heart, soul, and mind." His face quivered, and his eyes grew misty. He leaned his head back. With a deep sigh he mourned the death of his most cherished dream.

Jakop struggled to rise from his chair.

"Father, let me welcome myself into the family with a hug." Wils leaned down to grasp the old man under the arms and wrapped his own arms around the frail torso. He helped the count with the care he would have given anyone, which was the same care he gave to an honored host. He gave Jakop a hug and kissed his cheek.

When he stood on his own feet Jakop shouted, "Rutelyn, I'm a father again! I have adopted an heir."

Count Jakop pledged Heri and Wils to keep the secret of Wils's new standing—unbetrothed, full heir. "Rutelyn is the one other person who knows this. The fewer chances for confusion and upset, the better. My daughter will lose her precious but now imaginary future, and I don't want that to become gossip."

*__*__*__*

Wils wanted to avoid the prince. *I can feign enjoyment of everyone else's now false expectation that Janalei and I remain betrothed, but facing Ordowahl will be very difficult.*

But Ordowahl accompanied Wils wherever he went as vice-count in Utrecht's stead, "until she could recover"—just one of them knowing that she was no longer bespoke. Worse, Wils needed the prince's help.

Each time they went out in the vice-count's stead, Ordowahl showed unwavering calm courtesy. It left Wils marveling at the prince's grace. Household staff had long since told him that Ordowahl, after Hammerfoot drove the dragon away, was heard pledging deep love for Janalei while scooping her up and rushing to carry her inside.

That curses me, Wils thought. *My comfort in this deep pain is knowing that I, not he, have earned the agony. God grant me forgiveness.*

Wils dreaded the moment when Prince Ordowahl realized that

they stood beside each other, on the lip of a great chasm. On the far side, an unreachable Lady Janalei. That would be too much to bear—receiving heartfelt and full condolence from the man whose beloved he had tried so hard - and managed - to usurp.

How selfish of the prince to mourn his loss,

at first believing Janalei might die.

The moment she began to mend, his cross

held not just sins but lonely "bye-and-bye."

     Alike do Wils and Jakop rue the fact

     that Janalei will never bear Wils' child.

     Count Jakop, bless him, knows just how attacked

     poor son-in-law would wind up. She'd be wild.

So what of Ordowahl in "brother" role?

And Janalei, no longer with a part?

What blessing might she find from God, now whole

in frame and spirit, though at sea in heart?

     When everything is thrown up in the air,

     whatever lands and's right-side-up? Beware!

Redoubled

Janalei's torment came and went. Her sweats and green suppurations abated during the second night. Emluyn sat watch in her mistress's room, sleeping in catnaps. She marveled at the rapid change. Near evening of the third day Janalei stirred and tried to sit up. Emluyn caressed her brow with a damp cloth and eased her to a sitting position.

"Mistress Jana, the fever has left, and your wounds are already beginning to heal."

"Yes, Emmi, but please be very careful when you lift me up. I have a broken rib."

"My lady, I am so sorry."

"I had no way to tell you, did I? I want to lie on my side for a while—facing the window, to see the jackdaw that brought me comfort."

Emluyn had noticed the bird, too. "At least once that feathered thing popped through the window and had a peck at you. I shooed it out, but it's kept a flinty eye on you ever since. It still sits on your windowsill, as if waiting to ask you a question."

Ordowahl said the same about his healing. The Black Mage used a raven, and I seem to recall a dream in which a raven shepherded my jackdaw to come and keep watch.

Will that awkward giant never free me from his debt? What must I do, sacrifice past and future just to satisfy his awful obsession? I wish he had never come.

The thought opened a void in her soul. She knew her need of him was a prison she had never sensed before, and at least as great as his plain need of her.

Joop had showed her as much.

I used Markus as a stopgap, a smile and nice shoulders, a buffer to shield me from a terrifying truth.

And Wils? More than that, but still somehow enclosing. He will demand that I remove myself from governance. That's written on him in large letters. County Vendink will keep me, but to what end? Bear children, perhaps. No matter where I go, motherhood finds me. But, God have mercy, Ordowahl's *children? Daddy would cry if he believed that his grandchildren might never see Vendink. No! I block that road.*

Within a week the claw punctures became scars, which shrank day by day. The broken rib knit so well she needed thought to recall which side, much less which rib. As soon as she felt able, Janalei got Emmi to help her into day clothes. "Do you recall that odd word the prince picked up from Father Danelagh?"

"Breakfast?" asked Emmi.

"It means breaking the night's fast. Break fast or 'brekfist,' as Father Danelagh has it. Let's go down to take breakfast."

"Yes, my lady. Oh, Jani, it's so refreshing to hear you remember the prince in a fond way."

"Hmmph," she snorted. "Father Dan, *not* Ordowahl. While I am unready to go about as Utrecht, the giant-child can't pester me."

"Janalei," her father exclaimed, when she came into view. "So soon!"

Emluyn, following her down the stairs, gave a shrug. Her mistress had never yet surrendered to anyone else's notion of her limits or condition. She just *was.* Joop had been the first to learn this. A still-babbling youngster had driven that message home—at around the time she still bumped into sharp edges.

"Good morning, Daddy, Mama," she said.

Jakop said, "I see you've gone back to clothing from your

tomboy days, and it still fits." He nodded at her to sit beside him.

"I am not ready to go about the city, but a good breakfast will be wonderful."

Her parents watched while she began to eat. Emluyn knew that no one had told her about Wils's new standing as adopted heir, but sooner was always better than later with Janalei. In fact, they feared her uncanny foreknowledge; but challenge the crisis if there was to be one. Count and Countess had told Emmi as much when she first came to serve Janalei as lady-in-waiting.

"Jana, dear," began her mother, "there is something you should know."

She looked up; her face went pale. *I cannot tell what Mama means, what she feels. Nor Daddy!* She gulped. "Mama, this is an actual surprise. What is it that I don't know, but should?"

Jakop said, "I have adopted Wils. He is my son."

Janalei paused, absorbing the information. "Daddy, does that mean I am to marry a brother? The idea is odd, to say the least. Or does it also mean that he and I are no longer betrothed?"

"Jana, dear one," her mother said, "not only are you not betrothed, but the county will never again need its Vice-Count Utrecht."

She dropped her spoon and stared at them for a long, tense moment.

"There is nothing left for me to say, is there?" Her dull stare continued, as though speech had left her.

Her parents' concerned faces waited for her to explode.

"My duty of respect, *Father*, keeps me civil. You have erred, and in haste. But if you repent yourself, I will listen."

She glared at her mother and father both. One sat dumb in shock; the other's temper began to rise.

She cut him off. "I obey you in all things, Father, but do not expect to extinguish me like wet fingers on a candle wick. I have been Utrecht for five and one-half years. Doesn't Common Law make a thing permanent after seven?" She paused to calm herself then continued. "You have acted in time. You have done what was yours to do. But it has cost you every bit of your daughter's affection. All of it."

Jakop, like Rutelyn, now sat stunned, more by the loss of his daughter's love than by her disrespect. As explosions went, this one dwarfed them all.

Janalei struggled back up the stairs, with Emluyn trying hard to help her.

"Joop!" Janalei shouted. "Joop!"

In short minutes he came and knocked at her door. "Yes, Mistress Jana?" He trembled.

"Joopi," she said, "come in and close the door behind you. Please sit on the bed next to me. Let me put my arms on your shoulders, for I am weak."

Joop sat beside her. Emmi pulled up a chair and sat down.

"Joopi, Emmi, I am undone. Father has cast me aside. I am without a purpose, all at once!" Her eyes wore the dry glaze of shock. It was too early for tears.

"The pair of you knew this. Thank God I heard it from Father first. I am no longer Utrecht. Wils is an adopted brother, not a future husband."

From their faces, she knew the secret had found them. "I am severed from my life. I am become nothing in Daddy's eyes. God help me from becoming nothing in my own eyes."

Joop said, "Is a woman's private room the place for me? Whether or not I've been your nanny footman for twenty years and a lover of men not women." He rose to leave.

"Joopi, please stay for awhile. Emmi, I will take all my meals in this room, just as though I were still convalescing." *And oh, Father God in heaven, how ill I am.*

Resigned to the tempest called Janalei, and in her own quiet way adoring her mistress, Emmi waited for further shoes to drop.

"My word to my parents is this: 'Please do not tell me anything. Please do not ask me anything. I will obey you always, but know that I have no desire for your company.' Is that clear, Emmi?"

She nodded, shunning panic because lady Janalei's reactions often ran the gamut from vivid to violent, before returning to calm and reason.

"Perhaps Mama, in a few days. But not *Daddy*! Him I will obey as any serf obeys her master, and no more than that. He is dead to me."

Then she realized that her second sight into her father hadn't just faded, it was gone. The emptiness of it terrified her. She felt the last wisps of her mother slipping away as she spoke. In a week or so she might rediscover how to be a loving daughter, but in the most important way they lay as dead to her as though in the grave. She imagined herself in a tiny boat out of sight of land, afloat on waves too smooth and too large to comprehend. She felt sick to her stomach.

The starkness of that isolation dropped her into bereft misery. It shaded not being vice-count to a flimsy whisper. She waved Joop and Emmi out of the room and buried her head under a pillow. She felt strangled and had to force herself to breathe.

——*—*

"Joop! Let's saddle up and go for a romp."

They were in the stable yard. After over a week cooped up in her room, she could no longer endure the walled-in horizons, no exertion, no air in her face.

The memory of the dragon's attack worked an instant discredit to Ordowahl for drawing her into his web of magic and trials. Even if ignorant of that, *he* had cost her the title of Vice-Count Utrecht.

The dragon's claws, too. *Saints above, that was painful. I wonder if childbirth is anything next to that. Mama always blocked that memory. Thank God for that, because her miscarriages were dreadful agony.*

"Mistress Jana, the sun climbs the sky. Where shall we go?"

"Where? Out, just *out*."

While saddling her horse he noticed her saddling *his* mount and doing a vigorous job. Hefting the saddle from its tree and shoving it up onto his horse's back looked effortless, and this mere weeks after breaking a rib.

He stared in wonder, watching her breathe deep to get the cold air into her lungs, then got busy with her saddle,. He couldn't let her finish before him. He glowed amazement at her recovered good health. "Mistress, I hope I can keep pace with you today."

She smiled and said, "Even the smell of horse shit lifts my spirits!" She wore the old tomboy clothes so was not mistakable as either Vice-Count or lady. She gave a happy grin, leapt into the saddle, and trotted out the gate with Joop doing his best to come up alongside. She sounded like her childhood self, shouting "Wheeeee," and making her way into the nearby city square.

It was a market day, and the marketplace teemed with buyers and sellers. When she appeared, everyone leapt to their feet, stared, clapped, and sent up a huge cheer. The sudden noise began to spook her mount, but she reached down to caress her mare's cheek.

"Thank you," she shouted to the people, and halted amid a gathering throng.

Joop stayed next to her to guard one side from the crush. "Mistress," he said in a stage whisper, "I think they missed you."

"What a marvelous day this is, Joopi. I feel so happy."

Someone had removed his gaze from the radiant vice-count to look up at the mottled sky. He peered up and spotted a strange dark shape among the mid-morning clouds. He shouted in sudden alarm, "Look!" and pointed low in the west.

No one paid attention, so he cried out, "*Dragon.*" A few heard him, and tore their eyes away from their beloved Lady Janalei. Her joy, her return to fresh vigor, moved them.

He cried out again, his voice ragged with fear, "*DRAGON!*"

Now everyone looked. This dragon loomed much larger than the first. It also headed straight for Janalei. She leapt off her horse and pushed through the crowd to reach the cathedral door. The dragon swooshed by just as she went in. One wing smacked a pillar at the entryway. The dragon screeched and flew away, favoring that wing.

Inside the cathedral no sound could be heard other than the crowd noise outside. She looked into the dimness, saw no one, and tiptoed back out to get a look at the square. "Joopi!" she shouted, and found him standing in a shadow just behind her. "I will stay in this holy place until that dragon is also dead."

Joop, always gentle, laid a consoling hand on her shoulder.

"Say this to the *verdoemte* prince. Vice-Count Utrecht demands that he hunt this new dragon and slay it, no matter the cost to him."

Joop pulled his hand away. She seemed very tense.

"It belongs to his path through this world. If God allows it to plague him, in the name of County Vendink I exile the prince for drawing it here to plague us."

Joop looked out at the square. Those few remaining in the open began a low buzz. Heads, hands shading brows, scanned the sky to see whether the dragon might swoop in from a new direction.

"Yes, Mistress, I will find him and tell him this."

"Go back to the castle gate. He and Wils are of course out doing their insufficient best to handle whatever county business has come."

"Yes, mistress, they went out today."

"Ask where they went. Find them. Tell the prince he is to slay this dragon and, if he survives, vacate County Vendink." She paused. "Forever."

As she said it, a trap door fell open in the pit of her stomach. Rage yanked it shut again. "Tell him!" she shouted at Joop's retreating back.

The lady heals and harrows both the same,

her body whole but parents in the fire.

Small bit by bit her lion's heart goes tame—

when Joop says 'Go' he's preaching to the choir.

    In tomboy clothes, plain both in face and dress,

    the dragon spies her going out, but this

    means all the prince's love is meaningless.

    Her final word to him? Bane's emphasis.

Who's sinless now? Whose soul is white and pure?

Who wishes death on one who was "a friend,"

his love now moved from mute to overture?

Whichever, soft connections meet their end.

    She knows a crisis falls on her this day;

    the prince's massive arms are put in play.

Banished

Two hours later Wils found Janalei inside the cathedral. She stood in the darkness near a sliver of light breaking through the almost-shut doorway.

"Jana, while we were pursuing a boundary dispute between two barons—I'm sure you're acquainted with their disagreement—Joop arrived."

Still wrapped in tense fury, she asked him, "The second dragon?"

"Ordowahl, to his great credit, only asked Joop which way the dragon had flown, and went to kill it."

In the dun-colored daylight leaking into the sanctuary, she guarded her language and spat out, "Credit, you say?" Her clenched jaw, tight eyes, and rigid posture were like a silent scream. She wasn't ready to hear anything at all about her one-time devoted "baby brother."

"Jana, your request changed something in him. He obeyed without a moment's pause. His eyes went hard like flint. He will kill this dragon, or die. I think the dragon's doom is likelier."

"What of that, Wils? Eh? What of it? The dragon is his doing. I want no further part of anyone so drenched in evil and black magic. If God protects him, then let him belong to God. I am through with him."

This time, Wils could see the glistening in her eyes that might have become tears, if she would let them. Her face stayed dry, but Prince Ordowahl's gracious leave-taking haunted Wils.

"I wish you a long and happy life as Count, Wils, and many children with your beloved Janalei." Just that much. Wils remembered how he wheeled Hammerfoot about and went to seek the second dragon. *He did this anticipating a lifelong, inconsolable sense of loss, a life without her, not suspecting that I am also the reality of that.*

*__*__*__*

Late afternoon's air fell to bitter cold. Ordowahl knew he would still need food and water, and Hammerfoot was spent. He made camp beside a small, flowing creek. Each morning Klarenz placed a ration of journeycake in one saddlebag. Now he chewed at the hard, unflavored things until hunger began to fade.

Approaching winter gave the weather cold claws. He pulled off Hammerfoot's saddle and blanket and apologized to the loyal stallion for leaving him uncovered in the night.

When the sun fell from the sky, he draped the blanket over his body and slept. All night he fought dark dreams of dragons tearing holes in things, spewing fire, and Janalei hurling dank banishment.

In the same moonless dusk Wils, Joop, and Janalei walked back to the castle. After spending the day with an empty pit of a heart, battered between tides of helpless rage and loss alternating with pleading and prayer, she fell onto her bed and slept.

*__*__*__*

Ordowahl awoke well before dawn. A waning half-moon at the top of the sky helped him finish the last of the journeycake.

His trials with Janalei clouded his mind. She had healed, and Wils was to marry her. Blaming the dragon on him, she took offense so great that he would never again see either one. If and when the second dragon died, he was banished. At last the burden of dashed hope had left him. A door had closed. In its place he found peace, and with it hard, calm resolve.

Father God in heaven, You have protected me through many trials. Please bring me through this one. You have made me for many things, and I trust You now for help.

Joop said the second dragon is twice the size of the first one. My sword skewered that one's belly while its claw grazed my shoulder and its flame blistered me. How to take one twice as large? A direct thrust up into the belly between grasping claws will have a bad outcome. The dragon might die, but my own death will be certain.

Father God, is this my purpose? Killing these two dragons will be more than worth a life, because they can slay many and cause great havoc. Or is this a penalty for failing to control my fascination with Janalei? Death, Father, if it is Your choice, would be gentle, but save me from a foolish one.

Father in heaven, life may stretch out far before me. In time You will heal all hurts. Guide me now, in the name of my Savior Jesus Christ, Amen.

He looked up. In the east, a sky creeping from black to deep purple seemed to doom his day. Prince Ordowahl, ninth son of Stegnwahl, still king of Nordweg, as far as he knew. With a quick prayer for his parents and brothers, he mounted Hammerfoot.

He drew his sword, this one a three-foot curved razor, and held it upright in front of his face to salute the outcome of his quest.

Yesterday's long trek had been hard on Hammerfoot. The stallion carried him back out onto the road at a walking pace. Rome, it was said, both spread and governed itself at the speed of a walking horse.

He would find his fate in the same manner.

An hour passed, and Ordowahl halted Hammerfoot in a small cove at the bank of a stream. There the still-weary horse could graze and drink. He dismounted, laid the reins over a bush at the stream's edge, and bent down to take his own drink. As he began his crouch, a heavy rustling noise drew his attention.

He looked high up into the trees a few paces away. An indistinct shape stirred up there, masked by intervening layers of branches and still-clinging leaves.

He froze. *Even with fire inside, the thing must need the sun's heat to move about. I see it stretch its enormous wings to catch the sun, still low in the sky.*

His arrival with Hammerfoot had alerted the beast, and it was moving around on its roost, trying to see through the branches below it.

Will it breathe fire? Climbing up through kindling could be a poor choice. It's too bad I don't have a good hunting bow. Getting through all those twigs without spoiling the shot would be tricky, but even so, better than anything else I can think of.

The dragon solved the prince's quandary by flapping its way up and out of the treetop. Huge wing-beats blew the few remaining leaves off the swaying branches. A cloud of dust and autumn detritus showered man and horse. Ordowahl shielded his eyes.

When he looked again the dragon was high up, scanning the ground, searching for him.

That same cloud of dust and leaves hid him until the dragon spotted Hammerfoot. Its screech told any living thing within a mile or more, *Flee or die!*

Hammerfoot's instant rage drew him out onto the road. Heedless of the reins draped over a low bush, he reared up, front legs pawing the air, to issue a stallion's scream of challenge.

Ordowahl ran out to stand beside his horse, giving those hooves a close eye. Hammerfoot lowered his pawing hooves and looked about for the dragon. It may have gone somewhere behind the trees. The giant horse showed the height of animal alertness.

Ordowahl kept his gaze on the tops of those trees they had stopped under. Both horse and rider waited for the dragon to appear. If larger than the first dragon might this one be slower and clumsier, but what good could that bring, given its reach and strength?

He tried to out-think the dragon. Would it make a direct run along the treetops then swoop up at the last moment to pounce on them from above? He coaxed Hammerfoot over to just out of the leaf-fall of the nearest tree then climbed up to stand once again in the saddle.

Raising Klarenz's razor-sharp, gleaming, curved sword to his arms' reach, Ordowahl hoped not to slice off his own nose. A screech came from just overhead—he slashed out by reflex to catch whatever part of the dragon he could.

Banished

The dragon hadn't been able to come down at a sharp enough angle and overshot its mark. The curved razor met some resistance; he knew he'd wounded the thing. Half of one wing and part of the claw on that side lay in front of him, dripping green goo while the dragon struggled back into the sky on a wing and a half.

Ordowahl anticipated that the horse would move. He dropped more or less onto the saddle when Hammerfoot shied away from the severed parts. He dismounted and kicked at the half-claw.

One talon looked big enough to span his palm, and the half-wing could have been tanned down to made him a large shield. As soon as those were off the roadway, he went back to thinking like a dragon, one wounded and overcome by fury.

Was it the sort that got cold when angry, cold and devious? How to tell? Where had the damned thing gone to ground? Or was it somehow still in the air?

Ordowahl turned to Hammerfoot, whose keen nose caught the scent of dragon blood. To Ordowahl the stench blended wintergreen with warm dung.

The stallion seemed to search the breezes, but of course the dragon would arrive moving upwind, ahead of its own scent and into theirs.

He stuck a wet finger in the air, and turned just in time to see the awkward thing alight and limp toward him, shooting a horizontal gush of flame.

Hoping that the flames impeded the dragon's sight, Ordowahl charged into a drop-and-roll as though the dragon were another half-drunk Torwulf. He got past the flames and slashed the underside of its neck. Fire spewed from the wound. He hewed off the good claw and kept rolling, coming to his feet behind the thing.

Hammerfoot backed away, torn between rage and panic. The dragon's head fell onto the roadway. Wisps of smoky flame flickered at its mouth. The stallion rose up, half-danced forward, and with two great pounding hooves reduced the dragon's head to skin and jagged shards of bone.

Ordowahl came and threw an arm over Hammerfoot's withers. In just a few minutes the horse became calm then returned to grazing—the destroyed thing no longer held his attention.

Ordowahl went to the horse. He dipped into a saddlebag to retrieve the same rope used on the first dragon. He tipped the new dragon's heavy body onto its good wing and rolled it up, tucking in the half-wing and claws. He bound the crude bundle with two loops of rope.

Tying the free end of the rope to the saddle brought the dragon close to Hammerfoot, but since it was behind him thus out of sight, the stallion seemed eager to drag it home.

Even after half a hundred treks with Utrecht to every spot in the county, Ordowahl still needed the help of astonished peasants along the way to navigate the mesh of lanes and roads. He at last returned to the city square.

Hammerfoot, though still tired from the previous day's trek, pranced with evident pride at towing a second victim into public view. The first carcass still lay under its month-old shrine of black lace. It had desiccated, but no mold, maggots or worms found the husk tasty. A good breeze could still waft hints of its odd stink around the square.

Ordowahl undid the rope and rolled the second dragon onto the first, with no more ceremony than heaving one dead weight onto another.

Someone came up close and asked him, "I see the singed hair on your head and forearms, your face and neck. You look as if you just ran through a cooking fire."

"I hadn't noticed, my friend, but the dragon and I did have a heated argument," he said and smiled. But the smile fell away.

Ordowahl turned to examine the pile of two dragons. The second dragon's head had fallen back, leaving its throat open. Now a small flame licked out, eating at both dead bodies. The fire spread, and he backed away from its heat to stare at the growing pyre. In minutes a crowd collected to gape at the reeking, popping spectacle. Their own quiet buzz compressed awe, fear, and prayer.

With blank face and stiff neck Ordowahl let Hammerfoot pick his own slow pace along the familiar way back to Haus Hangendro. Tomorrow his steed would rest. The next day he would leave.

Banished

The two dragons produced tarry cinders and curly flakes of black, oily ash, and billowing smoke. Ash dotted half the city and all of the castle grounds. Each flake carried the dragon's unique scent—burned pine and roasted dung.

The end of things has come to pass, the door

that brings tomorrow suddenly ajar.

Leave-takings wash final'ty's nearer shore;

a good night's sleep and sail is set, fare far.

    The prince will never scale her wet-ice mount,

    the beauty of her youthful face ne'er fade.

    That tantalizing kiss is tantamount

    to promises unkept for never made.

A youth is soft and plastic like a pine,

which, felled and dried, becomes both strong and hard.

So Ordowahl, still pithy, asinine

with ref'rence to his lady, went die-hard.

    This day a door will open wide. We'll see

    the change from what has been, to what will be.

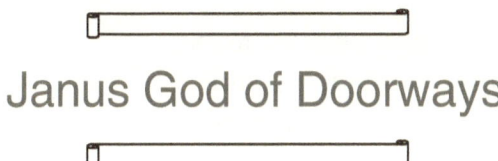

Janus God of Doorways

Janalei once again sequestered herself. Silent, in the one place that would always be hers alone, she saw layers of significance in the scattered black flakes. For one last time the giant interloper had made a fat mess of something. She couldn't put her finger on the one before, but he was always such a bumblebee among regular bees, unpredictable, teetering on the edge of clumsy.

It's as though he turned my command to kill the second dragon into a nasty farewell, something to remind me of him every time I see a black flake of ash. Detestable.

Emluyn came into the bedchamber.

Janalei turned to face her. "Emmi, I came to sense him whenever he was near, but while I did the county's governing I couldn't, didn't want to see the depth of his and my connection. Yet now I'll never be Utrecht again. Each place I go, with anyone you can imagine, will forever be damned and empty."

"Mistress, Joop and I tried many times to show you how deeply you cared for the prince. Why did you always refuse to open your understanding?"

"Emmi, if I had listened, it would have meant letting go of everything I've ever been. I could not surrender being Vice-Count Utrecht."

"My lady? You are not Utrecht as it is. And to keep the prince a brother not a lover, you dangled Lords Markus and Wils in front of him."

"What of it? He *was* a brother to me."

"You certainly weren't his sister. Whenever you thought he might have a woman on his arm, your jealousy mimicked a cat's spread claws."

"Cat's claws? Emmi, you are bold. Be sad with me. Bereft of my future, I wallow in a dreary marsh of madness and regret. The irony of it, refusing to just marry someone before the Bad Prince came along?"

"You had dozens of handsome suitors."

"One could in time have gotten past being a bore. Oh, who am I kidding? Even Wils was growing tiresome."

Emluyn sighed. "Mistress, of all the people to see that, you are the last. Even Wils knew it, brave soul."

"Daddy was right to break our betrothal. I shall spinster my way through humdrums and hats and gowns, and go husbandless because no man can displace Prince Ordowahl."

Emluyn looked at her mistress, close and face to face, to gauge her state of mind.

"I cannot marry my adopted brother. I have no other choice beyond the outlandish, outsized royal intruder. Must I do the unthinkable, come to a man as *his* suitor, bend *my* knee? Must *I* beg acceptance? And not just that, but join with someone who will take me far away? And one I know as a *friend*?"

"Mistress, was that a friend you kissed at Marcus's party? I only ask one thing. When you see things in a clear light, please take me with you. Joop might also want to come."

"Leave me."

Emluyn left the chamber.

Father God in heaven, hear my prayer. Send your angel to guide me. Holy Mother Mary, hear my prayer. Tell me whether to take Holy Orders in your name and, like you, live a virgin in service to God. Amen.

*__*__*__*

An impromptu gathering thronged Haus Hangendro and spilled

out beyond the porch, into the damp courtyard of a chilly early October midday. Occasional splashes of sun broke through a congress of high, sky-filling white-and-gray clouds that made it look like summer. News of the prince's necessary hasty departure from County Vendink had traveled far.

Stories of dragon ash popped up in every conversation, and a number of people had collected the evil-smelling flakes between pieces of cloth.

Ordowahl seemed at complete ease alongside Heri and Fretheldin. As much host as honoree, he showed a facility for light-hearted conversation.

Torwulf tried to explain things to a fellow free knight. "See how calm, how relaxed he is. Surely he looks forward, not back. We'll find a new start in some far-off place. I for one am relieved that he'll find a quiet spot to heal." The tale of Ordowahl's year-plus attempt to court the immovable Vice-Count Utrecht moved the other knight to a sad smile.

One man was heard saying to another, "Y'know, Utrecht never could find her way past him. The two of them looked paired for most of the time since he appeared, a year ago."

"Yah, didn't they?" another man said.

"And now whether or not he tried to woo her she's sent him away just like those who had the better fortune of a few small kisses."

"Ohhh, I just hope Wils doesn't have the same fate fall on him!" The other man roared his laughter.

"Wils is cool and thoughtful. He hardly looks the part of a man who can hold Lady Janalei's attention for more than a heartbeat past the moment she finds him boring, and so she will—just as she has every other man she's kissed."

"Ahh, my friend, what I wouldn't have given for one or two of those kisses myself," and they slapped each other on the back. "Indeed, to be close up, face to face, get a real kiss, oh, and a hug!"

Bright young women came up to the prince, often several at once. Each beamed a smile at him and offered a lover's embrace. They yearned for ham-sized biceps to crush them against an oaken abdomen. Desperate longing, that he would return fascination of his own, rose up among them like incense.

Each time he would smile, say something very polite, but without the hoped-for interest.

"Prince," one of them said, "I am so sad that we never managed to spend time together. I am sure that, once you see me smile at you a dozen times, a hundred more will be inevitable."

And he answered, "Dear Annelijke, your smile is a true gift, and I shall keep it with me forever."

Like all the others she glowed with hope, for just a moment.

"Yes," he said, "it is a pity that we have just this one chance to smile at each other. I thank you for your kindness." And that was that. Not so much as a pecky kiss on the top of her head.

All the men made sure to regale the prince with their praise for his gallantry, his derring-do, his constant wisdom in making certain that Utrecht avoided making a mess of some issue of governance.

They would smile, share a laugh, clap him on the back, and make way for the next man. Ordowahl didn't have a moment to himself to reflect, and he deemed it a gift. *Time spent in sparse company will be my bane. After today I will be glad to find a crowd like this one.*

By and by all the guests had chatted with the prince, given him their well wishes, and made their exit. The sun stood low above the western horizon when Fretheldin approached him.

"What mischief do I see in your eye, Mother Baroness? Is there some surprise you've held back, at day's end? I think I've run out of goodbyes."

"Have you?" she asked. Her eye twinkled.

"Baroness Mother, tomorrow at dawn you and Heri will hear my last and most heartfelt farewells. Then by the grace of God, Sir Torwulf and Klarenz will go off with me, to find another something-to-do."

"Ordowahl, someone waits for you in the front parlor. It's been empty for a while, so I ushered a late guest into it, someone you haven't seen yet." She took his arm.

Not one, but three people faced him through the parlor doorway:

Count Jakop, Countess Rutelyn, and Lady Janalei. He stopped, eyes wide, mouth open. He starved for air and took a huge, noisy breath.

"Jakop, Rutelyn, I am so gratified to see you. And Lady Janalei, I believed I would never again greet you in this life." Regaining his poise, he bent low to clear the doorway and went in.

Count and Countess sat on a loveseat. Lady Janalei sat on another, opposite them. With a careful glance to ask permission, he sat down beside her.

Ordowahl focused his gaze on Jakop. "Count, you honor me more than I can say by your journey here, just to bid farewell to a vagabond slayer of things that become black ash."

He felt, but dared not react to, Janalei sliding next to him, pressing hip to hip.

"Prince," said the count, "please listen to what I say. We are a thousand ways grateful for the attention you've given County Vendink. No man in generations has accomplished so much to secure peace and stable alliances. We are forever indebted to you and bring a very difficult sacrifice."

The prince asked, "Do you bring me a puzzle? I cannot imagine what would require you to surrender anything of value."

They smiled back, but sadness etched their faces. "Son, the day after Janalei fell to the first dragon, I severed her betrothal to Wils. He is now my heir. When I pass from this life, he will become Count."

The prince asked, "Wils? As your son-in-law he would do that anyway. Why, this evening I wished him a long and happy life, and many children with Janalei."

"Yes," said Rutelyn, "and not for the first time, either. He told me about that, and I know him for a brave man."

Ordowahl tried to understand their conversation. Count Jakop had addressed him as "son." *Son?* "Why do you call me 'son'? After this evening we will not see each other again in this life." His thoughts ground to a halt. A year of the count's acquaintance, more than that dealing with Vice-Count Utrecht, the endless turmoil, finalized and resolved - -

Jakop ignored that. "Our daughter has a dire effect on the

happiness of any young man who comes to court her. We rejoiced when she at last seemed to accept Wils."

"Wils, yes. County Vendink's best."

"By accepting him, she gave me such hope." Rutelyn cast a glance at Janalei from under pursed eyebrows.

Ordowahl refused to look, but Janalei now wrapped both arms around his arm. That made it hard to focus. *What is this?* "Forgive me if I am so blind, Count, but what can your sacrifice, your wonderful gift, be?"

"She has brought us here, and she will explain it." Rutelyn helped Jakop rise to a full stand. They left the parlor without a backward glance.

Ordowahl and Janalei stood as they left, but when he sat down again, she put herself on his lap and hid her face on his shoulder. As if confessing dismay she said, "Ordowahl, you still smell of scorched hair."

This further action, her presence in his lap, stunned him, and he reacted by rote. "Yes, I suppose I do." He longed to wrap his arms around her but didn't dare, so he sat on his hands instead. A deep, calming breath let him reflect for a moment. "But, Lady Janalei, I have forsworn seeking your company, and I leave in the morning. What is it that I can do for you now?" He couldn't let himself surrender to her intoxicating presence and forgot the mentioned gift. "I will be your friend forever but have cleansed my feelings toward you. If Wils bores you, then perhaps I would, too. And if Wils doesn't bore you, you should go back to him." *What am I saying? How can I suddenly long for her?*

She looked up into his face, and a tear rolled down one cheek. "I am so sorry, Ordowahl. I am so very, very sorry."

"What do *you* have to be sorry for?"

"I heard you when you picked me up, after the dragon wounded me. You spoke your yearning while you carried me indoors. I've also carried deep feelings for you, and for a long time."

"Lady Janalei, my Klarenz and your Joop kept trying to persuade me that was true. As Utrecht you insisted on the opposite. And your ladyship reinforced it at every opportunity."

"Oh, how I struggled to sustain my need to become the Virgin Countess. I had to choose between life and not-life and didn't realize that parting from you would begin a long death. The time at Lord Markus's birthday celebration when we kissed, something overwhelmed me."

He stared at her, trying to understand.

"Ordowahl, soon after you arrived I found myself entangled with you, too soon to get a glimpse of what was happening. Since then I have fought to defeat a bright, glowing ache for the time I could be your intimate, tell you we were past wooing, if you will. But first, I had to accept one thing: while we are knit as close as family, you'll never be a brother."

She managed a tiny smile then rose up and kissed him, this time without asking for it to look real. Ordowahl didn't notice the softness of her lifting off his lap, her thighs squeezing his, as she rose to bring her face up.

Like that first kiss, nothing had ever felt as intimate, pure, loving, as her lips. A weight that still lay on his soul floated off. An inner lightness raised him up, and he found himself standing, one hand under her while the other held her against him with shy tenderness as though she might break.

Her fingers tugged fistfuls of his hair, knuckles pressing against his skull. He was dizzy, his ears roared, his face burned, and he felt a desperate need to breathe.

He inhaled, and she with him, like two parts of the same being. He rested his forehead against hers, eyes closed, just to absorb the gift of her.

His heart pounded against her belly, and she pushed a hand between them to experience it. She marveled at his body's force. Ordowahl sat back down, cradling her in his lap. She wiped a wet cheek on his chest.

"Janalei, we kissed at Markus's party. You turned away, but I could feel God's small finger caressing my ear. It told me to stay. Arid, alone, yearning, but stay and wait upon you. I chose to endure that until His will would be clear."

She looked at him, her face unreadable. "When you went to

Haus Maihoff at the start of the summer, I was terrified that you would never return."

"Jana, even then I knew that some bond linked us, in a way I could never break. Your command to leave County Vendink was like a knife heated in the fire. It sealed an open wound. Now I struggle to undo that, and after this kiss you don't turn away. Tell me what has changed."

She bowed her head again and spoke in a tiny voice. "Ordo, my only, you need to know something. I have had the ability to see into two people's lives since I was very, very young. I could tell what Mama and Daddy were doing, and why, every moment I was awake. And I had all of their memories, even from both their childhoods. Not only that, a third was my own. I had glimpses of what I would become."

"I see," he said, struggling to make himself understand this new way of seeing.

"When I kissed you that first time, Ordi my Only, a rush of this same sight into you flooded me. I struggled to contain the exhilaration, but a great terror came down and pressed hard. I knew that I would have to choose between a long life and a long death, but I could not tell which choice meant life. I had to break away from you to find safe ground. But now?"

"Jana, that first kiss, no matter the use you intended for it, was the most intimate, wonderful moment I had ever known, with any woman. Afterward I wished Wils good luck when it happened to him."

"Wils? No, beloved, you only. Yes, I have kissed many. Each time I saw, well, nothing much. You, Ordi?" She shivered. "Now hear this warning my gift provided, in my sixth year of life. A journeying stranger, an imposing giant in fact, would arrive when I became an adult. He would come from far to the north and take me away with him, back to the distant place that grew him."

Ordowahl looked into her eyes.

"I would never again see County Vendink, or my parents, or anyone else here. That part still overwhelms me. A brute would drag me into exile, away from every part of my former life. The day you arrived, Ordowahl Prince Nordweg, I knew you would do that. I hated you for it."

"Hated? Really? You did have a sharpness about you, but over time the spikes and jagged edges faded from claws to small calluses on a friend's palm. I knew you as a tease." He kissed her forehead, her nose. "The day I met you, Janalei, and I never told anyone at all, not even myself. I prayed that God had brought me to my Other Half."

Her face relaxed, calm and radiant.

"Jana, none who came to court you ever found success. I knew that but didn't pull back. So, yes, blame me for selfishly trying to gather in, to possess someone like you, who cannot and will not ever be owned."

She looked down again, at hands folded into a knot. He waited for her to relax. When she did, he used one tender finger to lift her face He stared into shiny eyes, trying to read what lay behind the glisten of unspilt tears. His other arm had been a backstop. Now he slid that hand under her, caressing hip, then cheek, and thigh. She snuggled deeper into his caress.

"You have owned my innermost being, Janalei, despite every effort to govern myself. That will never change. I feel whole at no other time than when you are close to me."

"Do I own you? Here is my invitation, Ordowahl. Own *me*."

"How do I do that? Once I am become part of your private life, will that be to own you?"

"I have never lived without having family around me whom I know in full, by second sight. I've been privy to all of their being, yet not owned them, nor did they own me."

"So, precious Jana, if I become part of your private life, I won't own you, either?"

"You would, you will, you do, because *I* know. I barred you from my real self, from ignorance and dread. If I let you in, I knew I would give myself over to you without limit. I would no longer be the person I have trained to be for my entire life."

"Sweet woman, I always felt some part of you beckoning me on."

"Yes, but I couldn't bear that. Instead I treated you like a pariah. My God, I showed you a woman both fickle and callous, remote in what should have been close moments. I was a foolish child."

"Jana, how sweet to use your familiar name. I have always seen you as an adult, a woman. Maddening, challenging, frustrating, but always fascinating. Even at your thorniest, your most dismissive, just having your attention kept you precious to me."

"I am flawed, Ordowahl, and always will be. But I pray that your fascination never ends. Become my husband, because I give you myself. Then I will be privy into the life of the most significant man I will ever meet."

"Janalei, yes, please join your life to mine. But, how will you gain second sight into your husband?"

"You ask, after two kisses?" She turned and rose, kneeling on his thighs, elbows on his shoulders, hands toying with the hair on his head, her forehead pressed against his.

The intimate physicality of her breath's scent swelled his spirit. For a moment his whole vision resolved into one tawny-green orb. He looked into depths he would try to understand all the rest of his life.

She cocked her head to one side, her lips fondling his. "Ordi my beloved, you once made a comparison between a woman and unmasterable iron. Do you recall that? See, you have melted me. Now, strong soul, find me a priest!"

Instead of morning, he departs anon

with treasure that he cannot understand.

His pressed-down, expurgated heart is drawn

to hers. Her kiss is power, wields command.

> So what's the meaning of "We need a priest?"

> The day is dimming, why the rush, the haste?

> The lady Jana's moods are sudden, say the least.

> Now comes their partnership's first hasty taste.

She is both melted and in full control.

She uses Ordowahl to meet a need

that only she can see; it's not his role,

this time, but hers that God decreed.

> The prince has always met what met him first.

> Tonight he'll meet her need and slake his thirst.

Pledge

Lady Janalei struggled out of giant Prince Ordowahl's lap. She dragged him by one hand while brushing half-dry cheeks and now radiant eyes. "Beloved, I meant it! This is a time of great portent. We need a priest."

They emerged into Haus Hangendro's front hallway. Janalei called out, "Baroness Mother, we must leave at once." She dried her free hand on the shoulder of footman Joop, who'd been snooping by the doorway. "Joopi, Klarenz, return with me and the prince."

The two men exchanged brief glances and sprinted toward the back part of the Haus. They sped past the slender, elegant Mother Baroness Fretheldin, also listening at the doorway.

Two and a quarter decades had passed since Fretheldin saw Janalei born. She had helped Countess Rutleyn birth a furious, red-haired, red-faced newborn child. As time passed she watched Jakop Count Vendink's sole heir unfurl herself from baptized newborn to precocious toddler to fierce tomboy, and last to man-dressed Vice-Count Utrecht handling the business of County Vendink—at other times the spectacular Lady Janalei.

Prince Ordowahl, a cherished guest in her Haus from the day he arrived, would not be leaving Utrecht. Yes, two days ago Lady Janalei had banished him. Yes, his farewells were complete. Now Fretheldin marveled at the mash up of fear and excitement parading across Janalei's face—*that* had never been there before. Furrowed brow, bright cheeks, pulse bursting at her neck, a smile that seemed torn halfway between soaring joy and abject terror.

"My dears," the baroness mother addressed the huge foreigner and the count's daughter, "what upsets you?" A woman's intuition, plus the intimate conversation she'd just overheard, told her the Prince was un-banished and the once-imperious Janalei had abandoned her oft-professed plan never to give herself to a man, much less marry one.

Giddy with joy, Fretheldin peered up into the prince's face. Having him as houseguest for over a year meant she could read him at a glance. She saw relief, as though a world-sized weight were gone. She stepped backward into the plum-colored wool drapes lining the hall to let them pass.

Man-tall Janalei still needed to stand on toe-tips to gaze up into the prince's eyes. "Beloved, I need to be with my parents! I am—we are—on the cusp of terrifying events. We must see Father Henck immediately then spend the night at Vendink Keep."

As though he understood that she could see into his mind, he nodded toward the entrance door. Then with long strides he ran the other direction, chasing Joop and Klarenz.

Janalei turned toward the baroness mother. "Dear Auntie Fretheldin, you saw me come in with my parents a short while ago. You saw them leave; I cannot tell you how wonderful a thing has happened, there simply isn't time. Please lend me a wrap, for I left mine in Mama and Daddy's carriage. I will ride with the prince now, without so much as a saddle." Before the baroness could react, Lady Janalei stepped out the door and into the brisk pre-evening chill of autumn. A moment later a servant ran out to wrap a soft shawl around her shoulders.

Riding without a saddle was something Lady Janalei had thought would be both easier and more difficult than this. Stallion Hammerfoot's enormous stride, the huge risings and fallings of his gait, brought both fear and exhilaration. The implacable yet somehow tender clamp of the prince's wrist and palm across her abdomen, his fingers a protective wrap over one hip, their bodies rising and falling to the horse's pulse, her thighs against the prince's—it became difficult to think. She simply let the horse and prince carry her along the road back to the City and to Vendink Keep.

She could overhear Ordowahl's thoughts. Her second sight into him was growing, and she reveled in it. Her newly discovered life centered on this man she had banished. He had not anticipated her return to Haus Hangendro. He hadn't considered that she could reclaim him. Now she wrapped herself in the devotion he offered, his patience as large as himself.

At first sight more than a year ago she knew that he would tear her away from County Vendink. She had stifled, denied, murdered his male devotion a hundred times in a hundred casual ways. At the same time she found herself first enjoying his presence, then relying on it. Their bond grew and deepened. She understood it as a friendship, albeit one unlike any she'd ever known.

This day she had come to him, sun low in the afternoon sky, to repent—to undo her grave mistake. Clarity undid misery and confusion, showed what would bring life, drove her. She felt giddy contemplating what lay ahead. But terror also froze her bones. A great trial loomed. An evil being had sent the dragons for *her*. Each one Ordowahl slew out of hand, reaching into fire.

Guilt rose up in her throat. It nearly choked her. The prince heard her groans and bent his head down close to hers.

"Beloved, what is wrong?" His guarding arm softened then drew her closer to him, tighter.

She shook her head, craning her neck to look back at him, to smile. He slowed Hammerfoot from a half-gallop to a canter. They cuddled, enjoying a new intimacy through the simple closeness of their bodies, sharing the familiar rhythmic exercise of riding a horse.

Her life-long gift of concurrent, full awareness of her parents had taught her about shared intimate motions. This more innocent synchrony with Ordowahl added a fresh, personal dimension. Even the stallion's enormity seemed to complement her giant lover as she sat back against his chest. She struggled against the temptation to have him caress her breasts.

Pledge

She was aghast to know that she had drawn him into her peril. Its scale beggared description. Ordowahl was both her love and her rescue—so let it be what it might be, moment by moment.

After healing from that first dragon's deep claw punctures, she had thrown away her second sight. That loss was more terrifying than any dragon.

Two months ago she'd given Ordowahl a peck on the lips. She gave all sorts of men, Lady Janalei's continual parade of suitors, that same peck. Each time it conferred a glimpse of their limits. Nothing about any of them enticed her forward.

When she touched Ordowahl's lips, it swelled into a kiss unlike any she'd ever given or received. A glimpse of her future involved him in the most intimate way, but also made her recoil in terror. She caught glimpses of something not just evil but terrifying.

Had the second dragon cauterized her heart? Even then, her need of Prince Ordowahl was visceral.

This afternoon she dared a second kiss. Like the first, it overpowered them both. But this one built bliss. It sealed them together, showed her their linked future. No question need be asked: she would face an attack. Only he could defend her from it. And he would fight for her to the end of the world. *Dear Father in Heaven,* she prayed, *do not let his or my world fall to an evil fate. Bring us through the trial that looms tomorrow.*

——*—*

As they neared the City she lifted her head and spoke to him. "Beloved, when you take me to wife you take huge troubles with me."

He looked at her. "Those dragons weren't coming for me, were they?"

She looked back in shock. He had realized as much in less time than it took him to say it. She hadn't anticipated that. "Ordowahl, I tell you true. A great evil hunts me, and only you have a way to defend me against it."

"I have felt God's small finger caressing my ear, yet this time it burns. I am more ready to protect you than I ever have been ready to do anything. A new evil sent the dragons. But God saved me from falling to them, and to prior evils. I pray that He protects me again—this time, *us*."

He means it! I believe, with him, that he can sense God's protection when it involves him. He trusts that, as is necessary to follow it. "Ordo! Don't take this lightly."

"Never, Jana. Whatever the burden, if God leads me to it, He will help me carry it. A Black Mage capable of making dragons terrifies me. But you can't run, and I won't."

She had never found such a level outlook, and shivered. "We must go to Father Henck. Joop and Klarenz will be at the castle when we return. Father Henck comes first." *I am already giving him instructions; he seemed patient enough when we were vice-count and foreigner to each other. In an hour we will be man and wife. He yearned for this almost from the day I met him, and so did I, even while thinking him an ass!.*

How many wives command their husbands in casual speech? She snickered. *More than one! Father God, help me always when I deal with the man I'm about to join as one flesh.*

They reached the central square under a dimming sky. The rectory stood in deep shadow. Ordowahl laid Hammerfoot's reins over a tree limb; they went up the steps and knocked. A dim light shone from under the door.

Father Petur's familiar face looked out at them through the opened door. His brows flew up, eyes wide with surprise. He backed away to invite them in. "My lady, my prince, what brings you here?"

"Father," Janalei said to him, "we must see the abbot, and it is urgent."

The priest said no more. He turned from the small room and hurried down a hallway. They could hear his quiet but impassioned plea. After several minutes they heard Father Henck, abbot of St. Martin's, shuffle down the hall.

He came in, alone. He held out his ring to be kissed and asked, "My children, what am I to learn from this? Ordowahl, since I didn't attend your celebration this afternoon, have you come to wish *me* farewell?"

Ordowahl knelt, as much out of respect as to put his eyes below

Fr. Henck's. "Father, my banishment is lifted. Now Lady Janalei has agreed to become wife, mother to my children, and mistress to my worldly affairs."

Janalei added, "My parents have consented to this. They made it clear by taking me to Haus Hangendro this afternoon, to release me into the prince's hands. Marry us, Father. Do it now. Do not hesitate or delay. On behalf of my father the Count I waive all notice. We must be joined as husband and wife this night. Tomorrow may be too late."

Father Henck stared at them. He'd been napping, and sleep still rode his face. One firm old hand massaged his face for a moment, and he stood up straighter.

"Prince, even serving Lady Janalei as her confessor for more years than I can say, I have lost any hope of understanding her. Now I wish you a better insight. Come this way, my children." Holding a lit candle, he led them through the rectory and into a small chapel. "The sanctuary is a bit much for what we are about. The wedding of a prince and a count's daughter wasn't a use planned for this chapel, but it will serve."

He set the candle down, and the three of them stood there, holding hands to make a ring.

"On becoming one flesh you are also one heart and can have no objection to your spouse hearing your sins." He heard their confessions and forbore to assign a penance. "The constraint of marriage, each of you to a far stronger person than the other can possibly imagine, will be penance enough. Join now in God's love."

He recited a few verses from Matthew, guessed that both man and woman understood his Latin, and put their right hands between his two hands. "My children, pledge now with me that you will love, honor, and keep yourselves chaste from all others, from this day forward until death separates you."

They spoke the vows he laid out, and he said simply, "God now sees you as one. Go your way in peace."

Good Abbot Henck has named them married 'fore

the eyes of God. He knows it's pointless to

enquire of Janalei. Her purpose for

forever's gone away from Abbot's view.

> Her second sight required a circumspect

> behavior to preserve the status quo,

> lest something slip, unguarded, and deflect

> her day from play, to go malapropos.

Close-held, her thoughts and feelings came to be

her own with none the wiser, mom or priest.

Her sins she phrased in fog, thus secrecy

encloaked her sinful acts—no dough, just yeast.

> But now she has a partner, she must ope

> her agency, her inmost mind, her hope.

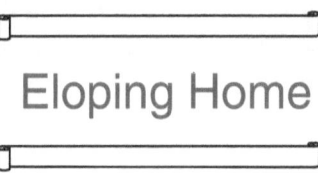

Eloping Home

A sliver of distant sunlight reflected off open water in marshes along the western shore beneath pinked evening clouds. Then it was gone, and night fell on them like a hangman's hood. Astride Hammerfoot, he wrapped an arm around her, with her shawl pulled tight against the cold. He let Hammerfoot walk past the alehouse, the spot of their second conversation. Then a further hundred yards along the castle wall and to the gate. The drawbridge stood level across the moat as always, and they went in. Klarenz and Joop stood waiting for them.

Ordowahl and Janalei tried to stifle the emotional moment, but several giggles escaped as tiny snorts. Joop and Klarenz stood still and gaped. Their masters' utterly changed affections left them speechless—and oddly joyful. The newly married couple walked around to the rear while footman Joop went with bondman, jack-of-all-trades-and-master-of-each Klarenz. He led the stallion into the stables to be curried, cozened, and fed.

"Beloved," she said, "in rage I separated myself from both my parents, scant weeks ago. But now I again love them. Poor Mother! She will weep to know that she has missed my wedding!"

"No matter, Jani, she will stage a complete betrothal to list all the gifts and appurtenances. Only she will know, and your father, that we have reversed the usual order. Everyone else in Utrecht can wink and nudge a friend in the ribs, but they will believe what they want anyway."

"Liar!" she called him, knowing that he'd never be one.

They used the servants' entrance. A sleepy groom hadn't expected them, but nothing Lady Janalei ever did would surprise him. She was impossible to predict. He gave them a candle; they crept up the back stairs and past her parents' room. Emluyn had already turned down the nuptial bed.

Janalei stood on the bed to drape her arms over Ordowahl's shoulders. She was ready for another kiss. But she turned her head and said, "Emmi, please come undo me. I want to be Eve, even in the cold of night." She snuggled closer to Ordowahl and said, "I understand the power of a man to warm a maiden. I think you'll do!" and giggled again.

Emmi, as best she could by the light of the candle Ordowahl still held in one hand, untied and loosened and unfastened and lifted off, until Janalei wore nothing. She left and quietly re-closed the door.

Janalei crooned, "Ordo," a gentle, soothing sound. She breathed on his face, a soft warmth on his cold nose. "Kiss me, this third time."

*__*__*__*

Ordowahl lay on the bed, also naked. Janalei luxuriated in his animal warmth, crushed under half his weight. A dozen more deep kisses had drained him. Each expanded her second sight into him. She knew him from birth now, all his family, all his deeds. His first women, that entrapping vixen in Hammaborg, and last a tutor in relating, more than just "relations." *And you, my completing man, have been faithful to me since the day we crossed paths on the road into Utrecht.* She knew her father's history and loved him. Now she knew the history of her husband, the man she had married, and loved him, too.

"Jana," he mumbled, "I'm hot, exhausted, and can't even tell where I am. What have you done to me?"

"Ordi, my beloved younger man—I am your senior by two years plus more than a fortnight—I have been making you family. If you are too hot, I shiver. Cover me. Provide some of your heat. Understand this: my second sight extends to family, and you are now as known to me as the innermost parts of my own mind."

"Yet to me you will ever be a mystery, Jana. I am Samson, you Delilah, and you have shorn my head."

She chuckled. "You still have Samson's hair and strength, my love. Take a deep breath and kiss me again."

The kiss began tenderly, mouths touching. Offset noses let them sustain the kiss, face caressing face, hands wandering and caressing, for minutes. When they separated she pushed on his shoulder. He rolled onto his back, and she clambered up to sit astride his loins.

He looked up; the flickering candle played shadows for him across her joyful smile. "I am no longer terrified by your kisses, Jana my love. I am the happiest man in the world, and we haven't yet joined as man and wife."

"Husband, I come to you a virgin, but with knowledge of the arts of sex that would take far too long to tell. Daddy, bless his randy soul, found whores who wrote books with their bodies. You have no idea." She pushed back on his knees. "Lie flat. I don't want your full weight on me—not yet."

Undulating hips brought her down onto his flaccid manhood. It went stiff.

"I am relieved, my love. Your limbs are twice the size of most men's, but the most important part of you seems, well, not ordinary, but..." She lifted herself up, then slowly settled down onto him. They came together, and were one flesh.

Her inner parts protested. She ignored the burning sensation, stretching to take something into a place that had been quiet all her life. Her inner part relaxed, then expanded. She had all of him and wanted every bit. She even felt a moment's disappointment that, while he could make two of most men, the manhood part of him, well, merely fit. Snugly. Their pelvic bones began making solid contact; her breath caught each time.

She realized that the shock, the newness, of this experience had drawn her away from second sight, inward to the solitude of her own senses. She looked at Ordowahl and knew that he, too, had surrendered much of his attention to his body, to the primal completion that coitus is to a man.

Under it, though, she saw astonishment and gratitude that *she* had accepted him, it was *she* who joined with him. Being her choice moved him in a way that he had never experienced before. She sensed him approaching climax, and purred at him, "Slow down, my Ordi. Take me with you." She was glad to see she'd broken his concentration. It magnified his amazement at the intimacy of their becoming one.

She moved in frenzied wriggles, under the candle's glow. While Ordowahl couldn't imagine her gift of second sight, he saw her openness and surrender. They demanded that he protect her from this day forth and forever more.

Her own excitement radiated outward from her center, a fiery tingling moving from hips down legs, up her belly to arms, fingers, toes, scalp. She began to lose control. Her eyes rolled up into the back of her head. She cried out, a long wordless moan . . . Her world shrank into ecstatic delirium that traveled through her in waves. She fell forward onto him while continuing to thrash and squirm.

She felt a fluid rush from him, inside her; she dissolved into rapture; time ceased to pass.

Completion for a man is rapid, and Ordowahl soon fell into a warm torpor. He rolled onto his side, being careful to move her thigh out of the way. His arms curled around all of her, to keep her body close.

While taking him into herself she had felt empty as an ancient seabed, then she felt filled up. Her excitement waned by small degrees to a tingling glow. She cuddled against his chest, wrapped in arms bigger than she had dreamed of. He drew a blanket over both of them.

When he did withdraw from her loins she asked, "How long have we been like this?" His eyes opened; a distant star gleaming through a window glinted on his eyeball, and she kissed his chin. "I have never known before how cherished a woman can feel."

"Jana, I've never been moved to such tenderness. Your body is a blessing I hope to receive a thousandfold, time to come." He kissed her forehead. "Holding you like this, I know that I will forever protect you the way a fortress guards the crown, the way Christ guards the Church and all saints, the way a mother hen guards her chicks."

"Hen?!" she snorted. "Yet I know your meaning. Husband, but I am the hen, and you are a father. In late July you, we, will have a daughter."

She sensed his puzzlement. She cuddled into him and murmured, "You will be a wonderful father."

"You say that like you know it for fact."

"Wonderful or not, you have just become a father. I told you we had to find a priest—to give our child an honest name. I know this as certainly as I knew, while still a child, that you would appear." She wriggled a bit. "It's a pity I'll have to keep telling you what to do, but I've seen you grow accustomed to it."

"Next time I see Father Henck I will thank him for making sure our child has parents who are married, and to each other." But he sensed that her need to become wife and mother arose from some unguessable purpose. He didn't know how to ask her that, and she didn't provide an answer.

They slept then and didn't awaken when Emmi came in to cover them with straightened blankets and lay a warm hearthstone atop the foot of their nuptial bed.

*__*__*__*

They awoke in deep night, between first and second sleep. The candle had long since guttered and Emmi had closed the window.

Janalei pulled herself onto his chest. "I know you are a strong man, Ordowahl. Can you Samson me a second, third, or even fourth time? Your Delilah lies next to you. Come in unto me again, press me down, keep filling me up. Try to make it hard for me to walk on the morrow." She smiled to herself, knowing his gentleness. She also knew his ferocity, and how soon they both would depend on that, and on Almighty God.

What secrets has she learned, and may learn more?

She knows that she's with child; 'twill be a girl.

She owns the giant former bachelor—

he landed in *her* lap, this erstwhile churl?

    Tomorrow they will face her Mom and Daddy,

    showing up at breakfast with a smile.

    'Twill be no great surprise—the princely laddie

    has no choice; they'll stay at home awhile.

She cannot travel north, away from here.

She told him she has troubles that are dire

and he's the only thing to keep her clear

of death, and worse. Her nemesis brings fire.

    As fine as fine can be, the wedded pair

    both dread black magery: it's in the air.

COMING

Mourner

A Dark Mage comes seeking vengeance for his scaly children, so rudely slain by the prince, but also to first understand then steal Janalei's gift of second sight. Prince Ordowahl will need her gift to combat him. Janalei loses her father. Threat averted and father mourned, the couple and their child journey to Nordweg to settle a certain amount of family business.

Monarch

Of nine brothers, five lost their lives trying to murder the ninth. King Stegnwahl absorbs the loss then rejoices to see Ordowahl, with wife and child. Within a year, he also dies. "Let the best son reign". The death of King Stegnwahl leaves Ordowahl, still in his twenties, to replace murderous brothers as sustainer to their widows. His kingship begins by healing five widows' bleakness. At the same time neighbors sense a ripe opportunity. Nordweg's king so young, his realm so eviscerated, keeping chaos at bay runs Ordowahl to his limit as he deals with fatalistic and violent neighbors

Mage

King Ordowahl must keep his standing within this framework to manage his extended kingdom. He also learns from White mage Heorald, who seems not to age. Heorald must take this royal pupil under wing to withstand a great danger that looms in Queen Janalei's future, thus also his. Heorald labors to complete the king's training.

Martyr

Heorald succumbs to time. Broaching old age and without Heorald's help, mage-king Ordowahl must confront a final black mage, one for whom dragons are common as fleas. Ordowahl must heal many rifts, including with his beloved wife, to hand down the kingdom while it, and he, are still whole. Confronting the Blackest Mage will be his final challenge.

Titles:

Joel Hinrichs

An Adult's Garden of Verses (2017)

Christ – Cosmology   (November 2021)

Ordowahl : Mourner   (2022)

Ordowahl : Monarch   (TBD)

Ordowahl : Mage   (TBD)

Ordowahl : Martyr   (TBD)

Jody Glittenberg

SAVING MOTHER EARTH   THE PROMISE SEED

(2018)

Words With a Mission (wordswithamission.com)

oh-and-another-thing.blog

www.ingramcontent.com/pod-product-compliance
Lightning Source LLC
Chambersburg PA
CBHW051326250626
47155CB00007B/2469